# The Man Who Ate His Book

## The Best of Ducts.org

Volume II

Edited by

Jonathan Kravetz and Charles Salzberg

GREENPOINT PRESS
NEW YORK, NY

**Aaron Morgan Brown**
***The Itinerant***
Oil on canvas, 30"x40"
*(Featured Artist, Issue 24)*

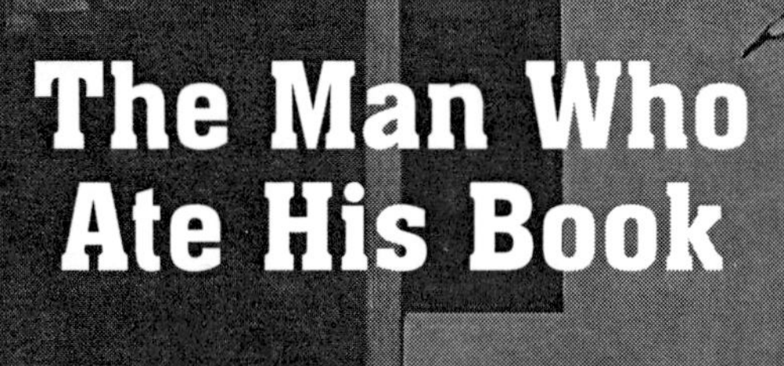

# The Man Who Ate His Book

*The Best of Ducts.org*

Volume II

Part One—ESSAYS
Part Two—MEMOIR
Part Three—FICTION
Part Four—HUMOR
Part Five—POETRY
Part Six—ART GALLERY

The Man Who Ate His Book—The Best of Ducts.org, Volume II
Edited by Jonathan Kravetz and Charles Salzberg



ISBN 978-0-9886968-4-6

Library of Congress Cataloging-in-Publication Data

Ducts.org and Greenpoint Press,
Divisions of New York Writers Resources
PO Box 2062
Lenox Hill Station
New York, NY 10021

New York Writers Resources:
- newyorkwritersresources.com
- newyorkwritersworkshop.com
- greenpointpress.org
- ducts.org

Book Designer: Robert L. Lascaro
Art Editor: Cindy Stockton Moore
Cover Artist: Aaron Morgan Brown

Printed in the United States
on acid-free paper

# TABLE OF CONTENTS

PART THREE

## FICTION



PART FOUR

## HUMOR



PART FIVE

## POETRY

Part Six

## ART GALLERY

INTRODUCTION

# The Hunger Game

HE CAME FROM OUT OF TOWN and the first thing he said after introducing himself was, "I'm planning to do a little something different tonight."

"Great," I said, because that's what I say to all our writers.

He must have imagined KGB Bar in the East Village of New York City, where we hold our readings for Ducts.org, to be an exotic land full of hip artist sorts who nod approvingly when writers strip naked or swallow live rodents. Or maybe he thought he was making a statement about the transient nature of existence compared to the seeming permanence of ideas. Whatever he thought, he didn't hesitate. He ripped out half a page and began eating his book.

"I brought ten copies with me," he said. "I'm going to eat this one here until I've sold them all." And he went back to chomping.

I'm guessing his thin volume didn't taste very good because his jaw worked slowly. Very, very slowly. I think he could have won a few hearts if he'd asked for salt, but Hungry Man was already losing courage. No one was getting up to buy his book and it must have dawned on him that whatever his plan had been—the plan he'd hatched on a long car ride to the big city—was turning to cod liver oil. I wanted to rescue him, but I didn't know how. While several solutions crossed my mind, I was mostly hoping for the thermonuclear destruction of New York City. Finally I asked if he'd mind if I read aloud from his book and he nodded and stepped aside. I read a short story of his—I can't remember a word of it—while he stood behind me still chewing that first half-page. What does it mean to eat your own words and discover they're indigestible?

I sat him down and moved on to the next, more typical author, who managed to read from his book without eating a single syllable. After the reading Hungry Man shook my hand and shrugged. I said, "Well, it was worth a shot." He nodded, said thanks and vanished.

I mention this story not because I want to humiliate him. I mention it because it was a crazy thing to do. And interesting. And poetic. And desperate. And human. And it reminds me why we started Ducts.org in the first place back in 1999 when "Internet" was a shiny new word and no one had heard of Facebook or blogging. We launched Ducts to give writers of all sizes, shapes, ages, races and dispositions toward book-eating a chance to be nuts. We began because sometimes you need a place where you can make a big, sloppy mistake and find there's someone there to say, "Good try." And after fifteen years, we're proud of our small corner of the literary world. Our writers are messy, smart, daring, thoughtful and, yes, hungry. Ducts.org owes its existence to them and this book is our small way of saying thank you for making us taste so good.

I would also like to thank the many editors who have contributed their time, energy and brilliance to our cause over the years. First, our current editors: Derek Alger, Lisa Kirchner, Amy Lemmon, Kat Rodies, Cindy Stockton Moore and Tim Tomlinson. Thank you for continuing to collect and edit some of the best writing on the web, and I owe each of you a chocolate-covered dictionary. Our past editors all contributed their own unique insights to our cause, and Ducts continues to feel their impact. So thank you Laura Buchholz (who gave us the name of our first anthology), Gail Eisenberg, Dan McCoy, Elizabeth Rosen, Dana Benningfield and Ryan van Winkle. This book would never have come to life without the efforts of our tireless Editorial Assistant, Anne Posten, who went digging far and wide to put this creature together. Thank you, Anne, for making a difficult job fun. Our new tome wouldn't look as delicious as it does without the hard work of our designer, Bob Lascaro, who has a talent for uttering encouraging words like no one else, and our meticulous copy editor, Gini Kopecky Wallace, who held the hold thing together when it could have crumbled to pieces. And, finally, I'd like to offer special thanks to Charles Salzberg. Charles and I launched Greenpoint Press with our first "Best of Ducts" book, How Not to Greet Famous People, back in 2004. The Press has survived because Charles flat-out loves this messy process and its practitioners more than anyone I've known. So we (I'm allowing myself to speak for all Ducts.org contributors) thank Charles and dedicate this book to him.

We hope you'll enjoy reading it as much as we enjoyed writing it. We doubt you will, but if you get bored and hungry, we hope you'll find something else to snack on.

— Jonathan Kravetz, Editor-in-Chief, Ducts.org

# Part One

# ESSAYS

# The Stupid Things You Do When Your Mom's Not Around

BY ALICIA FINN NOACK *(ISSUE 16)*

YOU'RE IN THE BASEMENT and you're bored. Andy and Molly are playing dive bomb on the old couch. They stand on the arm and yell, "Dive bomb!" and let themselves fall face-first into the cushions. It was your favorite game last year, but now you're too tall. Your head brushes the ceiling when you stand on the arm, and dive bomb isn't as much fun when you have to squat. Andy's kind of too tall for it, too, but he's pretending.

You tell Andy that he should try jumping on your stomach, just to see what happens. You kind of know what's going to happen—it's going to hurt. But you have to find out for sure. You just can't know unless you try.

So you lie on the floor next to the couch, flat on your back. Andy leaps off the couch with both feet together, like jumping into the deep end of a pool. There's a huge pain right in your gut and you're crying. Andy and Molly run away and later Mom discovers you on the ground. "Who did this to you?" she asks. She has that bite to her voice that means business. "Andy," you say, and he gets sent to his room for it.

At dinner that night, he stares at you with an amazed look on his face. It's like he doesn't know why he did it, like you don't know why you asked. You don't tell Mom what really happened.

* * * *

It's Saturday and you're roller-skating at school. It's got the best sidewalks for roller skating. Andy comes on his skateboard and Jodi from next door rides her bike. You go in front of the Dock Door, which is where the fourth and fifth graders line up in the mornings before the bell rings. You love it here, because it's smooth and flat and kind of dangerous. On one side of the loading dock is a five-foot drop to the parking lot. You see how close you can get to the edge, how fast you can skate without falling off. You're so good at it that today it seems kind of boring.

On the other side of the loading dock is a railing and after that, a thirty-foot drop down to the basketball court. Sometimes, you throw trash and rocks over the side, just to see how they splat and scrape up the brick wall. You only do this on Saturdays because teachers always yell at you when they catch you doing it before school. The railing side is very dangerous, they say. A few feet past the railing is a windowsill, a narrow little strip just one brick wide.

This is the best part about playing at the Dock Door. On Saturdays when no one's here, you strip down to your bare feet and climb onto the windowsill. When Andy did it the first time, you thought for sure he was going to die. But then you tried it once and it's not that hard. Molly and Jodi are the only ones too scared to try. Today, you think, you'll try it on your roller skates. Even Andy hasn't done that before.

Andy and Jodi watch you carefully. They stand close, but not too close– you don't want to be crowded, you say. The roller skates are heavy and they make climbing over the railing harder than before. The wheels get stuck in the rungs the first time you try. When you put your first foot down on the windowsill, you roll a little, kind of unsteady. But by the time you get your second foot down, you're fine. It's almost like being in bare feet, easy as pie.

From here, you can see all the way across the roof of the kindergarten building, all the way to the trees at the edge of Mr. Hall's yard. Maybe you pretend that one of the treetops beyond that is the one in your own front yard. Everything is quiet except for the wind in your ears. You're pretty high up.

Then you turn your head and look into the classroom behind you. Every time you come to the school, you and Andy and Jodi test all the windows you can reach to see if they are unlocked, and if they are, then sometimes you crawl inside. Andy broke in through this window once.

The sun is bright and it takes a long time for your eyes to adjust. A teacher is sitting at a desk, writing something. She pauses, looks up, and then she sees you in the window. The terrified look on her face breaks the spell. There's just enough time to see her mouth, "Oh my god," and then she jumps up and runs for the door.

You grab for the railing again, pulling yourself over it as fast as you can. If she catches you, you're going to be in big trouble, worse than anything before. Andy and Jodi are already gone.

You make it over the railing and down the stairs and then you're skating as fast as you can, pumping your arms. Andy and Jodi wait for you around the corner at another window. This one is only a foot off the ground, the one you always rest at. There's a waterspout next to it that you have been stuffing with treasures like kite string and dandelions, trying to see how long it takes to fill it up.

But today there's no time to check it. You and Andy and Jodi inch back the way you came, slowly, until you can just make out the back of that teacher's head. She's leaning over the railing and looking down into the basketball court, looking for a broken little girl in roller skates. You try to skate the rest of the way home like nothing happened, but your heart is pounding. Jodi won't even look at you.

* * * *

You're in stupid daycare for the summer. You're old enough to take care of yourself, even Mom says so, but not old enough to take care of Andy and Molly, too. So all three of you are stuck in this stupid Project Kids Day Camp at the school. It's like spending summer vacation at school only less fun. You're the oldest kid there.

To pass the time, you and Andy read the *Black Cauldron* books. They're good, so much better than the *Wrinkle in Time* books the librarian tried to give you last year. These ones make sense.

The counselors encourage you to do crafts in the mornings. One day everyone makes tie-dye shirts. You and Andy ask if you may sit in the corner and read instead of making shirts you will never wear. Sometimes you ask if you may visit the room where the younger kids are, so you can check on Molly, but they always say no. "Molly is fine," they tell you. But you and Andy are pretty sure that something sinister is going on.

Molly can be a real crybaby around people she doesn't know or like very much. Sometimes you hope she is OK and not crying. But during tie-dye shirt day, you hope she is bawling her head off nonstop just to teach them all a lesson.

Andy is so good at checkers that he's banned from playing by the other kids. This also happens with tic-tac-toe and Uno. You try to play Monopoly with him one day, but most of the pieces are missing. There are only two hotels and no five hundreds.

For lunch, you always have boring food from home. You beg for drink boxes and pudding, but you always get peanut butter sandwiches and apples. You look for Molly in the lunchroom, because her age group eats right before yours. One time you see her, dawdling at the end of the hallway, trying to catch your eye without drawing any attention to herself. Soon after that, the counselors tell you about the new "buddy system," which means that no one is allowed to walk through the halls without a buddy. You ask if you and Andy can be buddies, but they say only girls can be buddies with girls, boys with boys. The counselors give you a reason for this, but you suspect they're trying to keep you separated on purpose.

You never see Molly in the hall again.

After lunch you spend Siesta Time reading. Across the hall, the little kids get to watch movies in the air-conditioned library. Sometimes you sit near the door and Molly sits near the library window and you can see the back of her head. They get to watch *Bambi*.

Some days, instead of Siesta, you and the other kids in your class have to walk two miles to Vista View Elementary, where there's another Project Kids. When the Vista View kids come to your school, they ride in a bus, but you always have to walk. You walk right past your own house on the way. It would be so easy to climb the maple tree in the backyard, just to get away. You know where the spare key is on top of the back door. You could hide in the basement until Mom came home.

You say something to Andy at lunch one day, which is the only time the counselors won't overhear. He's worried about Molly. We can't leave her behind, he says. She'll be all alone.

So you'll just have to ditch them both. You plot exactly when you'll make a run for it—right when you pass the pine trees in the front yard. You'll hide there until the group is past your driveway, then run around to the back.

But somehow it's like they know something's up. Jimbo, the only counselor who treats you like a normal person, the only one who doesn't laugh at you for reading all the time, he walks right next to you the whole way to Vista View. He keeps between you and the pine trees. You try hard to keep your mind clear, ready for flight—you are faster than Jimbo, you can outrun him—but you end up seeing Andy in front of you and that brings back poor Molly, stuck with all the little kids in the library. Maybe she is crying. So you don't do anything, you just keep walking.

At Vista View, you watch a movie called *Hardware Wars* about a flying toaster and a magic flashlight. You watch and don't watch at the same time, let your eyes slowly die until you are looking and not seeing. You can hold this pose forever, you think.

* * * *

You're finally in sixth grade. You're in charge of the school! Finally, people treat you like you know what you're doing. You get to walk down the hall to band practice alone. No one asks you where you're going.

But when you get to band practice, you realize with a sinking stomach that you forgot something. The flutes won a contest for practicing the most hours and today there's the pizza party for a prize. Mrs. Tarabeck's ordering the pizza right now. All you had to bring was a can of pop, and you forgot.

You excuse yourself to go to the bathroom and say you'll be right back. In the hallway, you walk past the bathrooms and keep going until you reach the Stairway Door where the third and sixth graders line up every morning.

It's only a few yards of green grass to get to the trees around Mr. Hall's yard. And beyond that, it's only two more backyards and one street to cross to reach your house. If you run, you think, you can go home and get a pop and be back before anyone knows you are gone.

Of course, if you get caught, it'll be the worst trouble ever. You don't know what the punishment is for skipping school, but it's probably pretty bad. But you're in sixth grade now and you're not supposed to be afraid of these things anymore. So you run as fast as you can and hope no one's looking out any of the windows.

The real world outside school is quiet. No one's home in any of the houses you pass. All the dogs are locked up inside. No one drives down the street. It's kind of scary. You expect to meet someone from school, like a teacher or Mr. Hall, who is the principal at the high school.

And then you're running up to your own back porch. You stand on a bench to reach the hidden key and then you're inside. Mom only buys Diet Coke, which is the worst kind of pop, but maybe the other flute girls will think are you on a diet. That's always cool.

You run back, pumping your legs as hard as you can. You stop for a moment on the edge of Mr. Hall's trees, looking for signs of danger. Nothing. You run back inside and calmly walk down the hall. It's so easy that you wonder why you haven't done it before. You could do it every day.

And then you're back in the band room, where everyone's still waiting for the pizza to arrive. Jaimie Reiner's the only one who notices when you come in because you act so cool. You just went down the hall to wash your hands, no big deal. Then she notices that you're out of breath, and you think, Uh-oh, she knows. But the look on her face is the best, the way her eyes get wide for second and then real small and squinty. Then she smiles like you have a secret. She wants to know how you did it.

* * * *

You get into a fight with Andy while Mom's at work. She's only just started letting you stay home without a babysitter because you begged and promised to be good. But today you run inside and lock Andy out. You even lock the screen door, which doesn't have a key. His friends are on the front lawn and you think, Good, now he'll be embarrassed. You run around to all the windows and lock them tight. Good thing Mom had them replaced a few months ago, because Andy could pry open the old ones.

When Andy climbs onto the roof, you run upstairs and lock all the upstairs windows, too. You look at him through the glass and that's when you know you've gone too far. He's not allowed on the roof, and you should open the front door and say you're sorry. But that would be giving him the upper hand and you just can't do it.

And then you see it, Mom's car coming around the corner. Andy turns when he sees the look on your face and that's when he falls. He goes right off the edge, through the lilac bush, into the landscaping rocks. You don't see it, but you can hear a nasty crunch when he lands. His friends disappear from the front yard. Mom pulls into the driveway. You go around to all the windows and unlock them. You even crack a few of them open the way Mom left them, so it looks like Andy was goofing off on the roof for no reason.

Later, you go downstairs and see them in the kitchen. Mom's in a chair and Andy's kneeling in front of her. She has a bag of ice and a bloody towel pressed to his head. He's crying that it's all your fault and Mom doesn't believe him for a second. You walk through the kitchen like nothing's wrong, sneak down into the basement and turn the TV up loud enough so that you don't hear him crying anymore. He has a scar under his hair for the rest of his life.

You do, too, kind of, when you let yourself think about it. ▪

# The Last Visit, or Just Being on Broadway

## What the living can learn from those who are dying

BY MINDY GREENSTEIN *(Issue 17)*

I DIDN'T KNOW WHAT A DEATH RATTLE was the first time I saw it. It didn't sound like a rattle at all, more like a sustained attempt to breathe and spit at the same time, khhkhhkhhkhhkhhkhh. Tony Pastorini's eyes were wide open, looking vacantly at the empty hole filled with hallway that was his doorway. He'd been facing that doorway for weeks now, even though his doctors had wanted to move him to a hospice long before. They needed his bed for someone who still had a chance. Though I'd known that his death was imminent, I still wasn't quite prepared to see him this way, hovering quietly and helplessly between life and death. He looked weary and emaciated, with a few lonely strands of hair jutting out of his otherwise bald pate. Tony's esophageal cancer had metastasized to his bones, and he had been bedridden for over a month. He appeared decades older than his fifty-three years and was now in the end stage. My feeling of shock was itself a surprise to me, as he already had been quite sick on the day of my first session with him months earlier. I didn't need to look at his chart to know he was going to die very soon.

I had been in such a good mood only moments before. I'd just been named the Chief Clinical Fellow in the Psychiatry Service, despite the fact that I was a psychologist and not a medical doctor. I felt proud and honored and a little full of myself even though my schedule was so difficult. In addition to full-time hours, I was also on call some evenings and weekends, and I had a two-year-old son at home. But I loved my work, and I had strong hopes of a future there after my fellowship ended. I'll never know whether I was right, because things changed dramatically soon after this brief visit.

Illustration: Jenah Pelley

I had been seeing Tony regularly since his admission to the hospital. He loved to talk about his life, and our sessions often consisted of long monologues by him, occasionally interspersed with comments or questions by me. He spoke always in a slow, quiet voice, sometimes looking at me and sometimes looking off into space. And when I asked about subjects he didn't want to discuss, like his doctor's suggestion that he start looking into hospice care, he just looked at me and waited a few seconds. "You know," he would start while I'd wait for an answer, 'did I ever tell you about my favorite Madame Butterflys?" Tony was very much an avoider, and, like many people in desperate situations, he held on to the coping style he knew best. He preferred to stay in the hospital rather than move anywhere, and simply avoided the question of why hospice might be more appropriate. And Tony was perfectly happy to coast in his bed, blithely reminiscing with familiar faces about the old days, whether those faces seemed to want him there or not. If he'd paid attention, he might have noticed that many of them didn't. They wanted to save their beds for the fighters, and with the unused Ensure cans piling up on his side table and his ever-decreasing weight, he wasn't fighting anymore.

Tony's style was very different from my own, as I tend to go far in the other direction, looking for trouble before it starts and taking a proactive role in trying to hold it at bay or meet it head on. It could be hard sometimes to relate to Tony, for me and for the rest of his medical team. We were all so busy doing, it could be hard to understand someone who seemed content just to be. But I couldn't help noticing how Tony's voice would come alive when he was reconstructing his life outside the hospital, even when the subject was painful. Or how his face would brighten when telling stories of his overprotective brothers, or recalling his great lost love, a fiancée who had died in a car crash twenty years before, or describing his favorite paintings and operas. Besides, my style took its toll too. It takes a lot of mental energy to be always conscious of the things that can go wrong in a day, the things you need to do to feel like you're accomplishing something.

Tony's room was low enough that he could hear the bustle of the noisy narrow street beneath his window, and he liked to fantasize about the people below, imagining them walking down the block blissfully unaware of how quickly their time was passing. I imagined they probably were more aware than Tony thought, since many of them were the doctors, nurses and families of people like him. On the other hand, some of those people weren't walking at all, but instead were leaning against the hospital wall getting in a quick ironic smoke before putting on their white coats and scrubs and getting back to work.

It felt odd now suddenly to encounter Tony without words. Instead, all I could hear was the heavy sound of his breathing over the whir of the machines connected to him. As this was likely the last time I'd see him, I chose to stay awhile on the off chance that he might be comforted by my presence. I spoke to him a little, but mostly I sat by his side, feeling somewhat awed by the encounter. At least there was one battle he'd won; he clearly wouldn't be going into any hospice program. Although I'd worked with many terminally ill patients, I rarely had the chance to say goodbye at the end like this. A quote came to mind, by Samuel Beckett. "Astride of a grave and a difficult birth." And Tony certainly looked astride of a grave at that moment. Then, I thought of all the people trying to live their lives while fighting to survive their ordeal, and I envisioned a day when I would be the one lying in a bed just like theirs. What would I be reminiscing about?

I wondered if Tony sensed my presence, and, if he did, whether he considered it a comfort or an intrusion. I got up to leave, when I had a sudden insight that was as powerful as it was ordinary. Beckett wasn't referring only to people in Tony's situation. He was describing how we all live our lives, with our mortality hanging over our heads from the moment we're born. I caught a glimpse of myself through Tony's envying eyes—one of those healthy people walking down the street, oblivious to the real facts of life: that it's short and precious and you'd better know what matters to you now. I suddenly knew where I wanted to be in my life, but it wasn't the course I'd set for myself.

I thought of the previous weekend when I'd been on call, seeing to a delirious patient in the hospital in the middle of the night. Soon after I'd arrived at the hospital, my husband had called to tell me our son was sick. His temperature would soon climb to one hundred and six. I stayed with my patient until his delirium stabilized, but spent the next sixty hours shuttling back and forth between the hospital and our apartment, juggling phone calls to my husband, our pediatrician and the hospital's team, trying to give my all to both people in my care. Both ended up feeling fine. I was less so.

Sitting now beside Tony, I knew that what I wanted most was to spend more time with my son before his toddlerhood completely passed me by. I wanted moments that I could reconstruct from my own deathbed one day, a lot of them. And I also wanted the time to digest the unarticulated impact my work was having on me. More than that, I wanted to write about it. Ever since I'd been a child, I'd wanted to write, but it had been a vague and unfulfilled desire. I knew I was now having an experience worth sharing, but was unsure what I had to say about it. I wanted the time to find out what it was I wanted to express.

I turned my attention back to Tony. He was lying there just as he had when I first had walked into the room, breathing loudly, eyes wide open but looking vacant. I leaned over him and touched his arm slightly as I said goodbye. He never regained consciousness and died quietly in the middle of the night.

At first, I tried to ignore my inconvenient epiphany. It was clear what the consequences would be for my status at the hospital if I tried to cut back my hours. One senior psychiatrist suggested that if I couldn't give the three hundred percent expected of me, perhaps I ought not to be working there at all. But the vividness of my experience stayed with me; I cut back at the end of my fellowship year anyway and made a connection with a psychiatrist at the hospital who wanted to start a new kind of group therapy for cancer patients. I studied the work of existentialists and scientific researchers, ultimately designing an existential group therapy and writing the manual for future research. It was and remains one of the most fulfilling experiences of my entire career.

But I also reveled in the time I got to spend with my son. I had to smile when a member of our therapy group told us about how illness had changed his priorities. "You're not going to find yourself on your deathbed saying, 'Oh shit, what about that meeting I missed.' No, you're going to think of all the times you missed being with the people you love."

I ultimately had a second son, and decided to stay home with my children for a while, consulting when I had the time. Then I began writing a book about my experiences at both ends of the life cycle. And the final catalyst for this sea change was a man whom I was supposed to be helping, a man who could not even speak and who was totally unaware of the effect he was having on me.

The famous psychiatrist Viktor Frankl described the desire for meaning as a basic biological need, a craving for a sense of belonging in the world and of having a personal impact on it. He thought there were three avenues open to us in our search for meaning. The first is the most common, our work or our art. Not only our jobs, but what we do, the causes we fight for, the things we make. For Tony, this avenue had been closed off long before I'd met him. But all wasn't lost. Another path to meaning in Frankl's view is through our experiences: how we relate to other people or to beautiful things in the world; our ability to appreciate what Beckett once called "...the beauty of the way. And the goodness of the wayfarers." Even in the bowels of a concentration camp, Frankl could appreciate a luminous sunset over the mountains of Salzburg, and he felt more whole simply for knowing he could. Just as Tony could still appreciate his favorite sopranos and the people he loved. And as I could appreciate his appreciating them, even when he could no longer tell me himself. And when that ability is also lost to us, Frankl suggested we could still experience meaning through nothing more than our attitudes toward the unavoidable things that happen to us. Just being alive, just being, meant you had an impact.

I especially thought of Tony when I walked my older son to his preschool class each day. Before, taking him to school had been a source of nothing but tension, as we would struggle to make it out on time, yet another stress-filled chore. I am not a morning person, and, in addition to getting both of us dressed and out the door, I had to make sure I had whatever papers, articles, phone numbers, etc., that I would need afterward at work. Invariably, I would forget something on the way and would start calculating—whether I had enough time to go back, whether I could substitute one thing for another, how long separation would take at preschool.

After I cut back at work, the walk to school became the most treasured part of my day. I was aware on one level that there were many aspects of my career that were going to suffer in addition to the financial burden. I couldn't put these walks on my vitae, I wouldn't publish articles about them (except perhaps now), wouldn't get promoted for conducting them well. And those were things that mattered to me, and still do. I had a particularly vivid taste of the conflict between my personal and professional lives when I received a call from a therapist. He had read my journal articles and wanted to discuss the therapy group he was starting. While we were busy discussing existential issues like death, hope and meaning, he heard a tiny voice call out from my end, "Oops! Sorry about your bedspread, Mom. I forgot to wipe! Could you help?"

But my feelings about my lost status paled in comparison to the new feeling I had walking arm-in-arm with my boy. To my surprise, my favorite moments were completely uneventful, the more mundane the better, like talking about what he'd have for snack or what color Play-Doh he'd be making in school that day. We talked about the different colors of the trees, found shapes in the clouds, and ate steaming H & H bagels with no yucky stuff in them. Just walking with him on Broadway made me feel alive. Even when I tried to kiss him in public and he recoiled in quasi-disgust. Even when he stumped me by asking if I would ever get dead, and followed it up by asking if he would get dead, too. I answered briefly and almost honestly. Yes, I told him, one day, like his frog Eric, we would both get dead. But, I added, I didn't expect that to happen for a long, long time. "That'll be a bummer,' he responded casually. I wasn't satisfied with my answer, though it was the best I could do on the spot.

But I hope to do better than that one day, for both my children. I hope I can convey to them what I've learned from the people with whom I've worked. Frankl believed that we could find meaning no matter what the circumstances, even in Auschwitz, even unto our last breath. Even lying in our deathbed unaware of life going on around us, we can make an unexpected difference in someone else's life. Whether it's through our work, or our art, or the children we raise, or the example we set simply by living our lives and working with the cards we're dealt, we make our mark. It's hard to deny Beckett's point that from the time we're born, every moment of our living brings us that much closer to our death. But the converse is also true—every moment we're dying is also a moment we're still alive. ▪

# Into the Promised Land

## From Tennessee to Brooklyn, the Land of Milk and Honey

BY BENJAMIN FELDMAN *(Issue 18)*

THE TORAH SAYS that the land of milk and honey lies thousands of miles east of Brooklyn's Borough Park neighborhood. It's up to each of us, though, to gaze from our chosen mountaintops, out over the fertile plains we long for. For me, an Ashkenazic Jewish boy born and raised in East Tennessee, return from the diaspora required no overseas trip. The Greyhound to New York would do just fine. I rode the overnight bus to New York in the mid-1960s, once, twice, then for good. I didn't feel I had a choice. For decades, just being in the City sufficed, among so many Jewish people. Then my need to connect grew even stronger. I sated my desire by fulfilling a lifelong dream: learning fluent Yiddish has lit my path anew (albeit to a place hardly known for its physical beauty). I go to Borough Park often, seeking something, perhaps redemption. Maybe I'll find it, one day soon.

My wife tells me that learning Yiddish has enlightened and enlarged me in a way that I have been unable to accomplish in English. "You sound so alive, so excited, so happy when you turn a phrase," she tells me. "I love to listen even if I don't understand each word. I hear and see you in a different way...." Yiddish for me is poetry in motion, a torrent of music and connection with the many things that only God can determine. I end so many English sentences (ostensibly about what Frances and I will do together the next day, how we will get to visit with our grown daughters) with "*imertsHashem*," if God wills it, with God's help. This phrase conveys the larger meaning of each utterance, conveys that life is not *bashert*, not predetermined by man. The Yiddish word connects me with uncountable generations of ancestors who knew so well through lives of deprivation and unavoidable violence what I am only now learning at advanced middle age.

I visited the cemetery in my East Tennessee hometown last year, where my father, may his memory be blessed, has lain for sixteen years in the tiny Jewish section. Many others who knew and loved me as a child lie close by. In that small congregation, I felt the warmth and caring of a family, of parents who watch over their children with the same intensity I imagine in the faces of Borough Park fathers and mothers. Though I have no desire to become orthodox, much less Hasidic, and though I find distasteful many of the values and practices of ultra-observant Jews, nonetheless I am warmed and inspired when I wander in the streets of *frum* communities. My days in Borough Park and Williamsburg enveloped me as I gazed from a bench near my father's grave over the few dozen Jewish plots nestled together in kosher ground among the thousands of *goyim* surrounding them. What a strange place to lie for all eternity.... Why did he and my mother flee so far from their Philadelphia homes?

It's late December 1960. Scrubbed little Southern Baptist faces stare wide-eyed at Miss Eula Mae Crabtree, my third grade teacher. They'd never known that I was different, never laid eyes on one of *them* before. I kept my secret deeply hidden, going silent at *"Christ, our Savior"* as we sang verse after verse of "Silent Night." I'd have rather choked to death than say those words. All of the sudden, six-foot-tall Miss Crabtree singled me out with her hill-country twang: "Benjy, will you please stand up and tell the other children about the Jeeew-ish Chriss-mas?" Decades have passed, but I still burn with shame. Fleeing to New York was a matter of survival.

Since learning Yiddish, I've made a habit of going to New York's Hasidic neighborhoods and nearby waterfronts during the intervening days of the Jewish Feast of Tabernacles (*hol hamoed Sukkes* the period is called). In the streets and by the shore, families observe the holiday's tradition of enjoying nature together, marveling at God's many gifts. Street fairs and circuses abound, as well as sex-segregated performances of moralistic tales. This past October, I tried to think ahead for once, how best to enjoy the holiday. On a wall near Thirteenth Avenue, I spied a poster advertising a three-performance run of a play entitled *Dos Zaydene Hemdl*, "The Little Silk Shirt," to be performed in Yiddish in a giant auditorium at Brooklyn College. Two performances had already passed, so I decided to try for the final show, late Saturday evening. Tickets were said to be available at electronics emporia and bookstores in many orthodox Jewish neighborhoods. I put off making a decision until I could discuss it with my wife. Being apart on a Saturday night would have to be a joint decision. Sitting with the few women attending in the segregated *vayber benklekh*, the women's seats, would be distasteful to Frances. She'd be in the dark, amidst a Babel of Yiddish and suspicious stares. With her endless generosity, Frances gave me leave.

I decided to avoid a pointless 90-minute round trip the following evening if the show was already sold out, and called the number I'd scribbled down from the theater broadside. The phone recording brought good news: "*S'blaybt nor getseylte tikets far mener,*" there are only a few tickets left for men. But was there a human being to talk to? A website to consult? A Yiddish-language Ticketmaster maybe? Not a chance. The only way to make sure of a seat was to run back out to Borough Park, and I'd better hustle. *Shabbes* comes early in the autumn. At 1:30 p.m. the gates would close on me. So I jumped in my van and headed out on the Brooklyn-Queens Expressway once again, bent on a mission.

After first staring in disbelief, the white shirted yeshiva boy at the gift shop-cum-box office decided to accept my eager request at face value. He stepped into the back of the store and retrieved a crumpled white envelope, packed with soiled greenbacks. Five or six tickets were all that remained. "You have a top-price seat for me near the front, perhaps?" I was careful to employ the formal "you" and speak my Yiddish words clearly. Tickets ranged from $29 to $46, and I naively assumed that the mostly lower middle-class theatergoers would eschew the high-price seats. Not. Only a few cheap places high up in the balcony remained. The religious significance of the occasion began to sink in. The usual rules of economy were reversed. One makes a show of paying what one needs to so as to approach the *kisey ha'kuved,* the throne of honor. This Johnny-come-lately took what I could get, telling the young man to stuff the change from the two twenties into the *pushkes*, the traditional tin charity boxes that lined the counter in his and his neighbors' stores and adorn many a Hasidic kitchen table. Out I ran with my prize: a glitter-rimmed, pink-banded piece of stiff paper would take me where I wanted to go.

That Friday evening and the following Sabbath day I felt the promise of a spiritual experience reserved for the truly religious. On *Shabbes*, observant Jews do no work, carry no money, and concentrate as much as humanly possible on awareness of God's presence all about. Appreciation that life is not controlled by man, that so much is beyond our imagination, much less our control, is all important. As the hours passed, I meditated over and over on what was coming, this opportunity to immerse myself deeply in a true Yiddish-speaking environment, where the language is neither an academic experience nor a recreation. Just what one speaks, day in, day out. I headed out to Brooklyn that Saturday at sunset, clutching my precious ticket in one hand and the steering wheel in the other, preparing myself for another try.

Though certain that the show would not start anywhere near on time, I jogged the few blocks from my parking spot to the Brooklyn College campus, overwhelmed with excitement. The concession counter inside the lobby bustled with activity. Black-clad teenage boys shouted and pushed, grabbing candy in sealed packages to sustain them through what promised to be a long evening's entertainment. I'd brought my own sweets, though—ones these youngsters could not enjoy. Yiddish is just a language to these people, for the most part; it's the medium of daily commerce. Prohibited from reading most classic Yiddish literature because of its worldly impurities, proscribed by strict Rabbis from attending the so-called mainstream offerings of Yiddish song and drama in the New York area, Hasidim are denied the opportunity to taste choice fruit of their own language. But I carry my little supply of treasure in my own kit bag. There lies my knowledge of literary Yiddish. No Rabbi looks over my shoulder, no avenging angel looms behind me. I can pray quietly, all on my own.

When I arrived at the auditorium, a few minutes remained before the scheduled start. I decided to use them wisely and make myself comfortable. The men's restroom turned out to be its own one-acter. Standing at the row of urinals was as good as using the john at Yankee Stadium. When the Bombers hold a big lead in the top of the ninth, the lines for the men's room are out the door. Guys wait ten deep behind each piece of porcelain. One hunk of manhood is more beer-soused than the next. Wisecracks assault the man at the plate, "Wussamattuh, big guy? Havin' some trouble *findin'* it?" Average time with your unit out: sixty seconds. Then the elaborate hitching up. A stop at the washstand is only for sissies.

For my Hasidic brothers in similar need, though, the process is completely different. Religious men are, in general, very uncomfortable with their own bodies, all the more so with their genitals. Whether it's sex or just *oyspishen,* handling your member is done briefly, and certainly without a look down *there.* No one stands behind anyone, no one goes near anyone, no one says a single word. Clusters of men gather at the doorway, waiting a turn at the gleaming fonts. Furtive glances fill the air, dicks are barely touched. One by one they rush up, do their business and depart. Elapsed time per squirt: fifteen seconds, max. *No one* could possibly piss so quickly. But 100 percent wash their hands, many taking longer at the sink than at the urinal.

I stepped up to bat, and the surreptitious looks I got darn near constricted me. My ponytail must have done them in. It's a wonder a *mashgiakh*, a kosher certification expert, wasn't summoned after I flushed. The porcelain probably had to be blessed to make it fit for further use. What if my *bris* was performed by a Reform *moyel*? [1]

I hightailed it out of there, brushing by a gaggle of boys wearing astonished looks. Up the stairs I climbed, one flight after another, until I finally reached the upper balcony. After some effort, I found my seat in the last row. A sea of black-hatted disarray stretched below me. Not a woman in sight. Outside I'd seen a few teenage girls furtively smoking and talking with their male friends. The entry lobby was divided by a gigantic floor to ceiling white curtain, the *mekhitse,* divided in the middle to create a clandestine entrance to the tiny women's section in the theater. A stern-looking *shoymer*, a chaperone, watched over the part in the folds to prevent illegal mingling. From my seat I couldn't see a trace of the women's section.

Nine-thirty p.m. was advertised as show time, and I made sure to be prompt so as not to miss even a crumb. What a joke that was. The appointed hour came and went: 9:45, 10:00, and no sign of settling down. Up on stage, men with their coats off and their *kipes*[2] askew ran back and forth, adjusting video cameras, arguing over heaven knows what. At 10:15, with most of the audience inside the auditorium (albeit unseated), Hasidic rock music began to blare. The audience went wild, clapping and cheering as if the late, great Rebbe, the Lubavitch Reb Schneerson, was expected on a return visit from *yener velt*, the other world. Then an announcement boomed out: *Hoshever fraynd, mir bagrisn aykh tsu undzer vorshtelung* ... Respected friends, we welcome you to our presentation. The show would start in just a few minutes....

To my left and in front of me sat a half-dozen teenage religious dayschool students. None had even a sprout of a beard, and few wore *peyes.* These boys attend modern orthodox *yeshives* in Brooklyn, and although they speak Yiddish poorly, if at all, they nonetheless comprehend it. I exchanged a few polite sentences, but we soon fell silent. Whether the age difference made it tough to converse or simply my being a *fremd,* someone from outside the culture, our interchange soon failed, and the boys moved down to be with the rest of their compatriots.

Two minutes later an overweight, bearded man strode through the entrance nearest me and rushed into his seat. Dressed in full Hasidic garb, the thirtyish fellow gave off a scent like the Bronx Zoo monkey house. I could smell him clear over the cushioned row that separated us. In his right hand the fellow clutched a wrinkled black plastic bag. With the left he wiped the sweat off his brow. Rivulets ran down onto the filthy glasses perched on his nose. Once he settled in, the contents of the black sack were revealed: a new, expensive looking pair of binoculars emerged together with a crumpled instruction booklet.

My neighbor grasped the specs, first with one hand and then the other, tentatively raising them to his eyes to peer at the stage. Each time, nothing. A blank stare of incomprehension. Down the instrument went and back up. Again nothing. The instructions were consulted. The language gap between English (translated from Chinese by a factory manual writer) and this fellow's Yiddish train of thought was too much for me to bear. I leaned over, tapped my neighbor on the shoulder, and told him politely in Yiddish to look through the other end of the binocs. Perhaps he'd have better luck. The fellow took a shot at it, smiled with joy, and bestowed upon me his profuse thanks and God's blessings (with apologies for being so naive). I closed my eyes and tried to remember how old I was when I first learned the magic residing between the two ends of a pair of binoculars.

Again the balcony door opened. Another young Hasid came up the stairs, looking wildly to the left and to the right, anxious to take his seat before the show started. Sure enough, he plunked himself down next to me, though first recoiling at the sight of the *shtik treyf*, the piece of impurity, fated to be his seatmate for the evening. Dressed in a long, dull *kapote* and black slacks, a dirty-collared, long-sleeve white shirt, white socks and scuffed black dress shoes, the young man looked like he had stepped straight out of a 19th century study hall. He settled uncomfortably beside me and removed his broad-brimmed black hat.

We must have made quite a sight, me looking like some cleanly dressed refugee from Tompkins Square Park, and my neighbor in full regalia, *oysgeputst*, as his people say. This boy had two of the longest, most elaborately curled and coiffed, blond silk *peyes* I have ever seen. Absent was any intention, though, of making himself sexually attractive, regardless of his elaborate coiffure. Wearing *peyes* is a *mitsveh*, a commandment. The more you do it up, the larger your *zkhus*, your spiritual account, will increase, towards ultimate weighing in *oylem habe,* the world to come.

I took a breath and launched right in. "*Sholem Aleykhem*," I offered, and got the customary mirror reply. But it didn't take long for my seatmate to go on the offensive. With an insistent "*Vi bistu du?*" the pastiest of faces held me to account: "What the bleep are you *doing* here?" is a serviceable translation of the young man's politesse. But nothing I said would satisfy this *bokher*. In a world clothed in black and white, gray cannot exist. All my *plopl*, my careless rant, about being a Yiddishist, being interested in all manner of theater pieces done in my favorite language, it was all *puste reyd* to this fellow: empty talk. We were on to the next and main subject forthwith.

His arms and neck gyrating wildly, the astonished boy laid into me with the *klotz kashe*, the difficult question. I've come to expect it in all extended interchanges, the inquiry that interests them most. First one way, then another (due to my inability to comprehend the verb this boy used in his first formulation), I was asked to furnish the details of my personal financial statement to a complete stranger. *"Vi basheftigstu?* (How are you employed?)" came out over and over, and when three repetitions and my blank stares and requests for slower pronunciation had gotten him good and enraged, my interrogator used a phrase I recognized: *"Vi nemstu parnose?"* How is it you make a living? I understood those words just fine, but it pleased him not a bit when he heard that I was retired at an obviously young age. *"Host shoyn genig gelt?"* You have enough money, *already*? He stared with incredulity as his eyes bugged out.

For a people so deeply involved in the world of the spirit, this obsession with others' pocket linings is strange to me, but it's a totally predictable part of my forays. Like so many of the grown men in the auditorium, I have no visible means of support, and live my life studying and seeking enlightenment. They go on foot, I by bike, they to *yeshives* and I to the New York Public Library. Our heads are both in the clouds, though, chasing wonder. Somehow, on some level, despite the total disconnect in dress and religious observance, I know we're close, and I'm at the ready with as oblique but polite an answer a guy can muster who is obviously not from the *frum* world. But my neighbor didn't buy my story. Ashmoday himself might as well have been his neighbor in row S.[3] My new acquaintance was not to last: the boy jumped the seat backs in front of us forthwith, brushing my bacon-bit breath from his dandruff-coated collar.

Twenty minutes of Hasidic folk-rock later, the lights finally dimmed, and we were told to please turn off all cellphones, pagers, and other electronic devices. Not since the days of the golden calf have Jewish people so roundly and soundly disobeyed a commandment. Despite the cacophony of ringtones, darkness filled the auditorium, and the curtain rose. Sitting in a stone dwelling, *Yankev Avinu*, the patriarch Jacob of Genesis, bent over a table, squinting his dim eyes at a scroll. Dressed in Bedouin attire, our holy ancestor consulted with his manservant over what to do about the fighting among his twelve sons.

The play progressed in a Yiddish so thickly accented I could barely understand it, one scene more wooden than the next. Production values and thespian skills were of no concern to this audience, though. Each entrance of even a minor Old Testament figure was greeted with joyous hooting and applause. Again the stadium came to mind: Root, root, root for the home team.

Jacob's manservant provided the strangest counterpoint. The authors of the script had improved on the traditional story in many places, carefully announcing at the outset that the version presented was not intended to portray what actually occurred nor be totally faithful to the holy words *vos shteyt in posek geshribn*, those written in the holy verses themselves. *Fartaysht un farbessert* ruled the day: the drama was translated into Yiddish and improved, which in this case meant the confabulation of the story of Joseph and his brothers with Grampa from the TV program "Hee Haw." A witless ancient bumbler in bib overalls speaking Galitzianer Yiddish a mile a minute was interjected into desert scenes at his master Jacob's side as if nothing could be more plausible. Had women been permitted on stage, Minnie Pearl would have stepped from the wings as a housemaid, price tag still dangling from her new straw hat. Yiddish, English, what's the difference: the distance between poor folks in the hills of my childhood Appalachia and the Polish *shtetl* people in front of me amounted to a mere *katzen-shpring.*

I tried my best, now alone in my row, straining to understand the actors' words, watching dramatic technique straight from a typical high school play. But the clock got the better of me. Half past midnight rolled around, and though I'd only made it through 30 percent of the scenes listed in the program, I was exhausted. Few new opportunities would present themselves to interact with my fellow theatergoers, or so it seemed. A kind of quarantine zone had formed around me. I felt a little defeated, but glad I'd tried. This promised land certainly didn't measure up to the one that had beckoned to me from my personal Mount Nebo. I slipped out the balcony doors unnoticed, and headed down into the chilly black night. Wearily, I stumbled down Nostrand Avenue, alone and confused, condemned again to look upon Canaan only from a distance.

Maybe it will come to me one day, why I love to keep trying, to approach and involve myself in interactions with native Yiddish speakers, how it acts as a palliative for my soul. Each time I try, though, for better or worse, I know I feel better than I did in days gone by. That graveyard in the Appalachian foothills sat nearly empty forty-six years ago while I did Miss Crabtree's bidding, trying my best to tell my classmates the Maccabean tale. The few stones then set in the fescued burying ground bore names I didn't recognize. Back then, the *yizkor* plaque in our *shul*, the bronze tablet of remembrance, hung almost empty on the sanctuary wall. The sockets for electric lamps by each blank name strip stared creepily at eight-year-old me while I fidgeted through services on Friday night before we got to the cake and grape juice part I craved.

The cemetery section is well-tenanted now, and the words of the *kaddish* are heard every *Shabbes* at Temple Beth-el. I walk the rows and read the names in disbelief during my visits, laying a pebble on the graves of those I loved, warding off by magic the evil spirits that would steal my mind. But in my appointed task, that of living and dying, I've taken on a more powerful tool than a little rock. Language is lighter than a feather but mightier than a stone, easier to wield a thousandfold.

Learning Yiddish will entitle me to a proper Jewish burial, even though I do not observe all of God's commandments, despite the theatergoers avoiding me. My grave will now be where it should, among Jewish people, in sanctified ground, *nisht hintern ployt,* not under the fence near suicides and excommunicants. Soon one day I'll take my rest, and then no longer be alone. When I arrive in the world to come, I'll talk and joke in the language of my forefathers. God will listen, and I'll be blessed. ▪

1. The Jewish rite of circumcision, the *bris,* short for *bris milah*, the covenant of the word, is performed on Jewish male infants in memory of Abraham's word given to God at the altar where Isaac was to be sacrificed. The surgical procedure is performed by a *moyel*, a man trained in religious as well as applicable medical technique.

2. Skullcaps are referred to either by their Hebrew name, here rendered in the plural with the Yiddish inflection, or in the traditional Yiddish as *yarmulkes.*

3. Ashmoday (pronounced ah-shmo-dye) is one of the many Hebrew names for Satan, taken from a three letter Hebrew root that pertains to annihilation. The great annihilator does countless evil deeds; likewise the infinitive of the reflexive Yiddish verb employed for a Jew who converts to Christianity is *shmadn zikh*, literally to annihilate oneself.

Note on transliteration: In transliterating the Yiddish words above, I have used the system devised by YIVO, the preeminent secular Yiddish-language cultural and linguistic organization, founded in Vilnius, Lithuania, in the late 1920s, and transplanted to New York in 1940. The overwhelming majority of modern academic Yiddishists employ this transliteration system, known to them as "*di klal transliteratsiye system*," the rulebook transliteration system. ▪

# Mindanao

## Travels with my aunt

BY NITA NOVENO *(Issue 18)*

AS OUR PLANE DESCENDS for Davao City, I am looking at this aunt of mine who has fallen into her perpetual somnolent state. Nothing about this phenomenon has changed. Except perhaps an increase in frequency over the years. Her eyelids slide shut, her head sways in half circles, until finally, body solidly in seat, her head slumps forward or back or to one side, and she is asleep. Out cold until someone wakes her.

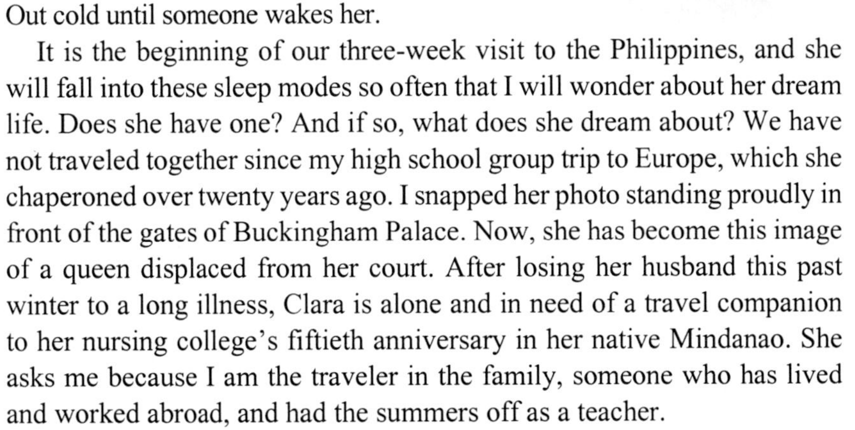

It is the beginning of our three-week visit to the Philippines, and she will fall into these sleep modes so often that I will wonder about her dream life. Does she have one? And if so, what does she dream about? We have not traveled together since my high school group trip to Europe, which she chaperoned over twenty years ago. I snapped her photo standing proudly in front of the gates of Buckingham Palace. Now, she has become this image of a queen displaced from her court. After losing her husband this past winter to a long illness, Clara is alone and in need of a travel companion to her nursing college's fiftieth anniversary in her native Mindanao. She asks me because I am the traveler in the family, someone who has lived and worked abroad, and had the summers off as a teacher.

It is a double-edged offer, generous and exciting on the one hand, and questionable and risky on the other. I know her as a sometimes-difficult personality—competitive and prone to biting comments, yet I am drawn to the opportunity, curious to meet my father's side of the family. I have been in search of my father these last few years; or, rather, I've been looking for traces of his past life, his life before he had a family. I was either too

Illustration: Jenah Pelley

young or too ignorant to ask him about his past, of which he offered few details when he was alive. Ours was a contentious relationship whose marquee could have read "Old Stubborn versus Young Stubborn." Then, when I was curious, it was too late. He died of congestive heart failure at the age of seventy-nine. I was in college, spending my junior year in France, discovering what the world had to offer, and, in the next moment, take away.

Since then, I find myself wanting to recover this part of my father like a set of lost keys. I look for him in places he used to live and in people who knew him, a glimpse of another life in a story or in a house on an old street. I am anxious to meet the families of his siblings on this trip to Mindanao. They live in a region where Muslim separatists have been known to bomb crowded, commercial areas and kidnap Western tourists. Their history, so different from my own peaceful, American upbringing, makes me curious. We are alien to one another, yet the blood that runs through our veins and the name we share beg to differ. My aunt is the thorny, dubious bridge to this place, but a bridge nevertheless. I accept her offer.

"Hey, Auntie Clara," I nudge her arm, "we're landing."

I was eight when I learned that my Aunt Clara came from Mindanao. What did I know of Mindanao then? Nothing. I thought it some vague region in the Philippines, when in fact it is the second largest island in the country. Of my parents' native country I was just beginning to take notice, like a young bird awakening to the fact that it is part of a flock.

"Mindanao is where the Moros live," a family member once told me, "and the Moros are a fierce people, capable of cutting off your head."

As she made the remark, this relative sliced the air with her hand like an axe meant to scare and amuse me. I did not laugh. Moro is a Filipino word for Muslim. I did not know that then, nor did I know what a Muslim was. I wonder now if she was trying to tell me something about my aunt. Not that Clara was of a different religion, because she is Catholic, but that when you are around her, you had better keep your guard up.

Aunt Clara ran the family restaurant, the Diaz Café, where my father played cards in the backroom well into the night with his old time cigar-smoking compadres from the Philippines. It was her second career. After twenty-five years as a nurse, she put away her white uniform for good and donned a shoulder to knee-length floral print apron, replacing her mother-in-law in the business. She became the new "Mama Diaz," the perfect job for someone outspoken, for someone who liked being the center of attention. As if it were part of the restaurant's service, Clara doled out advice to friends and family members alike. No need to ask. It came free with the meal.

During her breaks in the back of the restaurant, she would fall into a predictable napping mode, sitting upright on the sofa. These fits of sleep knocked her out as if she'd just inhaled anesthesia. My mother believed she was exposed to too much of this gas while working in the surgery room. Sometimes, Clara would snore loudly, waking herself with a start.

A memory I have as a teenager comes to mind. In this memory, I am in the small back room of the Diaz Café, waiting for my parents to finish chopping vegetables in the restaurant's kitchen. I am watching television, the volume turned low so as not to disturb Aunt Clara who is napping on the small sofa. She mumbles something in her sleep. Then, the mumbling takes on a panicked edge. I look over once or twice, thinking she is having a strange dream. She wakes up startled, then realizing she is no longer where she believed herself to be, breathes a sigh of relief.

"I had a bad dream," she says, her eyes squinting to identify the other person in the room with her. She sees me, sees that she is safe. She recounts her dream of her drunken father who chased her around a fire, a butcher knife clenched in his hand. Is this true? I wonder. Was her father an alcoholic? Why would he be chasing Clara around with a knife? Had Clara done something to provoke him or had he tormented all his children this way? She has never before spoken to me about her father or about her past life for that matter. For a moment I am a disembodied visitor, being led through the thick walls of my aunt's concrete personality to a secret place. I listen quietly, no questions asked so as not to disturb the memory of this dream, before the secret disappears in her next breath.

"My father used to weave our clothes," she would recall as we walked along the main road that ran through her Mindanao village, "and make my shoes out of wood."

When Aunt Clara speaks of her father on this trip so many years later, it is only out of admiration. He was an industrious farmer, constructing simple mechanisms out of bamboo to water the land, and providing for his family with meticulous care. I listened to her story, her reconstruction of the past, alert to the large trucks speeding dangerously by us. The father in her dream is nowhere in sight.

At the start of our journey, while waiting for our transpacific flight at the Seattle International Airport, I asked Aunt Clara how we were related, a long-accepted fact that had been confusing to me since there were many people whom I addressed as "Aunt" or "Uncle" but were not blood relations. She informed me, as I drew stick-figure representations on a napkin, that her mother and my father's father were siblings, which made us second cousins.

When I asked her about my father's immigration to the States she recalled facts I'd already known: that he'd arrived in the 1920s or 30s and that he'd picked asparagus and onion as a fieldworker in California. I felt her gaze of jealousy as I scribbled notes in my pocket notebook. When she heard I was writing a book, my aunt, never one to be outdone, took on a literary project of her own. With the help of a local newspaper reporter, she wrote a small book about being a pioneer nurse in our hometown and had it self-published.

"Is there anything else you remember about my father's past?" I asked.

"Ask your relatives in Mindanao," she answered curtly, having grown impatient with my questions. I was reminded of my parameters.

Before Clara Noble was born in the early 1930s, her family of poor Ilocano farmers was part of a great migration from the northern island of Luzon to the "Land of Promise" known as Mindanao. The promise was location. The island lies below the typhoon belt, creating ideal conditions for year-round cultivation of mangoes, pineapples, and a bounty of other tropical crops. The Nobles and Novenos settled alongside other Catholic families to cultivate their plots of land into vast rice fields in the frontier areas of the island.

Clara was the youngest of eight children. She and her siblings attended school in the Muslim city of South Cotabato an hour away from their small village. Clara was the only one in her family to attend college: a nursing school called Brokenshire College in the city of Davao. She was in its first graduating class. The year was 1956. After two years working in the college hospital, she left for the United States with the help of her cousin, my father, Benito, who'd become an American citizen.

"When I arrived in Seattle, your father had a special dinner in my honor," my aunt told me during our twelve-hour flight to the Philippines, her memories released in a sudden, warm flow, "It was my first time to taste goat meat." She recounted how her small floatplane from Seattle slapped down onto the black waters of Southeast Alaska, water spraying up to the windows.

"I thought the plane had crashed."

I am surprised by this revelation of her past, a scene suddenly come to life of someone I've never known, my aunt, young and vulnerable. Clara became one of a handful of Filipinas in the community and one of the four nurses at Ketchikan General Hospital. These pioneering nurses treated fishermen and lumberjacks who lost limbs. It was brave, noble work. Yet, it did not stave off the loneliness Clara felt in those first few years on the island.

"Your father hid my boyfriend's love letters," she claimed. I wondered if this was true. I pictured my father secretly slipping envelopes into his coat pocket. Was he afraid Clara would return to Mindanao? Or was Clara just making up an excuse for why she hadn't received any news from her sweetheart back home? Had she stayed, I imagine she would have married this boyfriend and lived the rest of her life in Mindanao. Instead, Clara had the opportunity to attend Johns Hopkins University to study surgery nursing. When she returned to Ketchikan, she was introduced to Manuel, the stepson of my father's good friend, whom he had met as a migrant worker in Seattle. Joe had persuaded Ben to find work in the salmon canneries in Alaska. Joe had married "Mama" Diaz, a windowed Filipina restaurant owner with three children. Manuel, the second child, was an American-born Filipino with a stutter and an easy laugh. Manuel and Clara married and had two boys.

As we fly under the clouds, I catch a glimpse of Davao City, green and lush right up to the white coast. Just when I think we are ready to land, the plane follows the U-shaped coastline and I observe as if through a magnifying lens the long pointy palms of the trees and the sandy beaches, unlike the smog-filled, billboard-stacked landscape of urban Manila, in which we landed the day before. The plane touches down on the runway, lined on both sides by dark walls of vegetation.

Last year, a bomb had gone off in the Davao City International Airport, killing twenty-one people. I was in the Philippines at the time, visiting relatives on the southern island of Luzon, a safe distance from the tragedy. The Moro Islamic Liberation Front (MILF), a politically separatist, supposedly anti-terrorist group, was responsible for the bombing. This shocking event only added to my impressions of the place based on relatives' stated fears and actual reports of killings in the past. As I watched the grievous news unfold on the television with my cousins, I envisioned walking through a hostile Muslim community that could smell my American scent, and being kidnapped and killed. Any interest I had in going to Mindanao was cast aside for the moment.

Aunt Clara and I make our way through the newly built airport, relocated from its original site. It feels like I have entered a large sculpture of metal and glass. Clara has put on her custom-designed red baseball cap, which reads on its front, "Brokenshire College—Class of 1953." She had a dozen made for the classmates she knew would be attending, classmates who started reuniting over the past ten years. We haven't walked far when a woman wearing bright red lipstick runs up to her. They both cry out in recognition and hug. Suddenly, Clara is being whisked towards a group of women holding a large welcoming sign, "Brokenshire College / celebrates Golden Jubilee Anniversary / 1953-2004." Between profuse hugs and cries, a round of photos are taken, while I stand by smiling. Then, after a brief wait for our luggage, we step out of the airport.

Warm air surrounds us as we climb inside the van that takes us to our hotel in downtown Davao. I feel less like a tourist on this island as I listen to the conversation of a young French couple from the back of the van and take in the view from my window, similar to what I've seen on the island of Luzon—a lush, dark green vegetation, roadside stands of grapefruit-like pomelos and mangoes, crude wagons drawn by water buffaloes, Nissan pickups with tinted windows, and people crammed into the uniquely Filipino mode of transportation called jeepneys: long-ended jeeps painted in the owner's vision, an often flashy design and a side or front placard with the name of the vehicle (often a family member's name) or a religious pronouncement like "God is here" or "Save your soul." As we approach the city and the streets become congested with cars and trucks, I try to imagine what the place might have looked like when Aunt Clara lived here and during the years of my father's visit. I imagine a scene taken straight out of a black-and-white photo with fewer wheeled vehicles and unpaved roads. I scan the city for any signs of Muslim culture or people and spot one mosque amongst the buildings.

For the first two nights, we stay at the large Chinese-owned Grand Men Seng Hotel, before we transfer to the new alumni house, or "Bahay" Alumni, built on the new college campus. Brokenshire College had recently relocated from its original building damaged by fire to its present hilltop grounds overlooking a dense forest of palm trees. Compared to our spacious hotel room, with a king-sized bed and a front room large enough to park a car, our alumni room is cramped, no bigger than my own 8' x 10' childhood bedroom, which I shared with my sister. Are you kidding? I think to myself as Aunt Clara and I entered. In it are five slim twin beds with enough space between each bed to slide a suitcase in sideways. I notice two beds with clothes piled on them and two closet doors ajar. I peek in the closets and see clothes hanging inside and suitcases on the shelves. Suddenly, I feel like I'm a character in a children's story, a composite of "Little Red Riding Hood" and "The Old Woman Who Lived in a Shoe." I look out the slatted windows to the garden below and then begin to unpack, wondering if all the rooms are this small and how much smaller these beds are than the standard twin-size in the U.S. and how I have lost my space for the next week or more but will not complain because I refuse to be a spoiled American.

For the next week, Aunt Clara and I share our tight sleeping quarters with three other women, two of her former classmates and one classmate's sister, who all flew in from the United States or Canada. "Mami," as everyone calls her, is the reputed leader of the group. She and her sister, who is also a nurse, arrived a day earlier. Mami, I learn, married for the first time a few years ago at the age of sixty-six. Until then, the thrifty woman who claims her nickname growing up was "ugly duckling" had been working to support her other siblings. I think her a saint. Later, our fifth roommate arrives, a silver-haired, sultry-voiced woman from Daly City, California who has left her ill husband at home to attend this big reunion. The women are ecstatic to see each other and their perfume and stories of their flights and arrivals fill the air in the room that evening.

The women get up at the rooster's crow—4:30 a.m.—every morning. When I join them and other alumnae downstairs for breakfast later in the morning, they are almost always finished eating. As I serve myself eggs, toast, pineapple slices, and coffee, I am transported back in time, listening to stories of their college days when they lived in rooms with ten beds in a row and washed their soiled uniforms in a long sink located outside behind their dormitory. These sixty- and seventy-year-old women transform before my eyes and become their mischievous, playful twenty-something selves who pulled pranks on one another and on their professors. They laugh, they shriek. Not yet wives or mothers, they are students again until one of their husbands or the reunion director pops her head in the doorway and reminds them of the day's schedule. Then, everyone piles out of the dining area and returns to the present day.

The "reunioners" have a busy schedule and I accompany Aunt Clara to many but not all of the events—an opening reunion ceremony, a tour of the new hospital, various luncheons with guest speakers that include doctors, nurses, and city officials, excursions to see Davao's gardens and beautiful homes. During the opening ceremony, an outdoor "Filipiniana" evening, all the guests wear their traditional Filipino clothing, women in their Imelda Marcos butterfly-sleeve gowns and men in their translucent Barong Tagalog shirts. We are entertained by traditional singers and dancers costumed in mixtures of indigenous and Spanish styles. It is all so formal and familiar, an event I recognize from growing up in a Filipino-American community that taught children the dances and the music of a country and culture removed from everyday American existence. At the beginning of the festive dinner, everyone stands to sing the national anthem.

"That was a nice-sounding tune," I observe to Jerry, a friendly white-haired Filipino-American gentleman from North Carolina who is sitting next to me. His quiet, stern-looking wife is an alumna.

"I don't know the words," he tells me in his happy-go-lucky American English. He sees the look on my face and tells me that he joined the Navy as a young man and traveled the world. He and his wife came to the Philippines four months ago for his brother-in-law's funeral and had been touring around the island before the reunion. I am not sure what surprises me more: Jerry's American-ness or his ignorance of the Filipino national anthem. It seems we have more in common than I first thought. His independence, his love for travel and for America, remind me of my father, a man who only bought American-made cars, in which we took family road trips through British Columbia and down the California coast.

The ethnic Chinese couple that I met earlier has joined our table. The wife is the youngest of five children of a prominent Chinese businessman. Her mother had died at her birth and the Chinese businessman asked Mami, who was working at the local hospital at the time, to take care of his daughter. She came to know Mami as her own mother so she and her husband, a tall, light-skinned man with a moustache, dutifully attend all the reunion events with Mami. During the dinner, I learn from the husband that their family originated from the Fukian province of China. They both attended Chinese school in Davao, speak fluent Fukian, and have visited China. While the musician on stage sings traditional Filipino ballads, the husband teaches me a few greetings in Fukian. I admire how the Chinese maintain their culture and language abroad.

"But I am Filipino through and through," he grins proudly, throwing a wrench into any conclusions I was forming in my mind on identity and culture. Or perhaps he was confirming something I already knew, that place can define you more than skin.

During a two-day break between the college reunion festivities and the grand finale, Aunt Clara and I attend our first family reunion at a simple beach resort in Davao. I am anxious to finally meet my father's side of the family. Under a large open-air pavilion with the ocean's surf a short distance away, I encounter what seems like a small city of Clara's relatives and some of my relatives who have come from near and far to see Aunt Clara and this mystery cousin from New York. I watch as Clara and her two older brothers hug each other and laugh. I take a digital photo of Clara, pale and chubby, between her two thin, dark-skinned brothers and dub it the "oreo cookie" photo. They speak English with a seeming propriety and a lack of self-consciousness, unlike some of the younger distant cousins whom I meet later.

The self-appointed MC for the evening, a comical middle-aged cousin with a missing front tooth, welcomes Clara and me to the reunion repeatedly, announcing the different family members as they arrive and the names of the families represented: "Noble" (Clara's maiden name), "Noveno," "Soriano," he says over the microphone again and again.

I am unmoored in this sea of faces, until I come face to face with a Noveno. Two Novenos in fact. Someone introduces me to my first cousins, Victorina and Ibing, petite dark-skinned women in their late 50s who have my father's smile and dimple. I grip their hands gently, in recognition, as if to say, At last, you've arrived. They speak little English and I speak scant Ilocano so we rely on smiles to communicate this newfound connection. A distant cousin with an excellent memory for family names translates my questions and their soft-spoken responses. I write down names and dates and other small familiarizing details in my notebook to finally replenish the empty branches of a family tree.

While we gather to eat under the pavilion, which the family has rented along with the cottages where some of us will sleep, clouds start to gather above and it is dark when the family "program" begins.

"Please tell us about yourself, daughter of Benit Noveno," the announcer keeps unknowingly shortening my father's name, Benito. I ask if they understand my English, adding that sometimes I speak quickly. They all nod eagerly. After an explanation of who I am, where I grew up, where I live currently, and what I have been doing in the past few years, the drunk cousin announcer asks the dreaded question, "Are you married or single?"

From my past visits to the Philippines, I've grown defiant and impatient with this question. In a country where women my age are already married and have teenage children, I feel alien.

"Single," I reply.

"Do you want to tell us more about yourself?"

"I'd be happy to answer anyone's questions personally," I say, cutting off any possibility for further public inquisition. Better to handle it one on one.

It starts to rain when Clara and I are asked to sit up front for a session of picture taking. After the first photo with the first set of families is taken, I stand up to return to my seat.

"No, stay here, all the families will take photos with us," Clara explains to me, laughing. Then, for the next hour, we sit like royalty as more families come up one by one and stand behind us. A representative of the family introduces each member and then our group photo is taken. Clara and I keep a royal-like composure, our hands crossed on our laps. I am flattered and amused for the most part, but also feel as though I should be someone more important.

Then, Clara's turn arrives. In front of this curious, eager family audience, Clara is asked to tell her story. At first she refuses, whispering to a nearby nephew that she will break down because of her recent loss. At the insistence of our drunk MC, Clara takes the mike and speaks of her husband's passing.

"You don't understand what it is like to be alone," she says, her voice like a sudden burst in a quiet universe, "You are all lucky, you have each other."

I shift in my seat, look up once to read any reactions from the audience, and, unable to find any, look back down at my hands. Her familiar sharp tone rings in my ears.

"You have each other and I am alone," her voice cracks this time. I shift in my seat again. After a moment of heavy silence I lean over to her and whisper reassuringly, "No, they don't understand, do they?" wanting to convey a mutual understanding of the large, extended family in this country and how fortunate they are in their ignorance. I feel pity, not so much for my lonely aunt, but for these innocent listeners having to take the blame for her current emotional state and I think I shouldn't be thinking this way because, after all, she has lost her husband of more than forty years, but I do think this way because I see the familiar queen has returned.

The years have not softened so much as slowed down her bark. Her remark feels like a slap in the face. I scan the audience for other offended parties, but find not a hint. Afterwards, as I talk to individual relatives, I notice groups of people sitting around Aunt Clara, some leaning forward to talk to her, some bowing their head in reverence. A queen recovered. I wonder if the people in her court are just being polite.

We return to the Bahay Alumni the next afternoon, and I am feeling more at home on the island. While Aunt Clara participates in the last two days of her college reunion activities, I am happy to go sightseeing with an older cousin who volunteered at our family reunion to be my tour guide.

"I am always the last to know of Aunt Clara's visits here," he claims to me a few times during our tours and each time I shrug in ignorance. It seems the opposition has found me.

He openly expresses his disappointment with Clara and how she once promised to bring him to the United States. After piecing it together, I come to think that Clara's marriage and starting a family probably distracted her from any promises she might have made while she was on one of her visits back home in Mindanao. This cousin had been a hopeful teenager at the time. I didn't realize until much later that he probably viewed me as the last chance to somehow connect him or one of his grown sons to Aunt Clara and life in the United States, a life he'd dreamt would make him a millionaire

He takes me to Philippine Eagle farm an hour away from the city in the mountains to see the once-endangered species with the punk-like feather-do on its head, and we walk around a hilltop resort with an impressive view of Davao City and Mt. Apo, the second highest mountain in the country and an active volcano.

One day, after a morning tour of a local museum, Tour Guide cousin and I join my aunt and others for lunch at the Grand Men Seng Hotel. When we arrive, the large group has just finished eating. We sit ourselves at a half-occupied table and I try to catch the eye of Aunt Clara but she is asleep. After eating, I finally manage to get her attention.

"Where have you been?" she asks in an admonishing tone.

Stunned, and feeling like a child, I stammer out my reply. She had not mentioned before needing company and seemed fine with me touring separately for the past two days. In an attempt to impress her, Tour Guide cousin begins listing off the places we visited that day.

"I don't care!" she cuts him off and says to me, "I brought you here to be with me, not to go off on your own!"

I am speechless. Tour Guide cousin is speechless. One of her classmates attempts to defend me by saying something about how I need to enjoy myself too, but Clara won't hear it. As Clara joins her departing party, I rise from my seat in humiliation. I discover that Clara is having a hard time moving around, her feet have become swollen again. Even though others assist her, she is still angry with me and doesn't talk to me for the rest of the day. I feel guilty for not being the attentive niece, but am shocked by her response. A dark cloud threatens to loom over the rest of our journey together, and I just want to escape it.

Fortunately, what vexes my aunt dissipates with the arrival of the reunion finale, a glamorous dinner and awards ceremony at a large hall of a municipal building. Before the event, back at the Bahay Alumni, a group of makeup artists of "bakla," or gay men, transform my Aunt Clara and her classmates into Hollywood beauties, coating and layering them with hairspray, eyeliner, powder, blush and lipstick. They are all in high spirits. Once they don their beaded and silk finery, I barely recognize my retired roommates. Aunt Clara's graying hair has been swept tight up to the side and cemented with hairspray. In her red sequined gown and red shoes, she resembles a celebrity of sorts.

"You look like Nancy Reagan!" I say and the name takes affectionately with her and her classmates.

On the spacious stage, professional singers croon the latest American and Filipino songs, nursing school alums and administrators perform humorous skits, and a set of three older couples affiliated with the nursing college slide smoothly through the tango and various ballroom dances. The spectrum of ages of alums are represented, honored, awarded, and cheered during the formal announcements. I feel like I am watching a talent show turned roast.

While waiting in the dinner line, I stand behind one of Aunt Clara's former classmates, Jainab. She is Muslim, one of two in her graduating class, from the city of South Cotabato on the western side of the island some six to seven hours away by car. She is the first Muslim I talk to and I begin to wonder how she felt going to school with her Catholic classmates. She wears a sequined cap on her head that covers all of her hair and bright red lipstick. She is matronly and handsome and has a deep voice of conviction when she speaks. I secretly nickname her the Filipino Maya Angelou.

"I lost my husband two years ago. He was shot and killed."

"I'm so sorry," I'm taken by her openness, "What happened?"

"It was politically motivated. My husband's younger brother is the mayor in our region…he was killed by his brother's enemies. The ones that don't like his politics."

"Why would they shoot your husband?"

"These enemies believed that my husband told his brother what to do. That the mayor was consulting his big brother."

"Do they know who did it?"

"Yes."

"Has he been caught?"

She shakes her head in defiance. "At large."

I had yet not witnessed the ferocious, sword-wielding Muslims of my dark childhood imagination or as reported at the airport, in the markets, or on the streets. In fact, the first Muslims I meet are the quiet, scarf-clad women selling pearls in the alumni hotel's garden. Jainab has made me privy to her corner of the world, where Moros are not only fighting and killing Western tourists or their Catholic neighbors like I had feared, but also each other. I run out of questions, but the conversation takes another turn as Jainab invites me to her hometown where she says her daughter, a city worker, will be my guide and bring me to the city's museum with a collection of interesting Moro artifacts and costumes.

"I will give you my daughter's number," she says, urging me to call her if I make it to South Cotabato. I feel like I've just been handed the keys to a private kingdom.

When we reach the buffet table covered with savory smelling dishes of chicken and fish, vegetables and rice, I notice that Jainab, in following her religious practices, doesn't take any of the young suckling pig, which has been served at every formal dinner I've been to so far. Although the unappealing appearance of this creature, roasted whole until its skin is brown and unusually shiny doesn't make it appetizing, I know from dinners past what's underneath and fork out chunks of the soft, juicy, fatty meat.

The night is full of flashing lights from cameras, award speeches, and dancing to the electric slide, disco and swing music. This is a special night for the college and its well-heeled alumnae. I know the rest of my trip on this island of oppositions will not look anything like this.

When the cousins come to pick us up at the Bahay Alumni, Aunt Clara and her classmates are saying their goodbyes and planning to see each other at the next reunion in two years in Las Vegas.

The drive to the cousin's town is just under two hours on a well-paved road. As we leave Davao, the view of the ocean gives way to plantations of pungent-smelling durian and sweet mango trees. The fruits are sold in neat piles in small shacks or tables on the side of the road. We stop to buy some, eat one in the car, and continue on. The mountains draw near and then disappear in the distance.

"It used to take seven or eight hours to travel on these roads before," Clara remembers. These days the travel time has been cut in half. She credits the former President Marcos, a man of grand deeds and scathing misdeeds, exiled from his country, for the paved roads and electricity brought to the then-hard-to-reach areas of the island.

We arrive at a small city and stay the night with the talkative cousin who had become my translator at the beach reunion. She lives with her husband in a simple, spacious home on walled property on which she maintains an impressive garden of over two hundred potted plants and some fruit trees. She insists on showing me each one, pinching leaves and fluffing up dirt with her fingers.

"I heard Clara was mad at you for leaving her alone at the reunion," she says. Word has traveled to the countryside, and Clara's reputation, or rather mine is being tested. I shrug, wanting to convey a mixture of innocence and indifference.

"You know Clara," she responds, and I nod in relief.

It is the first night on this trip that I do not have to share a room or a bed with Aunt Clara or wake up to her mumbling in her sleep. I relish my time alone before dinner, listening to the rain scattering across the metal roof.

We continue our drive the next morning. Small, wood homes dot the side of road and beyond them lie vast rice fields. After an hour, we arrive in Pikit, my aunt's birthplace, more recently known as the conflict zone. We turn onto a narrow dirt road and into a graveled driveway. At the end of this long driveway stands a big wooden house, the house where my Aunt Clara grew up. Two years prior to our visit, Muslim rebels attacked this small village, killing Christian residents. The Noble men guarded the property with rifles just outside its chain-link fence and the women and children stayed inside the three-story house. The road became the dividing line. Rebels invaded and occupied the other side. Anyone unfortunate enough to live on this side had to abandon their home in the evenings and find shelter with others on safer ground or risk being shot and killed.

The conflict between Muslims and Christians in the area went back to land disputes and claims by the Muslims of unjust treatment by the government in the 1950s with the influx of immigrants from other islands, like my father's and Clara's families.

Islam first arrived on the island of Mindanao in the 14th century after spreading from neighboring Malaya, Borneo, and the Sulu Archipelago through traders, missionaries, and teachers. Its opportunity to expand to the rest of the country was cut short by the arrival of Spanish colonizers and their Christian faith two centuries later. The different Muslim groups on the island united to resist these colonizers for the next three hundred years, continuing their resistance against the American forces.

The signs of war are pointed out to me—mortar holes in the road, bullet holes in houses, the building of a makeshift church on the other side of the road so it is closer to the Noble residence, the widows and mothers who lost their husbands and sons. Instead of fleeing their homes altogether, the cousins of Pikit, fiercely attached to their land, chose to stay and guard their homes and farms.

The night before the family reunion at this large weathered house, a group of men transform the parking shed into an assembly-line butchery. They set up tables and build a fire to prepare to kill and roast two enormous pigs and a goat. I am familiar with these rituals. I had witnessed them before in my childhood in Alaska when my father and the other Filipino men would gather in our yard and hold the animal—a pig or a goat—as still as possible while someone would pry open its mouth and pour vinegar down its throat. As the creature guzzled, its throat was sliced and out gushed blood and vinegar into a big silver bowl. This blood would be used to cook a thick soup called *dinaguan*.

Here in Pikit as I speak to relatives in the living room, sitting in front of the TV and videoke machine, I hear the hair-raising screech of pigs being killed and, afterwards, chopping sounds that last all night. I go out later to take photos of the happily liquored assembly of workers and a huge silver bowl of animal guts. The smoke from the fires, which act as a natural mosquito repellant, spare us the swarms of mosquitoes that fly into the house on the other late evenings. They enter freely through spaces between the roof and areas of wall that do not meet. These short walls I can only guess were built prior to the era of ceiling fans, allowing air to flow in naturally and keep the house cool. The fans do little to keep the mosquitoes away.

Aunt Clara's eldest living brother, white-haired, pale and homebound because of his weakening legs, becomes teary-eyed when he recognizes his sister. I notice how the Noble brothers differ in temperament from Clara. Like his other darker brothers whom I met at the reunion on the beach, the eldest is quiet and good-humored.

At the big family reunion in Pikit, I meet members of my family's namesake who are practically thrown at me once they enter the house.

"Here is another Noveno," they say excitedly, bringing the innocents by the elbow to me. I take pictures of them in groups and pairs, and I write down names, ask what they do—farmer, student, wife. There are no revelations about my father in my meetings with these strangers. Most of them are of my generation and thus had never met him.

My cousins Victorina and Ibing also make an appearance and we smile at each other from across the room. Our exchange is limited to my complimenting their beautiful part of the island.

We eat pork and goat and steamed rice and vegetables. I take more pictures. Outside, a man is turning the spit on which a large pig is being roasted over an open fire. I ask if I can take his picture. People begin to laugh and joke with the man. I smile along not knowing why people are laughing. Then, someone tells me that this man is Muslim, that he won't be eating the pig that is roasting over the fire. Oh, I say, and the man smiles.

In the next few days, I tour the village on foot, visiting people's houses and meeting neighbors. I notice the neighbors who are wearing small caps and vests. I know they are Muslim. They look at us as we pass. I hear stories of how the Muslims do not want to do any work on the land and think about the man roasting the pig at the reunion.

I meet Aunt Clara's childhood friends who have jet-black hair and deeply wrinkled skin darkened by the sun. One of them has returned from cutting grass out in the fields. Another one recounts the story of how she managed to escape the rebel attack.

"They would have to shoot me if they wanted me to leave," she says bravely.

I admire their fortitude. They are young compared to Clara, who appears so much older and slower despite her comfortable American life.

With the sweep of a hand, I am shown the other Noveno households hidden behind trees beyond the rice fields, too far it seems for us to stroll so that I can only wonder about them. It occurs to me then that this was the jungle someone referred to when I was younger and was told that my father's sister lived "deep in the jungle." Certain things will remain just out of reach. In the quiet surrounding, between the laughter of my family guides, the memories of war have been replaced by stories of youth.

Sunday, late morning, we attend the new makeshift church down the road. The original cement brick church, which is located on the rebel side of the street, is riddled with bullets and boarded up. The pleasant priest is from the island of Bohol and conducts mass in Cebuano and Tagalog. I realize my search here will not reveal more than I already know, but it is enough to see what my father saw too. I understand the Mass in bits and pieces. Accustomed to this holy celebration, I do not need to know the language, something beyond the words and rituals seeps in. In bits and pieces. This is how I will understand life in Mindanao and my Aunt Clara, both possessed with a complicated duality. This too is how I will understand my father's history that is becoming my own. ▪

# Pitt Street Pool

A leisurely pastime yields to a competitive drive.

BY JESSICA HALL *(Issue 19)*

I ROLL OUT OF BED, have a quick cup of coffee, throw on my bathing suit, wrap a towel around my waist, and head out the door to join the morning pilgrimage to the Pitt Street pool. Approaching Houston Street, I see the regulars merging from the southeast corner. Some are in their slippers and robes, others wear elegant kaftans or sundresses, and many of the men just come in their trunks. Entering through the tall iron gates, I am greeted by the friendly park ranger who knows me by sight now, and I give a knowing nod of swimmer solidarity to my fellow morning swimmers, all quietly converging at the lockers and under the showers.

The Olympic-sized pool is a grand sight to behold in the bright morning sun. It is stretched out shimmering and inviting under the Ginkgo trees. Hamilton Fish is a city gym. A long, majestic building which sits like a temple at the end of the pool, it was built at the turn of the century and designed to look like a garden pavilion in Paris. The pool was added by the Works Progress Administration in 1936, one of eleven city pools that opened in a single summer. In recent years, the city park and gym has been renovated, one of the few ways—aside from better garbage pick up—that the neighborhood has benefited from gentrification.

The pool is divided into thirds. Slow, medium and fast lanes. Until this summer, I have always preferred the slow lane. In addition to feeling no pressure, I get to closely observe the colorful characters who, like me, favor that lane: elderly ladies doing Esther Williams-style morning exercises in flowered bathing caps; a few younger people who push themselves along with their feet, pretending to swim (the pool is three feet deep all the way across); and, one morning, a woman with a swim mask searching the bottom for change. In the middle lane, decent swimmers do their laps, while the fast lane is a constant uproar of sleek bodies slicing through the water at a breakneck pace. I did, one time, venture into the fast lane because there seemed to be more room there, but I was in fear of being swum over and quickly retreated back to the slow lane where I could relax and still feel like I was moving fast.

Every weekday I wait, along with other eager bathers, for the gates to open at 7 a.m. Once, I attempted to go to the pool during the day, but so many kids were jumping and diving that the lifeguards were constantly blowing their whistles. When they finally gave up and kicked everyone out of the pool, a riot almost ensued. Each morning, I put my stuff in one of the outdoor lockers, then take the required freezing cold shower out in the wide open. The showers make a funny groaning sound, which makes everyone laugh.

This year, as I was signing up, I was told if I swam 25 miles in the course of the summer I would get a free t-shirt. In the past, my idea of fun in the pool was to just go in for about twenty minutes. I'd read somewhere that more than fifteen minutes in the chlorine is unhealthy, so I figured twenty minutes to be an acceptable risk. Last summer, I tried to swim a mile in an hour to qualify for a special swim race in the Hudson off the pier, but there was a thunder shower just as I approached my goal and everyone had to evacuate the pool. I was the last person out and still didn't complete the 32 laps that make a mile.

I never considered trying again because it seemed to be an unobtainable goal. So I continued with my twenty-minute morning paddles, laps uncounted. It is my time for meditation. One day, I found myself reflecting on a really great conversation I'd had with someone, but I couldn't remember who. After a few moments, I realized I'd had it with myself while swimming in the pool! But now, suddenly, the idea of getting a free t-shirt really excited me, and I decided that first day the pool opened that I would make it my summer's goal.

The first day I swam a mere ten laps; the next, 22; and the day after, 28. The fourth day, I swam 32 laps, my first mile, in about 45 minutes. I went to work and eagerly calculated the number of laps I'd have to swim each day to achieve my goal. It would have to be about a mile a day, and I would have to swim 800 laps by the end of August to achieve the 25 miles required for a t-shirt. I started keeping track on my calendar. Last Monday, I had 748 remaining. Now I have 558.

I had never worn goggles during my swim, but now, because the extended pool time made my eyes burn half the day, I started wearing them. As a result, I was able to see the humungous hairballs, scrunchies and Band-Aids that I had to share the pool with. It's always apparent when it's been a busy day at the pool because the morning after, the water is particularly cloudy and not only do I have to swim around the hairballs, but often long strands of hair wrap around my arms, which is particularly aggravating.

I've discovered that I can swim, meditate, have conversations with myself, and count laps all at the same time. After my swim is over, I report my laps and eagerly watch the girls at the table by the poolside record them next to my name and number. They have a graph charting the swimmers' progress hanging on the fence next to the pool and my name is listed there with my miles next to it. There are a lot of women ahead of me, but quite a few behind me, as well. I am securely in the middle, and so have finally moved to the middle lane, where I've found my groove.

Today, in the middle lane, I ran into an old friend from the neighborhood. She wanted to chat about our kids, but I was anxiously watching the clock. It was ten minutes to eight and I still had twelve laps to do. "I'm sorry, but I'm trying to swim a mile a day, and I still have twelve laps to go."

"You're going for the t-shirt?" she asked with a smile.

"Yes, I am."

"I did that one summer," she said, "and at the end of the summer there's a big ceremony where all the early birds, and night owls, from all the city pools come to get their t-shirts. They hand out awards and trophies, but try not to get one; they're really big! And when a swimmer from Hamilton Fish gets a t-shirt or prize, everyone hollers 'FISH! FISH!'"

But I wasn't really listening. I was back to splashing, furious and focused. ■

# Why I Return to M.F.K. Fisher

## The enduring sensuality of food

BY LEE UPTON *(Issue 20)*

I AM THE DAUGHTER of a hospital cook. If you've experienced much hospital cooking, please don't hold that against me or my mother. As a cook she had one day off a week—she was up at 5 a.m. to head for work. For twenty-three years she worked as a cook, with a seventeen-mile drive to work each way. And when she retired, at last, she lacked ten cents of making five dollars an hour. I can't begin to tell you how much I admire her. To give you a sense of the sort of woman she is, here's a story. When she was first married, she and my father raised chickens. One day she drove in the driveway and saw the chickens staggering, their wattles all white. And then she saw something that struck her with horror: a weasel sucking blood from under a chicken's wing. She ran out of the car, took off one of her high heels, beat the weasel off the chicken with her heel, saved the chicken, and at last gained the respect of her in-laws.

Illustration: Jenah Pelley

My mother cooked very early, as a young child. I too cooked—not as early as she did, but I cooked dinners regularly before I was fourteen. I confess.

I cooked with irritation bordering on rage. Until I began to experiment. I made meat loaves of my own invention. Meat loaf with cheese inside, meat loaf with mashed potatoes inside, meat loaf with peppers inside, meat loaf with meat loaf inside. But although I couldn't claim culinary sophistication, I knew of the great rewards of enjoying a meal, and that's why I return to M.F.K. Fisher. I'm a reader with an appetite.

As a culinary artist, Fisher enlivened the senses through almost thirty books. Perhaps one day we'll have great writers of decoupage, crochet and wood burning, but it seems that writing about fulfilling the appetites offers distinct advantages over writing about many other human activities. For one thing, such writing appeals to virtually every sense. Taste, smell, sight, even sound. And touch. It's so basic as to sound idiotic but we can't eat without touching our food—it's not possible.

And I think too that there's something about the way we make food disappear that suggests a magical transformation for a writer like Fisher. If we're successful as cooks, we don't see our creations for long. If we're successful as animals, we don't see food in front of us for long either. There's the pie. Now it's gone. Where can it be? I seem to have eaten it. That simple fact—that eating is the act of making a substance disappear, of internalizing the external—comes alive for Fisher. A meal is a sequence of fulfillments and, like fictional plot as the novelist Walter Mosley describes it, a meal for Fisher is a "structure of revelations."

The nature of what she calls her major symbol, her generative device, hunger, is a metaphor of return. We don't rid ourselves of hunger. Hunger is the guest that always comes back. And while a good meal is like a departure when it surprises us, a good meal may also be deeply realized as a fulfilled expectation. And what is a recipe but a buffer against disorder? A recipe allows us to anticipate, to meld the past into the present, to return to our senses. The poet Robert Hass has something to say about the peculiarly satisfying quality of repeating an experience. He tells us, "The first fact of the world is that it repeats itself. Though predictable is an ugly little word in daily life, in our first experience of it we are clued to the hope of a shapeliness in things. To see that power working on adults, you have to catch them out: the look of foolish happiness on the faces of people who have just sat down to dinner is their knowledge that dinner will be served."

Let me tell you a story that has nothing to do—you'll see why, thank goodness—with eating. It's a story about sea monkeys. If you have never succumbed to the glamour of sea monkeys, I can't say I pity you. Sea monkeys are relatives of brine shrimp. They're so small they're almost invisible. They're less than the size of a comma. After we bought a packet of sea monkeys, my younger daughter and I started our little colony in an old mason jar filled with water. In a couple of weeks we had the most wonderful sea monkeys. We didn't even need to use a magnifying glass to see them. We held the jar close to our eyes and watched the monkeys wheeling about. It was very exciting. Too exciting.

I decided I was going to give these sea monkeys the most beautiful new home. I ordered the executive sea monkey set—with a glittering gold rim, a statue of a crowned sea monkey, magnified viewing portholes. My daughter and I followed all directions. We carefully transferred our sea monkeys from their old mason jar into their deluxe executive accommodations. A few days later my daughter cried out, "Mom, where are the sea monkeys?" They were dead. My point here isn't about sea monkeys, but about the value of simplicity. I should have listened to those sea monkeys. They were thriving in a mason jar. They didn't need to live like Donald Trump.

Why am I telling you this? I want to underscore how merciful Fisher can be in her injunctions. "The best way to eat is simply, without affectation and adulteration," she argues. It refreshes and reassures me to think how simple her recipes are. Not all, of course. She has at least one recipe that calls for a calf's head. But she was able to appreciate not only the most complex meals, but the most basic, as well.

She makes me think of the painter Agnes Martin. Martin's paintings are remarkable—fine lines that look like graph paper, minute discriminations in shading. Like Fisher, she was another long-lived artist. Martin, who lived to the age of 91, wrote: "The function of the art work is the stimulation of sensibilities, the renewal of memories of moments of perfection." How often those words apply to Fisher, for even when she writes of terrible losses, those moments are poised against memories of times when the whole of life bursts with promise. Martin tells us "Those who depend upon the intellect are the many. Those who depend upon perception alone are the few." We could argue that Martin is creating a false dichotomy, that the intellect and perception are braided, but the spirit of Martin's remark is right. Being attentive to her perceptions, honoring them in writing, was Fisher's trade and the particular source of her distinctiveness.

There's a pose in which M.F. K. Fisher is often seen in casual photos from virtually every stage of her life. Whether sitting in a chair or lying on the ground, her hands are behind her head. It's the universal pose of luxuriating, undefended, unguarded. She seems to be breathing in everything around her. But, of course, writing can't be done in that particular posture, only the incubation, the gestation of writing can be. When Fisher writes she translates and transforms experience, using words not only to awaken the senses, but to make us experience words themselves as more fully sensuous. I recently heard a speaker declare that writing is not a generally sensual activity—he argued that we tend to move immediately from word to concept—but my own experience and, I suspect, Fisher's is quite different. Often her words are not transparent windows facing outward. Instead, the words in and of themselves conjure not only sound but color and even tactile sensations. She may loll around in photographs, but her food doesn't, nor do the words she uses. In her prose, soufflés "sigh voluptuously." A sugar replica of the cathedral of Milano becomes "a flag flying for the chef, a bulwark all in spun sugar against the breath of corruption." Beer explodes. "Peaches [shine] like translucent stained glass," and "a big tureen of hot borsht" is capable of "blasting … safe tidy little lives." Tea is "strong enough to trot a mouse on." Trout endure more varieties of fate than villains in an action movie. And for all her delicacy of feeling, Fisher can confess to possessing nothing short of an outrageous appetite. She coins a phrase for her youthful ability to eat: "husky gutted." She notes falling into a "digestive coma." And she certainly recognized in those she met the capacities for outsized enjoyment. A Burgundian woman is "almost frighteningly fanatical about food, like a medieval woman possessed by the devil." Another eats so much "she was like a squirrel, with hidden pouches...."

In her last years, brutalized by Parkinson's and arthritis and unable to use her fingers to write, her voice reduced to a whisper, Fisher worked with a tape recorder and an assistant, continuing to return to her senses to write her inimitable prose. She told interviewers and claimed often in her prose that when she wrote of food, she wrote of love—and what she called the hunger for love. Her capacity for love was also a capacity to endure the inevitable suffering that attends the loss of those we love. But it is most important to recall that she is one of the writers on the side of happiness. Agnes Martin tells us "what we really want to do is serve happiness." Those words might have been Fisher's: she served happiness. Whenever I return to her work, I find again her refusal to forego what satisfaction could be found through food and love. Our store of happiness may always be in danger of being depleted. She remains one of the replenishing artists. ■

# Processing Image: The Paintings of Aaron M. Brown

BY CINDY STOCKTON MOORE *(Issue 24)*

IN THE CONTEMPORARY MEDIA CLIMATE—overwrought with tweets and live-feeds, links and newsflashes—oil painting can seem anachronistic, a simultaneously quaint and frivolous throwback to a former era of static imagery. The work of Aaron M. Brown openly challenges that assumption, using traditional media to speak directly to the complex visual realities of today. In his layered body of work, painting becomes a language that is evolving with technology. Brown's latest series confronts the realities of viewing in a digital era, but—beyond that—it attests to the continued alchemical power of images.

***Dancer Dreams of Becoming a Pilot***, Oil on canvas, 40"x30"

The paintings are photo-referent, but not dependant on the camera's monocular viewpoint. Rather than concealing their means of illusion, they reveal tools of digital manipulation: cropping shields, transparencies, fills and filters. Seemingly disparate layers of visual imagery are hierarchically sorted and formally arranged. In this multifaceted work, simultaneity does not dilute the impact of images; it decants it. By arresting the movement of visual stimuli into concrete compositions, Aaron M. Brown offers a respite for contemplation and connection. It is a rare chance to process.

In the theatrical painting "Borderland Revisited," a vaguely academic

***Borderland Revisited, Number 1***, Oil on panel, 15"x30"

room houses family heirlooms, tagged for resale. Two children gesture towards the center of the space, the boy's countenance both framed and obscured by a semi-opaque rectangle. The exterior of a non-descript building is reflected in the surface of the painting, along with the face of a viewer that is not our own. In the midst of this dense, untenable environment, runs a figure first depicted by Eadweard Muybridge in the 1880s.

The suspended man is a product of Muybridge's (then revolutionary) photographic technique of freezing motion. Now thawed and recast as a contemplative artifact of visual history, the man runs in a liminal space between seeing and recalling. The black-and-white figure is a fitting signifier of the ongoing pursuit of "capturing" an image, his perpetual effort embodying both the futility and the nobility of the artistic practice. In this painting, history is both reflection and projection.

The flattened geography of Aaron M. Brown's parallel world is ultimately asynchronous. Past, present and future exist concurrently and create an archive of interconnected narratives. As viewers, we are left to excavate the layers and decipher their relational meaning; it is a process that invites self-examination, akin to analyzing the fraèents of a particularly lucid dream.

Aaron M. Brown's paintings remind us that active viewing is always an interactive experience. They call upon fundamentally human forms of processing, exposing the fallibility and wonder of our corrupted memories and fraèented drives. ▪

# Tattoo You

He pointed to his right arm and explained,
"Dad, this is my Jewish arm."

BY CARL SCHINASI *(Issue 25)*

ON A GLORIOUS AFTERNOON in 1995, my nine-year-old son, Noah, and I strolled into a street fair on Birmingham's Southside. Amidst all the hoopla and colors and curls, a tattooed young man danced down the street in front of us. His bright tattoos seemed to swirl and twirl sinuously about his arms and over his chest. Noah was entranced. His beautiful blue eyes snapped to attention as he intently watched the tattooed man cavort and leap along. He watched until the young man disappeared into the crowd.

Moments later, Noah stopped dead in his tracks. He looked me straight in the eyes and announced authoritatively: "Dad, I want a tattoo!"

It's always a tough moment when you have to turn down your kid. Gently, I explained to him that he was too young to have a tattoo inked into his flesh. I told him that Jews don't ordinarily wear tattoos. I told him this hoping he would understand, even though he was only half-Jewish. I explained the biblical reason: tattoos are considered unclean and a desecration of the body. Then I unfolded what I thought would be the most compelling reason, the matter of that nasty Nazi, Mr. Hitler. Noah knew about Hitler and the Holocaust. He did not yet know about the tattoos.

On that busy street, on a wondrous spring day, I explained to my son how Hitler mistook Jews and some other groups of people for the lower order animals and, before killing them, had branded numbers into their arms.

Noah seemed to understand. As we continued walking, I could see him thinking furiously. I figured he was mulling over my explanation of Hitler and the tattooed numbers. I did not anticipate what he was actually thinking.

Finally, he stopped again and fixed me with his shining blue eyes. He held out both arms. He pointed to his left arm. "Dad, I'll put the tattoo on this arm." I quickly gave him that cross "didn't you understand what I just told you" look. Immediately, he pointed to his right arm and explained, "Dad, this is my Jewish arm."

I was puzzled. I didn't quite get it. Then, just as quickly, he raised his left arm and declared with all the confidence of a seasoned lawyer, "And this is my Christian arm. I'll have the tattoo on this arm."

I cracked up. I figured, if the kid's that sharp he deserves a tattoo on this arm, that arm, or anywhere else he wants one on his precious little body. Thankfully, like so many youthful wishes, this one soon went the way of all flesh.

Several years later, we browsed through the local grocery store, picking over the vegetables. We were searching for the freshest ones to mix into our famous "Super Dooper Salad." As chance would have it, we noticed the tattooed man, the same young man we'd seen at the street fair some years earlier. He was not twirling now. He was just quietly shopping. He had a basket slung over his arm. He wore a string-strapped t-shirt. His tattoos stood out on display still, and although they were fading, they still shone vibrantly enough to catch anyone's attention, especially Noah's.

About that time, tattoos (or body art as it was then known) had begun gaining popularity. Coincidently, Noah had recently told me some of his friends had been tattooed. Jean had a small rose on her ankle. Andrea sported a heart shot through with an arrow on her upper left arm. And his close friend, Gus, had a fierce face with its nose pierced by a bone tattooed on his forearm. When Noah told me this, I rolled my eyes and commented, "Oh, brother."

As we picked over the vegetables, I could see Noah eyeing the tattooed man with more than a little curiosity. I remembered the recent mention of his friends and anticipated his question. As he turned to me, before he could utter a word, I snapped with sufficient parental authority, "No!"

I reminded him of our conversation concerning the tattooed man at the street fair. "Dad," he said, "I'm fourteen."

"So?" I asked, playing dumb, as if not understanding what he meant. I knew he thought that at fourteen he was old enough to make his own decisions, especially ones concerning his body.

Then he held out his left arm. He pointed to it and said, "This is Noah's arm." Almost simultaneously, he lifted the other arm, nodded his head in its direction and announced, "This is Noah's arm, too."

Even though he was only fourteen, it was becoming increasingly difficult to argue with such reasoning. All I could do was stare him down with that hard "I'm still the Dad here" look. He gave me a big grin and happily did not press the issue.

The following year Noah turned fifteen. He was now a teenager in full bloom. And, as teenagers will do to their parents, he shocked me. One day he announced he was a born-again Christian. He had decided he was going to be baptized. No words can express my disappointment. I argued with him vehemently. I tried reasoning with him until the reason well ran dry. He remained unmoved. So what could I do? He is my son.

Like any parent worthy of that honored title, on the day of his baptism, though heavy-hearted, I marched into his church. I watched him get baptized. It is difficult to describe my sense of loss at that moment, or my sense of defeat. I felt like Tevye must have felt losing his beloved daughter Chava. I felt like my parents must have felt when I married a non-Jew. I believed I had failed completely as a parent.

Life is like this. All the time it deals us lemons. So what to do? We make lemonade.

The years following were not easy ones for me with my son. He continually spoke to me about strange ideas I could not understand. He worshipped in a church, not the Temple. He wore a heavy cross around his neck, not the Star of David. I was surely being punished for my sins. But he was a good boy, growing into a responsible man. So, I reasoned, at least he has faith. So, I thought, maybe some day he will see who he really is.

He graduated from high school and went off to college. I thought somehow he would discover there what it means to be a Jew. He would come to understand the Jewish blood that stirs in his deepest soul.

Before I knew it, he was a sophomore. Over the winter holiday, he brought home Juanita, his exotic Argentinean girlfriend. She was a gentle, beautiful girl. She had the smile of a bright summer's day. She was also a girl who sported a colorful tattoo that began at her neck. It ran halfway down her back. It appeared to be the size of a giant condor.

One evening, I took Noah and Juanita to dinner. We dined at the Thai restaurant Noah and I had frequented for years, through good times and bad. During dinner, I asked Juanita about her tattoo. Why did you get it? Why one so large? Did it take long to ink it into your skin? Did the needle hurt when it bore into your flesh? Juanita was not offended by my questions. Finally, I asked, "Did it occur to you how that will look when you are older?"

To that she replied with a logic that I'm proud to say I still understood at my age: "Everyone has one." She turned to Noah. Her smile radiated like a sunburst. "Noah," she said, "you should get a tattoo."

Noah looked at me for a long, pregnant moment. He turned back to Juanita and answered in evident good humor, "Tattoo you. Not me." He followed his retort with a simple, "Jews don't wear tattoos."

That night I returned home and lay down to sleep. In my bed, alone in my dark bedroom, I thought about the pleasant evening I had spent with Noah, my son, and Juanita. Then suddenly and unexpectedly, without shame in front of God, softly and quietly I cried the happy tears that only a loved and loving parent can cry. ▪

# Considering the Alternative

BY DEREK ALGER *(Issue 27)*

I WAS STUNNED when a letter from AARP arrived informing me I was eligible to join. I wasn't that old and not even close to retirement. I knew of people in their forties who had retired, but most of them were cops or firemen and had chosen their career paths shortly after graduating high school. My sister, a year younger than me, reacted in a different way when I told her about the AARP solicitation. "I can't wait," she said. "Think of all the discounts."

The mystery of time, and aging, has been an obsession for me. At the age of twelve or fifteen, I remember continuously reminding myself to stay alert so I would recognize the precise moment when I became an adult. Of course I missed it, and though my life can be presented in some semblance of a narrative flow, with A leading to B and so forth, I can't pinpoint precise moments of change.

My father was a renowned psychiatrist, and my mother was a devoted wife who, to her four children, myself being the oldest, represented the epitome of unconditional love and encouragement. From an early age, I thought my father was nuts, but he was revered and honored, so I came to what I thought was the only sensible conclusion: I was doomed and would never fit in or succeed, since the grown-up world celebrated my father's accomplishments as if he was a contemporary celebrity version of Freud.

We lived in Flushing, Queens when I was three through six, and, for some reason, snapshots of that period remain very clear in my mind. On Saturdays, my father would see patients in the morning in his office in our house, and I would spend time with Mr. Florio, the gardener, until it was lunchtime and I was required to join my father in the quality bonding activity, or so he genuinely thought, of making model Aurora airplanes or aircraft carriers, which were so complicated, with such intricate pieces, that my future panic of trigonometry, much less calculus, was deeply ingrained at an early age.

One morning Mr. Florio didn't come at the usual time. I was about five, and time stretched out for what seemed forever, creating great impatience, as well as curiosity, about why Mr. Florio, who was always so punctual, was late. I sat on the front step of our house after my mother had reassured me that Mr. Florio would be arriving soon. Still, I bothered my father between each of his patients. "Where's Mr. Florio?" I asked. "Why isn't he here?" My father told me I shouldn't worry, that Mr. Florio was on his way, but by the time my father finished with his patients, Mr. Florio still hadn't come. To this day, I don't know why my father didn't call Mr. Florio's house, or maybe he did and there was no answer. Anyway, after lunch, my father finally relented and decided that we would drive over to Mr. Florio's house to see what was what.

There was an ambulance parked in front of a small house at the top of what seemed like a small mountain of steps. My father and I started up to the house holding hands. Just as we reached the top, the front door opened and two men in white were coming down a flight of stairs, carrying a stretcher with what turned out to be Mr. Florio's dead body covered with a sheet. As the men passed, my father reached out and shook a young man's hand, simultaneously placing his other hand around the man's back. "I'm so sorry," my father said. I asked if Mr. Florio would be coming next Saturday. That's when I was told Mr. Florio was dead.

The past lays the foundation for the future, and I came from anything but a traditional religious background. While some find solace in the roots of childhood religion and others may feel more comfort in a so-called "spiritual" approach to life, I was stuck at an early age pondering the word "infinity" and trying to grasp its meaning. I made the mistake of asking my father what happens when you die. His answer was remarkably straightforward—that you don't exist anymore. "Not exist, what do you mean?" I asked. "How long?" And then my father hit me with the word "infinity," the meaning of which I didn't have a clue. Infinity, according to my father, meant forever and ever, and then, once you thought you'd reached forever, infinity meant continuing even more. I was more intrigued than scared. I remember lying in bed and trying to put myself in a simulated state of death, a state of my perception of "infinity" in which I would be nothing. The few times I thought I had succeeded in reaching such a state, I promptly realized I hadn't because I was consciously aware that I thought I had.

I should feel grateful. So far the signs of aging have not hit me too hard. I have no indications of arthritis, no back pain, and my neck still looks basically the same as when I was a teen, meaning no rooster folds of baggy skin or fear of anything close to resembling a double chin. True, I don't bounce out of bed in the morning, and my energy level is not especially high, and I must confess that from time to time I can hear the click and snap of my cartilage when I rise.

A major shock hit my family six years ago when health problems came crashing down without warning on unsuspecting members. First, my mother learned she had breast cancer, Stage 4, advanced, and shortly after that, my brother-in-law was diagnosed with non-Hodgkins lymphoma, and then, my sister also discovered she had breast cancer.

At one point, my mother stayed at my sister's house in Ontario while my sister recovered from chemo treatments in the basement and her husband lay dying in the upstairs bedroom. But someone had to take care of the kids, ages eight and three, and provide some semblance of continuity and normalcy, and that's what my mother did, without complaint.

I don't know why, but I was sure my mother would be okay, though, of course, I recognized there was a possibility she would die, but an abstract possibility as far as I was concerned, because I couldn't imagine the world without her. My sister had a double mastectomy and my mother underwent surgery, and then, with stoic optimism, endured her rounds of chemotherapy. In a snap, I went from being part of a family to seeing the ravages and realities of mortality on a personal basis.

I moved my sister and her kids down from Canada to live with my mother in New Jersey after my sister's husband died. My mother spent most of her time in bed, but she was great with the kids, a true source of comfort and support, but also fun to be around. I knew my mother's illness was fatal, but she never complained, or felt sorry for herself, not about the ongoing chemo, or the chronic diarrhea, or the endless visits to doctors. My mother always made a small joke out of it, cheerfully saying, "Well, considering the alternative," and then shrugging her shoulders as if to say, "What can you do?"

My mother had great difficulty finding an oncologist willing to treat her. No one wanted to treat a woman over seventy with Stage 4 breast cancer because the outcome was bleak and the recovery period, the time undergoing chemotherapy and the resulting side effects, were too much for anyone that age. Finally, one oncologist, Dr. Gabriel Sara, stepped forward, a straightforward yet compassionate doctor, genuinely aware of suffering and pain. Dr. Sara said the situation was indeed dire, the odds were not good, but he would treat my mother because he liked her outlook, he could tell she was optimistic but realistic, and somehow he recognized my mother would fight tenaciously to stay alive as long as she could help her children and grandchildren. Dr. Sara helped my mother live seven years longer than she would have without the combination of his dedication and her determination.

Over those years, those valuable but painful years, it was a continual case of one large step forward and two small steps back. Dr. Sara said to me once, about a year before my mother died, right in the room with my mother, "Things are going very well, and will continue to do so, until at some point things will turn south and kill Joyce." Not comforting to hear, but it was important, the recognition that my mother was going to die, and, of course, that meant that someday I would as well.

My mother's life changed. She became dependent on me. I took her to chemo treatments and tried to encourage her to have a bit of soup or sip grape soda through a straw as she slowly recovered after each bout. I always treated her the same, talking to her as I always had, because I knew her mind was still extremely sharp, much more so than most of any age, even when she was overcome by fatigue.

The exact moment where our roles changed forever was when my mother needed a blood transfusion. She seemed listless and confused, which was very uncharacteristic, when I took her for chemo. It was a Thursday. My youngest sister was bringing her daughter down from Massachusetts for the weekend, and my mother was really looking forward to it because she had a special kinship with Katy, who apparently was quite a bit like my mother as a little girl. At Dr. Sara's office, blood was drawn from my mother and the white cell count was too high so it was decided that she shouldn't have her scheduled chemo treatment that day. Then the nurse in charge said my mother needed a blood transfusion and we should go down the block to the hospital to make arrangements for the next day. My usually agreeable mother wanted no part of it, mumbling that she'd wait till Monday. Suddenly my mother was standing before Dr. Sara. "I want to wait 'til Monday," my mother said. "You must have the transfusion tomorrow," Dr. Sara said, and that was that. One word from him and my mother immediately agreed to have the blood transfusion.

My mother hated hospitals, as do most sane people. The summer before, she had been admitted because of an infection caused after a port was implanted in her chest so the chemo could be poured directly into her body. She was miserable and told me firmly afterwards, "No hospital." In fact, while in the hospital, she told me she had witnessed how older people were treated as if they were stupid. One night, a nurse came into my mother's room with a glass of water for my mother's false teeth. The only problem was my mother still had all her original teeth. My mother and I laughed over the image of the nurse trying to yank out my mother's real teeth.

The day of the transfusion was horrendous: the length of time spent sitting with a plastic bag pinned by a thin tube into my mother's arm; the drip, drip, with the bag seeming to take forever before there was any true sign it was beginning to drain. My mother, whom I'd never known to complain outwardly, and who was stalwart in her acceptance of reality, seemed like a little kid as she kept softly saying to me, "I want to go home." Finally, the bag was almost drained of blood and I could tell my mother was excited over the anticipation of release and awaiting freedom. The nurse came up to where my mother was sitting patiently and unhooked the empty plastic bag with traces of blood streaking about, only to replace it with another one filled with blood, and my mother and I both knew that the transfusion procedure was at most only half over.

There was no way I could accurately measure my mother's diminishing body. Each time I took her to chemo, as I walked with her the one block from the parking garage to Dr. Sara's office, I noticed her arms were becoming thinner and thinner, similar to a tree branch shrinking to a twig. Where was I and why couldn't I stop it? And, of course, that she could age so imperceptibly, what did that mean for all of us? The reality that my mother was dying whacked me right in the face: there was no escape from mortality.

I couldn't imagine that my mother could really die, just as the inevitability of my own death somewhere down the line remained an abstraction. My mother was aware she was dying and handled it with brave acceptance. I remember, after Dr. Sara told her the cancer had spread to her liver and her life span could be measured in months, my mother said to me, almost in a voice of cheery wonderment, "It's funny, I don't feel like I'm dying." But she was.

My mother was given a choice: do nothing and wait for the end, or continue chemo and try to delay the inevitable. My mother wasn't scared of death, far from it, but she chose to continue fighting, and Dr. Sara seemed pleased with her decision.

I was caught off guard, wasn't prepared for my mother to die the day she did. A visiting nurse arrived that Saturday morning, September 10, to hook my mother up to an IV and, while examining my mother, said, "She's not going to make it through the night."

Once, on my birthday, I think my fortieth, my mother said, in glowing awe, "I was there at the beginning." And she had been there, and continued to be there, as a source of comfort to me just knowing that she was in the world. And now, while she had been there at my beginning, I was there at her end. I watched my mother's eyes, her beautiful blue eyes, and I'm still haunted by how they moved from side to side, and I kept saying, "I'm here, Mom, I'm here" and wondering what she felt and remembering that despite the kind clarity on the surface, she had been blind in her right eye since the age of ten and could barely see out of her left. Still, I sensed, even through the morphine patch and lack of sight, my mother realized I was there.

My mother wanted to die at home in her bed. There was no way she wanted her life prolonged in a hospital through the wonders of science and medicine. I had watched my mother only a month before standing up to my father, and the visiting physical therapist, and anyone and everyone advising her to wear a life-alert alarm around her wrist. She wanted no part of it. She was alive and operated in a specific time and space and had no desire to try and extend such boundaries through artificial technological advancements.

Using a prearranged code word, through the answering service, I was able to reach Dr. Sara. He was calm and forthright. The end was here. He respected my mother's wishes. Increase the morphine patch, let her slip away peacefully.

I came up the stairs at about three in the afternoon and entered my mother's bedroom. I approached the bed and instinctively dropped down on one knee, taking her hand in mine. She looked peaceful, and then I sensed an eerie silence. I looked closely at my mother and her eyes were open and her mouth was also open, frozen, a small oval with nothing coming out. I was still holding her hand and the unbelievable hit me: my mother had just taken her last breath. I stared down at my beloved mother's face, so restful and calm, and I waited to see if by some miracle she might blink or speak, but, of course, she didn't. I cried out to my sister, "I think Mom's gone!"

still unable to say "dead" or "died," and a moment later my sister was in the room. Sitting on the bed, without saying anything, in quiet tears, my sister and I acknowledged that our worlds would never be the same.

My mother died on September 10, and then, shortly after, I learned that her horrible eye accident had occurred on September 9, 1937 when her cousin zapped her with a paper clip zipping from a slingshot. My mother and I had a common bond due to eye accidents: when I was eighteen, a drunk in a deli in Manhattan dropped a quart bottle of beer and glass shattered, a piece piercing up through my right eye. Major surgery within the hour saved the eye, and I have memories of my mother diligently sitting by my hospital bed every day, content to be silent or, at times, the two of us talking about the Knicks' chances in the playoffs.

The one story my mother delighted in telling me was how she obtained her driver's license. She was an excellent driver, but according to the uniform rules of the State of New York, she should never have received a license. The bureaucrat at Motor Vehicles asked her to cover her right eye, the blind one, and read the eye chart. Then, for whatever reason, the Motor Vehicles guy was interrupted and stepped away for a moment. When he came back, he made a fortuitous mistake for my mother by asking her to cover her right eye and read the chart again. So, my mother, who over the years drove her four kids numerous places and came rushing whenever we were in jams, obtained her driver's license because she was able to read the eye chart twice with her left eye instead of sitting in helpless darkness if she had been asked to read with her right.

Though now I've experienced a sorrow I hoped would never come, I am left with only good memories of my mother, what she was like and what she wanted for me and her other children and grandchildren. And I laugh to myself, knowing that she would agree, that she died on September 10 instead of the following day, 9/11, so she would never have to share a day of grieving and remorse with the multitude. But that's the way she was. She was always one of a kind to me. ■

# On Swimming

Smell of chlorine and slick seal-like clinging of wet suits....

BY DEWITT HENRY *(Issue 28)*

I WAS A GOOD SWIMMER as a teenager, in a swimming family. My mother had been good and loved swimming still, even after operations in her shoulders and elbows for bursitis. She told stories about diving off cliffs at Cornell. My older brother, Chuck, was on the team at Martin's Dam and also at Haverford School. He swam a hard crawl and also butterfly and I don't remember if he ever won. My sister, Judy, however, was more than good. She was a star on the Martin's Dam team, doing crawl, butterfly and backstroke, and practicing for hours in the lanes set up for fifty yards between the diving float and racing dock. At Baldwin School she swam races but also water ballet. She and her best friends, Kathleen and Cathy, practiced maniacally, and I went to their meets. I remember the smell of chlorine and slick seal-like clinging of wet suits, as well as the inane music of Blue Tango they used for ballet. For racing she specialized in racing dives and for backstroke in flip turns.

I tried to imitate all this on my own, as a junior at Martin's Dam. I don't remember if I ever placed. But I must have at some meet, second or third. We were given ribbons and badges. I remember the practices, grueling, under the aegis of the Martin's coach, Jules Provost, who was also my science teacher at the public school. I imitated Judy's water-ballet smoothness in my crawl stroke, turning my wrist to slide into the water, and cupping my hand for thrust, rather than slapping the water. When she swam, she seemed streamlined and effortless, gliding. She would pull ahead of her rivals so smoothly. Just the steady, powerful glide and pull, and she would surge ahead. I tried my best. But my wind, even after hours of practice, laps and laps, was never good for swimming. I could push myself to the brink of nausea, but that was never the equal of the gifted.

I remember J.V. meets at Martin's. The shivery dawn. The butterflies in the stomach, which Judy had too and tried to calm with jelly beans. The pretense and pomp of a real race, team to team. Standing on the block, arms back, ready for a racing dive. The tense expectation of the starter's gun, then crack! And spring forward for a shallow splash and already churning kick, and stroke, pulling deep. My damnedest. Trying to keep in my lane. Barely aware of anyone ahead or behind. Plunging, digging each stroke, pull, kicking hard. Heart wild. Gasping every third stroke for breath. Harder. Hitting the slimy edge of the diving dock and ducking under for a tuck and turn, then push, glide, and back, pulling, digging, as my strength failed, arms ached, gasping, keeping in the lane, between the floats, kicking my best, can I make it, harder, one hundred yards, gasping, failing, and dimly aware of splashing in the adjacent lanes ahead of me, all body, all effort, finishing fourth, fifth, sixth, my hand hitting the dock. Heaving breath at the finish, hardly able to lift myself out. We had no swimming team, as Chuck did at Haverford, in school. This was only at the summer swimming club, Martin's Dam. Perhaps 9th and 10th grade. The meets were tense with other clubs, sometimes away. I remember Colonial Village, just down the street from Martin's. The different format, different pool. And shivering, having to show up early, early, Saturday at 8 a.m.

When I got to college, swimming was too difficult a sport. Not only in muscle and stamina, but in time. At Amherst freshman year there seemed barely time to breathe and think, let alone go out for demanding sports, and swimming was one of the most demanding. I went to a couple of meets. I remember a star, Jack Quigley, now a doctor. The conditioning, the regimen, the dedication, and the performance were utterly beyond me. As for Chuck, I think he tried swimming at Franklin and Marshall, after he had flunked out of Cornell, but then he quit. Judy, I think, tried too at

Swarthmore freshman year, but then she quit when she got pregnant and married an upperclassman. We never amounted to much, as swimmers. My mother, after our father died, lived alone in their suburban Philadelphia ranch house, and had the notion to install a swimming pool for health. In her late seventies, she said she was too fragile to travel anymore, so she wanted to make her house a spa, where we all would visit. The pool, in a sheltering Plexiglas enclosure, became our baptismal pleasure, and we all clamored in, splashing, playing, with our wives and children. Alone, she swam laps for as long as she could.

I don't swim much anymore, I confess. In my pre-retirement sixties, I am dedicated athletically to workouts in a gym. Neither my wife, my daughter, nor my son is a serious swimmer. Our New England waters are mainly Walden Pond (inland) or various beaches south of Boston and on the Cape, or the local MDC pool, less than a mile from our house. Walden for our family has spiritual connotations. From the time our children were young, we and friends would go there, stunned by the privacy no matter how crowded the park. Our family's best friends also swam there and had appropriated a beach near the original Thoreau cabin, on the far shore of the pond. Sometimes we joined them for picnics. Sometimes they went with their children and ours without us. My daughter, always precocious, sneaked into Walden as a teenager for illegal skinny dips. Years after these family friends had suffered untimely losses to cancer, first their nine-year-old son (best friend to our son), and then the father, Pat (a second father to our son), we rarely swam at all, and rarely took the trip together to a beach or to Walden.

Now summers, in the heat, I may run ten or twelve miles around the Charles River, then dip in the MDC pool alone on the way back home. It is a shallow pool, crowded with frolicking teens and sub-teens, but exhausted and hot, I find it a blessing on a long run. I try a few laps in the old freestyle crawl of my sister, but my stamina is only good for twenty yards, if that. Sometimes, special times, my wife Connie joins me, and we swim together in these shallow, neighborhood waters. One of the lifeguards is Caitlin, sister and daughter of the family friends with losses to cancer. We are middle-aged. Two teachers: my wife at an elementary-through-sixth-grade school, to which she has given her life and where she now is assistant director; and me at Emerson College, to which I have given my professional life.

Two summers ago we are alone at Walden. We both feel the losses and the toll of time. But there is a lovely buoyancy. We wend our way through the paths around the rim of the pond and discover that our favorite spit has been reclaimed for conservation. We slip into the waters from a nearby beach. And the waters are warm. We swim together. The bottom falls away to the deep of the pond. I love my wife. I cannot speak to her or to others in words how much. She is a pure, constant and affirming soul against all the doubts and contradictions of living. My loving is not worthy of her. But in this twilight we swim as newlyweds. ▪

PART TWO

# MEMOIR

# The Moments Between

BY HELEN ZELON *(Issues 12,13)*

*Across cultures and centuries, certain narratives persist: stories of creation; of the battle between good and evil, love and hate, the righteous and the damned. This story is not universal but particular, a specific myth-that's-not, a true legend peculiar to my family and rehearsed all the years of my childhood, as my mother told and retold her tale. It unfolds in four parts and reveals layer after layer of truth, received memoir and longing for a lost time, a lost world, a life less complicated and dark.*

**Rudolf Natter, Part I: The Ghetto**

Tuhk tuhk, tuhk tuhk.
Silence.
Then again: tuhk tuhk, tuhk tuhk, tuhk tuhk.

Getting closer. The sounds of hard heels on cobblestones, the sharp clatter of an officer's walk on ancient, uneven streets. Now fading: tuhk tuhk, tuhk tuhk, soft in the gaining distance.

Rudolf Natter, on his evening rounds, walking on Mila Street, passing the blocks of crammed apartments, lingering on the corner, near Pawiak Prison. Deliberately he steps, his oiled leather boots gleaming silver in the moonlight. The boots are his pride; he steps over muddy gutters and choleric beggars to avoid soiling their hand-stitched soles. Tuhk tuhk, tuhk tuhk, then a little sigh of exertion as he hoists himself over just such an obstacle, and again, tuhk tuhk, tuhk tuhk, tuhk tuhk.

Natter was an SS man. Assigned to the Warsaw Ghetto, he prowled the streets with a pistol on one hip and a bullwhip curled on the other. No one saw him actually use the whip; it seemed permanently coiled in its place, more trophy than weapon. But the pistol, well, he did not hesitate when the time to shoot was at hand.

The time to shoot was a flexible thing. Sometimes, of course, one had to shoot unbidden—say, when a laborer leaving the Ghetto for a shift at the Derringwerke munitions plant stepped out of line or clumsily, idiotically, tried to slip away. Then, Natter shot. A single shot, usually, sometimes to hurt, sometimes to kill, but always—or nearly so—a hit. People saw him shoot and laugh; heard him hold a conversation with barely a breath-stop for shooting and then saw a limp body crumple, or heard the cry of a man in hot, searing pain. Natter shot. He was good at his job. Took pride in it. He kept his pistol as clean as his boots.

Natter also wore a jacket, which—like so much else during wartime—was good for more than one thing. First, of course, it kept him warm against the bitter, wet months of a Warsaw winter—gray days, black nights, seeping damp that never dried out of woolen trousers. Also leather, like his boots, but the jacket was brown, whereas the boots were ink-black. It was the badge of a German officer, and no one, it seemed, was more born to the role of the Aryan overlord than Rudolf Natter.

The jacket also helped Natter in his entrepreneurial adventures, for everyone knows, an officer's salary, while greater than an ordinary soldier's, buys precious few nylon stockings or bottles of whisky. Not to mention a future he had to consider: the war wouldn't last forever, he knew, and even when his side won, it couldn't hurt to set something by for his civilian burgher life. So Natter smuggled: He traded gold, jewels and coins, for extra food-ration tickets, waiting with his boot heels clicking while a woman ripped the hem of her skirt to reveal the gold rings stitched in its lining. Quickly, she passed them to him. As quickly again, he passed her the ration vouchers. She put them in her bag, mumbling, "Thank you," as he struck her on the shoulder, sending her to the pavement.

Even though he was a ranking officer, Natter knew he was surrounded by other eyes, eager to expose any deviation from official orders, all too ready to report a senior officer if it meant a chance at improving their own commission. He had to make the street exchanges look good, or good enough—that's why he struck the women. But, in his own act of kindness, he always struck them on the shoulder, or in the gut. No marks on the face; he wanted no scars, no gashes traced to Natter's hands.

So Natter's jacket smuggled goods out of the Ghetto. Gold and diamonds; money; letters impossible to mail within the Ghetto walls. And occasionally, Natter's jacket smuggled things into the Ghetto, too. Very occasionally, and always at tremendous risk to himself—not to mention his family at home, who knew nothing of his black-market exploits, save for the spoils—Natter brought something inside the Jewish world. Aspirin tablets, for the right price. Cheap potato vodka, again for a price. Very occasionally, he brought guns. It was not that he supported the Jewish resistance—they were puny, weak, utterly deluded even to imagine they stood a shred of a chance against the far superior Nazi troops. But the trade was good; gold and stones for simple guns. Portable, liquid, universal currency—always best in wartime.

On a day when Natter was bringing a gun, everyone who knew the plan—the machers who arranged such deals—knew to lay low, clear of the streets and of Natter's path. Tuhk tuhk, tuhk tuhk his stride announced itself on the stones, and then a scuffle, seemingly from nowhere. In most cases, Natter grabbed a man by the lapel of his coat, accused him of theft. The man, unwitting, denied the infraction. A second man, and a third, and soon a fourth and even a fifth, inevitably rose to defend the "thief." In the midst of the scene, one who knew slipped from a doorway's shadows to Natter's left side, near the whip, trading a flannel pouch of stones for a pistol. Slip away, quickly—for in the next instant, Natter's pistol was out and flashing fire. The thief lay splayed on the paving stones; or sometimes a defender, it didn't matter.

Natter knew the eyes on him; knew he had to mask his "humanitarian" efforts to arm the Ghetto fighters. One life or another mattered little. They were all headed for Treblinka; Natter knew that even if they didn't. When a fate of naked incineration awaited you, perhaps it was a kind of mercy to die in an instant on a city street. In any case, Natter shot. The calculus was simple: to gain the weapon cost a life; impressions had to be maintained.

In addition to his own private business concerns, Natter also had SS work to do. Beside the everyday chore of keeping order among the forced laborers as they left the Ghetto and returned at night—troops saw to their escort to and from the factory, but Natter was responsible, Natter was the man who made sure that as many came back in the evening as went out that morning—and in addition to keeping the streets free of robbers and thieves—for even in the Ghetto, petty crime persisted, life went on, along with measly concerts and anemic celebrations—Natter had to nag the Jewish burial society, it seemed every day, to clear the sidewalks of corpses. With typhus and cholera rampant, and people crammed 40 to an apartment, he wondered that so many were still left alive to ship out to Treblinka when the time came. Every morning, the bodies lay on the sidewalks: in winter, as solid as statues, literal frozen stiffs; in summer, stinking and rotting on the paving stones. They came with wheelbarrows, these Jewish body-chasers, and heaped the corpses like so many sacks of wheat, until the barrows overflowed. No matter how vigilant Natter was in his pursuit of the Jew morticians, there were always more bodies. This bothered him; the scent and the mess offended him. And of course, his boots got dirty in the filth. The sidewalks were a mess, entirely.

Once every week or so, Natter and his unit received special orders. In characteristically precise detail, Natter's men approached a specific Ghetto block. The Ghetto was in the oldest part of Warsaw, and the apartments were built on a U-shaped model, so that the open side of the U faced the street, and three sides of apartments surrounded a sheltered courtyard, used in better times for laundry and soap-making and games of tag.

"Raus! Raus! Alles raus!" the soldier's voices would call in the courtyard. Out, out, everyone out.

No one came outside, of course. Who would go out when a Nazi invited you? A few peeked from windows. Others hid in secret spaces, behind stoves, in ceiling panels. And waited for the next invitation from the courtyard.

"Attention, everyone with a blue Kennekarte! Holders of the blue Kennekarte, this message is for you."

Kennekarten, or identity cards, were issued by the Nazis to Jews living within the Ghetto. Color-coded to indicate family status, place of origin, and date of arrival, the Kennekarte was like a flimsy Ouija board for its holder: Was yellow better than blue, 1940 better than '41? What about those signed by Natter, or by his underlings? Everyone looked to the Kennekarte for clues to their Ghetto lives. Also, the little cardboard rectangle gave comfort. If you had an official paper, how bad could things be? If it was signed, and stamped, and had your name and a date, too, certainly you were secure—for the time being, at least, if not for good. The Kennekarte was proof of your existence; losing it was nearly as great a disaster as dying itself, for there was no replacing it, and without it, no food rations, no nothing at all.

The day that Natter and his men arrived at the apartment block on Mila Street was sunny and warm; spring had come to the Ghetto, its trees blooming pink, a sudden yet entirely welcome respite in the crowded stench. That day, before coming to Mila Street, Natter had enjoyed his second cup of coffee after watching and counting the columns of exiting day laborers. It was midmorning when the officer and his soldiers clattered into the courtyard and began to call out to the residents.

"If you have a blue Kennekarte, listen now, for good news awaits. If your karte is yellow, this announcement is not for you. For those with orange Kennekarten, we expect news later, perhaps next week. Today, we have a message only for those with blue Kennekarten."

Inside the apartments, hurried conversations whirled at half-whispered volume. "Should we go down?" one asked, one who held the blue card.

"I would never," spat another, but he held a yellow card, so who expected him to go?

"Maybe I will go down, and the children can hide," a mother reasoned. "At least they will be safe upstairs, even if I go down."

"Achtung, Juden!" called Natter. "Holders of blue Kennekarten, into the courtyard. Present your card and you will receive rail tickets for you and for your families. We will resettle you in the East. You will be safe." Silence from the apartments; no one moved.

"Everyone who comes now will not only receive rail passage, but also a kilo of margarine and two loaves of bread. If you do not come, we will come for you. It is better, you will see, to come now."

Natter's voice resounded off the brick apartment block and bounced up to the open windows. Slowly, heads came into view, looking down to try to discern the soldiers' intent. No guns were drawn. There was a wheelbarrow with bread, its scent sweet on the spring breeze, and wrapped bricks of oleo stacked on an upturned box. The soldiers stood, smoking, relaxed. Natter held a clipboard, and shouted up again to the apartment residents.

Slowly, a few people came to the courtyard and presented their blue Kennekarten. They reached for the bread, but soldiers stood in their way.

"You must come down with your things, ready to travel," Natter explained, in the soft voice used to coax a shy child. "You are going on a journey, you must prepare yourselves."

Soon the courtyard buzzed with activity. People packed their valises with their dearest treasures—the trains, Natter said, would be crowded, one bag for each family only—and kissed the unlucky goodbye. Who knew the blue card would be a ticket out of the squalor? A passage to the East, to safety, to farms with geese and chickens and a cow or two? How lucky to have a blue card!

One woman hesitated upstairs longer than the others. Her husband was at work in the Derringwerke factory; how could she leave him? And then there was the matter of her daughter Cesia, who was nowhere to be found. The littlest girl, Renia, was right with her at home—where she belonged—but Cesia, who could know where she was? She had a boyfriend now, her mother knew, a handsome boy about her age, who had even begun to shave with a razor, and with whom Cesia spent her daytime hours.

Where was Cesia? Leaving the Ghetto behind would be good, the mother reasoned; maybe they could start over, east of Bialystok, make a life apart from the city they had always known. But she was unwilling to go without her whole family, so she and Renia stayed, hidden behind the ceramic panels of the large kitchen stove.

Tuhk, tuhk—Natter's boots on the stairs, followed by a stomping herd of soldier's heels. She heard them on the landing of the floor below; heard them break the door and move through the rooms shouting "Raus, raus!" heard the neighbor children's cries fading as they were led down the stairs into the courtyard. Then, as easily as one breath gives way to the next, Natter was in her apartment—in the living room, in his tall black boots. Tuhk tuhk, louder now, his steps took him into the kitchen.

Looking for someone, anyone, hidden. Whether he found her behind the stove, or whether she emerged on her own, will never be known. What is clear is that she went downstairs, with her child Renia and her blue Kennekarte, accepted the bread and the margarine, and rode off to the East with the others from her apartment block. The train left from the Umschlagplatz, in the center of Warsaw, and headed northeast to Treblinka, where, finally, no one needed the things they brought from home.

* * * *

At dusk, the columns of workers marched back through the Ghetto gates from the Derringwerke factory. All men and boys older than 18 had to work, according to the laws of the Ghetto, created by the SS administrators and enforced, with a devotion bordering on obsession, by the Judenrat, the self-elected body of Jewish leaders who, at least theoretically, governed the world of the Ghetto.

Cesia and her boyfriend were among the workers marching in. In a move so brazen it could only have been borne of the naïve, willful invulnerability of teenagers during wartime, she and her boyfriend had sneaked into the factory line in the morning. They had made a bet they'd go to Ogrusatzky Park, an elegant formal greensward, where swans glided on ponds and linden trees stretched in long parallel rows, shading lacy ironwork benches. It helped that she was tall, for a girl, and always skinny, even before the war and the food shortages and the rotten potatoes and the bad milk. For once, she had been glad to be flat-chested, too, as she borrowed her boyfriend's second suit of clothes and his cloth cap to hide her hair. In her clever disguise and with her boyfriend at her side, she marched out of the Ghetto to Derringwerke. He knew a door at the back of the factory, where they wouldn't be seen, and through which they left, into the broad streets and bright sunlight of Warsaw early on an innocent spring morning.

Now, at dusk, they returned, hiding among the ranks of weary laborers. Natter stood just inside the gate, counting again, by twos, as the workers returned. Ja, the count was square—the ranks of workers scattered to their homes.

Cesia avoided her father on the way home. She reached the courtyard on Mila Street after he did, shaking the hair loose from under her cap and trying to imagine how she would explain her appearance, in men's clothing. He stood in the courtyard, talking with a neighbor. Cesia saw him turn his head up to their apartment window. She wondered why the courtyard was so quiet; where were the children squabbling before suppertime? And where was her mother's face in the window? A stab of colossal guilt seized her—how she must have worried her mother, how frightened she must be—until she looked again at her father, whose shoulders were bent and shaking.

She ran to him. Her father looked pale, his eyes wild, as if she was someone else, or someone not real at all. "Cesia," he said, "is it you?"

"Who else?" she answered, afraid.

"You didn't go?"

"Where?" She was afraid again, sure he knew of her illicit day in the city.

"To the East, with them all. With your mother and your sister, you didn't go?"

"Where did they go?" she asked, uncomprehending.

"Natter came and went," her father said, nodding to the neighbor that had given him the news.

"And with him went everyone from our building—all with the blue Kennekarten were granted permission to go."

"And Mama? And Renia?"

"They had the blue cards; they went."

* * * *

That night, Cesia didn't sleep. Her father sat up, too, staring out the window, watching for the dawn, hours away. He didn't eat dinner, refused his breakfast—sat in silence by the window, staring east.

From that day forward, Cesia and her father were alone. He didn't speak much after the first day or so, just worked and stared and slept, in snatches, sitting up by the window. He had lost his will, and lived now only to see Cesia live, to see her survive. She could, he said. She held all his hopes—his upstart, his scholar, his firstborn, winning a place in Warsaw's technical high school in 1938, the first girl to win such an honor, not to mention the first Jew, boy or girl, who studied with the goyim scientists there. Lithe and headstrong, speaking a beautiful patrician Polish (no shtetl Yiddish for his girl), Cesia was the vessel into which he poured his scant hope. All he wanted—and for this, he went again to Natter, with the last valuables he had, the last of the gold—was false papers for his daughter. With another identity, with her intelligence and her youth, she would survive. This hope sustained him even as it burned in her. She would, she promised, live.

For a price, Natter came through. Cesia Dymetman, Warsaw Jew, became Czeslawa Dvorakovska, Warsaw Pole. Shadowed by guilt, sure she could have saved her mother and sister if she hadn't been larking about Warsaw on a dare, Cesia swore she would survive. For better or for worse, she swore to her father and to herself, she would live.

### Rudolf Natter, Part II: No Turning Back

The father and the daughter soon settled into a new, confined routine. Cesia, eighteen at last, registered for compulsory factory work at Derringwerke. The false papers stayed hidden in their room, wedged into a small hollow space behind a row of ceramic tiles, padded by a thick cover of old newspaper. Just as some of their neighbors hoarded cyanide tablets—also available on the black market, for the right price—Cesia and her father safeguarded her papers. Let the neighbors find their way to death, she thought. She would fight, even shoot, or so she imagined. She had no gun, of course, and no chance to fight, only to work and to sleep and to barter her mother's empty leather shoes for carrots and parsnips.

She heard talk of resistance among the youth. Natter was not the only small arms merchant in the Ghetto, and the boys especially bragged of stockpiles of pistols, grenades, gasoline for firebombs buried deep in earthen bunkers. Cesia never knew what to believe, but she listened. Perhaps one in five were telling the truth, she thought; perhaps, perhaps, perhaps. Day by day, she worked, she lived, and she listened.

Occasionally at night, her father's breathing a wheezing metronome, Cesia pried the tile hiding place open to study the papers. Now, her papers. He had forbidden this, fearful that even the smallest sound after curfew could raise suspicion, that the slightest movement could attract attention, a search, arrest. He had changed, her father. Though hardly 40, he had become frail and remote, an old man stooped with sorrow. Cesia had always listened to him, but now she didn't. She had to see who she might become.

She studied her new name, so odd matched with her own photo. Was Dvorakovska a real person? Had she once been real, a girl like Cesia? The birth date was a new one—Cesia learned it quickly—but the hometown was Warsaw, her own. Did she play volleyball in the summer, too? Go to school, flirt with boys? That the name and identity could be real meant that the real Dvorakovska, the authentic one, was probably not real any more—that is, not even alive. Cesia traced the photo's sharp corners with her fingernail and wondered, could she simply step into another life and out of her own by spelling a new name, learning a new birth date?

Some of the glue used to stick the photo onto the heavy ivory stock had spattered into the type; would that be a problem? The letters were typed but uneven, o's sitting slightly higher on the line. Would that reveal her? And what about the stamp—it was slightly crooked; was that right? The work of a careless forger, or the well-placed mark of one who knew well the practiced slam of the official's stamp?

What if, one day, she was asked for information the real Dvorakovska would know—her school, her mother's family name, her church, of course. What if she had to say the Rosary, or take Communion? Cesia remembered how her maid used to cross herself, and tried to practice the smooth pattern of vertical and horizontal gesture, the kiss to the fingertips. Could she pass? Even with practice, could she leave this life behind?

The papers grew darker where she handled them, smudged by the oil of her hands; would that be a problem as well? Nothing was without questions. Nothing could be known, for certain, save that she had to live; and to do so, she had to have these papers. One night, with the sky beginning to pink up toward dawn, she put the papers away, shoved them deep into the hollow space. There, she thought, now they are gone. They do not exist, not until I need them. This was the first time Cesia found a way to keep a secret so secret that she herself could forget it—too many questions, answers that led to more confusion, all could be resolved if the thing itself never happened. So the papers went away.

She chose to stay within the life she knew, within the Ghetto. She would live with her father, work now that she was old enough, and together they would manage.

Daily, father and daughter left the apartment block and walked together to the main Ghetto gate. There was little conversation; Cesia's attempts to engage her father met with steady silence. She soon grew self-conscious, choosing instead to keep the talk-stream flowing inside her head, but not aloud. As they walked, she registered familiar sights: the beggars; the rigid corpses, stripped of their still-useful garments and covered in newsprint; the Nazi soldiers posted near Pawiak; the streetcar tracks. The Ghetto lay in the heart of the city of Warsaw and, although its walls kept Jews in and others mainly out, regular Polish streetcars passed through the Ghetto a few times every day, loaded with Poles shuttling to work. They gawked at the Jews as the streetcar rumbled through. That it raced through quickly, without stopping at all, was some kind of mercy. Count ten, count twenty, the streetcar would be gone, and with it the jeering, whistling passengers. Count thirty and the dusty cinders in the streetcar's wake would have settled into the cobblestones. Cesia could pretend the streetcar hadn't passed at all.

Every morning, Rudolf Natter waited for the workers at the main gate. The responsibility of counting the workers was an important one, and he entrusted it to no junior soldier—the consequences of error were too great. A man could lose his rank, Natter knew, or his family could suffer the consequences at home. More than one had been sent to the front, far to the East, where life was very bad indeed.

Natter counted people in pairs. Two by two, the workers lined up and were led out to the factory. Natter, who had been at the job a while, sought out some familiar faces amid the pale and stony stares. He would shake one man's hand every morning—a factory man, not a one-time rabbi or a pious man, but one of the regular workers—and enquire as to his health. As the charade unfolded, the lines waited. When Natter finished, the lines moved.

Natter also watched the women. After the liquidation efforts, so many women were gone, and those who remained had grown so scrawny that they looked less like women than eunuchs, skinny scarecrows in worn dresses. Only the young ones were anything to look at these days. They managed, pinching their cheeks and biting their lips to raise the color before they passed Natter's watch, to favor him with a smile, a glance, what he imagined were tender looks. He was a man of some principle, and on this he prided himself: No Derringwerke woman would be his. Let the others mix duty with pleasure; Natter, the consummate soldier, would not follow that route to professional doom. Besides, he was too much a man to take a Jew, and plenty of Polish girls were more than willing, for extra rations or even without, to entertain an officer. But still, he was a man. He looked. And many, many looked back.

Cesia was one who looked, too. She liked Natter; he had done something good for her, had gotten the papers that might save her. If revealed, the act—dearly bought and motivated far more by economics than by humanitarian impulses—could cost him at least his commission, at most his life. She knew he shot, had seen his pistol gleam dully as he aimed over the workers' heads, taking target practice at the Ghetto's brick walls. She had seen him suddenly turn, lower the barrel, and end the life of a beggar kneeling at his high black boots. This was Natter; he shot, he helped, he shot again. Even so, Cesia looked.

Natter looked back, met her eyes every morning going out, and every evening coming back. He never spoke to her, and she never to him. A single syllable might reveal the collusion that got her the papers. They looked, twice a day, then looked away.

* * * *

Work in the munitions factory was a good way to spend the time, Cesia thought, as she moved bits of metal into a press, punched them with two holes, and slid them to the next woman. Working, she didn't think, she didn't wonder as much where her mother was living—for Cesia only believed she was alive, no matter what the Bund boys said in the bunker meetings most nights. They talked of resistance, of armed struggle within the Ghetto, of Jews fighting the Nazis and winning. This was rubbish, she knew; there was no winning, only living. If she could just stamp and slide and count and punch, she didn't have to imagine Renia, could box her thoughts into another secret cask and work, stop for soup in the middle of the day, then stamp and punch until the evening whistle blew shrill and the machines sighed to a stop.

Cesia worked on the second floor, the finishing area. Most of the women worked there, too, as their smaller fingers—and greater dexterity, the more experienced women bragged—better suited them for the fine work of metal finishing. Her father worked downstairs, on the ground floor. A silversmith and jeweler by trade, he now hauled pallets of raw metal destined to be worked into shell casings and perfectly smooth bullets, packed and capped by the ladies on the third floor, above the finishers. A hive of munitions manufacture, it was a better living than many others in the Ghetto. At least there was a bowl of real soup at noon; the best, and for many the only, meal of the day. There were always potatoes in the soup, barley, too. Better than most.

Among the workers, there was conversation. Cesia listened more than she spoke, as was her way. Around her, the women spoke, less of their present situation than of the lives they lived—the meals they cooked, the holidays they celebrated, the tablecloths, the baking. On Fridays, the few pious women swapped recipes for challah. No one baked, but they debated: Sugar or honey? And how many eggs? How long to rise? As if the talking would bring the food into their mouths.

Spring meant one thing, in the lives they had left behind: Passover. Cleaning, cooking, more potatoes and eggs than there were poppy seeds on an onion roll. April was upon them all. Cesia hated all the talk of food: It was not her life, this religious attachment, and it only made her hungrier, made her long more deeply for her mother. She preferred the Bundists who were, this April, not talking food. They were talking, with equal passion, of war. People, they said, were gathering "cold" weapons—iron pipes; brass knuckles; any hard, metal hitting thing—and "hot" weapons, too, caching knives, guns and smuggled grenades in the same kind of hiding niches where Cesia's papers were hidden. Every night she went to the Bund meetings, the talk continued, the plans grew more detailed. Expect annihilation, said the organizers. No one should hope to survive, simply to resist and die fighting. Of the half-million Jews who crowded the Ghetto at its peak, 40,000 remained. This remnant, this fraèent, was honor-bound to fight.

On April 19—the first day of Passover, except that it was 2 a.m., the middle of the night—soldiers surrounded the Ghetto walls. Nazis and conscripts, Poles, Ukranians, Letts, civilian police pressed into service, each man stood 20 paces apart around the perimeter of the Ghetto. By 5, when the black marketeers were usually rousing from sleep to begin their negotiations before the light of day, it was altogether too quiet. No one was out; only the soldiers, outside the walls, standing sentry. The gates of the Ghetto were barred shut.

By 6, the sun was up and bright. Cesia was awake, her father asleep, as battalions of black-uniformed troops—full battle dress, regalia gleaming—carrying not pistols but machine guns, flanked by Panzers and military tanks, assembled outside the gates. When the gates opened and the troops marched in, the Uprising began.

First from the soldiers, who shot their introduction into each courtyard, spraying machine gun fire like swaths of black pepper. Then from the rooftops, where snipers hidden by chimneys and smokestacks killed, too, one man at a time. Cesia heard the machine guns, heard single shots ring out, but saw little from her upstairs window. A platoon marched past on Mila Street, and she felt as if her heart had stopped beating: Pass, pass, pass us, she willed, pass us by. You took everyone from here long ago, there is no one for you. Pass us by.

Fires were set all around the Ghetto. Some were set by Jews, to distract the attacking army—a brush-factory in flames, a stack of dray wagons soaked in gasoline and torched, mid-street. Hard to get a tank past that kind of obstacle. Then fires began from the shooting, as sparks caught the timbered beams of the apartment houses. Fire was everywhere from Cesia's window. All morning, her father slept, and she watched the fires burning. All afternoon, they sat together at the window, watching the fires, until the sun set and the fires lit the lowering gray sky at dusk.

The next day, the Nazis came again, but this time, they did not parade in the streets. They came as single soldiers, or small knots, clinging close to walls, leaping across doorways, shooting machine gun spray into every open window, door, alley, archway. A trio of soldiers came into Cesia's courtyard, sprayed a hail of fire at the ground floor apartments. Everyone still living there was either hidden in a bunker, dug to a double depth below a false cellar floor, or hiding in a ceiling space—an attic, a bathroom, a kitchen vent. Cesia and her father hid themselves behind part of the same tile wall where her papers were hidden; a section two meters square had been pried loose even before her mother and sister left. Before they hid, Cesia took the papers from the small hiding place.

"Not there—away, under your dress," he said, as he strained to lift the tile panel from the wall.

Cesia tucked the folded paper next to her skin; she pushed it down, under the waistband of her underwear, and felt it begin to soften and bend as she and her father sat, cramped, in the dark, small hollow space behind the kitchen wall.

They sat in silence and in darkness. They sat for hours. Then, like thunder, boots in the courtyard.

“Achtung , Derringwerke laborers!” Natter’s voice bounced around the yard.

“Derringwerke will shelter its workers during this situation. All Derringwerke workers, assemble in the courtyard in a quarter hour.”

Tuhk tuhk, tuhk tuhk on the stairs, followed by the galloping boots of soldiers in his wake.

Tuhk tuhk, tuhk tukh, the nightstick on the door resounded in the empty room. The knock sounded again, then the sound of battering, of many hits of metal against wood, until a splintering and the door was open. Slowly, then, tuhk tuhk in the apartment; tuhk tuhk, tuhk tuhk, pause.

“If you can hear me, listen now,” began Natter, in his deliberate, gentle tone. “If you are hiding here, come out. Come to safety. Save your lives. The Ghetto is in flames. The streets are full of fire. Come to the courtyard; be quick, or be lost.”

Cesia heard fabric tearing—the curtain at the window? The thin sheet that covered her father’s bed? She heard gunfire so close it pinged off the enamel kitchen stove, big enough to hide a small child. A stream of bullets sounded, like a woodpecker striking metal, and then, as suddenly, stopped. Tuhk tuhk, tuhk tuhk, tuhk tuhk, receding now, with the chorus of boot heels in pursuit. They did not bother to close the battered door.

Cesia and her father sat still in the silence. They sat until the sound of footsteps faded from the stairwell, and until they heard voices above them coming down the stairs, headed for the courtyard. At the sound of familiar voices, Cesia’s father slid the panel away from their hiding place, unfolded his tall frame into the trashed room, and stretched his cramped back. Cesia followed his example. She stepped out into the room. It was the curtain they had torn down, and the stove was neatly punctured with bullet holes. Her father didn’t move for a long time, just stood, slowly turning his head this way and that, half surveying the wreckage, half memorizing the space that he would never see again.

“We will go down,” he said at last. “With them, we may live; without them, we surely die. We will go down.”

Cesia, mute, fingered the papers in her waistband. Now was the time, she suddenly knew, now was when and why her father had insisted on the papers, had bartered the last of his own mother’s jewelry, had bought Natter’s help in procuring the precious documents. Now, only now—there was no more “before the war,” no more “after” to look forward to. There was only now, this present, this moment, and Cesia knew, they would go downstairs—to Natter, and into whatever mystery lay ahead.

They packed no suitcases; they were under no illusions—this was not resettlement, but survival. Cesia took only her mother's old leather satchel. She wrapped a packet of photos—happy pictures, carefree years, with her mother and sister on the carousel, riding the streetcar, visiting family—in a handkerchief, and knotted the bundle closed. She put a piece of soap inside a sock, rolled it up, and put it in the satchel. Thus packed, she and her father went down the stairs.

In the courtyard stood perhaps two dozen workers. Fires burned on Mila Street, right in front of their apartment, and across the street as well, but Natter had his checklist, and the workers lined up, dutiful as dogs, to present their names for his inspection.

"Dymentman," said Cesia's father.

"Dymentman," said Cesia, in her turn.

Natter looked at her. "Dvorakovska, do you mean? Or Dymentman? Which shall it be?"

"Dvorakovska," Cesia answered, a sudden fire burning in her cheeks, as the next person behind her in line waited for his turn to speak.

* * * *

Natter led the group out in two neat columns. He led them out the main Ghetto gate, and marched them directly to Derringwerke, where the floors had been spread with fresh hay, sweet-smelling and soft enough to pillow many exhausted heads while they slept. Cesia stared again, from a different window. The sky over the Ghetto turned red at night as the fires raged. Five days they burned, black smoke all day, then furnace-red at night. Five nights she wondered, why did Natter bring us out? Who paid him? None of the Jews had said they'd done it—and, oh, how they would brag if they had, just to build themselves up in this puny, dreary hell of a life. So if none of the workers paid, did Derringwerke? Pay to get their slaves out of the Ghetto inferno? Another question without an answer, another mystery. Who was behind their rescue? Could Natter have simply walked them out on a whim, to prove once again his immense power, his singular mastery, in the world of the Ghetto Jew?

After five days, the factory began production again. Cesia returned to the second floor, to the finishing room. She kept her papers under her dress, and strapped the satchel underneath, too. The dress hung loose on her skinny frame, as loose as a sack—there was plenty of room for her mother's bag, and she liked how the leather grew warm next to her skin, how it gave off a scent that smelled, in some distant way, like the inside of her mother's armoire at home.

There was little talk among the workers now; work was steady, work was calm, amid the thrumming machines. The soup came at midday, still with potatoes; one day, even with beef. Life resumed a new normal, contracting again to a world as small as the factory itself, where the workers ate, slept, occasionally prayed and regularly squabbled, while the Ghetto burned and burned.

One morning, Cesia stood at the metal press. The bits of metal moved quickly in her hands. She daydreamed a little as she worked; it helped to have the satchel. Waking into alertness, she bristled to hear the sound of feet on the stairs, rushing up, sounding like dozens—running up, not down, no order or march-cadence, but rushing, helter-skelter, up to the factory roof. Suddenly mobile, she left the punch press running, smacking empty bits of nothing between its plates, and went to the landing. She saw a man she knew, a Bundist from the nighttime meetings and ambitious plots, and grabbed him by the sleeve.

"What is it? Where are you going?"

"Up, to the roof. People are jumping to the next building. Or out the window, if you like. It's no matter, it is the end. There is no place to go. Natter and his troops have returned, shooting as they walk. People are running or dead. You must run, too."

Cesia looked up the stairs, clogged with people, and down again, thick with pushing, crying workers. She looked at the open window. Outside was Warsaw; the streets were full of traffic and people and pushcarts. She felt for her papers, still at her waist, and felt the strap of her satchel tight against her body. Without another look, she jumped. ▪

• *Read* **Part III: On the Brink—New Life** *at: ducts.org/12_04/html/memoirs/zelon.htm*

• *Read* **Part IV: Awakening** *at: ducts.org/06_05/html/memoirs/zelon.html*

# Surviving Homicide

When her boyfriend is murdered, a woman tries to come to grips with his death and the justice system.

BY FREDRICKA R. MAISTER *(Issue 19)*

*March 11, 1986.*

WHEN MY BOYFRIEND, Richard,* in his usual upbeat mood, phoned me at work around lunchtime to make dinner plans at our favorite restaurant in Chinatown, I was in a real snit. The day had been insanely busy and I detested my job. For the last few months, Richard and I had discussed my job predicament, so he was not particularly bent-out-of-shape when I yelled, "How can you think about dinner when it isn't even lunch? It's a zoo here and I can't talk!"

Illustration: Jenah Pelley

"No problem," he said. "I'll call you at three-thirty and we'll make the plan." Before he hung up, he tried to calm me down. "You'll be out of that place soon. Stop being so negative. Come on, I just want you to be happy. And you know what, I'm going to come pick you up at work and we'll go down to Chinatown together."

"That's absurd, " I protested. "I'll meet you in Chinatown like I always do. Why take the subway from Queens, get off, come to my office, then get on the subway again. That's two fares. What for?"

"Because you're special. I'll call you at three-thirty," he said, hanging up.

**Some names have been changed to protect privacy.*

Those were Richard's final words to me. I often wonder whether some unconscious inner knowing that this would be our last conversation prompted Richard to want to do something out of the ordinary for me, to make me feel cared about and loved. To be sure, Richard sometimes went to extremes to accommodate me, but his insistence on picking me up was well beyond the call of amorous duty.

My behavior was also inexplicable that day when I went out during lunch and bought Richard a gift for no apparent reason. I had come across a bar of men's soap-on-a-rope. I hemmed and hawed over buying it. Did Richard really need something else to clutter up his already cluttered apartment? Was I going to buy it out of guilt for having been so bitchy when he called? Why should I feel guilty when he understood the way I felt? But he's a great guy. Why not give him a gift? I kept leaving the display only to be drawn back to it. A flash-forward to our dinner that evening and Richard's expression of surprise when I would ceremoniously present him with his soap-on-a-rope finally convinced me to purchase it.

I returned to my office at about two-fifteen…two thirty…or was it three o'clock? The authorities would later ask me when I went out to lunch and when I returned. My timing regarding that day was so skewed that I could not say with any certainty. All I remember is that three-thirty… three-forty…four o'clock passed with no word from Richard. I called his apartment. There was no answer. Something was not right. I knew Richard. If he said he would call at three-thirty, he did not mean four o'clock. It crossed my mind that perhaps there was a medical emergency involving his daughter, who lived in Philadelphia and had just undergone knee surgery, but Richard would have called me before rushing off.

I kept calling Richard's apartment, letting the phone ring an inordinate number of times. I was sorry that I did not have his friend Bill's unlisted phone number with me. Bill lived in the building and might have a clue to Richard's whereabouts.

Bill and Richard were polar opposites. While Richard was a highly intellectual and creative type with a genius I.Q., a practitioner of Zen Buddhism and a witty, charismatic presence wherever he went, Bill was an auto mechanic and body builder totally absorbed in his good looks, overly developed muscles and female conquests. According to Richard, Bill was always busy working out or "servicing" a steady stream of adoring women.

Richard and I used to speculate about what drew them together, but we never came up with anything conclusive. In retrospect, what bonded them was their mutual attraction to drugs, mainly cocaine.

For years when they were mere acquaintances, Richard had gotten Bill marijuana. It wasn't until coke became the prevailing drug of the early '80s, the pre-crack era, that their friendship solidified.

Richard had access to a dealer friend with a regular drug store and Bill could never get enough. Richard soon became alarmed about Bill's overindulgence and confronted him. Bill then admitted that he was sharing his purchases with members of The Family. Even though recession had hit the Garment Center where Richard worked as a designer/patternmaker and he found himself unemployed, he was soon making a better living supplying Bill and his family.

From what I gathered from Richard, The Family was an organized crime family, Irish-style. Richard had never met any of its members with the exception of Maureen, who sometimes visited Bill. Maureen was Bill's sister-in-law, the wife of his brother Jerry, the head of The Family. Jerry was also our connection to Mel Brooks in Hollywood. Richard and I had written a screenplay, which Bill had given to Jerry to pass on to Mel, a childhood friend from Brooklyn.

Bill was always running off to take care of Family Business. I remember he once stopped by, dressed to the nines, briefcase in hand, before hopping The Family Plane to South Carolina to supposedly avenge the murder of a young nephew. There was also talk of The Family Compound in Tahiti, to which Richard and I were invited but then disinvited when we were ready to accept the invitation. The Family even offered Richard a job as a warehouse manager, but when he seriously considered taking it, the warehouse suddenly burnt to the ground in a suspicious fire.

After hearing some of Bill's Family Tales, I would ask Richard, "Did you really believe that?"

His response: "You're asking me? Who knows with Bill? He's just weird."

Weirdness aside, Richard trusted Bill. He even gave Bill a set of keys so he could have access to the closet where the cocaine was stashed. Richard once told me, "Bill would do anything for me. If someone tried to hurt me, that man would risk his life for me."

Because Richard trusted Bill, so did I.

When five o'clock passed and I was still unable to contact Richard, I was beside myself, emotionally torn between anger at him for leaving me in the lurch and worry that something had happened to him. I raced home to call Bill.

When I arrived, I checked my machine, half-expecting to hear "Hello, machine, this is Ricardo…" followed by an elaborate explanatory message. When there was no such message, I frantically started dialing, alternating between Richard and Bill. There was no answer anywhere. Finally, after a half hour or so, a female voice answered Bill's phone. I introduced myself and explained why I was calling. She said her name was Marlene, and that Bill was also concerned about Richard and was downstairs checking his apartment. They'd get back to me as soon as they could.

Within three minutes, Bill called. "Get over here," he said. "What's the matter?" I asked. "I'm your friend, get over here," he answered. "Oh, my God. Is he dead?" I blurted out. He wouldn't answer me. "Bill, is he dead?" I repeated. "Just get your ass out here!" he ordered.

I fled my apartment in a panic. My hand shaking, I could barely lock the door. As I proceeded down the stairs to the street to summon a cab, I knew I was moving forward into an unspeakable reality, into a world in which Richard would be irreversibly gone. I just wanted to return to the security of my apartment and set the clock back to my life a few minutes before when the truth was still unrevealed to me.

The cab driver who took me to Queens must have initially thought me mad. Overwrought, I kept screaming," My boyfriend is dead, I just know it," to which he kept saying, "How do you know that? Why would you say such a thing?"

The ride seemed endless. My mind raced, my chest tightened as I tried to come to grips with what I was about to face. I felt as if I was going to choke with emotion or worse, have a panic attack and not be able to breathe.

I struggled to be rational. How could Richard be dead? It made no sense. He was not the heart attack type; his heart, cholesterol and blood pressure, according to his latest medical exam, were in enviable condition. It must have been something that killed him instantly without warning—an embolism or massive stroke.

As we turned into Richard's street, I saw an ambulance and two police cars parked in front of his building. I was right: Richard was dead. I burst into tears and paid the driver, a stunned look on his face. As I ran towards the building, I heard him call after me, "Take care of yourself, okay?"

Crying and hysterical, I rushed into Richard's building past the doorman and took the elevator to Bill's apartment.

I knocked on Bill's door. When he opened it, I screamed, "I need a Valium!" I felt as if I was jumping out of my skin. Marlene, the woman who had answered the phone, was with him and apologetically explained,

"There isn't any Valium left. Bill took the last of it in the car."

Some of what subsequently transpired is a blur or missing from memory. For example, I have no recollection of who told me that Richard had been murdered. That was one of the first questions the District Attorney posed to me and I simply could not remember whether it was Bill, Marlene or a police officer.

What I vividly recall is crying out, "Murder? Murder just happens to people in the headlines!" and later sitting on a couch across from Officer Wang, a rookie cop who appeared shaken, as if this was his first murder. I later learned that he was the first cop to arrive at the crime scene.

I asked Officer Wang if Richard had been shot, to which he replied, "No, there were no gunshot wounds." After an uncomfortable silence, I reluctantly asked, "Was he stabbed?" His reply: "Yes. Multiple stab wounds." I felt as if Officer Wang had punched me in the stomach. I wanted to keel over. Multiple stab wounds! What did that mean? Two? Maybe five? The autopsy report later revealed that Richard had been stabbed ten times and had a fractured skull from a blow to the head.

I still try to visualize what Richard looked like lying on the floor, mutilated, his blood splattered about the room. Sometimes I hear the phone ringing—my frantic calls to contact him. Would it have been better if I had seen him? At least I would have known and not have to imagine the worst. But maybe Sergeant Schmidt, one of the homicide detectives in charge of the investigation, did me a favor.

Later that evening, as swarms of police and detectives descended on Richard's apartment, I kept thinking of Richard, dead and defenseless, surrounded by all the mayhem, his apartment ransacked and overrun by strangers looking for clues. I wanted to be there with him, to protect him from this onslaught, so I went down to his apartment. When I announced that I was going inside, Sergeant Schmidt stopped me dead in my tracks. "I don't think you should go. It will be unpleasant for you," he said, his voice authoritative and firm.

During the course of the evening, Bill, Marlene and I were repetitively interrogated by a number of police officers, then by Sergeant Schmidt and his partner, Sergeant Palumbo. We told them about the threatening calls Richard had received.

I was at Richard's when the first call came in at three o'clock one Sunday morning in January, a few days before we went on vacation to Mexico. The caller had said, "You're a dead man." Richard took it in stride, saying, "It must be some kind of joke, but who? I don't have any enemies." I wanted to call the police. He thought I was being foolish. "What do you think the cops will do? Listen, no one's going to call you up if they really want to do you in," he reasoned.

When we returned from Mexico, Bill, who had been watering Richard's bonsai trees and feeding the fish, reported that when he had stayed over a few nights, three more threatening calls had come in. It was never clear why Bill stayed in Richard's apartment. (He also said he wore some of Richard's clothes.) Richard and I simply shrugged his behavior away, attributing it to his "weirdness."

There was talk that it had been a crime of passion because of the nature of the stab wounds, possibly the brutal work of a homosexual killer. Sergeant Schmidt told me it had to have been someone Richard knew (there was no forced entry), someone who came at him from behind, someone strong (one of Richard's ribs was broken). The detectives thought money had been stolen. A few dollars had been found scattered in the closet as if someone had been in a rush.

There were no drugs to be found, only a scale and other low-level drug paraphernalia. That was contrary to what Bill had told me shortly after I arrived. He had said that Richard's apartment was a mess, that there were drugs all over, so he didn't go in. Bill also advised me not to say anything about drugs, Jerry, The Family, Mel Brooks or the screenplay.

At that point, I should have been suspicious of Bill, but my thoughts and emotions were not focused on Richard's killer. It was Richard and what he had suffered that mattered to me.

Because of that, I often found myself at odds with the detectives. They wanted to probe and I just wanted to be left alone to mourn Richard's sudden, violent death.

Some of their questions—"Did Richard have women in the afternoons?"; "Isn't it strange that you were together fourteen years and weren't married?"; or "Why did you each have your own apartment?"—were hurtful and invasive of my privacy, but I was too traumatized to protest. There was never an expression of sympathy or inquiry about my emotional condition, though I was obviously in shock and in great pain.

It was becoming evident, even at this early stage in the investigation, that my status as a girlfriend did not remotely approximate that of a widow in the mindset of the authorities, and that I would be treated accordingly.

Whereas I was greatly bothered by the interrogation and the police presence, Bill and Marlene took it calmly, even joking at times with the detectives. Bill, who was wired and talked nonstop, seemed overly enthusiastic about lending a helping hand in the investigation. He was constantly going down to Richard's apartment and engaging in tête-à-têtes with the detectives. It annoyed me that he was privy to what was happening and I had to stay upstairs and wait to be informed. What I did not know was that Bill was "invited" down to the crime scene because he was a suspect. As one detective later put it, "We just let him talk."

Marlene, a very articulate, in-control type person, who I learned was also Bill's realtor, stayed upstairs with me and was, in the absence of family and friends, my sole support system. She helped with the calls I needed to make and the calls that came in. That evening I slept at her apartment where she went out of her way to make me comfortable. I could not thank her or apologize enough for imposing on her kindness. I felt sorry that she had unwittingly become involved in what was happening—just because she had spent the afternoon with Bill and was at his apartment when he discovered Richard's body.

In my vulnerable, disoriented state, I bonded with Marlene, thinking for sure that, because of the uncommon experience we shared, this was the beginning of a lifelong friendship. In fact, when my former therapist (I called her that evening after not having seen her professionally for over a year) advised me, "No matter what, don't stay alone tonight." I responded, "That's no problem. I'm with my friends Bill and Marlene."

Despite the Valium Marlene gave me when we arrived at her apartment, I could not sleep that night. Tormented with questions—Why Richard? How could murder happen to someone so nonviolent? Who wanted Richard dead? What human being could have possibly chosen to pick up a knife and deliberately end Richard's life?—I had no answers. I lay awake, struggling with the few facts and details I had to make sense of an act that defied all reason.

The detectives came early the next morning and interviewed Marlene and me, then escorted us to the station house for more intensive questioning. Bill was already there. Once we arrived, Sergeant Schmidt fingerprinted me because, as he explained, my fingerprints were most likely all over Richard's apartment and they needed to distinguish mine from any others they might find. Even with this explanation, I felt ill at ease as he pressed my fingers into the black powder to make the impression. Was I paranoid in thinking that I was a possible suspect in Richard's murder? According to the entertainment and news media, which dictated all my perceptions regarding homicide, wasn't it only the "bad guys" that got fingerprinted?

Marlene was also fingerprinted because she said she had been in

Richard's apartment once. I did, in fact, recall Richard telling me that Bill once brought his realtor to the apartment.

The interrogation at the precinct seemed interminable. My relationship with the authorities was becoming strained, almost adversarial. Accusing me of being uncooperative and withholding information, they looked upon me as an anti-establishment type with an attitude, and I viewed them as callous, case-hardened bureaucrats who would not let me mourn Richard.

I wanted and needed to grieve at home with family and friends, not in a station house with strangers. There were funeral arrangements to be made, obituaries to be placed, and relatives and friends to be notified. And my parents were flying in from Florida that afternoon.

Everything was put on hold as I fielded questions about Richard and Bill's relationship, drugs, and people whose names appeared in Richard's address book and personal papers. They asked if Richard had dealings with loan sharks. They wanted to know whom Richard and I met when we were in Mexico. Did we smuggle in drugs? Someone had told them Richard had been to Mexico six times, and that we went on many vacations. Who fed them such lies? Bill? Or were they concocted by the detectives to see how I might react?

The only respite from the interrogation was the trip to the morgue to identify Richard's body. The day was dreary, damp, and very gray—in sync with what I was about to do. I could not help but recall a similar day years before when I visited the Dachau Concentration Camp.

I had never seen a dead person before. In Judaism, the religion in which I was raised, closed coffins were the norm, so I did not know what to expect when Richard was wheeled into view. Separated from me by a glass partition, he was wrapped in a sheet, only his face showing. His mouth was open as if he had been taken by surprise. He did not look peaceful or even human. What I saw was a body, a bag of skin and bones that had nothing to do with the Richard I knew; that realization was very comforting.

After the visit to the morgue, I went with Bill and the detectives to Richard's apartment to remove the valuables. Because a homicide had been committed, the apartment was to be sealed for a month, barring all access to it.

As I waited in the hall, Bill and the detectives brought out the various items. When Bill asked me if he could have Richard's flamingo, a beautifully handcrafted piece that Richard had brought back from Mexico, I looked at him askance and he put it down. How inappropriate, I thought.

There had been another incident earlier that day at the station house that disturbed me. Emerging from an interrogation session, I noticed that Bill and Marlene suddenly looked worried. I approached Bill and, in a nonaccusatory, pleading voice, asked, "Do you know who could have done this?" "No, I don't," he muttered under his breath. There was something angry and menacing in his repressed tone, as if he was being pushed too far.

After removing the valuables from Richard's apartment, I was driven back to the station house for more of the same questioning, this time with the precinct captain in attendance. I was eventually dismissed about six-thirty that evening.

I stayed that night at a friend's apartment, where I was to stay for the next month—at her insistence. While I thought I was functioning well enough to stay alone, no one else agreed, and I felt too emotionally battered to argue.

I will never forget the experience of trying to eat an English muffin the next morning, my friend coaxing and coaching me as I force-fed myself for two hours. Food never tasted so awful. I felt as if I would choke with every bite. I lost seven pounds that week.

Operating on sheer emotional adrenalin, I attended to the memorial service and notification of relatives and friends with phenomenal efficiency and stamina. My phone rang nonstop with people calling to help or wanting to hear about Richard's murder and the police investigation.

Everyone had difficulty assimilating what had happened to Richard. A few people even called back to confirm the reality of what they had just heard. After the initial expressions of shock, horror, silence or condolences, inevitably the conversation shifted to the particulars of the death. I spent hours on the phone rehashing and reliving my story of Richard's murder. People needed to know and I needed to ventilate. This obsession with details was all we had to convince ourselves that murder had happened to someone we knew.

I spoke with Bill that day, mostly about the arrangements for Richard's service. He offered to help find a hall and said he wanted to have a private mass for Richard at his church. I told him I thought that was a nice gesture, and that I would attend.

Marlene also called later that day, very upset. The police had followed her to her mother's house and had taken Bill for a polygraph. I did not know what to think. Although I clung to the belief that the polygraph would ultimately clear Bill of any involvement, I intentionally did not return his call later that evening. I was at a friend's house when my mother called to say that Bill, sounding distraught, wanted to talk to me. He had told her, "Imagine them interrogating me like that. I was Richard's friend." The next morning, I was whisked away by my parents to my aunt and uncle's suburban New Jersey home for what was to be a weekend of peace and quiet. Free at last to mourn what had happened to Richard, I thought. Was I wrong!

A day after I arrived, I learned Bill had been arrested for Richard's murder. He had "flunked the polygraph with flying colors" and Marlene had broken down and confessed she had lied when she said that she had been with Bill all afternoon on the day of Richard's murder.

"You're going to be involved in a murder trial!" was my aunt's immediate reaction to the news. I was too overwhelmed by a sudden rush of anger to consider the implications of her statement.

Ever since Richard was murdered, I had been feeling a kind of free-floating, low-key anger, but, mixed with the myriad of other emotions and without a specific face to rage against, it never manifested with the intensity it did when I heard that it was Bill who had snuffed out Richard's life. I suddenly hated this man who had dared to call himself our friend.

Why? I had to know why. Had Bill been freebasing cocaine and lost all human perspective? They said it was a crime of passion. Did Richard say or do something that provoked him? Did Richard "bug" him about Mel Brooks and the screenplay? Could Bill have been a closet homosexual who suddenly made advances that Richard rejected?

Was it over money? I knew that Bill was always behind in paying Richard for his cocaine and at one time had given Richard a deed to a condo he owned as collateral, but I thought that had been squared away. In fact, I had asked Bill that first evening if he owed Richard any money. "Two thousand dollars," he had said without hesitation. Did he murder Richard because of two thousand dollars? Or was there something inherent in Bill's personality that Richard and I had overlooked or dismissed as "weirdness," a pathology that could inspire Bill to commit murder? I groped for answers but only found more questions.

I returned to New York, physically and emotionally exhausted. Pushed to the limit, I thought. I was wrong about that, too.

Awaiting me in my apartment was a phone message from the detectives to call the precinct. "I don't believe this. Now what do they want from me!" I protested to a friend who had met me at the bus station. I immediately called them. They asked me to come out to Queens for more questioning. They needed to be sure of their information before the case against Bill went to the Grand Jury the following week. Like a Pavlovian dog, I heeded their call, and my friend and I were off to Queens, an hour-and-a-half, two-bus trek from where I lived.

This was the most unpleasant of my encounters with the detectives. For four hours straight, I was made to feel more like a suspect than the mourner of a homicide victim. In fact, my friend, who had to wait outside for me, said that when she inquired about what the detectives were doing with me for so long, the officer on duty jokingly responded, “Torturing her.”

The detectives told me that Bill, in maintaining his innocence, insisted that he was protecting someone. They wanted the names of Richard’s supplier and another friend, a legitimate Garment Center executive whose wife happened to be related to a reputed Mafia kingpin. I adamantly refused to divulge that information on the grounds that my policy was not to “rat on” friends and implicate them unnecessarily, but the detectives were unrelenting in their pursuit of these questions. I felt so stripped of my right to privacy that at one point I asked if I needed an attorney. Moreover, Sergeant Schmidt had the audacity to offer such evaluations as, “You’ll feel differently about this in six months,” as well as to blatantly come on to me: “If you cry, I’m going to kiss you” and “You look so sexy when you pout.”

One might argue that in light of Bill’s statement that he was protecting someone, the sergeant was just doing his job and checking me out as a suspect. His remarks were his way of testing my attachment to Richard. On the other hand, if I had been Richard’s wife, would the detectives have been so invasive of my privacy and ruthless in their questioning? Would they have even suspected me? And would the sergeant have taken such liberties and come on to a widow?

The detectives and I stayed locked in a tug of war. I refused to name names and they refused to stop probing and let me go home. But I was starved, overtired and emotionally vulnerable, with no one on “my” side—a perfect candidate out of whom to eventually extract information. In the end, I reluctantly gave the detectives what they wanted. “Now was that so bad? Look what you put yourself through for nothing,” was their reaction. They then admitted that they already had the names and merely needed my confirmation. I still felt like a traitor who had collaborated with the enemy.

Despite its grueling aspect, the session with the detectives did shed some light on the dark side of Bill’s personality. When I inquired about Jerry and The Family, the detectives did not give much credence to their existence. They doubted that the screenplay ever went anywhere, speculating that Bill had either discarded it or tore out the title page and submitted it as his own. I also learned that Bill’s Porsche actually belonged to a girlfriend who was using his garage privileges. Why did he tell Richard it was his

Porsche? I wondered what else he lied about. The threatening calls? The two thousand dollars? All those stories about The Family?

And what about Bill's daughter, a model who lived in California whose magazine photos suddenly appeared all over his apartment a few months before Richard was killed? Richard had even remarked, "All these years, I never knew Bill had a daughter." Those photos, especially the one with "I love you, Daddy" scribbled across it, used to haunt me for some reason I could not articulate, but it never occurred to me to question their authenticity. Why would someone invent a daughter if they didn't have one?

I also wondered about the meditation cushion, an exact replica of Richard's, the detectives said they found in Bill's apartment. I could not fathom why Bill would have use for a meditation cushion unless he wanted to be like Richard or…he wanted to be Richard.

That revelation startled me at first, but it did not seem so illogical and far-fetched a notion when I considered Bill's wearing of Richard's clothes while we were in Mexico, the sudden appearance of a daughter similar in age to Richard's daughter, not to mention his frequently expressed desire to have his nose fixed to resemble Richard's. (Richard had a fine nose, but not one a plastic surgeon might seek to emulate.)

Whenever I thought I had an interlude of calm to mourn Richard, an unexpected, anxiety-provoking disruption relating to the case against Bill inevitably arose to set me back. It was cruel punishment for being the survivor of a homicide victim. Wasn't I suffering enough? I felt victimized, powerless and resentful that homicide was ruling my life.

Those were my sentiments when I heard Assistant District Attorney Levine's voice on my answering machine summoning me to appear the very next day before the Grand Jury considering the murder indictment against Bill. I was furious over this turn of events. I did not anticipate having to testify until the murder trial, which, if there was one, was months away. Richard's memorial service was in two days and I did not feel emotionally prepared to go to court. Only a week had passed since Richard's murder. It was too soon; I still hadn't sorted out the details.

To ensure that I not forget anything, I stayed up most of the night writing down everything I could possibly remember that might be relevant to my testimony—from the chronology of events to my assessment of Bill's eccentric behavior.

Levine was young, perhaps a few years out of law school. He tried to be sympathetic and human, prefacing his interrogation with quick, garbled condolences, but then it was business-as-usual as he began firing questions at me: "When was the last time you talked to Richard? How did you know Richard was dead? Who told you Richard had been murdered?"

When I started reading my notes, he seemed visibly annoyed. He advised me not to write down anything else. As it was, he had to give a copy of the paper with my notes to Bill's defense attorney. I asked whether I could continue writing in my journal, which I had been keeping up-to-date with renewed diligence since Richard's murder. He cautioned against that, too. Naturally, being a writer, I did not heed his advice. How could my intimate writings be of interest to the Defense? If anything, they would undermine the case for Bill's innocence.

At the end of the meeting, I was required to sign a waiver of immunity, which I did like an automaton, thinking it standard procedure for anyone who took the stand. I later realized, after learning that other witnesses were not asked to sign such a document, that I was still regarded as a possible suspect in Richard's murder.

During the nerve-racking hours I sat waiting to testify, I felt as if I had descended into the underbelly of the criminal justice system—an almost surreal world inhabited by those who either worked for the justice system or transgressed against it. The criminally accused, cuffed and led around by armed guards or attorneys, at times sat only a few feet away from me.

Among those waiting to testify were the detectives and Richard's neighbor, who, on the afternoon of Richard's murder, saw Bill in the building at the time he said he was elsewhere. Marlene, who had been summoned by the prosecution, was conspicuously absent. I could not help but wonder where she might be.

My actual appearance before the Grand Jury lasted no more than 10 minutes. I told my story as I had countless times before. When I mentioned that upon arriving at Bill's apartment, I screamed out, "I need a Valium!" there was an explosion of laughter because of my presentation (I tend to get dramatic when nervous) or out of empathy. Whatever their motivation, I felt supported and confident that justice would be served on Richard's behalf. ■

• *Read* **Surviving Homicide, Part II** *at: ducts.org/content/surviving-homicide-part-ii/*

# Memoirs of a Chemist

## The bridge to my grandmother

BY ROGER LIPMAN *(Issue 20)*

IN THE 1990s THE IRA tried to blow it up. That hurt me, for Hammersmith Bridge provided access to the house on Clavering Avenue in Barnes, South West London, venue for my grandmother's Sunday lunches, and as a child I had assumed a proprietorial interest in it. Though the house was modest, it was as if the bridge were entrance to my grandmother's estate, a grand driveway, and we used to take the 9 bus across it from Hammersmith Broadway; in the 1940s the double-decker buses were allowed freely to rumble over.

During visits to Auntie Muriel in the 1980s, long after my grandmother's death but before the IRA bomb attempt, we walked the half mile from Hammersmith Broadway, my mother and I, across the splendid little suspension bridge. By then, only one single-decker bus at a time was permitted to cross, and the romance had gone out of the bus journey.

"It can't take it anymore," Muriel had said about the bridge when the weight restrictions were imposed, sorrowfully, as if talking of a revered and ancient draught horse. "No, it can't take it," and her voice quavered and tapered, the way their voices in old age always quavered and tapered, Muriel's and my mother's.

When I was much younger, about 8, in the mid-1940s, Muriel had a beautiful voice. In it's heyday it was BBC, the words strong, the syllables flawlessly enunciated, the accent perfect yet not posh. It greeted us after we rang the bell. The door opened slowly and she grinned conspiratorially, and then it opened wide to admit her younger sister and me—there were only the two of us since my parents were already separated.

"Hello, Roger. Hello, Blinky," she said—one of my mother's nicknames since childhood—and Muriel's grin became an abashed chuckle, as if she wished to excuse the strident notes of Liszt as his Hungarian Rhapsody

No. 2 thundered to its conclusion on the drawing room spinet. The music ended as we arrived, and my grandmother emerged into the hall to greet us, piano-practised and pinafored, and after exchanges of kisses she waddled into the kitchen to complete lunch preparation.

The three of us lingered in the hall, the sisters exchanging pleasantries, until their younger brother, Ronald, arrived from outside with the scuttle full of coal for the fire in the drawing room and said, "Hello, Phoebe. Hello, Roger.... Yeesss, well, how are you getting on at school, then?" (Ronald and my mother always said, "Yeesss.")

Satisfied with my answer he ushered me into the dining room, while the sisters moved slowly into the kitchen to continue with filial babble. Ronald sat me down at the long table that reached almost to the French window at the end of the dining room, overlooking the narrow back garden resplendent with snapdragons and dahlias and staked tomato plants. On the ochre table cover, along with the place settings, sat a silver tray with bottles of Crabbie's Ginger Wine and Sandeman's Tawny Port.

"Would you like some wine, Roger?"

He poured me a glass (I always chose the ginger wine) and then left to join his sisters and mother in the kitchen. I settled at the table, stroked the textured ochre cover, fingered the long ochre tassels that hung down and tickled my knees, comfortable on the plush velvet dining chair, its soft fuzz cushioning my short-trousered thighs. Behind me, on the tiled hearth next to the gas fire, stood a figurine, a mournful maid, her fine china features framed by her bonnet and her draped blue cloak. To my right stood the sideboard, under the gallery of which were oriental vases and a china boy who stood deep in thought, right elbow resting on his quiver and right hand supporting his chin.

I knew sooner or later the adults would come to the dining room and gather round the table for lunch, and I looked forward to the nice things to eat and drink. I was used to being alone, so the environment was not unusual. The adults treated me kindly but as the child I was. I knew my place—my mother was probably glad of the break from me—so I busied myself. I withdrew into my own little world, a silent world, a world of snapdragons and pansies, insects, tapestries, textures and tassels, designs, objets d'art, water colours of the Middle East that adorned the walls of the drawing room and engravings of composers on the walls of the hall. It was a rich environment. And I was mostly content in my separateness. One Sunday I ate a Brazil nut and discovered I was very allergic to them, and Uncle Ronald took me out for a walk for half an hour until the reaction subsided. That kind of togetherness was a rare event for me in my grandmother's house.

My grandmother, her thin hair showing the crown of her head and a handkerchief peeping from the pocket of her pinafore, came in to recover silver serving spoons from the sideboard drawer, and she placed them on the ochre cover near me, explaining their use before she returned to the kitchen. On the far wall, next to the French windows, a convex gilt-framed mirror captured this dining room scene: grandmother addressing grandson, the panoramic image Vermeer-like in its composition and virtue. Suddenly, the heat from the gas fire behind me became too fierce, and I left my chair to follow her to the rest of the adults.

I sought my mother in the kitchen; she was drinking a glass of sherry at the unfinished white oak table. Ronald was there, too, standing with his pint of stout and a frothy moustache and his back to the kitchen range; and from time to time he turned to shovel coke into its red-hot boiler, and he asked me again, "Well, you're getting on all right at school, then?"

I satisfied him again with my answer and approached my mother at the oak table while studying the flypaper spiral suspended above it, strung from the white plastic lampshade, twirling slowly in the thermal from the hot range, its latest victim trying in vain to extricate itself from the tacky mass while others remained motionless, glued to the paper, like museum specimens. I watched the fly in its death throes, sinking into the sticky adhesive as it tried to lever free first one leg, then another. Each attempt drove it deeper into the quaèire and exhausted it, until it moved no more.

"Filthy things," said my mother, and she smiled a wan smile.

My grandmother and Muriel bustled in and out of the kitchen to the pantry, where the black gas stove stood, full with its Sunday bird and roast potatoes. The adults talked of this and that, and I knew I was not to interrupt my mother, for that would bring a stern rebuke from Muriel. As a youngster, I was frightened of Muriel. Once, when the three of us were out walking and my mother went on ahead, I ran after her, leaving Muriel behind. "Oh, leave your mother alone," Muriel shouted at me, and I fell back, alongside my aunt, crestfallen.

The sloping front of the writing desk in the kitchen by the door to the hall hid all sorts of interesting things belonging to Ronald that were outside my permitted domain, but *The Jewish Chronicle*, which sat folded on top, on a brass trivet, I was allowed to take back to the dining room to read. So I returned with it to the quietude of the dining room, with its hot gas fire, its china maid, its quivered boy and textured ochre cloth and tassels and fuzzy chairs. But come the time when my glass of Crabbie's Ginger Wine was empty and necessity took precedence over caution, I would again go to the kitchen to ask for more.

"Yes," said Muriel, "but leave your mother alone," and I went back to the dining room and poured myself another draft.

When I was very young, Uncle Harold, my grandmother's eldest child, was sometimes present for lunch. Harold was something of a prodigy with the cello. My grandmother, who had been a professional pianist of some renown, had taken Harold to London from Edgbaston, near Birmingham in central England, early in the century to push his musical education. With some success it may be added. He gained a scholarship to the Royal College of Music, and the story has it that he was the youngest graduate ever from the College at the time. Harold had long since left the family home. He became a professional cellist and played in the symphony orchestra under Sir Henry Wood, who initiated the Promenade Concerts at London's Queen's Hall in the 1920—the Proms today, still the highlight of the London summer music season. But by the 1940s Harold had drifted away from the cello. His teacher had been cruel; the standard he reached to achieve his scholarship had been beaten into him. No wonder he ended up hating the instrument. According to one of my cousins, a clairvoyant had earlier foretold his academic success and unhappiness as a result of it.

I enjoyed it when Uncle Harold was visiting his mother while we were present. He entered the dining room with social intent to greet me—a slight figure, hands in pockets, stooped and bald and crow's feet around his eyes from his smile, just like Uncle Ronald.

"The best little ducky of the lot," he said, before turning and retiring to the drawing room. And a few seconds later he was back, saying again as he came into view from behind the door, "The best little ducky of the lot, and he's doing all right at school, then?"

He wanted to talk, just didn't know how. They all wanted to know my progress. I was the male grandson. No doubt they all expected me to do well academically and enter one of the professions.

Education in England in the 1940s and 1950s was selective. Children, especially those from lower- and middle-class backgrounds whose parents had no money for private schools, were sorted at age eleven into those who would follow an academic route in grammar school and have the chance to go on to university, and those who would pursue a vocational path in a secondary modern school. The dreaded eleven-plus examination was the culmination of this process, and was the reason behind this probing of my academic progress. Yet I do not remember stress or panic about the examination. It seemed preordained that I would pass. I had no doubts or questions about it in my mind. I am not sure, though, that this was testament to the ways of my grandmother and her family. It was my father who was the teacher, and he supervised my preparation.

At last the roast turkey or goose or chicken arrived, succulent and tasty, plump and juicy, on a big oval platter. Oh, what a splendid dinner! Ronald carved and my grandmother and Muriel served me and the others. I liked the breast meat, and the roast potatoes, their crispy crusts scrumptious when smothered with rich gravy from the boat, with Brussels sprouts and peas or carrots. Then they served afters, plum pudding with custard, and I'd have more ginger wine. I ate until I was ready to burst. There might be candied fruits and chocolates. During the war, delectable tidbits would arrive from distant relatives in South Africa, so the candied fruits were no novelty. And at Christmas time, for it was at Christmas and not at Chanukah, there were silver threepenny joeys in the plum pudding, two or three of them. I had no competition to secure them, no siblings with whom to squabble. I had only to eat my way to them. They were mine for the taking.

Conversation was circumscribed, and never directed at me. My mother said "Oohhh" and "Aahhh" and how tasty everything was. The ladies talked about clothes and fashion and colour and this shop and that shop. They talked about the relatives in South Africa, but I never knew who they were. My mother said, "How are things, then, Ronald?" and he said with animation and passion, "Yeesss, alright Phoebe, doesn't do any good to complain, does it?" And my mother said, with passion and animation, "Noohhh, indeed it doesn't," and I always wondered, without ever being able to put it into words, what there was to be so passionate and animated about, and why she was different with other people than she was with me.

Muriel talked to my mother about Mr. Savage, her boss at the photographic studio, where she managed the appointments for weddings and Bar Mitzvahs, and sometimes they talked about my father, but I could not understand the drift of what was said. Ronald gave the latest gossip from the print shop, where he set the type for the morning newspaper. Nor had I conversation with my grandmother. She just cooed and said what a good boy I was. I stayed silent, in the background, doing my epicurean duty. I was to be seen and not heard, and the ginger wine served its purpose admirably.

After dinner, when I got tired of the dining room, I wandered back to the hall and looked at the pictures of the composers adorning the walls. There was Mozart with his hair in a ribbon, and Liszt with big warts on his face, and Rachmaninoff, Beethoven, Chopin—all the composers of the Romantic period. I wandered up and down, studying their engraved faces with great interest. How I wish my grandmother, Licentiate of the Royal Academy of Music, had played the piano for me. But she never did. She, who in the 1890s with her violinist sister Fanny had played sonatas for Queen Victoria, never asked me, her only grandson, would I like to hear her play. The nearest I had gotten was the closing passage of the Liszt upon arrival, except for my surreptitious perusal of the score still in place on the piano in the drawing room, to which we would repair after lunch for a cup of instant coffee, Black Magic chocolates and a glass of port wine. The blackness of the notes on the stave, how on earth was she able to play them? It was a mystery to me. Those unfathomable hieroglyphics elicited in me a terrible awe.

I would have liked my grandmother to have sat down at the piano and played Liszt or Chopin or Rachmaninoff, something that she had been doing for 60 years and could have done in her sleep. If she examined the question at all, maybe she thought I wouldn't have been interested. Given the pressure she had placed on her firstborn to learn the cello, perhaps my grandmother also had felt pressure at a young age to play the piano; then the last thing she would have wanted was to inflict it on me? And what role did music play for her, I wonder? In my grandmother's family, music was not an avocation; it put the bread on the table. No, it was the academic path for me, she probably concluded; you cannot do both.

One Sunday I thought it was happening. I was in the drawing room on the window seat and she came in as if I were not present, sat down at the piano, adjusted the stool and started to play. Her hands moved quickly over the keyboard. I was swept along with the sounds, loud and rich. After a couple of minutes she stopped, got up from the stool, went into the kitchen, the Sunday bird vying for her attention, and never returned. She cannot have known how much I cared to hear her play. And I never knew if I had the right to ask, or whether she would have acceded.

In 1947, when I was nine, she got ill with pernicious anemia. I didn't know what it was but I knew "pernicious" was a bad word. My mother took me to see her in hospital, but when we got there I had to wait downstairs by the porter's office. I was too young, the staff said, to be allowed on the ward. I wished that I could have visited her in her sick bed. Instead, I sat in the entrance hall of the West London Hospital, contemplating that last little recital. I never made it across the bridge to my grandmother. She died a few weeks later, on August 3, aged 74.

"Poor Ma," her children said. "Yeesss, poor Ma." ■

# Sunshine Factory–Part 1

A summer job working in a greeting card factory turns into a nightmare.

BY COREE SPENCER *(Issue 22)*

A RITE OF PASSAGE for a sixteen-year-old in East Lonèeadow, Massachusetts is getting a summer job. This fits right in with our Spencer family work ethic. No fancy "sweet sixteen" celebration will make me feel as good about myself as holding down a full-time job. Many nights around our supper table my two sisters and I are reminded by our father of how our turning sixteen has given us a newly gained usefulness.

"See, now you can bring in your own money. If I were smart I'd start asking you girls to pay rent and foot your own bills. But I tell you what: I'm such a good guy, I'll let you keep your money to put toward your college. I put myself through college, and now I'm a better person for it. You want to be a better person, don't you?"

My father has left out the part about how his own father died when he was a toddler, forcing his mother to accept welfare to care for her three young sons, and that the government picked up my father's college tab. My mother told my sisters and me this once when we had lunch at Friendly's at the mall and made us promise never to mention that we knew this. We continue to let my father retell his "paying for college himself" story and of course never mention his "welfare years."

Getting a summer job will also introduce us to other members of our community's blue-collar society. For some teenagers it will pay for a coveted car and a super hi-fi stereo. For others, like my sisters and me, it will pay for college.

We get a choice between an indoor job and an outdoor job. The outdoor job is "tobacco field hand," meaning you're picked up at the end of our street in a cattle truck that looks like it's straight out of the prop department from the movie *The Grapes of Wrath*. The truck takes you to Enfield, Connecticut to pick tobacco across the street from a minimum-security prison where the prisoners also work the fields. The indoor job is "factory worker," where you have a choice of many factories lining Shaker Road, including American Saw, Milton Bradley and Springfield Gun and Rifle.

My eighteen-year-old sister, Anne, and I decide to become factory debutantes. Somehow this seems easier and less like hard labor than working in the tobacco fields. So far, the only jobs I've had are babysitting, paper routes and a failed lawn-mowing business with my father. I also helped my father teach tennis to kids for a couple of years, something he has done for the few months off in the summer from his high-school English teaching job. After the failed lawn-mowing business, I don't know what we were thinking by teaming up together once again. We hated each other, but our love of money brought us back together. We sabotaged each other. I would make faces behind his back as he lectured all the kids on the perfect backhand, then I'd intentionally aim for his stomach when I'd demonstrate volleying at the net. Soon, instead of letting me show off my fancy tennis moves, he just used me to chase tennis balls and pick them up after they were whacked by the kids. Then I put them back into a plastic bucket. He'd retaliate by firing me for mysterious reasons, like my bad attitude, my no-hustle on the courts, or for having a dirty look on my face. I was rehired when he needed me to help carry equipment back to our van or hand out water cups to the kids. I was fired and rehired so often I felt like Billy Martin, the manager of the New York Yankees.

I've never had a "real" paycheck job, but Anne has spent the last two summers working at Fenway Golf, serving up ice-cream cones and buckets of golf balls to the sporting citizens of Western Massachusetts. She has said she's had her fill of soft-serve ice cream and miniature golf, but I really think she won't go back because of Bob, a boy she met at Fenway Golf last summer. He shared her love of the band Journey. They quoted the songs to each other in love letters. I'd tear apart our shared bedroom looking for these letters, both feeling sorry for Anne that her life was reduced to corny love letters and feeling jealous over this boy Bob calling her his "Journey Girl" at the end of each love note. Bob disappeared at the beginning of fall last year, causing Anne to go on a three-week binge of eating only celery. Her shoulder blades stuck out and she'd taken to standing on our bathroom scale, watching for her weight go down. This summer, Anne decides a change is necessary.

My mother drives us to the employment office of one of the smaller factories, Sunshine Greeting Cards. All the other factories intimidate us. Milton Bradley is in a building so huge and scary it looks like the Pentagon, and, well, we actually can't figure out where the front entrance is. Then there is American Saw, and Springfield Gun and Rifle where we'd be working with things that can kill you, or at least give you a nasty wound. Sunshine Greeting Cards seems small and safe. The worst we could suffer is a paper cut.

Now, for me, there will be no more carefree summer days—days I had spent in a damp bathing suit, wandering the neighborhood in flip-flops, only changing into clothes to work a few hours babysitting or help my father toss tennis balls to kids a few times a week. I'm walking through this employment door to become an adult—an official, card-carrying nine-to-fiver.

At the reception desk sits a woman wearing a gray-blue wig that could be worn backwards and look just as good. She turns to us, crinkling her nose under heavy glasses. "Are you here for summer work? Fill out these papers, and I'll have you speak to Hal." I stare at the papers and see SSN and DOB written on them. It might as well be French for all I can understand them. I look over Anne's shoulder as if I'm cheating on a math exam. She glares at me, covers her paper and turns away from me. I twirl my pencil, tap it on my knee and stare at the wall.

When Anne is good and done, she turns to me and whispers, "DOB is date of birth and SSN is Social Security number, you idiot!" Finally, I get to use this nine-digit number that was sent to me typed onto a small white card. I see the person referred to as "Hal." He's a pale, waxy, perspiring man-child. I've never seen anyone so beaded-up with sweat outside of a tennis match. Hal is gesturing to three olive-skinned people. The three seem to have trouble with their English. I've heard about these people, these Portuguese people, but I've never seen any until now. None of them live in our hometown, but lots of them work in our factories.

Hal's translucent eyelids flutter as he reads our applications. My sister might make the cut; she's had a real "paycheck" job, while I've only had "pocket change" jobs. Anne sits next to me gnawing on her fingernails as if they provided the same delicious flavor as a Nutty Buddy ice-cream cone. Despite her professional skills, Anne remains silent as she turns her right thumb over and inspects it, finds the perfect spot for a nibble, then gorges herself on her own flesh. Maybe it was a fluke she worked for Mr. Palmer at Fenway Golf. It was kiddie work, selling tickets to the miniature pitch and putt course and sprinkling jimmies and nuts on sundaes. We're in the real world now, and all our extremely obvious shortcomings will be recognized as soon as someone will be paying us minimum wage, $3.35 an hour.

I'm transfixed by Hal's dampness. I wonder if it bothers him. Does he notice? My mind starts to drift off as his thin lips describe the job to us. Thank goodness my alert, nail-biting, older sister, Anne, is next to me, absorbing these important instructions, while I tune out like a radio caught between two stations. Hal's lips stop moving, and I'm snapped back to reality as I feel his damp, warm hand shaking mine. As soon as we exit the employment office, while I wipe Hal's sweat off my hand on to my cut-off shorts, I ask Anne, "So did we get the jobs?"

She turns to me and rolls her eyes. "God, Coree, weren't you listening? We report to somebody named Jane on Monday at 8:30! We've got four days left of freedom!"

I don't sleep for the next four nights. When I close my eyes, I have the sensation of being swept up into the whirlpool of the working force. I try to picture what the factory will look like. The only factory I've seen the inside of is "The Saltwater Taffy Factory" in Kennebunkport, Maine. The employees there wore colored-yarn, pigtail wigs and painted-on freckles. They laughed, and waved to us from behind a glassed-in conveyor belt filled with multicolored taffy. I could work there.

The 7:30 Monday-morning alarm bell rings, and I roll out of bed. I've slept in my clothes and made my peanut butter and jelly sandwich the night before. I join Anne on our front porch steps, waiting for our chronically late friends, Carol and Lori Kennedy, to join us for a ride to the factory. We see several pale, soon-to-be-sunburned boys from our neighborhood walk down the block to catch the truck to the tobacco fields. We give up waiting for the Kennedys, and our mother drives us to their house a few blocks away. She lays on the horn until the Kennedy girls lumber out of their house. Carol has a bag of Wonder Bread and Lori has a half package of bologna. They create their sandwiches in our car on the way to Sunshine.

We meet with a traffic jam moving down the long stretch of factories on Shaker Road. It's a long, slow procession of cars that could be mistaken for either a parade or a funeral. We're dropped off at the loading dock entrance in the back of Sunshine Greeting Card Factory. The opening of the loading dock looks like the cave entrance that opens and swallows up all the innocent, blond people in the 1960 film *The Time Machine*. The blond people end up becoming food for these horrible red-eyed Morlocks who toil beneath the earth. I'll be the first one eaten, since not only am I blond, I'm as pale as a corpse.

Once inside the factory, I realize that this won't be anything like "The Saltwater Taffy Factory." The people here don't look like cheerful Oompa Loompas from the movie *Willy Wonka & the Chocolate Factory*. In fact, the employees here look a lot more like the Morlocks from *The Time Machine*.

Right away, it becomes obvious who the new employees are. Once we walk about twenty feet from the entrance, all of us "new workers" bunch up together like ants on a Ritz cracker. Meanwhile, all the old time workers, "the lifers," crowd around a pole with a metal box attached. The lifers punch their time cards in the box and scuttle off to various parts of the dark, high-ceilinged, dimly lit factory. There are a few small windows at the very top of the factory walls, but they look like they've never been washed and allow for very little light and are up so high no one can look out of them to contemplate life or watch a bird build a nest. They probably only exist so Sunshine can save money on light bulbs, relying on whatever sunshine might get through the grimy window to illuminate the factory.

While I stare up at the tiny specks of outside light near the ceiling, our supervisor, Jane, appears before us like a silent apparition. Her pin-straight, bobbed, brown hair is heavily streaked with wiry gray strands. It's parted on the side, and playfully held in place with a pink plastic barrette shaped like a tiny bow. This pretty, pink bit of whimsy belies the real Jane; she is not cute, frilly or sweet. She opens her mouth to reveal teeth that haven't seen the business end of a toothbrush in years. They look like stalactites hanging from the roof of a cave. It seems as if working in this factory has stolen whatever beauty she's ever had. What strikes me most about Jane's appearance is when she raises her hands to separate us into groups: her skin is a patchwork quilt of livid white blotches and mottled brown color. It's as if God couldn't decide on a flesh tone for Jane, so he left her terribly spotted.

Jane takes a watch out of the pocket of her baby-blue checked smock and informs us that we're all late clocking in and that as a result we'll lose our first quarter hour of pay. I'm sure she must be joking with us, like this is factory humor, but she isn't laughing. She isn't even smiling. Somehow I get the feeling it's moments like this that get Jane to work every day.

She rolls her eyes at us, and points to the wall where the time cards are filed and instructs us, "Punch in, and report to your work stations!" All nineteen of us run to the wall, and I find my time card, "Spencer, Coree." I get to the punch-in clock first, and in my rush I stick my time card in upside down. When I pull it out, instead of clocking in on Monday morning, it looks like I've clocked out on Friday evening. I don't move. I stare at my time card until all the other workers push me out of the way of the time-card box, like we're all monkeys at the zoo and I'm blocking all my fellow chimps from getting to the feeding station.

I turn and address Jane. "I think I put my time card in wrong…."

She cuts me off with, "Just get to your station!"

Lori Kennedy and I have been put on the same assembly line, while my sister Anne is placed on the line in front of ours. Carol Kennedy is escorted off with two other girls to the shadowy wastelands of the factory, behind several skids of boxes. We learn "skids" in factory lingo means a large wooden pallet boxes are piled on that is then moved around the factory on forklifts.

Lori and I might be on the same line, but we aren't next to each other. Sunshine Factory has devised a way to keep production up and talking on the clock, down. On the assembly lines they place a Portuguese-speaking person next to each English-speaking person. Not only does this not cut down on talking during work, it makes things even noisier, because people must shout in Portuguese and English to reach the person they are speaking to, on the other side of the person next to them. Antigrassia is the barrier between Lori and me. She's a tiny, antique-jeweled, middle-aged Portuguese woman who speaks nonstop to her friend Ava on the other side of me.

Jane stands behind me to teach me "the skills." She must have an allotment of only twenty-five words a day, because she attempts to teach me like I'm Helen Keller and she's Anne Sullivan. One of her two-toned hands grabs my hand from behind, reaches over the conveyor belt and snatches up a "winking Santa" Christmas card. She glues glitter to the front of the card, then glues the back of the card and places it in the sales booklet coming down the line. I try to repeat her actions without her manhandling my arm. My card drips with excess glue and I miss the sales booklet coming down the assembly line and accidentally glue my card to the conveyor belt. I feel Jane's cold eyes on the back of my neck and hear Antigrassia jabbering loudly next to me, pushing my messy, gluey card back at me.

Jane assures me in English that I've done wrong. She says, "NO!"

Jane grabs another card, and repeats her motions. I'm still just mesmerized by her two-tone skin. Antigrassia tries to help me. She smiles, holds up a Santa card and then in rapid-fire Portuguese talks me through the gluing procedure. I don't know what's harder: trying to learn my job by having Jane forcefully manipulate my arm, or being instructed in a foreign language. I finally catch on and after only thirty minutes I feel like a machine. My arm, as if acting on it's own accord, repeats the same movement over and over. The death of all my ambitions is creeping up on me. I want to turn and run. This is all a huge mistake. I'm not meant to be here. This doesn't seem like the first step to my dream of becoming a famous movie star or Olympic gold medal athlete. Sally Field only had to endure this kind of humiliation for a couple of hours in the movie *Norma Rae.*

I'm not special. I'm really just a regular person. I'm so unspectacular that now I've become the lowest kicker on this blue-collar chorus line of greeting-card glitterers.

With one hand busy gluing cards and my second hand turning the page of the booklet, my brain has plenty of time to philosophize about my new environment. I ponder the question, "How can Jane be so grim when she's surrounded by glitter and happy Santa Claus cards all day?" Jane seems to be devoid of everything greeting cards represent. I also ponder the lack of men working in this factory. As if to keep the few doses of masculinity around here, I notice that the men have the easiest jobs. The seven or eight men I've seen so far aren't even good looking, but still all the women notice when one of them whizzes by on a forklift or carries a piece of paper from one end of the factory floor to the next. We all look up from the assembly lines as one of these "fetching" specimens walks by in overalls and safety glasses. One guy in particular catches my eye. His name is Jim. Jim's neck is perpetually twisted sideways, and he's cross-eyed, yet this doesn't stop the factory from letting him drive a forklift.

Time passes slowly here. But two hours into the workday, the conveyor belts speed up. I pile cards next to me that I can't glitter fast enough. I feel like Lucy and Ethel when they worked on the assembly line in the chocolate factory. Unfortunately, I can't shove these cards into my mouth or fill my hat with them, as Lucy and Ethel did with the chocolates.

Antigrassia sees this pile and points to the cards like it's a dead rat next to me. She's speaking to me, but I understand her Portuguese about as well as I understand our dog Brandy when she's barking at me. I try the same tactic I use on Brandy when communicating with a foreigner. I look at Antigrassia, and I speak very slowly and clearly. I tell her, "I'll—glitter—these—when—I—get—a—chance!" I'm sure that when I speak this distinctly, my English will make as much sense to her as Portuguese. My slow speech apparently seems to convince her that I might be learning disabled, and she smiles, repeating her earlier instructions in slower Portuguese.

A feeling a lot like I had last summer when I was dragged out by an undertow on a family vacation to Old Orchard beach comes over me. After my face scraped the bottom of the ocean floor, I almost suffocated when I couldn't figure out which way was up or down. Now I grab the Santa cards, which pass by as a red blur, spin them on the glue roller and just slap glitter down anywhere. Sometimes, I accidentally glitter over the poetry written inside: "Have a Ho—Ho—Ho—Happy Holiday!" Now both Antigrassia and Ava are chattering at me. Somewhere, Jane's ears pick up on this louder than usual Portuguese. It's an unofficial alarm bell for her. In a moment her silent pinched face is behind me.

"What's this?" she inquires, pointing a livid, speckled finger at a pile of unglittered cards at my side. Her eyes burn the back of my head like two red-hot nickels pressed to my skull.

Without turning around I tell her, "I'll do these, I promise!" She stands behind me, like she's watching me perform open-heart surgery. My armpits dampen. All 5'2" of Jane seems to glean delight from my near nervous breakdown at the young age of sixteen.

Just when I'm prepared to fake a fainting spell like actresses did in old movies, there's a bell. All the conveyor belts slog to a halt. It's 10:45—break time. I've heard about these things. People who work eight hours a day have breaks for the "three C's"—coffee, candy and cigarettes. There's a stampede as people fly off the assembly lines. Jane doesn't move from behind me. She watches as I glue and glitter the cards next to me.

When I'm done she says, "The boss needs to see you."

"*Oh my God,*" I think, "I'm going to be *fired*." I follow behind her blue, checked smock. Carol, Lori and Anne huddle together and watch me go past. I've already been separated from the pack, like I'm a deer hobbled by an injury, and now Jane is a mountain lion going in for the kill. She and I climb old cement stairs to a dingy, glassed-in room at the top of the factory. It looks like a hamster cage overlooking the whole factory. Waiting for us inside the hamster cage is the head Sunshine guy, Mr. Tampoon. He's so old he looks like he ran this factory before there were child labor laws. He's wearing a bow tie and suspenders, and in his hand he holds my time card.

He shakes it at me. "Who are you trying to fool? What's the meaning of clocking in this morning on the Friday clocking out space?"

As in all events where my intelligence is brought into question, I break into a huge, inane smile. "I'm sorry, I accidentally stuck my time card in upside down." Then to back myself up I add, "I didn't know there was a correct way to stick my time card in the box. It's my first day!" All time stops for a moment as Mr. Tampoon drinks in my chuckleheadedness.

With fire in his watery eyes he shakes the time card at me until his voice comes to him, "Let me tell you, Miss Spencer, if I catch you pulling a stunt like this again, I'll dock your paycheck! After that you're FIRED!" I like the way he called this a "stunt," as if I was Evil Knievel planning for months to jump Snake River Canyon on a motorbike. Mr. Tampoon dismisses me with a wave of my illegitimate time card.

Jane informs me at the bottom of the steps, "You have eight minutes left on break!" All eyes are on me as I join the rest of the workers in the cafeteria area, which consists of squeaky metal chairs and tables with "Discarded by the East Lonèeadow School System" printed on them. There are three vending machines: one for candy, one for coffee, and one for cigarettes. On all of these dull aqua-blue machines are painted stick figures, representing people enjoying all three of these things. I guess with one's wits so dulled from factory work, stick figures are necessary to understand what to do with a Hershey Bar, or which end of the cigarette goes in one's mouth.

On the candy bar machine there are even two stick figures of what appear to be '50s teenagers at a sock hop. I have no idea what dried-up old Baby Ruths and Clark Bars have to do with dancing, but one thing for sure is that no one here is doing the twist while they break their teeth on a petrified Milky Way.

There is much chatter in the cafeteria about my appearance in Mr. Tampoon's glass hamster cage office atop the factory. I didn't realize it until now, but everyone witnessed him shaking my time card at me. I also learn that Mr. Tampoon is cleverly nicknamed, "Mr. Tampon." Even the Portuguese workers are talking about me. I know this because, as my mother always claimed was bad manners, they are blatantly pointing at me and whispering to each other. I have a feeling that I'm quickly acquiring a reputation as a shifty troublemaker. I bite into my Charleston Chew candy bar, and it shatters like an icicle and all my favorite part, the chocolate coating, flakes off. I look down at the sad, stale chocolate flakes lying on my lap and littering the table, then I cover my face with my hands, and push my thumbs into my eyeballs to stop the tears.

On the ride home from work, I sit in the front seat next to my mother. Anne and the Kennedys are in the back seat. Even in the car I'm separated from others. Do they tolerate me only because they can't avoid me? As my mother discusses her day working as a dental receptionist, I sit with my eyes fixed, frozen and focused on the road in front of us, hoping our blue Pontiac is headed for a brick wall somewhere to bring me sweet relief from this job I've gotten myself into. My mother sounds a million miles away as she prattles on about her day.

"You know the Ramseys, right, girls? You know their son, Tommy, right? He's in the eleventh grade? Well, you'll never guess. He's got gingivitis! Such terrible gums, can you imagine? He comes from such a nice family, how can he not floss his teeth?"

In the past, I've always enjoyed my mother's gossiping about our town folk's oral hygiene habits, especially a popular boy with bleeding gums, but today, even though I hear her, I'm unable to respond, just as I've read happens to people in comas. As I stare at a dead bug splayed out on the windshield, I hear Carol Kennedy in the back seat explaining how she's working in the best part of the factory. She's in a far-off corner of the building, out of sight of Jane and Mr. Tampoon. Best of all she's off the assembly lines. Her job, it turns out, is packing prizes into boxes. These are the "valuable" prizes advertised at the back of the greeting cards sales booklets. Kids can win these prizes when they sell 20, 40 or 60 boxes of Sunshine greeting cards to their neighbors, family and friends. These prizes are mostly cheap, plastic stuff, like transistor radios, watches and pocketknives. By far the most interesting prize Carol packed today is the life-size Brooke Shields doll head. The head comes complete with blush, lipstick, combs and brushes so anyone at a whim can change Brooke Shields's hair, makeup, even her famous eyebrows. Carol tells us that, oddly enough, a lot of boys pass up transistor radios and pocketknives for the Brooke Shields head.

Once home Anne and I are greeted by our father, sitting in his La-Z-Boy in the living room with a Budweiser and his *Runner's World* magazine. We are well aware that we will receive very little sympathy from him about our grueling new jobs. He considers adversity the pathway to being a good person. If something is too easy he becomes suspicious and will make it harder for my sister's and my benefit. In the past he has had us walk off most of our injuries, also claiming band-aids were for sissies. It seems his main job as our father is making sure we never get too soft.

My whole body aches as I cross the threshold of our front door. I look at him sitting there, shoes off, feet kicked up on top of a ragged old hassock. I know he spent about two hours today teaching tennis lessons in Enfield, Connecticut. I have moved on because I need more than the $25 a week he used to give me for being his tennis slave.

He barely lifts his head from his magazine as he says, "Before you two girls lie down in front of the TV like slugs wasting the day, the patio needs to be swept and the clothes need to be brought in off the line." Anne slumps and heads for the backdoor, prepared as always to do as he says, no matter what.

I stop, jut out one hip, put my hand on it, using my other hand to point at him in case he's not sure who I'm talking to and I say, "We've been working hard all day, why can't you sweep the patio?" I know I shouldn't have said it, but I couldn't help myself, my exhaustion has made me bold and stupid. In a moment my father's *Runner's World* is on the floor, leaving his hands free to find their way around my neck.

He squeezes with emphasis as he asks, "What'd you say? What'd you say?" He presses more tightly as I struggle to remove his hands and I simultaneously kick at his shins.

I'm barely able to gasp out the words, "I'd tell you what I said if you'd get your hands off my neck!" In the meantime I've managed to knock over a pile of his *New Yorker* magazines.

For a second his grip loosens as he looks down to see the mess. Then he lets go as he warns me, "Just watch that smart mouth of yours!" As I turn to leave I feel his calling card, an open handed cuff on the back of my head. Somehow my father and I can't, as my mother says, get through the day without "throwing bouquets" at each other.

Out in our backyard Anne blandly pulls down the clothing off the clothesline, just tugging them off so that the clothespins either snap off the line, falling to the ground, or just remain on the line half broken. I grab the broom from our shed out back, smacking several trees over and over with it like I'm taking in batting practice. I stand in the middle of my father's homemade patio created from leftover, multi-colored cinder blocks he got from Kelly-Fradet lumber mart. Between each cinder block, ants have fastidiously built their homes by piling up sand one grain at a time, leaving a hole for the entrance. I smack the broom across several of these anthills, wiping them out. Ants frantically scatter. I look at the mayhem I've caused. In a minute I'm down on all fours poking with a stick, trying to reopen all the ant holes. I finish sweeping the patio, leaving the remaining anthills alone.

Later on, Anne and I do lie on the floor of our family room. It is carpeted with leftover two-foot-square carpet samples, making it fit in with the rest of the crazy-quilt, '70s look in this room. Anne and I fight over who gets to lie on top of the shag carpet-covered spots. I hurt more than the first day of soccer practice when our team was punished for being lazy by having to run wind sprints for an entire hour.

Our father looks in on us, shakes his head and clucks, "Are you two going to eat your supper lying there on the floor?"

While Anne looks at the ceiling as if actually contemplating this, I shoot back with, "We sure are!" We do make it to the supper table, my sullen attitude tempered by my stupendous exhaustion. I have my eyes closed when my father reminds me to chew with my mouth shut. My lower jaw feels like lead as I try to get it to meet its upper half.

I lie in bed thinking I can't possibly go through another day at Sunshine, but just like I believed I couldn't make it through another day of 10th grade, I'm up at 7:30 in the morning, and an hour later I'm back on the assembly line reliving the nightmare of the day before. Can I do this everyday for the next couple of months?

When I get home this second evening, I do what I do all the time when I have something to endure that I hate, which lasts any amount of time. I draw up a two-month calendar, and then I make two big, black X's over Monday and Tuesday. I stare at all the un-Xed out blocks left on my calendar.

There are still a few hours of daylight left in this lovely summer evening, yet, somehow, meeting up with other neighborhood kids for a softball game at the baseball diamond near our house seems too exhausting. I need to save my energy for standing on my pile of flattened cardboard boxes at my spot on the assembly line tomorrow. I've quickly taken a cue from my fellow workers to make a pile of cardboard to ease standing on cement flooring for eight hours a day. At the end of every shift, like squirrels hoarding nuts, we all hide our stash of cardboard for the next day. It's terrible when someone's stash goes missing, either through theft, or by being accidentally thrown out.

The following morning I hear two Portuguese women on the line behind me yelling at each other. I turn towards the angry conversation and see they both have their hands on opposite ends of a large, plush-looking piece of cardboard. The more they tug, the louder they get, until Jane shows up. This only quiets them somewhat, until Jane yanks the cardboard out of their hands and points to the conveyor belt as it starts up for the day. The two women's eyes tear up as they take their spots on either side of a teenage girl. Their eyes never leave the cardboard, which is now in Jane's hands, as if she took their pet bunny or firstborn child. We all watch as Jane simply creeps away with the cardboard and disappears behind a stack of boxes. Couldn't she have just taken out an exacto knife and cut it into two pieces and split it between the two women? But, no, she just takes the lovely piece of plump cardboard and takes off for who knows where. She probably has a huge stash of it somewhere deep in the factory where no one can find it and where she sits on a huge pile of confiscated cardboard while others suffer, standing on the cement floor.

It's weird; I've taken to looking at cardboard quite differently now. When I see a stray box at the supermarket, or lying discarded like trash on the side of the road, I think of how lovely it would be to have it flattened out and lying under my feet at Sunshine.

Anne and I have now learned to come into the house through the back door to avoid our father and his list of chores to extend our workday. If he doesn't actually see us, then I think he forgets we exist and sits blissfully in his bubble of magazines, poetry books and beer. We sneak in the back door, put on our swimsuits and slip silently into our above-the-ground swimming pool. We don't splash around, alerting our father to our presence—instead, we lie floating on our backs like two dead bodies.

After this first week on the assembly line at Sunshine I start to suffer from an illness that afflicts our whole family. It's called "I know they're going to fire me from this job" disease. My entire family has it, and now I do. My parents started this by coming home every evening with new tales of jobs that were teetering on the brink of total collapse. Their stories are creative and filled with a cast of characters that would make any soap-opera writer jealous. Apparently my parents' charms, especially my father's, cause other people to want to get rid of them. Conspiracies are huge, carefully plotted and soon to be carried out by the villains my parents work with. My mother plays defense at her job by being relentlessly cheerful, be-bopping around the dentist's office like a bagful of happiness, spilling over and covering the people who work there with a sugar coating. Who could ever get rid of someone who has a personality that is a combination of Santa Claus and Carol Burnett? My father, on the other hand, has taken a different approach. When his dander is up, he is like a rumbling volcano that threatens to erupt at any moment, covering his enemies with hot molten lava. The day my father loses it with his tormenters will be a day they will rue.

As for me, the hatred I have for this job is already outweighed by the shame and fear of actually losing it. This gives me headaches and keeps me up at night. I'm sure the Portuguese women on either side of me are actually a hit team disguised as two smock-wearing, middle-aged ladies using a foreign language to plot my downfall. Whenever they look at me and laugh, which is often, I'm sure they're discussing how funny it will be when Jane and Mr. Tampoon grab me by each arm and escort me from my spot on the assembly line and toss me into the parking lot. Then Antigrassia and Ava will divvy up my cardboard pile and celebrate how they no longer have their conversations obstructed by my presence.

By my second week, while working on the assembly line at Sunshine I ponder who else is plotting my downfall. I know I can put Jane at the top of the list. She just walked past me with her hands shoved deep into the pockets of her blue checked smock. She slows down when she gets to me, stopping twice to get a look at me from both sides. She is silent, like the fog we read about in "The Hound of the Baskervilles" this past year in English Lit class. As soon as Jane passes I see Lori Kennedy about five feet away from me. She looks up from the cards on the conveyor belt and smiles at me. What does that mean? I see my sister Anne on the line in front of me. Her face is a slack mask of dull concentration. Her slightly buck front teeth are fused over her bottom lip. I study the back of her head, which is covered by her dutifully straightened-and-curled-under version of the Dorothy Hamill wedge haircut. It is now in the midst of slowly curling up despite her earlier labor at taming it. It's looking a lot like plastic does when it's held over an open flame. Anne, our younger sister, Shannon, and I all have this haircut, but since we're cursed with raging curls, we have instead all ended up with atomic mushroom cloud versions of Dorothy's straight, shiny bob. Instead of commiserating over our shared beauty curse, my sisters and I torture each other constantly about the shameful fuzz that grows out of our heads. We hide each other's brushes, hog the blow dryer and regularly point at one another's head and laugh. I look at Anne with her tortured hair and know that our hair wars could now be extended to include our jobs. Maybe Anne wants me out of Sunshine, too? Maybe even Carol Kennedy, far off in the prize packing part of the factory, secretly hopes I'll be given my walking papers soon. According to my father, when it comes to your job, you can't trust anyone.

The lunch bell interrupts my paranoid mental meanderings. I play it cool with my co-workers. My father also tells us not to let your enemies know you're on to them. He regularly plays pick-up basketball with his enemies, who are disguised as co-workers, neighbors and friends. He bowls with them, and invites them over to our house so he can grill hotdogs and hamburgers for them. They'll never suspect he's aware of their plots to steal his job when he regularly feeds them picnic food. I won't let anyone know I'm onto his or her plans to get rid of me. I'll even take my chances and eat my peanut butter and jelly sandwich with my enemies.

At the sound of the lunch bell all the Portuguese and local women lifers head to the cafeteria. They sit at the tables, in their flowered work smocks, smoking and gossiping about us, the new summer help. A few of the men jump into their souped-up cars and burn rubber to get to Bruno's Pizzeria for beers and meatball grinders. The rest of us, summer help, about twenty teenagers, sit outside the back entrance. We lean up against the brick wall, soaking in the real sunshine, outside of Sunshine Factory.

We discuss our favorite topic of gossip—JANE! Maybe if I can get everyone thinking about how horrible Jane is, it will distract them from thinking how great it would be if I weren't here.

Once we're all gathered around, I tell everyone, "I bet that right now Jane is eating her lunch in her private office, you know, the broken-down stall in the ladies room!"

Lori points out, "You know, I've never seen her eat her lunch with anyone else. She must hide somewhere, or maybe she isn't really human and she doesn't eat food! She just crouches in a corner somewhere thinking up evil things to do to people!"

Anne leans in and whispers, "I heard Jane and cross-eyed Jim are boyfriend and girlfriend!"

We all scream as Lori Kennedy squeals, "What if they start having spotted, cross-eyed babies!"

"OOOhhh, gross!" I scream as I squeeze my eyes shut, "NNNooooo!"

I use the bathroom after lunch, making sure Jane isn't lurking in the broken-down stall near the back. I hold my breath as I check each stall, afraid she's waiting to pounce. I'm alone. I spend a full two minutes staring at my face in the mirror. With the greenish, fluorescent, prison lighting and the mirror that looks like a flattened out car fender, I look positively ghoulish. I'm afraid I'll end up looking like Jane by the end of the summer.

* * * *

After these first two weeks, to my surprise, I'm still here, and I'm slowly getting into the rhythm of sacrificing my life to the factory. We're supposed to get paid once a week, but since we're new, the Kennedy girls, Anne and I will receive our first paychecks this Friday after two weeks of work. This is the first time I've ever been taxed—it's weird, I'm giving money away that I've never seen. It's as if a silent hand has swept in and just taken fourteen dollars a week out of my check. Believe me, I've been multiplying over and over for two weeks now, $3.35 an hour x eight hours a day x five days a week. I should get $134 in each check, but when I open my envelope for the first time there are two checks for $120 each. Where's my $28! I feel robbed and violated.

Anne, who had taxes taken from her Fenway Golf checks the last two summers, smirks when she tells me, "I told ya, the government will find ya as soon as ya start making money!" I try to look at the bright side: this is the most money I've made all at once! I feel incredibly significant. I'm so important the government has not only located me, but they've located my source of money, and for their efforts they have taken $28. I close my eyes and try to think that my $14 a week will go to good things like helping nature and feeding poor people.

My father dispels this quickly when at supper he points a fork at Anne and me and tells us, "You wanna know were your tax money really ends up? You know all those deadbeats using food stamps to buy cigarettes and potato chips at the grocery store? Those criminals ripping off hardworking taxpayers with their welfare checks—that's where your money goes! Just think about that next time you see someone paying for their beer with food stamps. Once you start paying taxes you'll find out how many lazy, good-for-nothing people there are in the world! That's where your government sends all your money!"

Other than the government and welfare cheats, two other people are happy about Anne and me receiving weekly paychecks: our parents. On a regular basis they have borrowed from us, but paper-route and babysitting money is small potatoes compared to $120 a week. My mother is the one who asks to borrow the money, never my father, and she has always carefully written down on a 3X5 index card how much she owes us. She places these cards into our SIS Bank savings books. My mother pays us back every time, so I know it's okay when she asks Anne and me to hand over $100 each. My mother promptly creates two index cards with IOU's handwritten on them. We head to the A&P right after leaving the bank to buy groceries.

After buying a week's worth of food, we pile the bags into our VW van and at the last minute she announces, "We just need to make an emergency run to the liquor store to stock up!" At Kappy's Liquor Mart we grab another shopping cart and fill it with a case of Budweiser, gallon jugs of Ernest and Julio Gallo red and white wine, and jumbo bottles of gin, vodka and sweet vermouth.

At the checkout the cashier jokes, "Having a big party, huh?"

My mother smiles broadly. "Well, maybe, yes!"

This is what we buy every week and believe me: there is no party at our house. This is our regulation stock of liquor to keep my parents functioning in the manner they are accustomed to.

On the way home my mother assures us, "Listen, girls, as soon as your father's teacher's paycheck comes in the mail next week you'll get your money back!"

I have to say it is a little scary how quickly all my money changes hands. I never get to hold and caress the money or lay it out on the floor to obsessively count it and categorize it, like the cold hard cash I had in my hands after a night of babysitting or a week of delivering newspapers. It just went from a piece of paper with Sunshine Factory and my name printed on it and suddenly it's several bags of food and a shopping cart full of liquor that will take very little time for my family to devour! ▪

• *Read* **Sunshine Factory – Part Two** *at ducts.org/content/sunshine-factory.*

• *Read* **Sunshine Factory – Part Three** *at ducts.org/content/sunshine-factory—part-three.*

# What Is the Day For?

Like a light switched on, I get it. "Dying with dignity."

BY JENNIFER BERMAN *(Issues 24)*

I'M WALKING DOWN WEST END AVENUE, not troubled by where I am going, but happy because spring is finally here, and soon I will see my mother. As I cross 82nd Street, I dig the crumpled scrap of paper on which I've scribbled the address out of my front jeans pocket. I'm at the building twenty minutes early. My mother is always early too, but I have the feeling she's not here yet, and so I sit on the bench outside and watch for her and my sister.

I see someone way down the street, still just a speck, but I know it's my mom. My heart leaps! It's not easy to get to see my mother—a bit like negotiating your way into the castle to see the Queen. She's always been fiercely independent, and more so since she got sick—the opposite of what people expect from a Jewish mother, nudging her kids to call and visit. It's my sister and I who are always calling her, asking if we can come to the house and offering to go with her to doctors. Every once in a while she'll surprise us by letting us come, and we drop everything to meet her.

When she called and said she wanted Rachel and me to come with her to a meeting with a social worker at a place called "Dying with Dignity," I didn't ask questions. My mother doesn't like questions; I learned that as a girl. She likes clean and she likes order. She likes to iron. A question makes her face sour, like when I used to leave my toys out in my room. It's a burden that unsettles her, a mess she has to clean up.

I, on the other hand, am a bit of a slob. My college roommate used to say that I always looked like I just rolled out of bed, but had had a good time. At 40, I'm still very casual. I mostly wear jeans, and keep my hair long, letting the curls dry naturally and haphazardly, like an untended garden. I don't own a brush. I'm always asking questions, thinking out loud, reading self-help books and Eastern philosophy, trying to understand things that can't be explained. With my mother, I know that unless we are having an especially good moment, unless she's extremely relaxed, I have to contain myself. She may answer, "I don't know, Jen," a seemingly neutral statement to the untrained ear, but I hear the sigh of exasperation in her voice that warns, like thunder before rain, of the tension about to descend upon us that could last—especially if we are in a car—the rest of the day.

My mother is closer now. I stand up and wave my arms back and forth, but she doesn't see me yet. She looks like a movie star, dressed to the nines and wearing full make-up, which is something she started to do when she got sick. Her hair has grown back from her last round of treatments. It's not the sleek, straight, auburn bob from her pre-cancer life. It comes in grey and curly and when it grows past her scalp she colors it brown. It's still short, which she's told me she thinks makes her look butch, but I think she looks athletic and chic. She compensates by playing up her eyes. I've seen pictures of her when she was a young ballerina, with false lashes and eyeliner extending past her lids, and now her eyes look the same and her skin has a rosy glow. Whenever I see her I tell her how great she looks. And it's true. No one would guess she has cancer.

We embrace. Her back feels boney. I admire her bright pink suit and ask, "Is this the Harari?" She's told me about the Harari—a very expensive outfit she bought when visiting her friend Berta in Beverly Hills.

"Noooo, I wore the "Harr-rar-eee"—my mother over-enunciates the word to mock her extravagance, "to the opera last night." She bought herself a full season at The Met this year, also something she wouldn't have done before she got sick. She likes to get all dressed up and go by herself. She has also been wearing her best jewelry, as she says, "saving nothing for good."

My sister Rachel is running up the street towards us as quickly as she can in her strappy heels. As always, she is stylish and feminine, in a soft pink sweater set, gray slacks and French manicure, but her eyes look glassy and tired. She hugs my mother, and then me, and we file into the heavily air-conditioned lobby, where the doorman directs us to an old-fashioned elevator. The attendant slides the metal gate closed and pulls the lever, bringing us upstairs.

I had expected an office, but we are standing in the foyer of a quintessential prewar, Upper West Side apartment. Everything is big—the open kitchen to one side of us, the living room with French doors leading out onto a planted terrace on the other, the exotic long-haired dog barking at us, and Judy, the social worker herself—tall and expansive with brown, frizzy hair to her shoulders and a purple, baggy linen suit. She shakes my mother's hand, while I bend down to pet the dog. I can tell my mother is nervous because she's talking to Judy in the singsong voice she uses when she's self-conscious with strangers. I go to her and she puts her arms around Rachel's and my shoulders. "These are my daughters." I love when she introduces me with the word "daughter." She always sounds so proud.

Judy asks, "Which one of you is older?" It's always hard for people to tell because Rachel and I are only two years apart and look nothing alike. Rachel has a wider face, small and delicate features, and blond hair, which she usually wears up in a bun. I'm narrow and angular, like my father was. Growing up, I was always jealous of Rachel for being the pretty one, but she always wanted to be thin like me.

The doorbell rings and the dog starts barking all over again. A man—bald, very well-dressed in a Brooks Brothers sort of way, mid-fifties, round wire-framed glasses—comes in and hugs my mother. I remember now that she'd said a man had come up to her after an A.A. meeting and told her about Judy, but I'd had no idea he'd be joining us.

My mother introduces John to Rachel and me, and the five of us stand in the hallway and chat—about the dog (Judy tells us it's an Afghan Hound), the apartment (it was the terrace that sold her) and, like all good New Yorkers, about whether we think real estate will go up or down.

Then Judy says, "Let's go inside." My sister and John go to use the bathroom before we start, and my mother and I follow Judy into the living room. Judy sits in a black leather recliner and rests her feet on the ottoman. I sit on a small couch, expecting my mother will sit next to me, but instead she sits on an antique wooden chair on the other side of the room. I ask, "Mom why don't you sit here with me? I think it's more comfortable." But she says, "No, hon. I'm fine." Her eyes well up with tears. Rachel sits next to Judy, takes her thick Filofax out of her purse and opens to a section with notepaper. She has been taking notes whenever we go with my mother to medical appointments. Afterwards, she goes home and looks up the information on the Internet and calls me with statistics on how long our mother is likely to survive. John slumps in a chair on the other side of Judy, draping his leg over the side, which I think is odd.

Judy begins by asking, "So, girls, what do you think of your mother's situation?" This strikes me as cruel. Our mother has cancer in both lungs, her bones and her brain. The chemo has stopped working and the laser surgery failed, so now she faces full brain radiation. It may shrink the tumors temporarily, but there is the risk she will lose her mind.

I say, "I don't know how to respond to that." We are all silent. The dog comes into the room and flops down by Judy's chair. Birds chirp on the terrace. Judy says, "All we do is provide information that's all over the Internet. It's perfectly legal."

Again we are all quiet. I am lost. Then she says, almost casually, like we are chatting over tea, "Have you been following the Terri Schiavo case? I read in the *Times* that her parents may win the appeal." And like a light switched on I get it. "Dying with dignity." I thought Judy was going to teach us how to help my mother die as comfortably as possible, but she must be broaching the subject of a DNR so my mother won't wind up like Terri Schiavo, kept alive by a machine.

I say, "We want to support our mother in whatever she wants to do."

Judy asks, "Susan, what is your prognosis after the procedure?"

My mother clears her throat, "I expect there will be a process of diminishing cognition."

"Then you won't want to be having fancy conversations with doctors." Judy leans back in her chair. "There are directions for making gas machines on the Internet. But the best, and by far the simplest method is Seconal."

Slowly I grasp what is happening and wonder why my mother didn't warn me.

Rachel looks up from her notes and asks, "What is Seconal?"

"It's a sleep medication. Pills. Susan, you should get prescriptions right away. There's a limit on how much a doctor can legally give you, so you will need three different scripts. You'll tell the doctors you're having trouble sleeping. They'll try to give you Ambien. You'll say you've tried everything in the past and Seconal was the only thing that helped. They'll probably know what you're up to, but if they're sympathetic they'll cooperate. Are there three doctors you can ask?"

A tear runs down my mother's cheek, but her voice is steady. "I have a cousin who is a physician." Then she says to Rachel and me, "I don't think Phyllis would do it." Phyllis is a pediatrician, my Aunt Lee's best friend from childhood. Lee was my mother's only sibling. She died unexpectedly one year ago, just after my mother's diagnosis, while undergoing a medical test. Lee had been experiencing shortness of breath, and Phyllis had arranged for her to see doctors at Columbia Presbyterian during a family visit. The test was considered routine. Lee was supposed to fly home to Santa Fe the next day.

Ten months later, my grandmother died. Phyllis took the limousine with us from the funeral to the burial site. While we were in the car waiting for the rabbi, my mother asked Phyllis what she thought about hospice care. Phyllis said she was against it because often the nurses can't get enough morphine. And there could be a delay with finding a doctor to pronounce the patient dead. The family could get stuck with a corpse in the house for days.

My mother, who is a realtor in the Hamptons, where she lives, said that another drawback is when there's a death in the house the property value goes down. I wanted to tell my mother that Rachel and I didn't care about the value of the house, and that Grandpa Jack, my paternal grandfather, had hospice care at home without any problems. But I knew my mother would resent my interfering. She saw Phyllis as the expert and would think I was being a know-it-all, trying to tell her what to do.

After a moment, my mother looks at Judy and says, "Yes, I think I'll be able to get three prescriptions."

"Good. There should be one other person involved. Susan, do you have a friend you can ask to help?"

My mother thinks out loud. "Not Whitney, she's Catholic. Eileen. She lives across the street from me. She's the one I've asked to tell me when my judèent starts to go. I don't want the girls to have to do that."

Judy starts to say how important it is that we not tell anyone else, when she's interrupted by a blast of motorcycle engines outside. She waits for them to pass, but they just keep coming. I think it must be a group of Hells Angels. Judy jumps up, goes to the window and mimes a machine gun in her hands: "Eh-eh-eh-eh-eh. Don't you just want to shoot 'em?"

John, who hasn't said a word this whole time, laughs maniacally, and my sister and I lock eyes. I know we're thinking the same thing. She says it later, as soon as we get to talk: "Those people love death!" It is then that we coin Judy and John "the death people."

When the motorcycles pass, Judy explains the procedure for administering the drugs. My mother must ask for them on three different occasions. The third time Rachel or I will need to crush the pills into a glass of water.

"Can't I just swallow them?"

"No, there will be too many pills, hundreds. Susan, where do you plan to be?"

I don't know what she means, but my mother says, "A hospital in New York. It will be easiest for the girls."

I think it is Judy being there, knowing my mother won't blow up at me in front of her, that gives me the nerve to speak up, “Mom, we don’t care about what’s easiest for us. I know Phyllis said that there are problems with hospice getting enough pain medication, but Grandpa Jack had hospice care in the house and it was fine.”

“I’ve worked with hospice for many years, Susan. As long as the nurses order the morphine on time there will be plenty, and it will be a lot easier to give you the Seconal at home. They don’t do autopsies on hospice patients.”

My mother turns to Judy, “I want to protect my daughters.”

“But it doesn’t work, Mom. It’s like when you didn’t let Rachel and me come to the hospital before Lee died because you said you didn’t want us to see her like that, just staring out into space. It just makes it worse.”

Judy says, “Good for you!” like she’s our family therapist, which for the moment she is. She asks, “Susan, where are you most comfortable?”

“In my home. Definitely.”

“Mom, I’m not trying to tell you what to do. I’m just saying I think you should stay at home, because that’s what I’d want for myself.”

My mother gets up, walks over to the couch and sits beside me. I rest my hand on the back of the couch behind her. It’s very delicate with my mother. I don’t know how she’ll react if I put my arm around her, if it will be too much. I stay like that, almost touching her, until we leave.

The next day I get a voice mail. “Sweetheart, I would want to know you, I would love you, even if you weren’t my daughter. I’m so grateful you were there.”

I save that message on my answering machine for a very long time. ▪

# Breaking Up is Hard to Do

An essay from the memoir in progress,
*The Barracuda in the Attic & Other Memories*

BY KIPP FRIEDMAN *(Issue 25)*

THE FIRST TIME I SAW a woman naked was in late 1970 while attending the final performance of my father's off-Broadway play *Steambath* at the Truck and Warehouse Theater on the Lower East Side of Manhattan. I was 10 and my father thought it important that I see his satirical play depicting the afterlife as a steambath and God as a Puerto Rican attendant—despite its brief nudity and use of profanity—before it closed. My attention, however, was somewhat distracted by my older brothers' glowing accounts of the play's nude shower scene, so when an attractive blonde actress strolled across the stage, nonchalantly disrobed and quickly showered—making a gleeful squeal as the water splashed across her body—I should have felt more excitement. Instead, it

▸ **ABOVE: Not-So-Smooth Sailing**—The author and his family aboard the *S.S. Romantica*, circa Christmas, 1968. Pictured, left to right: novelist and playwright Bruce Jay Friedman; Kipp Friedman; Josh Friedman; Ginger Howard Friedman; Drew Friedman.

happened so suddenly and matter-of-factly that I felt more like a voyeur self-consciously peeping through a keyhole.

We left the theater and got into an awaiting limo and as we drove off my father asked the driver to stop momentarily and in hopped the pretty actress whom I had earlier seen naked. She was dressed in what appeared to be the same white terrycloth bathrobe that she wore in the play. As she took a seat next to us, I could detect the scent of herbal shampoo in her hair and feel the warmth her body still radiated as if she had just stepped out of a shower. In my giddiness I hardly noticed my mother's absence.

I'm not sure when it first dawned on me that my parents were having marriage problems. Growing up, I had heard the story about a party my parents held at a rented beach house while we were staying on Fire Island during the summer in 1963. With the alcohol flowing, my father left the party with an attractive blonde woman. Suspecting something was awry, my mother followed them onto the deck where she promptly found them and reached for a sprinkler hose, watering them down. The blonde woman screamed, "I'm a lesbian! I'm a lesbian! I don't even like men!" while my mother's girlfriend, Gerri, shouted, "Oy Vey!" Dripping wet, my father began laughing and the blonde woman ran off. My parents weathered that storm, and it even became a source of humor, but apparently there were other forces at work that would put greater strains on their marriage.

Maybe because I was the youngest and less observant than my older brothers, it never occurred to me that anything was out of the ordinary in my parents' marriage. Indeed, I knew a number of classmates whose parents were separated or divorced, so I reasoned that my parents' still intact marriage was somehow stable and secure. Looking back, though, as pleasant and magical as my memories were of a childhood as the son of a successful writer and an equally creative mother, there were a number of early warning signs of trouble brewing ahead.

One of my earliest memories of suspecting that all was not as it appeared occurred in 1968 when I was about seven. I had just returned home from school when my mother introduced me to a man who spoke with a German accent named Marc M., who turned out to be Swiss. He was handsome, in a Maximilian Schell sort of way, with dark wavy hair, and he had an old world, courtly charm. My father was away on business at the time. Marc was visiting, ostensibly, to view my mother's exhibit of Plexiglas art and jewelry creations that she kept stored in a large pantry room off the kitchen area of our home in Great Neck, New York. She was preparing for a showcase of her work at a Manhattan gallery and the room was teeming with odd-shaped bits of multicolored futuristic Plexiglas creations. Items scattered around the room included oversized rings, necklaces, bracelets, end tables, ash trays and decorative cubes, as well as sheets of bubble wrap which I enjoyed popping.

The only reason I recall this chance encounter back in 1968 was because my white corduroys were still wet and clingy from peeing in my pants on the long walk home from Clover Drive Elementary School, and I felt a rash forming on my inner thighs. With moist fingers I sheepishly shook Marc's hand and I could sense from his nervous smile that this was an awkward moment for him as well, only for different reasons. While tending to my wet corduroys I could tell our middle-aged housekeeper, Mrs. Sullivan, was clearly not pleased by Marc's presence. She came up with a nickname for Marc—"Nazi Monkey"—which she would utter a bit too loudly.

Marc, I would later learn, was a lounge singer whom my mother had met during the summer of 1967 at a restaurant where he was performing in Bridgehampton, Long Island. We were staying at a rented beach house in nearby Amagansett. During the fabled "Summer of Love" I memorized the words to the Beatles' latest album, *Sgt. Pepper's Lonely Hearts Club Band*, given to us by my father's friend, the writer Terry Southern, whose picture was on the celebrated album cover (shown standing in front of Lenny Bruce and next to Dylan Thomas and the singer Dion) and who was staying with his family in a beach house not far from ours. I was too busy singing "When I'm Sixty-Four" with Mrs. Sullivan to possibly notice that my mother had begun a relationship with another man. Most of the summer my father remained in Manhattan, working on the production of his play *Scuba Duba*, ironically, a tense comedy about a New York couple vacationing in the south of France when the wife decides to run off with a black scuba diver.

A few years later, while I was away at sleepaway camp, Marc and my mother would run off together—at least for the summer. Almost daily I would receive picture postcards as they traveled throughout Europe. The postcards first arrived from Switzerland, where she was staying with Marc's family. They showed idyllic images of the famous Alps, bars of Swiss chocolate, Swiss cheese and lots of dairy cows. Soon I would receive a flurry of postcards from Austria and Germany depicting medieval castles with moats, and then more castles and country scenes from Spain and Portugal. I would also receive occasional letters from my father who was on the road with his latest play, *Turtlenecks* starring Tony Curtis, which was having out-of-town runs along the East Coast. He was consumed with anxious hopes that his play would make it to Broadway. (It closed out of town). I remember he wrote optimistically of how Sammy Davis had loved one performance. Despite my parents' separate paths that summer, it still seemed all was business as usual, and I assumed our family would be back together when I returned from summer camp.

And my parents did return by the end of the summer, only I would soon discover that my mother had replaced their king-size bed with matching antique twin brass beds. Although the beds were spaced only a few feet apart, to me they represented a bigger gulf than the geographic distances that separated my parents the previous summer. Their bedroom had always been a refuge of sorts where my brothers and I spent evenings watching family movies on their color TV like *The Wizard of Oz* and *It's a Wonderful Life*. With the arrival of the twin beds, I remember feeling somewhat confused as to where to sit, thinking I would be showing disloyalty by choosing one bed over the other; instinctively, my brothers and I would soon retreat to our own rooms to watch TV.

Unbeknownst to me, my father had begun renting an apartment on the 30th floor of the ultra-modern Phoenix high-rise building on East 65th Street and Third Avenue in Manhattan. He would call it his "tower of steel and glass." This is where he holed up during his increasingly more frequent overnight stays. Somehow I failed to connect the dots and saw his absences as nothing more than his occasional business trips to Hollywood where he would work on screenplays. Despite several trial separations, my parents made a number of valiant attempts at reconciliation, although I'm not sure if they ever went to the extent of actually seeking marriage counseling. One such memory of this period sticks in my mind: my parents were sitting happily together on an overstuffed chair one summer morning in East Hampton. My mother was in her nightgown, with my father joking that this was their "third" attempt at reconciliation. They were laughing, even flirting with each other, and all seemed so natural to me; in retrospect, it was probably the last time I saw them so happy together.

By the fall of 1972 my mother would become more open with me and my brothers on how they were seeking ways to save their marriage, which had a ring of optimism—like saving the whales—at one point even raising the notion of moving the family to Italy, far from the distracting New York influences that she thought were pulling them apart. I think my father mostly indulged her ideas, but when push came to shove, we sold our house in Great Neck, New York, and moved into Manhattan. Just prior to our move, my mother held an estate sale and a line of neighbors and antique dealers queued outside our home one bright Saturday morning. I remember neighbors squabbling over our family's possessions; it was as if vultures had descended upon our living room, picking apart a carcass.

My parents' final attempt at reconciliation coincided with a mostly dispirited family vacation to Puerto Rico during the winter of 1972. We stayed at the San Juan Hilton and visited brown-sanded beaches dotted with palm trees and explored much of the verdant countryside as well as the capital city of San Juan. One night we visited a restaurant in downtown San Juan recommended to us by my father's friend Mario Puzo because of its reputation for wonderful paella. The restaurant was located in a Spanish Colonial-era home with a huge tree growing in the middle of the dining room. Leaving the restaurant, my father amusingly pointed out all the transvestites prowling the streets. They looked like heavily rouged stevedores and cab drivers in poorly fitted wigs and loud, patterned dresses. Unlike during previous family vacations, my parents' steady bickering, followed by long silences, became more obvious and we could see them literally splitting apart before our eyes. While visiting a rainforest, a guide pointed out a peculiar plant that shriveled and shied away from human contact called the Touch-Me-Not plant. This strange plant seemed to embody the fragile state of my parents' marriage at the time.

When we moved into Manhattan, I first stayed with my father in his apartment at the Phoenix for a few days while my mother and my older brothers prepared for the move into our apartment at the El Dorado twin-tower high-rise building on Central Park West and 90th Street. My father's apartment at the Phoenix offered a dizzying panorama of midtown Manhattan, especially at night, when the city seemed to light up like a million candles. He decorated the apartment sparingly with dark leather couches, contemporary track lighting and unfamiliar furniture and dinnerware, but I did recognize one item: an abstract painting made of overlaying white strips of plaster that my mother had purchased at an art gallery in East Hampton the previous summer. The piece reminded me of a body cast that had completely splintered apart with the plaster dripping white dust whenever it was touched. I remember how messy it was, clinging to your clothes as you passed, and he soon discarded it.

After a few days of living with my father like bachelors, I rejoined my mother and brothers at the El Dorado across town. My father, however, would remain at the Phoenix, choosing instead to visit us for dinner on weekends, and then leave. It was as if my parents were now dating, and my mother wanted to make sure he had a nice homemade meal (prepared by our housekeeper, Mrs. Sullivan, of course). After dinner, my father would relax in our apartment's living room and library where he would smoke his Macanudo cigars and sip cognac while reading or listening to records. The next morning the room would still smell of his cigars and sometimes I would relight the butts I found in ashtrays and turn green after a few ill-advised puffs.

My father soon stopped visiting us at our apartment altogether, and within a few months, my mother would announce that there would be "some changes" and "belt-tightening." The only change I noticed at first was that she had purchased about a dozen loaves of rye bread that quickly grew stale—my mother's futile attempt at economizing. She would, however, begin actively seeing other men. Mrs. Sullivan would pass judèent on her dates. David was a clean-cut, well-dressed businessman whom Mrs. Sullivan thought was marriage material for my mother, but whom my mother found "too boring." Mrs. Sullivan was clearly unimpressed with Steve, though, a long-haired acting student who rode a motorcycle and who was a Vietnam vet. Then there was a man whose name escapes me who looked to be no older than my oldest brother Josh, then about 18. In an attempt to win favor with me this latest suitor would tell me all about his belief in out-of-body experiences.

One day while my mother was talking with Steve on the phone in the kitchen, my brother Drew walked in and my mother, knowing Steve was an acting student, announced: "Oh, Drew just walked in! He does wonderful imitations. Would you like to hear one?" She handed Drew the phone and walked out of the kitchen briefly. Seizing the opportunity, Drew launched into a pitch-perfect Edward G. Robinson: "Listen, you!... Do you know how old my mother is...See?" When my mother returned, he handed her the phone. Steve must have been in shock, and said something that disturbed her because my mother screamed into the phone: "What did Drew say to you! What did he say! Oh my God!" Drew walked out of the kitchen with a look of contentment and that was the last we ever heard from Steve the actor.

Occasionally, Marc M. would reappear, like a long-lost uncle, with Mrs. Sullivan reprising the "Nazi Monkey" nickname she had given him years ago. Once, Marc and my mother even attempted to set up her slightly overweight girlfriend, Karen, on a double date with Marc's friend, Helmut. When Helmut finally met Karen, he backed away from her in a panic, stuttering in broken English: "No! No! Please! Please!" sweeping his hands defensively before making a hasty retreat.

My father also began dating more openly. He soon introduced us to his latest girlfriend, Hesu, a tall, attractive Korean woman with an oval face about half his age. One weekend, we spent the whole day with my father and Hesu, going to see a restored version of the film *Citizen Kane*, followed by dinner at a Korean restaurant where Hesu took over. I remember how she imperiously barked orders in Korean at the cowering wait staff. I wasn't sure what Hesu did for a living, but my father joked that she enjoyed partying with members of The Rolling Stones. He would also tease her in our presence, claiming that she was a Korean War orphan whom he had rescued off the streets of Seoul. By this time my father had moved into a studio apartment off of Madison Avenue and 63rd Street.

For several years I would shuttle back and forth between the apartment I lived in with my mother and brothers on the Upper West Side and my father's studio apartment on the East Side. Although long separated and clearly dating others, my parents' marriage still remained technically on the books. By the time they finally got around to the divorce in 1976, it seemed more of an afterthought. My father told the presiding civil court judge to give my mother whatever she wanted and my mother countered that she only wanted enough to live on. Noticing how amicable my parents were, the hardened judge asked, half jokingly, why they were getting a divorce. ▪

# In Wonder

I felt it as a certainty, as a stone inside my chest, that we would separate if I kept on drinking.
— Two excerpts from a memoir

BY MIA MATHER *(Issue 25)*

**Late Night**

I SAT DOWN ON THE FRONT STEPS. I wondered if I had my keys. I tried to remember if I'd come out through the downstairs door, in which case I would have needed the key to unlock the outside gate. But Warren had taken the garbage out earlier so maybe he hadn't locked the gate again. I couldn't remember opening the gate from the inside with the key, but I couldn't remember going out the upstairs door either. I was pretty drunk.

It was late, after eleven, but the summer night was still welcoming. I lay back on the steps and looked up. I couldn't see any stars. "There are no stars in the city," I thought. Outside the city, in the countryside where I'd grown up, there were stars and fireflies in the summer. Fireflies were nice. But the country was boring: long, slow days and long, desolate nights with the neighbors' dogs howling. I liked the city. Greenwich Village stayed awake on summer weekends. I liked that. I liked the sounds of voices and the street. Lying with my head back on the steps like this I couldn't see the people on the sidewalk or the passing cars, but I knew they were there.

"This is my stoop," I thought. "I own it." That still amazed me. Warren and I had bought this brownstone in the Village. I was 32 and I had money saved that we used for a down payment, and we both paid the mortgage, but Warren paid much more of it, and the rent from the upstairs helped a lot. We had the downstairs duplex. It had been Warren's idea. "Let's buy the brownstone that's for sale on Charles Street," he had said. He could do that, have thoughts like that and then act on them. He was wonderful. Our house had been a rooming house at one time, and most of the original detail was gone inside. There was a tenement on our left. The brownstones across the street were wider. The one directly across had been completely restored inside. Warren had told the owner how lucky he was to live on the nice side of the street. "Yes," the owner had replied, "but you've got the view." It was true: they looked at a tenement and we looked at brownstones. I sat up to study them but my head went around. I was very drunk. This was going to be a problem.

Warren and I weren't married, but we might as well have been. When you own property together you're going to need a lawyer to separate, so it's the same thing. I thought, "In 1972 you don't have to be married in the law to be married." I struggled with this concept but my mind wasn't holding on it to it very well so I let it drift up into the dark green branches above the street.

I had thought about what separating was because it was very hard to live with Warren. It was very hard for me to live with Warren. "You are too sensitive," he kept saying. Warren was a real person. He had an executive job, he had real thoughts. He didn't spend time contemplating himself and his moods and his feelings. He just moved in the world. I admired that. I supposed if you were used to getting your way during the day it would hard to get home at night and negotiate, even if you loved the other person.

And he was funny. I'd planned to roast a chicken for dinner. I had the whole chicken ready on the counter. The book said to tie the drumsticks together, but it kept slipping around. I was afraid I was going to get my nice dress dirty so I took it off, and my good bra and my uncomfortable panty hose and put on an apron. I tried to hold onto the chicken but it still kept sliding around on the counter. I grabbed it and it shot out of my hands and across the room. Just then Warren walked in, and looked at the bare chicken in one corner and me, naked, in the other. "It looks like you're winning on points," he said. We both starting laughing. "This is love," I thought, "when someone makes you laugh so hard you have to pee."

Where were my keys? I tried my shirt pocket and found a piece of paper. It looked like a list but I couldn't tell what sort of list so I tried to put it back, but it was hard to do because it had become too big. I folded it up very neatly, very small, and it fit nicely. I patted a pocket in the front of my pants, feeling for the keys, but it was too bunched up to tell anything, and I wasn't ready to stand up. I felt the other front pocket but it had the same problem. I stood up without thinking and patted my back pockets. Not there. I couldn't remember if I'd already tried my shirt. Or maybe I had put them in my bra? That was where I put them when I was jogging. It was too complicated and I couldn't remember where I'd already looked.

Beside, standing up wasn't a good idea. I sat down.

I tried to remember when I'd starting drinking tonight. It was after the chicken was finally in the oven, after dinner. It was while I was washing the dishes, and had remembered the glasses man. I had stopped in an optician's because I'd lost a little screw from my glasses. The man behind the counter searched in a drawer until he found the right size screw. He was putting it in with a tiny screwdriver. "Would you like to have an affair with me?" he asked. I was startled and scared. He was so ordinary looking. "No," I said, unable to think. "No. I'm married." I wanted to run out but he still had my glasses. He handed them back to me and as I turned away he said, "Many women like to suck my penis."

It seemed easier to think about this now, at a distance, less threatening. Who would want to suck his penis? Probably no one did anything with him unless he gave them money. One of the things that made it so strange was his saying "my penis." It should have been 'my cock," or "give me head" or "go down on me." It was as though English wasn't his native language, although he had no accent, and his intonations were correct. It must be a ritual phrase for him—suck my penis. It must mean something special to him, something exciting. He is compelled to say it. I wondered how often this happened, that he said this to strange women. Someday there would be real trouble for him because of it. He surely knew that, but he must have to do it.

The whole thing was frightening—the incident, and his need. I pushed it out of my mind, pushed it all away from me, and let the summer air come around me like a soft quilt. My hand moved over the warm, fine abrasive surface of the steps. "What I would like is to be in bed," I thought, "falling asleep." But I couldn't be in bed, because I had forgotten my keys, or couldn't find them, which was the same difficult thing.

A friend told me to try not drinking for a whole month. If you could go without a drink for a month then you weren't a drunk. Well I guess I was a drunk. It had been—I wasn't sure, but it hadn't been a whole month. It was hard not to drink. There was that feeling of ease, of something relaxing. It was so much nicer to be with other people when I was drinking. I liked the taste. I liked the bite of the gin and the strong, sweet tastes of liquors.

When I drank, I had hangovers in the mornings, and it made it hard to work. The one time I had tried to work when I really wasn't sober, I couldn't do it at all. It was impossible to make those quick, beautiful, slippery connections between one part of a computer program and another, between what I was coding now and what I had coded yesterday or would work on tomorrow. I was very good, I knew that, but not when I had been drinking. I wondered how long I could keep it up before they noticed at work. I didn't wonder what it would be like if they let me go. I could feel that in the pit of my stomach. I needed to work. I needed to know I had money coming in. I needed it to be safe. That was one of the things that drinking did—let me feel safe for a while. But then it made me even less safe.

Thinking about not being safe made me think about how hard it was to stand up and that I'd be in trouble if someone who saw me sprawled out like this decided I was passed out and wanted to rob me. I propped myself on my elbows. I should go inside. But I didn't know where my keys were so I'd have to ring the doorbell and Warren would have to let me in and then he'd say something. Something angry.

Warren could make me feel safe. Warren could help me act brave. I could buy a brownstone with Warren. But sometimes I felt as though he just didn't see me, or care, and then I felt like I was falling. I needed to keep working. I needed the money, my money, so I would have something if he ever got angry enough to let me fall away. My being drunk made him angry. My being drunk and not being able to find my keys would make him really angry. If I had my keys I could get back in, and maybe he'd still be in the upstairs front room and I could brush my teeth and slide into bed before he knew.

The same friend who had told me about not drinking for a month had told me that if you are a drunk and you stop drinking and then start again, it was as though you had never stopped, as though your drinking problem had progressed even though you weren't actually drinking. It was as though it was a disease inside you. Well I was very drunk, and it hadn't taken a lot to get me here.

I thought about drinking and what it would be like, living with Warren, and I knew we wouldn't be together. I felt it as a certainty, as a stone inside my chest, that we would separate if I kept on drinking. He wouldn't put up with it. We would separate and someday years from now I would look back and wonder what would have happened between us if I hadn't been drinking. It would be so terrible. I could see myself, maybe on a bus somewhere, maybe working in some dingy office with dirty windows, having his image expand and fill the space and having to just sit and wonder. We might not have lasted anyway because I was too sensitive, but I'd never know because I'd lost him for the drinking.

It was very difficult and now I was sick and exhausted, drunk, on the steps. I couldn't do this again. I couldn't lose my job, I couldn't lose him.

I would have to do something. AA? I hoped there was something else. I'd look in the phonebook tomorrow. I made myself think of not ever drinking. I made myself think, "This is possible. You can do this." I thought, "This is what real people do in the world. They do things that are hard for them."

I whimpered.

I heard the door open above me and I heard his voice. "Coming to bed?" I knew from his tone that I was safe, that he didn't know I had been drinking. It was a sign, a sign that I would be all right. I got up carefully and turned around. He stood at the top of the steps, tall, full, the light from the hall behind him. The shape of his head and the outline of the shirt collar on his neck moved me. "You forgot your keys," he said, and laughed.

"I know," I said, but I hadn't known and now I did. "Oh, Warren, you wouldn't leave me, would you?" I felt my desperation as a physical thing, as though my arms were stretched toward him.

"Of course not. How could I ever leave a naked chicken wrestler?" I took his hand. I would look in the phonebook tomorrow. I would ask someone.

**Passing Scenes**

I have just been to visit my sister, who lives on an island off the coast of Maine. Now I am riding in a van service from the Rockland ferry terminal to the Portland airport. There is another woman in the back seat who is also going to the airport. She is using a laptop. The keys go clickety clickety.

Just ahead is a house that used to be an antiques store. Warren, my husband, and I stopped there once, before the long drive home. He died almost three years ago. Warren could drive from the Rockland ferry terminal to New York City in seven hours. Everyone else takes nine. Fang, our car, was an old BMW with a sweet ride and an incredible engine. When Warren told Fang to overtake something, Fang did. If Warren got frustrated with a person who was driving too slowly in the left hand lane, he passed on the right, blowing his horn and giving the other driver the finger through the sunroof. I finally got him to give up the sunroof part when stories about road rage became so prevalent, but I couldn't keep him from passing on the right. I don't miss the speeding and the passing, but it makes me sad to think we will never drive up here together again.

We are coming through Thomaston, a small town with classic white houses lining the road. We are going past a wide-open space where a state prison used to stand. I wonder what having the prison torn down did for real estate values. When I was young I worried that my older brother, who had poor judèent and bad friends, would end up in prison. He didn't. He found Scientology and it took all his money and spit him back out. Now he lives in a tiny room in Los Angeles, on social security, California disability and money I send him. I think he is content, or at least not too sad. Maybe a little lonely, but so are we all. He likes the weather there and does not want to come live with me in New York where it gets cold.

I had a nice visit with my sister. She is twelve years younger. We look enough alike that people often recognize us as sisters, both of us tall and blonde. Her hair is cut very short and mine is long. She has a landscaper gardening business. She works outdoors four days a week and is the bookkeeper and general everything at the island's Land Trust one day a week. On weekends she digs in her own yard. Her house is a showpiece, a simple two story with two porches, fat cats draped on the steps, surrounded by gardens. In the winter she scrapes and paints her kitchen floor, or steams off the ancient wallpaper. She is very smart, and has self discipline; she eats her lobsters without butter, and confines herself to one piece of chocolate a night.

I think to myself that I am a slug. My favorite city bus is the Number 5, which stops just outside my building. There is something luxurious about being conveyed to my doorstep. I rarely visit the gym. I have houseplants, but only the strong survive, those that flourish on neglect. However, my sister and I both chose, completely independently, the same obscure stainless steel dish drainer. We buy, without consultation, the same sweaters from L.L. Bean and we like the same books. She is moderation in all things, but I believe that too much ain't enough. I think about all those little inheritable genes deciding where to go. "You get in this egg and I'll wait for the next one."

I am also a glutton—not a gourmet or a gourmand, but a glutton. I am failing Overeaters Anonymous. I don't know if you could say I failed Alcoholics Anonymous long ago. I did give up drinking, but I couldn't get into the spirit of the AA meetings. I was too shy to make friends and I never found a group where I felt at home. The main reason I stopped drinking was that I knew I'd lose Warren if I kept drinking. That was Warren the first time. I left him five years after I got sober, and fifteen years later we found each other again and that was Warren the second time. He had gotten softer and I had gotten harder, and we were a better fit.

I couldn't find my Higher Power in AA, and I can't find it in OA. I should look for a sponsor, someone who is experienced and can guide me in OA, but I am suspicious of giving myself up to another person's direction. A brilliant black woman spoke at one meeting, and I thought she might be the right person. She seemed clear and strong, but I have never seen her again. Meanwhile I subsist on self-disgust, cake and ice cream, and fear of the future.

There are patches of wild lupines in pink and blue beside the road. Warren died in the fall. There was a star outside the bedroom window in the early mornings, bright and still. Maybe it was a planet, or a satellite. I didn't care. I felt its calm, constancy as balm.

The road follows the coast and there are occasional glimpses of quiet bays. After a while we come to a bridge over shiny railroad tracks. This is the old freight railroad line from Rockland to Portland. They fixed it up and now they run a tourist train on it. On my left, the tracks curve around a large stand of pines. Warren and I came up here once long ago. The tracks were abandoned then, with rotting ties and dark, rusted rails. Around the curve behind the pines, out of sight of the road, we made love. We called the bend in the tracks, Pauline's Curve, after the old movies *The Perils of Pauline*. He took off my clothes and tied me to the rails. I put my blue jeans on the ties to protect myself from splinters. We were laughing so hard we almost couldn't do it, and then we could. I'd like to think Pauline is still down there, naked, laughing and gay, hiding in the woods when a train comes by.

Warren and I made love outdoors in other places too, in the backcountry. We liked to get off the highway anyway, maybe because Fang rode so beautifully on little roads, swinging around the curves, climbing the small, steep hills. There were streams running alongside, abandoned orchards, barns sinking into the earth. The only vehicles we needed to pass were occasional lumbering tractors.

What will become of me? I am too old. I wouldn't look lovely naked now, tied to the tracks. I count on my fingers. I have had six long love affairs, with five different people. (I count Warren twice.) I suppose that is a lot. I should be more grateful. I have friends who have only had one or two. But there were long periods without love also. I am tired, tired of myself. I could make a list of my failures: shyness, anger, nail-biting, being judèental, gluttony, etc., but it would be neither sufficiently sad nor sufficiently funny. When you are young everything seems momentous. When you are 69 it's not so easy.

We pass well-maintained white farmhouses with big old barns behind them. The grass is mowed, but there are few ploughed fields and no cows. These are summer places now. When I was a young girl I just assumed that someday I would have a white house, maybe with fields, maybe in town, and I would beat the rugs outside on the porch railing and hang the quilts on the line to air. Instead I lived in rent control apartments and learned to program computers. I liked the work. I liked the beautiful logic it took to do it well. I liked elegant code; statements to the computer that made it run faster. I liked working alone, doing something well. Later I became a manager. I was good at that too, but I missed the beautiful simplicity of programming. Now I am retired. Computers change so fast. It is painful to think that all those programs I wrote, all those huge systems I installed, are gone now. I cared too much. I wanted things to work; I wanted things to be right. I stayed late and worked weekends. I wonder what life I would have had if I had been able to leave work at five. Would I have found someone else who left at five, and married him and had a white house? I'm glad now I don't have one. It would be lonely out there at night. I would see the lights of one or two neighbors at most. One star outside the window was comforting, but a whole sky of indifferent constellations would have been frightening.

Warren was a city person. He didn't want a house in the country. He wanted to read the *Times* and watch the news and go to ball games. He followed politics and knew the governors and senators from every state, and their parties and where they stood on issues. He projected election results for the networks and the newspapers. He was famous and he loved that. He belonged to professional societies and was their president and served on their boards. I was so used to turning to him for information that it took me a long time after he died to realize I would have to learn these things for myself.

We have passed the place where Warren and I used to stop for lobster rolls. They were so good. It was our way of saying goodbye to Maine. I miss having one. We are entering the outskirts of Portland. The city has created a jogging and biking path along part of the bay. I like to think I would use it if I lived here, but I know better. I rarely use the parks in New York City. I wish I were someone else, someone who liked to take walks, who didn't want cake for breakfast. I can't blame who I am now on Warren's death. I was that way before. There is no way to explain anything.

In the first year after he died I would go to the theater. Sometimes the play would involve someone dying. After the death some of the people on stage would be upset. I would get angry. I wanted to say this is not what death is. It is not a plot device. It is not someone being there and then not being there, boo-hoo. It is not that simple. It is about never again. Do you understand never? What is it you don't understand about never? I would be angry and crying also. I learned to cry silently in public, just letting the tears run down my face. I stopped wearing silk, because the water made stains.

Soon there will be the airport and security. Take out my laptop, take off my shoes, take off my belt. It is disorderly; it is rude to make people take off their shoes and their belts. Some of the World Trade Center terrorists flew from the Portland airport to Boston and on to their grisly task. They used a cash machine in New Brunswick. We passed through there a few minutes ago. Warren had pointed out the cash machine to me, but now I can't remember which one it is.

The lady in the back seat has closed up her laptop. I hear her rooting around, putting it back into her carry on. I wonder what existential really means. I want to tell myself I am suffering an existential sorrow, but that is because it sounds better than saying I feel old, and sad, and lonely. I am rarely this way any more. It must be having to see once familiar things in a new way. The first year was the indescribable pain of enormous loss. The second was missing the company, the simple shared conversations, the rustling on the other side of the bed. Perhaps the third is when one mourns the collateral damage, the back-country drives, the place we stopped for a lobster roll. Grief comes and goes and time changes things. Someday I will not remember Pauline on the railroad tracks. And soon, today, I will be home, where loss is familiar and accepted. ▪

# Dispatch from Wonderland

The Granville—as one house is built, another crumbles.

BY JERICHO PARMS *(Issue 25)*

IN THE SUMMER OF 1989, my mother built a house. The Granville, as it was called, was a ready-to-construct Victorian dollhouse precisely modeled after the Granville Mansion in Frank Capra's *It's a Wonderful Life*. When my mother came across the advert in the local newspaper it read simply: "Experienced craftsperson wanted… excellent pay" and listed a telephone number which she soon learned belonged to some woman up in Yonkers who had purchased the dollhouse as a gift for her young niece and upon its delivery—packaged as a hefty boxed kit—realized she'd be best off hiring someone more apt to construct it. My mother had been searching the classifieds for months, taking odd jobs to make some extra money "for a rainy day." As a young girl of seven years old, I had no way of knowing what that meant. It rained every day that month. The summer was marked by the earthy metallic scent before a thunderstorm when the streets of the city burned with acidic thirst.

She was the only person to call about the job, and it was hers. Within a week, in the form of varying sheets of perforated balsa wood and blueprint instructions for assembly, the makings of the Granville dollhouse arrived. And so my mother set to work constructing a mansion, in a half-emptied room in our family's Bronx apartment.

* * * *

My mother sat looking over her supplies. Ever a curious young girl, I rose to my knees from my spot on the floor beside her and peered over the table where she had laid out the thin slabs of wood, several bottles of glue, small clamps, and a slick utility knife.

"How does that song go?" my mother asked, looking down at me with a half-vacant expression that I understood required no response. She hummed a few muffled words about a "very very very fine house." Little did I know then that Graham Nash's chorus to "Our House," written about his love affair with Joni Mitchell, was a constant soundtrack running through my mother's head. At the time, it just lightened the thickness in the air.

I sat examining the family—a set of four miniature dolls my mother sewed precisely to model our own family, their muslin faces painted in lifelike acrylic, a red heart stitched on the breast under each felted jumper.

A warm, sticky breeze entered the room and wafted the smell of the honeysuckle that lined the fence to the neighbor's garden. I watched my mother breathe in deeply. Then, worried the humidity might affect the balsa, she rose and stepped over me to shut the window. I asked her how big the house would be when was finished, if there would be room enough for all of us. "We'll have to wait and see," she said, studying the blueprint. Her patience was as soothing as her whispered song: "With two cats in the yard, life used to be so hard, now everything is easy 'cause of you…."

In her high school yearbook, just below Library Aide and Student Council, my mother's peers listed her most distinctive qualities: "fantastic seamstress, squeaky and feminine." Below her photograph reads a line from Walt Whitman's inquiring verse "O Me! O Life!": *That you are here—that life exists and identity. That the powerful play goes on, and you may contribute a verse.*

My mother began to align the thicker slabs of the Granville's foundation. Her hands were delicate, long. As she sanded smooth the edge of a floor panel, sawdust sprinkled her forearms. At 35, she still had the slender frame of her high school years, though no longer the mousy blonde hair. Now, her hair cropped short and prematurely grey, she stared off with the same lost wonder she held in her teenage years, the same strength of conviction waiting to bud from the flowers in her hair.

I looked down at the dolls in my lap. They were near perfect, though too small to bear the minor details—the hands and feet, the slight angle of a jaw—that compose the visual image of a family.

* * * *

My father has flat feet. They spared him service in the Vietnam War, and what may have been a risky trip across the Canadian border. I didn't inherit my father's feet, or his wrestler's build, or the fading halo of his black kinky hair. I have high arches, like my mother. We do share the same facial features—same nose, same cheekbones—which makes me, unmistakably, my father's daughter. But my skin is shades lighter, filtering somewhere between his walnut-brown and the fair white skin of my blue-eyed, Irish mother.

My parents married in the 1970s, a biracial marriage that defied their families and tested the conservative boundaries of their Pennsylvania suburbs. As college dropouts and art school graduates, they moved to New York for a breath of urban tolerance.

I was born in 1982 into the hands of a peace-loving midwife named Lorna Davis after 10 hours in a maternity center on East 92nd Street and Madison Avenue. At the time my mother held a steady stream of work as a seamstress, then found a secretarial position at a prestigious high school, where my brother and I later reaped the rewards of private education. My father was enrolled in seminary at Columbia Presbyterian because somewhere between art and religion he believed he might find his doctrine.

By the time I was five years old, we had moved into a small garden apartment in the Bronx, nestled due north of Manhattan. It was a yellow stucco house built into a hill. A house divided—about a quarter of which on the second story (reached by a set of stone steps along the south end) was our small back-facing apartment with access to a terraced yard and a small portion of the attic.

My mother fixed up the back yard into a wild green garden, grew tomatoes and peppers, sunflowers that dwarfed us all. There, we brought home paint swatches from the hardware store and painted each room a different color based on the beauty of its name—Shrimp Toast, Celadon Cloud, Rusted Persimmon—and danced barefoot on the patio when it rained. My mother nurtured her green thumb, wrote poetry and waited for the Solstice; my father composed music on his guitar and painted in the attic; and my older brother and I grew up sewing patches on our corduroys, worshipping Cat Stevens.

On the morning my older brother turned nine years old, we woke in our bunked beds draped in a web of colored string that crisscrossed our bedroom walls, led out to the hallway, and transformed the entire apartment into a labyrinth of died yarn and twine. We found our parents in the living room, taking their tea and newspaper amidst the wild tangle of threads, like two fish caught in a net.

"Good morning," was all my father said.

"Breakfast?" my mother asked.

I never understood how they managed to marvel us—to fool us—so straight-faced and composed.

In an hour or two my brother's friends arrived, raided our dress-up box for hunting caps and cowboy hats, disguised in oversized glasses, tweed coats and field vests, like a troop out of Sherlock Holmes, and my father read dramatic riddles to an epic scavenger hunt in which each string, attached with a written clue, lead to another, unraveling the great maze.

I helped my mother ice cupcakes as she prepared lunch. From the kitchen window, I licked at the bowl of icing, rolled my eyes and laughed as my brother and his friends played exaggerated detectives to the mastermind of the great mystery web, and tried to imagine my next birthday—a decadent Mad-Hatter Tea Party set in the garden.

We were happy. My parents provided enough opportunity—a handful of friends and family to visit with outside of the city—to toggle between urban streets and natural landscapes. In the summer we made sun tea and rock candy. My brother and I caught salamanders along the creek roads of Vermont, and collected sea glass and cowry shells on the shores of Cape Ann. In winter we decorated gingerbread men with licorice, candied molasses in the snow, and every other year went west to my grandfather's ranch in Tucson, where we baked fudge on Christmas, and weighed horse feed at dawn

But it was New York that grounded us. The city afforded my parents, with little to their name, freedom to craft an elaborate world of magic and possibility in which my brother and I—when not consumed with our own quarreling—were free to flourish, safe and supported.

We lived on the line where the affluent enclave of Riverdale dissolves into the massive borough of the Bronx. Tucked neatly below the suburbs of Westchester County, the neighborhood is bookended by the Hudson River to the west, and two-way traffic on Broadway to the east. Orthodox Jewish families stroll the tree-lined streets on Saturdays, while the Irish bagpipes sound off a game of hurling at Gaelic Park. On 238th Street, old couples with their Sunday hats and swollen ankles line up outside the diner at dawn for the bus to Atlantic City. Slow-moving trains creak along the elevated subway platform heading one stop north to retire, like gutted silver fish, in the train yard near Van Cortlandt Park, where on summer afternoons the air fills with the sound of salsa or merengue, and the smell of sweet-charred barbeque.

They say John F. Kennedy owned a house on Independence Avenue. The women in the laundromat would gossip about Ed Sullivan's home in the Whitehall building. And, though it meant little then—a real TV man in the same building as my dentist—it confirmed my suspicions that the closer my brother and I rode our bicycles toward the river, the larger the houses grew, and the richer the people inside. But despite my observations, our attentions were tuned in elsewhere. My parents kept a steady tap into the world of downtown city politics. Newspapers piled in the hallway. Public radio broadcasted through the kitchen while my mother washed dishes.

"Turn that up for me would you honey?" she would say, motioning a soapy hand toward the clock radio propped on the counter. And inevitably, my father's voice would bellow from the living room reminding "us kids" to "keep it down" each night during the McNeil Lehrer News Hour.

Ed Koch was in his third term as mayor. It had been nearly a year since the rioting in Tompkins Square, when the city dispatched police to enforce a curfew to rid the park of the homeless and street folk. Downtown New York was a ripe epicenter of creative chaos and evictions.

* * * *

My mother was squatting before her worktable, installing a banister along what was to become the Granville's front porch steps. She was dressed down to work in the heat. Her turquoise jersey, cut loose around the neck, hung slightly off her shoulder and billowed over a pair of cut-off shorts. Her ears, normally adorned with dangling stones and Mexican beads, were bare, her silvery grey hair wrapped neatly away in a pale bandana. Her legs were strong from running, her feet tan along the lines of her Birkenstock sandals. She knelt in close to look at what she had done.

The smell of wood glue tickled my nose. I marveled at the weightlessness of the balsa wood as my mother handed me a leftover scrap. I knelt down and scrawled my name in the thin coat of sawdust blanketing our own parquet floor, just enough to rouse my dust allergy and send me off with an incessant sneeze. My mother's half-amused expression seeped through her eyes, barely biting back a "serves you right" before she smiled and reached down to untwist a strap of my overalls. She knew how much I loved it there, with her, with The Granville. Still, I was careful not to be a bother. I knew even then, there was something in her silence that summer that suggested she needed to build the house alone.

Instead, I became more interested in the reality that the Granville represented than the house itself. It seemed we all did for a while. When we had nothing to talk about we talked about the Granville. At dinner my father would ask my mother how it was coming along. My mother issued steady progress reports as I watched her spoon green peas onto my plate, and glanced up at my brother silently daring me to eat them one by one.

"Who ever gets the dollhouse should paint it camouflage," my brother once said.

"That's ridiculous," I said as if knowing then that the mansion's grandiose refinement was fit for a scene out of Fitzgerald where the wealthy parvenus of Long Island Sound gather indoors while Gatsby's yellow roadster awaits outside. I hoped it would belong to a girl with a wagging ponytail, crisply pressed dresses, and enough sensibility to wallpaper the interior.

"The house will be one color and the shutters another. Just like the picture on the box. There are nine rooms," I explained.

"Yes, well let's just remember," my mother said softly. "The house is going to another family when it's all done."

Many of my friends lived in big houses that I visited on play dates as their invisible parents entertained in a distant dining room and checked in every hour. In our one-bedroom apartment we tripped over one another. I recognized, with a certain envy, what fun it might be to slide down a banister into a spacious foyer, or close the door to my very own bedroom. Like any young child, I filtered between my want of large houses, new toys, and all other concepts deemed "normal" at the time, and my own distinct pride in our family's differences. There was a certain comfort in our close quarters—each of us no more than a name call away. Yet that summer it seemed my parents hardly crossed paths. As if the humid air had swelled, not only the Balsa wood, but an invisible rift between them.

It was in those months I realized my parents rarely addressed one another, but instead spoke directly to my brother and me. I wondered if they were mad at each other, and why. It was like the silent treatment

I used with my brother when he pulled at my curls or teased me with his friends. I tried my hardest not to look him in the eye. But he would inevitably make me laugh for some reason or another and I always broke my silence.

"They could put jungle moss along the balcony, like canopy cover in case of attack," my brother continued.

"It's supposed to be beautiful. Stupid."

"Alright. Enough," my father said. "Eat your food."

As my brother offered far-fetched ideas for a secluded base camp for his G.I. Joe action figures, I countered with my own imaginings of a house filled with bright dreams and miniature armoires. And, like any well-loved children bathed in the unassuming ease of youth, we bickered wildly, played with our vegetables, and in our own oblivion, filled a deafening silence.

* * * *

Inside, our apartment was a near-perfect portrait of bohemian disorder. Books covered every surface. A pair of overalls pinned down to my size lay waiting for weeks near the Singer sewing machine, draped with a half-knit sweater. Color photographs of my parents when they first met at art school in Pittsburgh lined the bookshelves, the edges tawny, as if steeped in sepia. The walls were covered in mirrors, crocheted tapestries, my brother's drawings of amiable wizards and elves with crossbows—meticulously convincing scenes from Tolkien novels. Canvases leaned against the television set, an old wooden-box unit with a tight-clicking knob that ushered in one or two channels—three at best with the antenna propped just so. It was a small haven, cramped and cluttered. It was home. And I rarely thought to question it.

I remember one day I found my mother kneeling in the yard staking tomato plants along the stone wall of our garden, scanning the stems and leaves for aphids. The sunflowers had been growing steadily all summer. They hung in the awkward lankiness of their adolescence. By summer's end their stalks would thicken like torch handles stemming from their wide-seeded faces and petals of flame.

I watched our neighbor Frank—old, Italian, with kind eyes and a widowed heart—as he nursed a vine of cucumbers that crawled along the fence between our yards. He dropped a few, ripe and mature, on our side of the fence for my mother to chop for salad, and gave a quick wave to be sure she noticed. Frank's house was built farther up into the hill, so I rarely caught sight of him from level ground but rather from a sharp angle—a small old man looking down at us from above.

Next door to Frank, on the same hillside shelf where Waldo Avenue and Dash Place meet at a sharp curving bend, lived another young couple with two children. My brother and I played there often. Their house was large and creaky, built of stone and mortar with wide-planked mahogany floors.

"I get goose bumps all over," I once told my mother, as I was convinced the structure held the haunting residuals of an ancient ghost story.

"It is certainly very old. In fact, years ago that was likely the main house," my mother said. "And these two," she motioned a hand full of weeds pulled at the root towards our house, then Frank's, "probably belonged to the grown children." My mother continued, attempting to explain how in the 19th century, the Riverdale section of the Bronx was an estate district where Manhattan moguls built their country homes.

"Back then it was considered the country around here," she said.

"So we live in the daughter's house?" I asked.

"Not exactly. The entire house likely belonged to the daughter. Our apartment would have been the maid's quarters."

In some pockets of the neighborhood, historic mansions of the past remained more or less intact, though with the turn of the century—the dawn of rail commuting, and the advent of small houses and apartment living—several streets transformed to create a modern-day architectural hodgepodge of distinguished Georgian- and Tudor-revival style homes from the 20th century, prewar co-ops, multi-story buildings from the 1950s and 1960s, high-scale luxury condos, and mid-range housing projects.

We lived in the maid's quarters. I tried to imagine where we might fit in on the architectural scale, just how we measured up in the neighborhood, in life.

I had known from a young age that my parents were different. They expected more from the world and there was a certain radicalism about them, but their politics were not manifest in picket lines. I wasn't thrown on my father's back to attend protest rallies downtown. I have no lasting images of my mother perched on a soapbox amidst a swarming crowd. Theirs was a quiet defiance. It cried softly through their art. Members of society's voiceless underclass surfaced as protagonists of my mother's verse, which she scrawled in notebooks alongside nature poems and folk illustrations. Rebellion echoed from the graphite drawings that hung above my father's drafting table. In one, a young black boy peers up at a mounted officer, a small stone—the hinted promise of rebellion—clenched in the fist behind his back. For years, I tried to imagine, had it been a still frame from a motion picture, what might have happened next.

* * * *

"If you had three wishes, what would you wish for?" I asked my mother. She stood by her worktable sweeping matchsticks and sawdust from the floor, remnants of another day's work.

"That's a good question," she said as she stopped to prop her chin on the upright broomstick. The dollhouse sat on the nearby table. Each day it had slowly begun to take form. I circled around it peering in and around its skeletal frame of interior nooks and doorways, zig-zagging staircases. My mother leaned her broom against the wall and joined me, crouching down to inspect the innards of her mansion. On opposite sides we could see each other through the structure by way of the cavernous foyer, in between the slender columns. Small vertical beams, soon to be full walls, hid the full image of my mother's face, like the rosewood screen of a confessional.

"I would wish for a big house like this one," I whispered.

Through the Granville I could see only my mother's eyes, sharply blue as the light turned to evening and the air pressure hardened, bracing for the rain. I stood and ran around to her kneeling on the floor.

"I also wish that I had a cat, like my friend Susannah's," I said. "Her cat goes in circles before he sits in your lap. Like this—" I rolled my hands into paw-like fists and kneaded them gently into her thigh. My mother laughed and squeezed my hands.

"That does sound nice, doesn't it?" She stood and reached for the broom again, perusing the floor. "Meanwhile, what a mess."

I shrugged, happy to have made her laugh, and headed off to find my brother. Before I got too far, I stopped to listen: the broom swept against the wooden floor keeping time as my mother, left alone, began to hum her favorite song.

* * * *

By the end of the summer, the Granville was complete. My father carried the house out to the garden and placed it on a stool. My mother posed for a photograph, her arm draped awkwardly over the shingled roof. There was a melancholy blush of accomplishment in her otherwise stiff expression.

As my father and brother fussed about, tinkering with the flash on his old Pentax camera, my mother leaned down to me. "Go and bring the family," she said, fingering the curls at the nape of my neck. I ran in search of the dolls and propped them one by one around the exterior—my father and brother leaned forward on the second floor balcony, my own doll bent to sit on the front porch steps, my mother propped at a slant on the main threshold behind me. They were the perfect size for the otherwise unfurnished home.

After the last photograph, I collected the dolls from the house, stood them up in the front pocket of my overalls, and watched my father carry the house away.

"We wouldn't really fit in there, anyhow," I said crinkling my nose up to stifle a sneeze, or a shiver. "Too much dust."

My mother's smile was warm. I leaned back into her and pulled her arms tight around my neck. I realized how much she hated to see it go. In the crease of her elbow the faint smell of Patchouli oil, sawdust, and sweat turned to the earthy metallic of a coming rain.

* * * *

A few weeks later my mother announced at the dinner table that she had joined a female Outward Bound group and was heading off for a month to hike in the mountains of North Carolina. She said she needed to be in nature. She needed a change of pace. I looked over at my father nodding along silently as my mother spoke to us, looking down as he stacked a bite of food on the tines of his fork. I wished I could go with her. Before she left my mother took me in her arms. "When things start to feel too hard," she said burrowing her cheek against my head of curls, "remember to be kind to yourself." At the time, I was unsure what to make of her words, and it didn't occur to me to ask, though I carried them with me for years. In all likelihood, her trip was the "rainy day" she had been saving for along. And I now realize the irony of her spending a summer to build a model house in order to flee—for a short while, a stint of kindness—the four walls of her own. In her absence, I drew pictures of her climbing the tallest mountains. I wrote to her—proud letters with nowhere to send them. But the time went quickly, and before I grew too curious, my mother was back home.

After that there had been a period of relative normalcy. Sometimes I wonder at how little I remember of those years. Or rather, how well my parents masked the budding divide between them, because for us children it just read as a prolonged period of silence. We grew accustomed. My father spent more and more time holed away in the attic writing music, and my mother took night workshops at a nearby city college to hone her poetry and make new friends. Meanwhile, I entered the second grade and assumed a dose of healthy elementary-level diversions: pottery classes, extended recess, Laura Ingalls Wilder novels. And, likewise, more grappling concepts: friendship circles, crushes on boys, pop music. I came to ignore the hushed interactions in another room, the closed doors behind which my parents, young and disappointed, were desperately negotiating how to save their marriage.

* * * *

I was nine years old when my parents divorced. It was 1991, two years after the Granville dollhouse, and a late summer evening, when my father's clenched fist came down against the half-cleared kitchen table, cracking the white linoleum Formica finish, breaking the bones in his left hand. My brother and I sat in the family room staring at the changing grey glow of an old Marx Brothers film playing on the television set, a muted scene from *Horse Feathers*, when cigar-toting Groucho in his painted mustache and slapstick routine tries to get the girl. My brother and I listened, trying to piece together severed strips of our parents' muffled cries from the kitchen. But my father's deep barreling growls and my mother's angry shrills carried not as decipherable words, but as a disorienting noise that filled every corner of our apartment.

"What are they saying?" I whispered, tugging at my brother's shirt.

"I don't know. Shut up." He brushed my hand away so hard that it pinged through my arm. I heard the crash of dishes, the deep clink of broken pottery down the hall. I was angry with my brother for turning on me but I was too paralyzed by the sounds from the kitchen to fight back. I tried to slide away from him but my dress had risen up under me and, in the heat, the warm sticky skin of my bare legs felt glued to the wooden floor.

"I'm sorry," my brother's voice softened. "It's going to be okay." He inched closer to me on the floor and we sat, cross-legged with our backs touching, as if to fend of an attack on all sides. A hot gust of air entered the living room window and boiled around us. Beneath the rich humidity I felt the chill of my own sweat. We waited.

After a few minutes, I heard my parents' footsteps in the hallway. The next moment they were crouched on the floor beside us, wrapping my brother and me in their arms.

"I'm so sorry," my mother wept into my ear. "Everything is going to be alright."

In the tangle of our parents embrace, I felt my father's hand on my head, stroking my hair, and watched it move to cup and knead my brother's shoulder. "We are going to change things. Things will be better now," he said. His voice was heavy, smooth like tar.

We ate at the kitchen table for days after, setting our plates over the cracked divide left by my father's fist, trying to ignore the harsh way it interrupted the surface, until my mother opened the other side for us to use. My father's hand was in a cast for weeks while he moved into an apartment down the street.

A week or two later, my mother knelt on the floor with a newspaper spread out, packing a box of my father's odds and ends. She stopped to skim a news story before clipping the article and pinning it in her nearby notebook. The headline said something about bulldozing in the shantytowns. By then it was Mayor Dinkins holding the reigns of the city as police in riot gear escorted men and women from abandoned buildings and East Village squats. The half-faded picture in the newspaper showed a woman in a wheelchair cast onto the streets with her cat, Misty Blue. "The city doesn't know how to handle its homeless population," my mother said, wrapping up my father's favorite coffee mug. I nodded in agreement, trying to emulate her quiet scorn. I looked down again at the newspaper and studied the woman's face, photographed minutes after her eviction, with her belongings piled high into a metal shopping cart. I thought about my father moving out, his boxes piled by the front door ready to go. I understood the woman's grimacing expression, torn between resentment and fear. I felt a cringe of nausea at the sudden realization: now I had two homes. Our structure was not holding. The world I knew had fallen victim to a great demolition.

"Honey?" My mother reached down and threaded her long fingers in between mine. My heart raced quickly as a mound of tears swelled in the base of my throat. I couldn't bring myself to look up at her. I ran off to separate my things.

That evening, I pictured the dollhouse—the two-story tower, fancy cornices, and wrap-around porch—and the four family dolls, before I tucked the memory away.

It was the 1960s when Graham Nash penned his lyrics to "Our House," with evening sunshine in the windows, flowers in the vase, and "two cats in the yard," nodding to the complexity of domestic stability and family life in the era of free love. And though the song's scene belonged to a house in Laurel Canyon, it struck a chord from the hills of California to the streets of New York where, I have no doubt, my parents set forth to build a lasting future. But by the time I was seven years old I had learned about the transient properties of things. Just as the Granville, adorned in all its decadent possibility, would come and go, my parents were architects of their own Wonderland, but it was not built to last.

The 1990s arrived. We watched Bill Clinton's inauguration live on television at school, huddled on the reading carpet in the library. While New York City's homeless still took up lodging in the streets, news of Mayor Giuliani's crackdown aired on the radio. In time, my father worked a few jobs painting folk-tale illustrations for children's books, but made rent with a graphic design job. My mother charted her way from odd jobs and secretarial work to become an eighth-grade English teacher and brought home dog-eared copies of Steinbeck and Salinger. My brother and I settled into our routine shuffle between our parents' two apartments. Life went on. But we were all changed: my father stopped writing love songs on his guitar; my mother no longer gathered wildflowers along the side of the road; and though I cannot speak for my older brother, I spent years trying to understand what had gone wrong. ▪

# Kid Without a Jacket

Our house was always a mess....From a memoir about growing up with a mother struggling with mental illness

BY MELISSA LARSON *(Issue 26)*

KIM'S WHITE HIGH HEELS were at least two sizes too big for my eight-year-old feet. I stood in front of the full-length mirror, examining the gaps at the backs of my heels. Yep. Too big. Maybe some walking practice would help. After about fifteen minutes of strutting around my bedroom, I was able to keep them on my feet without plunging headfirst into the yellow shag carpeting. Had Kim been home to witness the runway show, she would have flipped. Her new shoes, purchased for Easter and her middle school band and chorus concerts, were off limits to me, her sticky younger sister. I don't see why, I thought, as I pulled on her new pink and white Madonna tee-shirt, the Material Girl's hair outlined with silver glitter. It's not like I would wear her shoes out of the house.

Oh. Wow. I could totally wear these to school today. A glance at the clock told me it was 10:03 a.m. Earlier, I had moaned to my mother that I was too sick to go to school, and she'd groaned her consent from underneath a scratchy wool blanket the color of rust. Mom spent way more time in bed than most mothers. Though I didn't fully get why, it was clear that she was sick in a "different" way. She sometimes used phrases like "manic-depression" and "anxiety" to explain how she felt, but the words were as mysterious to me as she was. What worked in my favor, however, was that she didn't get out of bed before noon on some days. Avoiding boring old school had become a cinch. But now, twirling in front of the mirror in "my" new outfit, hitting the third grade didn't seem so dull. I could always catch "The Price Is Right" tomorrow.

I considered the shoes. My big toe and its sidekick—alien toe, my brother Eric called it, as it was longer than the big toe—both peeked out happily through a thick, white leather strap. A white bow smiled up from the perfect white strap. In the midst of our jumble of a house, the shoes were perfect. Clean. Unblemished.

Our house was always a mess. While the folks across town had cleaning ladies, we…didn't. Between my mother's mental illness and my father's job in New York City, they weren't the best housekeepers. In short, she was too tired and he was too busy. The poor crib wasn't even nice enough to make "before" on one of those home makeover programs. The problem with the house wasn't just that things were antiquated or dirty or broken or cluttered. The problem was that all of those things were happening at the same time.

So when you had a new pair of shoes, like Kim had, you wanted them to stay pristine forever, kind of like a beacon of cleanliness and purity in the midst of dog hair and peeling wallpaper and distressed mothers and fathers.

But I took them anyway.

Within ten minutes, I was pedaling up Chesapeake Avenue, Kim's heels catching in the pedals of my yellow and white banana seat bike. Few cars were parked in the driveways of the Cape Cods and split levels that ruled the neighborhood, and the streets were as still and grey as a cemetery. Everyone else was where they were supposed to be on that weekday morning.

I pedaled along, my bike happily plunking on and off grey stone curbs. From my outfit to the pink lip gloss I had swiped onto my lips, I was ready to rock. Suddenly, the March wind stole through Kim's tee-shirt, breaking up the party. I looked down at my arm, where goose bumps neatly punctuated my freckles. I should have grabbed a jacket. I had been so pleased with my ensemble that I hadn't even considered outerwear. Madonna never wore a spring jacket onstage.

In the distance, the verdant soccer fields of Knollwood School greeted me in all their dewy glory. I excitedly pedaled up the concrete path to the bike rack, crashing my ride next to Jennifer Kaplan's as usual. Once old banana was locked up, I strode toward the school with the confidence of a corporate worker who'd taken the morning off, wandering into the office a few hours late.

Slup. What the? Slup slup slup. I looked down. Great. Kim's heels were sinking into the mud as I walked across the grass, brown quickly replacing white with every step. A wave of fear came over me. I looked back at the bike rack, realizing I could forget this whole idea, speed home, and still finish out the morning with Bob Barker.

*No.*

Madonna never ran off the stage before the set was finished.

By the time I settled into school and avoided the curious looks of my classmates, it was time for recess. I looked around for Jennifer Kaplan, the Beavis to my Butthead, to confirm our recess itinerary. Maybe some swings, followed by a little monkey bars? I caught sight of the back of her dark blond French braid, following Rachel Edelstein and Heather Hunt out the classroom door. Weird.

Jennifer and I were friends with Rachel and Heather, though I always felt like they were from another planet. Rachel and Heather always sat in the front row, their Trapper Keepers perfectly organized with completed homework. Teachers were in love with these two. Their brown-bagged lunches were neatly labeled with "Rachel E" or "HH," the tops of the bags folded down in precision, packed with, like, multiple food groups and CapriSun. Heather's hair looked different every day. Her mother really knocked herself out, combing and parting and braiding and the whole nine, coming up with new ways to arrange her Girl Scout's hair and always color-coordinating Heather's silk scrunchies with Heather's outfit du jour.

Because I was in charge of my own food and grooming, let's just say that those departments proved dicey for me at times. Between my mother not feeling well most of the time and my older brother and sister kept busy by all things high school and junior high, I was on my own, and sometimes got a little too inventive. One day in the third grade, tired of dragging myself to the water fountain at lunchtime, I actually swiped an empty Molson Golden from the counter where my parents stored recycled goods. I peeled off the label, rinsed the sucker out, and filled it with orange juice. Good as gold. When I ferreted the bottle out at lunchtime, a curly-haired lunch aide had yelled at me, even after I swore that I wasn't an alcoholic and that my dad refused to spend money on drink boxes. Something about commercialism and excessive packaging, I implored.

After that note home, Dad bought me a reusable water bottle the next day, words like "yuppies" and "capitalism" skidding over his bottom teeth. It must have been hard being a hippie during the 1980s.

But anyway, on Madonna Day, it looked like Jennifer was ditching me for the Wonderbread crowd. Not one to be ditched, I followed the trio out to the school playground, where a game of hopscotch was in full swing. A cold wind whipped across the blacktop as Jennifer jumped across three spaces on one foot, her hands in the pockets of her purple fleece hoodie. Teeth chattering, I looked down at Kim's heels and suddenly felt as garish as a fistfight in church. Everyone else on the playground was running around in sneakers and coats. Why had I worn this stupid outfit again?

As Rachel tossed her pebble, clapping as it landed neatly inside a chalk-lined box, the curly-haired aide who had called me out on the beer bottle blew her whistle from across the blacktop. Everyone turned around to see who had committed the latest offense.

She was heading for me.

She blew her whistle again. Oh God. Oh S-word.

"HEY!" She screeched. "HEY YOU!" Heather, Rachel, and Jennifer pretended they didn't know me.

"Uh…yes?" I eyed my bike at the rack, about a hundred meters away. I could outrun this broad even in my too-big heels, I thought.

"WHERE IS YOUR COAT?" The aide screamed. Her mousy frizz, cut into a mullet, didn't move even as she thundered across the blacktop.

I stared at Jennifer's hopscotch stone and shrugged like a kicked dog.

This woman was nowhere near done. "WHERE IS YOUR COAT?" she repeated. A circle of kids was beginning to form. "YOUR PARENTS LET YOU OUT OF THE HOUSE WITHOUT A COAT? YOUR MOTHER DOESN'T CARE IF YOU CATCH COLD?"

Clearly this lady had skipped Child Psychology in her quest to become a lunchtime aide. My lower lip began to tremble, but I bit it back and stared at her. I was not about to break my "no crying in school" policy for someone with a perm.

"DON'T YOU TALK?" She was really starting to lose it. "WHAT'S THE MATTER WITH YOU?"

"Hey, what is going on here?" A male voice broke in, interrupting the banshee's rant. Oh God. It was Mr. Scanlon, who had been Kim's sixth-grade teacher two years prior. He wasn't any nicer than Curly here, from what I'd heard. He had once called our house, complaining that Kim looked out the window during history lessons. Dad tried to make a joke about kids and windows, but before long was speaking into the phone in a tight voice, telling Mr. Scanlon that he'd rather raise a dreamer than a disciple before slamming the phone down.

And now, minutes after the hopscotch incident, I was sitting in Mr. Scanlon's classroom, unsure whether I was being punished or being saved from imminent pneumonia. Kim's shoes weren't looking so hot. They stared up at me accusingly. "What do you want from me?" I asked them. "I'm only eight."

Curly was stationed outside the classroom door, angrily guarding her convict. I heard Mr. Scanlon come back down the hall, returning from the men's room I suppose, and they spoke to each other in hushed whispers.

Mr. Scanlon marched into the room and made a beeline for where I sat. He was clearly not psyched about wasting his lunch hour on me and my desire to play dress up in public. I really didn't blame him. Halloween had long passed.

"OK, little Miss. Enough of this." He ran his hand over the widening part in his hair. "Didn't Mrs. Clifford speak to you about your ensemble when you got to school this morning?" Mrs. Clifford was my teacher, a woman who looked and acted well past retirement age. She was a bit of a loose cannon, Clifford, but had taken to ignoring me lately, a vast improvement over some of her previous tirades. It probably wasn't her fault that she wasn't as into me as the kids who were easy to like, the Rachels and the Heathers of the world. I was absent sometimes for no apparent reason. I forgot my homework frequently. The inside of my desk was about as organized as my snarled hair. Clifford had told me earlier in the month, a look of resignation on her face, that the only thing I had to do in life was die. I think I had forgotten my Lewis and Clark review questions or something.

I pretended to be really interested in twisting one of my blond curls around two fingers. "No. Mrs. Clifford didn't say anything."

Curly shifted her weight from one double-Velcro Reebok to the other and broke into our tête-à-tête. "HOW DID YOUR MOTHER LET YOU OUT OF THE HOUSE LIKE THAT?"

This woman had no clue of what an "indoor voice" was. Rather than voice this observation, I just shook my head. The truth was that my mother would not have let me out of the house "like this" had she been up and about, but I was too terrified to say as much. It's too bad my parents didn't just stick a note to my forehead, explaining me to people: "Please excuse my outfit, ma'am, but my mother has a mental illness that I don't even know the name of, and can't always care for me properly. Sometimes she hits a downward spiral and doesn't get out of bed for days. Plus my dad works in the city, and the poor man leaves too early in the morning to be of assistance to my morning routine. But let me assure you that they are loving parents who are doing the best they can with an unpleasant situation, and would definitely oppose my lack of a coat and suitable footwear today."

But I wore no such note, so I stood there like a dummy.

Mr. Scanlon, clearly disgusted by my silence, snipped, "Well, you can go outside for the rest of recess. You wore the clothing; you can be cold in the clothing." He and Curly ushered me outside, where I stood for the next ten minutes and silently watched Jennifer, Heather, and Rachel jump through their game of hopscotch, their sneakered feet hitting the pavement with as much force as my humiliation. ▪

# A Harlem Education

BY JACK WILLIS *(Issues 26, 27)*

**Part I**

IT WAS WITH SOME WONDER and overwhelming ignorance that I stood outside Louis Michaux's bookstore on the corner of 125th Street and Lenox Avenue in the heart of Harlem on a cold spring day in 1961, staring at the signage:

THE HOUSE OF COMMON SENSE
AND THE HOME OF PROPER PROPAGANDA
WORLD HISTORY
BOOK OUTLET ON
2,000,000,000
(/O BILLION)
AFRICANS AND NON-WHITE PEOPLES

Underneath it were pictures of African revolutionary Jomo Kenyatta, the father of Kenyan independence, and Marcus Garvey, the legendary Black Nationalist. Of course, I didn't know who they were; I only learned that later.

Beneath the pictures on the upper part of the large display window, were large graphic sun rays and the words:

NATIONAL MEMORIAL TO THE PROGRESS
OF THE
AFRICAN RACE IN AMERICA

And under that were pictures of the twelve heads of African states that had won their independence from colonial rule. I didn't recognize them either.

Posters hung at street level around the window. Two of them made me laugh: "The White Man's God" was a picture of a Hollywood idealization of Jesus, except he had kinky hair.

"This can't be him he has the wrong hair," it said. The other one was titled, "The Black Man's God" and had a Black Jesus.

"This could be him," it said. "He has the right hair."

Two other posters that I didn't think funny hung beneath them.

THE
GODDAMN
WHITE MAN
THIS IS THE TITLE OF THE BOOK
READ IT

And the other read:

LUMUMBA
LYING IN STATE
FROM 1 TO 7
PUBLIC INVITED

Patrice Lumumba, an African Nationalist, and leader in the Congo's fight for independence against Belgium, was the first democratically elected President of a newly independent Congo. He was the reason I was standing outside Michaux's bookstore that cold spring day.

Lumumba had been assassinated that February during a coup staged by African soldiers under the control of the Belgium government with the connivance of Britain and the CIA. His assassination shocked many.

Just a few days earlier a riot had broken out in the gallery of the United Nations' General Assembly, led by Black Nationalist James Lawson and singer/actress Abby Lincoln, protesting the murder. The riot at the U.N. introduced a new Black Nationalism to the United States and scared many white Americans. Lewis Michaux's bookstore was the main gathering place for Harlem's Black Nationalists.

At the time, I was working as a desk assistant (read copy boy) at CBS News. I was twenty-seven and it was my first job after coming to New York. It was still the glory days of CBS News. Edward R. Murrow had just left to head up the USIA, but the legendary staff he had assembled was still there.

My job was to do whatever chores anyone needed done. I got coffee for some of the icons of TV journalism, Charles Collingwood, Eric Severeid, Howard K. Smith and Richard C. Hottelett, picked up staff newspapers downstairs in Grand Central Terminal and ripped and posted the copy off the wire services. It was like my army experience: structured, no authority, but also, no real responsibility. After breaking my ass in law school, the menial work was a relief. I felt myself at the heart of something big and important, and even though I didn't know what I wanted to do with my life, or where this job would lead, I loved it. Every day I learned something new.

On my days off, instead of doing my laundry, cleaning my room and running errands, I went with reporters and crews as they covered breaking stories in and around New York. I sat in the editing rooms with them as they cut the stories, wrote narration and added voiceovers. It was the beginning of my news and production education.

On one of those days off Sam Jaffe, CBS's U.N. correspondent, got the assignment to cover the Lumumba story in Harlem and I tagged along.

As we entered the bookstore we were ushered into the back room. It was cramped and chaotic. There were no windows, the lighting was bad, there was a jumble of books and papers scattered about, and on the walls, tables and floor were dozens of framed photos of Negro celebrities, from W.E.B. DuBois and Paul Robeson to Louis Armstrong and Billie Holiday, as well as some prominent African Nationalist revolutionary leaders like Kenyatta and Kwame Nkrumah.

It was a little overwhelming, especially since my understanding of Negro (as we termed it then) culture, like that of most Americans of the 40s and 50s, came from listening to "Amos and Andy" on the radio and following the exploits of Joe Louis and Jackie Robinson. In my freshman year in college I would sometimes go with my friend Bernie to the Oasis, a Black-owned jazz and R&B club on south Western Avenue to listen to The Treniers and try to look as cool as the all-Black crowd. Afterwards, we'd sit in his car drinking from quarts of Pabst beer and feel sooo hip. I'd read a little while in the army: James Baldwin's *Go Tell it On A Mountain* and *Notes of a Native Son* and Richard Wright's *Native Son*. But the number of Negroes I knew personally you could count on the fingers of one hand. There was Timmy Devault, a slick center fielder whom I played Muni baseball with while in high school; and Sam Brown, another center fielder I played baseball with at UCLA and in the Army; and Ethel, whose last name I'm ashamed to say I don't remember even though she cleaned our house and cooked our meals from the time I was thirteen until I left for

New York after law school. She'd get up at five or six in the morning to take care of her family before boarding a bus for the ninety-minute ride to our house in west LA for her day's work. She'd leave around seven that evening after dinner and the dishes were done for the long bus ride back to Watts. My brother and I had no sense of her life outside of our home except that she was an avid churchgoer. She and her work were taken for granted. With scant experience of Negroes, the celebration of Blackness in the back room of the bookstore was both fascinating and strange to me.

Even stranger was an open coffin in the center of the room. Inside the coffin lay not a body, but a likeness of a body, a papier-mâché likeness of the body of Patrice Lumumba—a protest designed to call attention to the CIA's involvement in his assassination. The room was so small that I was in the way as the crew began setting up to film the coffin and interview Michaux. So I wandered out into the main room to explore the shelves.

The front room of the bookstore facing the street, featured books by American and Caribbean Negroes, Africans, and revolutionaries from around the world, and even though I considered myself pretty well read, most were new to me.

Above the bookshelves and along one wall were pictures of a Black Jesus surrounded by Black angels.

I was looking at those pictures when a man said, "I'll bet you've never seen a Black Jesus before."

I turned and saw a very tall, light-skinned Negro with a goatee watching me. He wore a dark overcoat which, even though we were inside, was buttoned and a dark suit, white shirt, dark tie, dark hat and rimless glasses that gave him a scholarly look. I admitted I hadn't seen a Black Jesus before.

"Nor Black angels," he said.

His manner was quiet and polite.

"Why do you think that is?" he asked

When I admitted I didn't know, he went on, "Because whites have stolen him… Jesus was a black man… Black people were the original people… Whites stole Jesus. They also stole the great African cultures like the Egyptian and Sumerian civilizations and made them appear as white Europeans."

I didn't know whether that was true or not, but he said it with such certainty that I wasn't going to argue, especially since I didn't know my ass about it, had never thought about it, and didn't have an opinion; so I decided just to listen.

Then, in the same even matter of fact voice, he quietly switched his focus.

"All white men are racists, " he said.

I felt myself get angry. Was he goading me? Was he picking a fight?

"I'm not a racist." I protested

"Yes you are. All white men are racists"

"What makes me a racist?" I demanded, trying to remain cool.

"Because you live in and prosper from a system of white supremacy."

I laughed. I had a menial job, made $60 a week and lived in a tiny rented room on 108th street and Riverside Drive. I could barely make ends meet.

"I hardly prosper," I shot back.

"Yes you do. How'd you get your job?"

He didn't wait for me to answer; he didn't have to. He knew I probably got my job through a connection. And he was right. Before I came to New York my Dad introduced me to a guy who introduced me to a guy who was visiting LA and was high up at CBS News. When I got to NY and needed a job I called him and the rest is history.

"How many so-called Negroes are there where you work?"

I didn't have to say anything; he knew the answer to that too. There weren't any Negroes or any people of color there.

"White men prosper, deny they're racist, and brainwash the Black man," he said.

I saw some truth in what he was saying but still felt personally attacked.

"How are they brainwashed?" I asked.

"The white man tricks Black people into thinking integration is good for them."

"You mean it's not good?" I said with more vehemence than I intended.

"It's only good for the white man." he said. "It deceives the Black man. It's like strong, black coffee. If you integrate it with cream it gets weak. And if you put a lot of cream in it, there's no more coffee. It's cool instead of hot, weak instead of strong. It puts you to sleep. That's what integration does to the Black man, it puts him to sleep."

He reached up and pulled a book off the shelf and handed it to me saying,

"Read this"

On the dust jacket was a picture of a fat black man with a mustache in three-quarter profile dressed in a comic opera emperor's jacket and tricorn hat, replete with gold braid and a medal, scowling out of the corner of his eye at the viewer. The book was *Black Moses: The Story of Marcus Garvey and the Universal Negro Improvement Association.*

I thought he was kidding.

The tall man saw me hesitate.

"Read it," he insisted. "You'll learn about Garvey and why the Black man doesn't need integration. He needs his own country."

If it weren't for his dress and even tone, I would have mistaken him for just another New York crazy. I started to argue about the sacrifices young Negroes in the South were making to bring down segregation, but before I could respond Sam and the crew came out of the back room and said it was a wrap. I went to the counter and paid for the book, and as I was leaving I turned to him and said, "Goodbye."

"If you want to know why the Black man needs his own country, read Garvey and come back on Saturday," he said.

That is how I met Malcolm X—and how he jolted me out of my comfortable whiteness.

* * * *

My parents would have been shocked if someone were to call them racist.

They were Roosevelt Democrats, proudly liberal. Yet, black people to them were *schvartzes*. My mother was especially prone to use the word, as in the schvartze did this or the schvartze did that. And, they often thought of Negroes as children. My dad told stories of how they played practical jokes on the Negro porter at the factory to frighten him and how he'd react just like Stepin Fetchit, the Negro character actor in the movies who made his white audiences laugh when he rolled his big eyes and acted scared.

But it was complicated. One day a man rang the bell of our modest house in west LA. I answered; I must have been about twelve. He asked to see my father. When my father came to the door the man, who was holding a clipboard with a petition on it, introduced himself to my father, said he lived around the corner on Westbourne Drive, and that he had been going door to door talking with all our neighbors. My father just looked at him, so the guy continued, "We've got a fine neighborhood here, and I don't want anything to happen to it," he said. "And I'm sure you don't either."

"What do you mean?" my father asked. I could hear the suspicion in his voice.

"A Mexican family has been looking at homes in the neighborhood,"

"So?" my father said.

"Well, if they should buy, do you know what would happen to our property values? They would plummet," he paused for emphasis, "and soon there'd be more Mexicans and then Negroes…and our property values would plummet even more. So I've gotten up a petition to keep these people out. I hope you'll join us by signing it."

My father, who had a temper, started to lose it.

"No! I'm not going to sign it!" he barked. "Those people have as much right to live here as you and I." And he all but slammed the door in the man's face and called to my mother.

"Libbie, do you know what that son-of-a-bitch wanted me to do?" I was so proud of him. Even though I didn't entirely understand it, I knew he had done something very right.

* * * *

After meeting Malcolm, I began hanging out in Harlem on Saturday afternoons—standing, along with dozens of others, all black except for me, listening to Malcolm and other Black Nationalist soap box orators (actually, they stood on ladders) outside of Michaux's bookstore, dubbed "Harlem Square." Malcolm was a fiery orator, and when he spoke he invoked the name of "the honorable Elijah Muhammad," the founder and leader of the Nation of Islam. Muhammad called white men "blue-eyed devils," and said that black people were blessed by God. He preached Black pride and the separation of the races. Muhammad may have been the Nation of Islam's leader, but Malcolm was the public face and chief spokesman for the movement.

Before I began listening to Malcolm the only knowledge I had of the Nation of Islam was through the polite young Negroes in black suits, white shirts, black bow ties and hats who handed out free copies of *Muhammed Speaks*, the Nation's newspaper, in Times Square. I barely glanced at the paper before dumping it in the nearest trash can. Listening to Malcolm speak I was embarrassed that I'd had so little curiosity

* * * *

Along with my friend, Irv, a writer at CBS News, I began interviewing other Black Nationalists, with the idea of writing about this new Black nationalism for *The Reporter* magazine. I interviewed James Lawson, head of the United African Nationalist Movement, who had led the protests around Lumumba's death at the U.N., and Carlos Cooks, head of the African Nationalist Pioneer Movement. Like Malcolm, they were Garveyites. Garvey had preached Black pride and separation of the races and led a Back to Africa Movement. Neither Lawson nor Cooks had large followings, but along with Malcolm they were the pillars upon which the Black Power movement of the '60s was to be built.

These were interesting men. Cooks was the first to clearly delineate Black from Negro and sought to abrogate Negro as a form of racial identity. He was the first to say, "Buy Black" and start a Harlem coop. It was Cooks who initiated the concept of natural hair as a source of Black pride by holding a Miss Natural Standard of Beauty Contest, and he supported various African Liberation movements.

Even if I didn't agree with their separatist notions (and sometimes thought they were full of it), I began to recognize certain things about America I'd not seen before. I began to see America as two separate countries: one white, the other black and brown; one prosperous, the other poor. I slowly began to see the pervasiveness of what today is called structural racism—how housing patterns affect health care and education; how access to jobs and services, like banks, grocery stores, cleaners—services I'd always taken for granted—impact the life of a community. They helped me become more aware of my environment, often in small ways. For example, when I got on the subway at 96th or 110th Street to go downtown to work, the cars were usually filled with black women. As we headed south those women got off to go to their jobs as nannies and maids in white people's apartments and their place was taken by white people on their way downtown to their office jobs. Malcolm had said that if you go to almost any ghetto in America you will find that the major stores are owned by whites. When I began looking along 125th Street I realized what he said was true. I also saw that those white-owned stores hired very few Negro salespeople. I also saw that except for 125th Street, there were almost no other amenities in Harlem like cleaners, shoe-repair shops or supermarkets that were in every other neighborhood in the city. I learned that Blacks in Harlem had to pay deposits to get telephones, and how store prices went up the first of every month when the welfare checks came out. For the first time in my life, I was becoming aware of the notion of white privilege, even though we didn't call it that, and started to pay attention to the history of racism in the country, racism that went back to before the revolution and was built into the Constitution.

**Part II: "The most dangerous creation of any society is the man who has nothing to lose." – James Baldwin**

I returned from Canada in the spring of '64 after making two films for the CBC (Canadian Broadcasting Corporation) with money to complete *The Streets of Greenwood*. Fred and I began cutting the film and I started looking for freelance work to pay the bills. I found it in May when a series of articles ripped like machine gun bullets across the pages of *The New York Times,* scaring many white New Yorkers already apprehensive about the rise of Black Nationalism and an increasingly militant, though nonviolent, Civil Rights Movement. The first article appeared on May 3,

1964 with this three-column headline:

> **WHITES ARE TARGET OF HARLEM GANG**
>
> A gang of about 60 young Negroes who call themselves, 'Blood Brothers' is roaming the streets of Harlem with the avowed intention of attacking white people. They are trained to maim and kill....

All the articles in the series were written by Junius Griffin, a former AP reporter hired by the *Times* to cover Harlem. Each article added more and more ominous details: the police suspected the Blood Brothers of murdering four white people; a researcher at Harlem Youth Opportunity Center (HARYOU), a government funded service organization, had taped hundreds of Harlem youth who had confirmed the existence of the Blood Brothers; the youth were trained in karate and other martial arts (a front page photo showed an alleged gang member practicing a karate chop to his teacher's Adam's apple); a police informer claimed that gang members who killed or maimed a white person got to use the letter X as their surname; the people who were indoctrinating the youth were dissident Black Muslims; and the gang could have as many as 400 members.

The NAACP and The Congress on Racial Equality (CORE) denied the existence of the Blood Brothers and challenged the State to find evidence that the gang existed. Unlike the front-page articles that claimed the existence of the gang, these stories were buried inside the paper.

Dr. Kenneth Clark, the noted educator, sociologist and Director of HARYOU, also challenged the veracity of the *Times* reports: "There is no specific evidence in the HARYOU files which supports the contention of the existence of an organized anti-white gang in the community and no such statement was made by a HARYOU staff member."

Despite the denials, a *Times* editorial began, "The existence of a Harlem gang indoctrinated in hatred of all white persons is chilling news. It is as indefensible as the Ku Klux Klan. It must be firmly repressed by the police. It should be extirpated, once and for all, by the aroused sentiment of the better elements of the Harlem community."

I wasn't surprised by the over-the-top editorial or the paternalistic tone in the phrase, "better elements of the Harlem community." Just weeks before a *Times* editorial had denounced civil rights activists' plans to draw attention to poverty in Harlem by picketing and blocking traffic to the opening day of the billion-dollar New York's World's Fair. *The*

*Times* warned that these actions would risk the Civil Rights Movement, alienating its "friends." Apparently it was okay to hold sit-ins, throw up pickets and stage boycotts in Charlotte, Memphis and Atlanta, but not in New York City.

Police Commissioner Michael J. Murphy, who believed force could solve everything (his stated police philosophy: "the substitution of a show of force for the actual use of force") reacted to the news of the Blood Brothers by sending forty Negro undercover detectives and assigning a Tactical Force Patrol to Harlem. Malcolm X cautioned the Police Commissioner that the additional forces and ongoing police brutality made Harlem a "powder keg" about to blow.

Murphy, acting defensively, tried to reassure an anxious public that there would be no explosion when the summer heat hit the city. The police continued to try to link Malcolm to the Blood Brothers.

Even if the gang existed, I was sure Malcolm had nothing to do with it. He preached self-defense, not murder. But I could also see how Malcolm's preaching could fuel kids who had nowhere to go and no jobs into violent action.

I called Doug Leiterman, my former boss at the CBC, who was producing a new television magazine show called "This Hour Has Seven Days," and offered to find the gang and produce a piece on them. He agreed to pay for research and production.

The first thing I did was move out of my apartment on West 96th Street and into the Hotel Theresa located in the heart of Harlem at Seventh Avenue and 125th Street. It was catty corner from Louis Michaux's bookstore, where I'd first met Malcolm three years earlier. The hotel was a vibrant hub of Harlem's black life. Many black entertainers and celebrities like Lena Horne, Muhammad Ali, Jimi Hendrix, Louis Armstrong, Duke Ellingon, Ray Charles and Sugar Ray Robinson stayed in the hotel or lived there for a while. And Fidel Castro stayed there while in New York for the 1960 opening session of the U.N. The hotel benefited greatly from major hotels downtown refusing to accept black people.

My first morning there, I entered the hotel's coffee shop and saw Malcolm dressed in his signature dark suit, white shirt and dark tie seated alone having breakfast. He had recently split from the Nation of Islam and opened his competing Organization of African Unity with headquarters in the hotel. He asked me to join him, clearly curious to know why I was in Harlem. When I told him I was trying to find the Blood Brothers, he said there was no such gang and even if there was, he had nothing to do with it.

"We don't preach violence," he said. "But we believe if a four-legged or two-legged dog attacks a Negro, the dog should be killed."

"But what about the article in the *Times*?"

"The Blood Brothers don't exist," he repeated, then added, "but that doesn't mean they shouldn't."

"But the writer of the articles is a Negro. Do you think he lied?"

"Being a Negro doesn't mean he can't be a fool. Or that his white editors won't believe him because that's what THEY believe about Negroes."

"I'm confused. You say 'the Blood Brothers don't exist, but that doesn't mean they shouldn't,'" I said. "I thought you only believed in violence to defend yourself."

"Consider police brutality," he said, shifting in his chair. "Blacks exist in a police state. We're routinely stopped, searched, beaten, and sometimes killed. That makes us brothers— blood brothers." He paused. Then rushed on. "Oppression make us blood brothers; exploitation makes us blood brothers; degradation makes us blood brothers; discrimination makes us blood brothers; segregation makes us blood brothers; humiliation makes us blood brothers—we're all blood brothers. And we have to do what's necessary to defend ourselves."

When I hit the streets after breakfast, the first thing I noticed were the number of cops. They were everywhere, sometimes three and four on a corner. Harlem was an occupied territory, occupied by overwhelmingly white policemen. And milling around the crowded streets were idle men standing on street corners and crowds of teenage kids with nothing to do and nowhere to go.

Harlem was one of the most densely populated areas of the country: 232,000 people, 94 percent of them black, were jammed into a 3.5 square mile wedge of Upper Manhattan. In the past two years numerous rent strikes had been called to publicize some of the worst housing conditions in America. Slumlords, many absentee and predominantly white, charged high rents for rat infested tenements with no electricity or hot water, no super to clean and collect the garbage. The rats and the slum lords got the white press's attention, and Mayor Robert F. Wagner called for a million-dollar campaign against rats. What they didn't deal with was the racism, both private and public, that caused the crisis.

The *New York Amsterdam News,* the leading black newspaper in the city, highlighted the real story: white landlords refused to rent to blacks in other parts of the city, and there weren't enough government-sponsored, low-income housing units in New York. And those that existed discriminated against the fast growing nonwhite population. Government-funded housing policies of the 50s and the open-housing movement of the 60s favored returning G.I.'s and upwardly mobile white immigrant groups.

At the same time, slum clearance projects spared unlivable, dangerous structures in white ethnic neighborhoods but tore down those same buildings in black neighborhoods. They were replaced with middle-income housing and luxury apartments. And black residents were forced into dangerous, unlivable tenements in the increasingly crowded Harlem.

It was no wonder that by the time a Harlem child reached the sixth grade, he was nearly two years behind a white child who lived downtown; that the school dropout rate was 55 percent and that unemployment among Negro teenagers lacking access to jobs was 40 percent.

Crime was higher in Harlem than the rest of the city. Yet people complained that the police were less intent on protecting the citizens of Harlem than in hassling them, and that the police committed acts of brutality with impunity. I began to understand what Malcolm meant when he said if there were no Blood Brothers perhaps there ought to be. But I still had to find them.

After spending a frustrating week running down dead leads as to the Brothers whereabouts I decided to move back home. I needed to find a guide, someone who knew his way around Harlem and the gang scene. A friend put me in touch with a social worker named Piri Thomas. Piri had been a gang member and ex-con, who was now straight and was helping rehabilitate gang members in Harlem. I called Piri and set up a meeting. I liked him as soon as I met him. He was a round-faced man of Puerto Rican and Cuban descent. He had a big smile and wore horn-rimmed glasses. He had an owly look about him. He was excited about working with me to find the Blood Brothers and assured me he knew his way around Black and Spanish Harlem.

A few days later we drove up to 114th Street in Harlem and parked in front of an old apartment building in a rundown neighborhood. I grabbed my tape recorder, hopped out and started to lock the car.

"Don't bother, man," Piri said. "If they want your car, they'll break the window. Just take everything out of the glove compartment."

The building was dilapidated, plaster hung from the ceiling, the walls were streaked with graffiti, the smell of cooking hung heavily in the halls. There was no elevator so we started up a garbage-strewn stairwell. I began to feel uneasy.

"Don't say a word," Piri said as we climbed up the stairs. "I'll do all the talking. And don't turn on the tape recorder unless I tell you."

I started to protest.

"I'm serious, man," Piri repeated, stopping me on the stairs. "Don't talk unless I tell you to."

Now I was really getting nervous, but I nodded okay.

When we got to the 4th floor, Piri knocked on a door. It was cracked open by a young guy who peered out at us without saying a word. Piri said something in Spanish. After a short discussion, the kid closed the door and Piri and I headed back up the stairs to the roof, where we interrupted a young guy in the middle of shooting up. He froze, the syringe in one hand, his other arm outstretched, his belt wrapped in a tourniquet just above the elbow with one end held tightly in his teeth. I thought he was going to bolt, but when he recognized Piri, he relaxed, and inserted the needle into his vein and pressed the plunger.

Piri and I stood there watching. When he was finished, he untied the belt and looped it into his pants, rolled down his sleeve and buttoned it. He didn't look much older than sixteen. He was short and so swathed in baby fat it was difficult to tell his age. It was an unusually chilly summer day but the boy stood calmly in his shirtsleeves and asked Piri who I was and what I wanted. When Piri said we were doing a story about the Blood Brothers he just shrugged and said, "Let's go downstairs."

There were six or seven kids, maybe fifteen or sixteen years old, hanging out in the apartment below. They were smoking weed, sipping cokes and talking quietly when we walked in. There was a beat-up couch, a coffee table, a few chairs scattered about the room. On the walls were pictures of Kennedy and Jesus, dirty curtains on the windows and paint peeling off the ceiling. Nobody said a word. They just stared at us. Piri motioned me towards the couch. I unzipped my jacket, placed the tape recorder on the coffee table and sat down. The kid from the roof pointed Piri toward the kitchen door and proceeded to nod off in a chair. Piri went into the kitchen, where I could hear a number of voices speaking Spanish. As I watched them in this sad room, afraid to speak to them, I felt as if I were in another country.

Suddenly Piri came out of the kitchen,

"Let's go," he said, heading toward the door.

I got up, grabbed the tape recorder and followed him out the door and into the hallway. He was halfway down the stairs when I caught up with him.

"What's going on?" I asked.

"There's a guy in there who says he wants to kill you."

"You serious? What for?"

"How the fuck do I know, man? He just doesn't like your looks"

"What about the Blood Brothers," I asked.

"They've never heard of them."

I didn't know whether to trust Piri, but I wasn't going back into that room to find out.

A few weeks later, just as Malcolm predicted, the city exploded. A group of Negro summer students from Robert F. Wagner Junior High School on East 76th Street were playing in front of an apartment building on Manhattan's posh upper east side. It was a hot July night and when the building custodian turned a hose on them, the boys began throwing garbage can covers and bottles at him. Thomas Gilligan, an off-duty police lieutenant in plain clothes, heard the ruckus and came running. Witnesses thought some words were exchanged between Gilligan and one of the boys, James Powell, but they weren't sure. Powell charged Gilligan who pulled out his revolver and fired at him three times; the last shot went wild, but the first two killed him. In his defense, Gilligan maintained Powell had a knife.

Two days later there were demonstrations in Harlem outside of New York's 28th Police Precinct. The angry crowd demanded that Gilligan be dismissed and that Police Commissioner Murphy and Mayor Wagner resign. There were screams of police brutality and demands that Powell's killer be prosecuted. Suddenly the Tactical Patrol Force guarding the precinct charged the demonstrators and despite all the police in Harlem (or because of them) or maybe because people were just tired of being sick and tired, riots broke out. They spread quickly from Harlem to the Bedford-Stuyvesant section of Brooklyn. It took Police Commissioner Murphy five days with a force of six thousand cops to put down the uprising. Stores were looted and burned, cars set on fire, people were beaten and an estimated five hundred were injured. One man died and 465 men and women were arrested. Property damage was estimated between $500,000 and $1 million.

Just as much of the southern press blamed the civil rights demonstrations on "outside agitators," *Time Magazine* and many in the mainstream media blamed the riots on "hate preaching demagogues," "raunchy radicals" and "veteran activists." It was easier for lazy journalists and editors to blame "outsiders" and "militants" than to be shaken out of their comfort zone and investigate and report on the poverty and racism that existed in their own backyard. That included the press's own complicity in helping create the conditions that led to the uprising.

Of the many complicated reasons for the riots, one most certainly was the *Times*' inflammatory articles and editorials on the Blood Brothers that resulted in heightened police activity in Harlem.

When the dust finally settled and we felt it was safe to go back to Harlem, Piri had me cruise the projects until he spotted a kid in his teens who was sitting alone on a bench. Piri went over to the boy, who recognized him and gave him a big hug. They chatted for a minute, then came over to the car. Piri opened the passenger door and slid into the back seat. The kid looked at me, nodded hello, got in and closed the door.

Without bothering to introduce us, Piri said, "Lets go."

I turned to the kid and stuck out my hand. He gave me a limp handshake, and turned away.

"Let's go," Piri said again, impatiently.

As I turned on the ignition, I asked, "Where to?"

"Downtown."

We headed down Broadway and Piri asked the kid if he was hungry.

He grunted "yes."

"Let's find a chink," Piri ordered.

I drove to the Harbin Inn, a Chinese restaurant I knew on 95th and Broadway. As the kid started to get out of the car, Piri stopped him with a hand on his shoulder.

"You better unpack," he said quietly.

Without saying a word, the kid reached under his shirt and pulled out a large knife and stuck it under the car seat.

I tried to act cool, as if this happened every day.

As we settled into a booth, Piri and the kid on one side, me on the other, I had a chance to take a real look at the boy. He was skinny, with a shock of dark hair, mahogany colored skin and dark brown eyes set in a baby face.

I sat quietly as Piri tried to warm things up by asking him about former gang members.

"How's your brother, Angel?"

"He's in jail."

"Robert?"

"Dead. He was shot."

"Samuel?"

"Shot dead, man"

"Corey?"

"Him, too"

"And Mical?

"In jail. They're almost all dead or in jail. There're a couple of guys around but the only one I see regularly is Tomas."

As if he hadn't heard, Piri pressed on.

"Yeh, man, but what about Gregory?"

"He's dead, man."

"And Kinky Sam?"

"Dead, too. I told you."

Of fifteen gang members, only three were alive or not in prison.

I had seen violence, and been threatened in Mississippi the year before. Mississippi was a violent society, a police state, where beatings and murder of black people were commonplace. Even as we were sitting there eating Chinese food on Manhattan's Upper West Side, divers were searching for the bodies of three civil rights workers—James Chaney, Michael Schwerner and Andrew Goodman, who had been missing since June 21st. While they were searching they discovered the bodies of seven other murdered black men whose disappearance hadn't been noted outside of their own community. And, when the bodies of the three young civil rights workers were finally found buried in an earthen dam, it was discovered that all three had been shot, but Chaney, the only black man among them, had also been horrendously beaten before he was shot. But THAT was Mississippi, THAT was the South, and even though I'd been there the year before and was cutting a film about the experience, it all felt light years removed from me and my life.

But this kid's nightmare existence was only thirty blocks north from where I lived. The people we were talking about were just a little younger than I was and his roll call of the dead and interned was one of the most chilling things I'd ever heard. Looking at the boy sitting across from me, I wondered, what was his future? What were the odds that he and his friends wouldn't end up dead or in prison too?

As we ate, Piri questioned the boy closely about the Blood Brothers. He said he didn't know anything. I then spent another couple of weeks with Piri working the phones, visiting the projects and interviewing people in Harlem, but never found a trace of the gang. Nor did anyone else. From start to finish the story had been a hoax.

Six months later, Griffin resigned from *The Times*, his career as a journalist over. Over time I came to believe that he'd been duped by the police or had made a lot of the story up (or both). I also came to believe that the *Times* editors accepted his story without question because the Blood Brothers fit their stereotype of the urban Negro.

I had wasted many weeks chasing the Blood Brothers story but I had gained real insights into urban America and learned an important journalistic ethic: When the press fails to portray marginalized communities in all their diversity and humanity, those communities become even more marginalized. And when the press projects its own racism and fears onto them, the consequences can be deadly.

Despite the lack of evidence that the Blood Brothers ever existed and the likelihood that Griffin may well have made it all up, *The Times* never admitted it had made a mistake. ▪

# White Coat

Tonight I take on the identity of Physician.

BY JENNIFER HASENYAGER SMITH *(Issue 27)*

ONE HUNDRED AND FOURTEEN brand-new medical students milled expectantly, many with their families, in a large university hall that reminded me of a hotel ballroom.

*Tonight I take on the identity of Physician.* The familiar chattering voice in my head was unusually somber that night. *Physician. Doctor. Really?*

The cavernous ceiling, ornately trimmed with dark wood moldings, arched over worn wooden floors and plaster walls hung with historic university photos. *This is my medical school.* The students were dressed up for the occasion in slacks and skirts. *These people are my classmates.* I scanned the college-kid faces, trying to see the doctors they would become.

It was our first week of medical school, and the entire freshman class of the University of Chicago Pritzker School of Medicine was gathered for the White Coat Ceremony in a drafty old stone building. I knew I was about to symbolically embark upon a life-changing journey, but

I felt like a college student at just one more university function. *Tonight I take on the identity of Physician.* It was surreal.

"Hi, Jennifer!" The classmate I'd sat with during that morning's orientation lecture waved and bounded over to me. She wore a grey skirt suit and had her hair pinned into a serious-looking bun at the back of her head. Her wide eyes and huge grin betrayed her little-girl excitement despite her effort to look professional. She was an honors graduate from one of the Ivy-League schools… Brown? Dartmouth? Her alma mater—and her name—evaporated from my memory.

"Hi…" I smiled back at her. *Oh God, what's your name?*

"So, what do you think will happen tonight?" Miss Ivy League half-whispered.

"I don't know. Seems like an initiation of sorts." *Name…? Ugh, does it start with a P?*

"A rite of passage—yeah, that makes sense," her grin faded reverently.

"Looks like we're really going to be doctors someday," I said, trying to sound reverent, too.

*Peggy? Patty? Shit!*

"I know. Can you believe it? And we're at Pritzker!" She giggled nervously, returning to her excited grin. "Did you know 6,000 people applied for our class of 114?"

"Wow. I didn't realize that." *6000 applications?? How the hell did I get in here?*

We both glanced around the room, studying our classmates.

There must be some amazing people here. I have no idea how I got in," said my nameless future colleague, giggling again.

I smiled at her, "I was just thinking the same thing." *Do we all feel this way?*

Our shared moment of self-doubt was interrupted by the announcement that the ceremony was about to begin. We made our way to one end of the hall, towards a low plywood stage with five rows of plastic folding chairs for the medical students and participating faculty. I took a seat in the second row near the heavy mahogany lectern adorned with the University seal. *Tonight I take on the identity of Physician.* My internal mantra continued, as if I was trying to convince myself. The fifteen rows of folding chairs facing our stage were now filling up with family and faculty. Single and far away from home, I had no family in the audience. Bathed in the gaze of those beaming strangers' faces, I fleetingly became a small, lost child. The loneliness ached far below my smiling excitement, but I didn't let it show.

The purpose of this ceremony was to formally welcome us medical students into the ranks of physicians. We were to be called up individually and given our white coats (a gift from the school) and a stethoscope (a gift from a medical equipment company). As the white coat slipped onto my shoulders, I would be admitted into an exclusive club of healers who serve at the highest level of knowledge and responsibility. By accepting that coat, I would commit to seeing a long, difficult journey through to its still-murky destination. I also committed to traveling that road with dedication to excellence.

We settled into our seats, and the ceremony began. Speeches about our shining futures and the importance of our chosen path wafted over me. I was pleasantly basking in the glow of my glorious potential when I was abruptly jarred by the Medical School Dean's deeply resonant voice: " … as you fulfill your calling…" *My calling???* I knew that I was interested in science and that I had a desire to work with people rather than alone in a lab. To me, medicine seemed like a good fit for my strengths and preferences in a career. It made a lot of sense to me. But was it a calling? Probably not. Was that required? I hoped not. I hoped that it would be enough for me to want to use my talents in the service of fellow human beings.

*Dad was disappointed in my choice. Maybe I shouldn't be here.* My thoughts drifted back to that painful phone call two years earlier. Until my junior year of college, I had been planning to get a PhD in genetics. My father, a brilliant man who had not had the opportunity to go to graduate school, was very enthusiastic about my PhD plan. It appealed to his sense of intellectual hierarchy—the PhD is the most advanced degree, and that seemed like just the right level of accomplishment for me, his highly accomplished oldest daughter. He loved the idea that I would be "Dr. Hasenyager," the first person in our family to earn a PhD.

As I dialed nervously, ready to tell him my news, I knew he would be surprised by my change in career plans. What I didn't expect, however, was the lasting impact of his words:

"Hi, Daddy,"

"Hello! How's my girl?"

"I'm good. I have some news for you,"

"OK. What's your news?"

"I've decided to go to medical school instead of getting a PhD. I learned a lot working in the lab this summer, but it was really lonely and isolating. I want to work with people. Medicine combines science and people."

Dad was briefly silent, and then I heard his controlled inhale as he prepared to speak. "You know, Jennifer, medicine isn't really science." He was matter-of-fact, almost chatty.

His casual disapproval sucked the breath out of my body and scattered my carefully constructed pyramid of logic like a house of cards. Medicine isn't science? It isn't good enough for him? Stunned, I somehow gathered my words back together and mumbled, "MDs can do research just like PhDs, Dad." I then lamely tacked on, "I'll still be Dr. Hasenyager." The tense conversation didn't last much longer, and my Dad never repeated his initial disapproving remark about medicine. Despite his rapid shift to supporting me, his early and honest reaction sowed the seeds of doubt that were in full bloom as my attention returned to the White Coat Ceremony.

*Do I belong here?*

I shifted in my wobbly chair, listening to the slow reading of our 114 names. I watched classmates summoned in turn to receive their white coat. Returning to their seats, some of them were shining with pride. Some of them were scared to death. Many looked as if they didn't quite inhabit their coats. A few seemed completely comfortable. One classmate was oddly blank—as if he were numb.

Lulled by the monotonous ceremony, I drifted into another memory from just a few months before: I was trying to read my smutty historic novel, passing the time on a flight back from Chicago to New York during the spring of my senior year of college. I'd been visiting the University of Chicago campus as an accepted medical student and was returning to Cornell to finish the last few weeks of classes. During my visit in Chicago, I had struggled to imagine myself walking the halls of the hospital dressed in scrubs and a white coat, on my way to take care of a patient. Until that visit, I'd been focused solely on getting into medical school. Now I was contending with the reality that I was about to become a physician. I read the same paragraph in my book several times over, unable to concentrate on the heroine's imminent deflowering—consumed instead with the mystery of my life as a doctor.

DING DING DING DING. I looked up from my book and saw, twenty rows ahead of me, a person's hand reaching up to the flight-attendant call button, pushing it over and over again. I'd never seen that before. I certainly never pushed that button. I'd always put flight-attendant call buttons in the same "emergency only" category as fire alarms and red STOP buttons in elevators. And I definitely would never consider pressing it repeatedly.

DING DING DING DING. *Wow, this person's persistent. They must really want another Coke.*

I tried to go back to my reading.

"May I have your attention, please. Is there a doctor on the plane?" The flight attendant's voice was clipped and tense. "If so, please ring your call button and identify yourself."

My head snapped back up. I looked to the front of the plane, where the call button had been ringing. There were two flight attendants standing in the aisle, lifting an unconscious passenger out of his seat and to the floor. I couldn't see much else from where I was sitting, but I could tell they were starting CPR.

"We have a medical emergency on the plane." The carefully controlled voice explained, "Please remain in your seats. If there is a doctor on board, please identify yourself."

*Thank God I'm not a doctor yet.*

The stunningly true thought slipped through my thin veneer of pre-med confidence too quickly for me to deny it.

*No one's ringing the button.*

I watched a tall man in a flannel shirt stand up and move forward down the aisle.

*Is he a doctor? He doesn't look like one. What's wrong with that guy? Did he have a stroke? A heart attack?*

No one else seemed to be crying or upset, and so I assumed that this sick passenger was traveling alone—dying alone. I was certain that he was dying.

*Oh my God, next time I hear someone call for a doctor, I'll be on the hook. A life will be in my hands. What the hell am I getting myself into? I don't want this. What if I can't save him? What if I don't know what to do?*

I watched the guy in the flannel shirt take over the chest compressions for the flight attendant. I didn't even know that they were called chest compressions then. I watched flannel shirt guy do CPR while the flight attendants got the cabin ready for landing. I couldn't stop watching.

*Thank God that's not me. What's wrong with me? I should want to help. Oh, thank God that's not me.*

The chattering voice in my head went on incessantly. I was breathing fast, my chest tight and heart pounding up into my throat. I couldn't look away from the increasingly hopeless resuscitation—none of us could. As we landed, we were all instructed to remain in our seats until the ambulance crew arrived. As the poor dead man was rolled off the plane, I wondered how the guy in flannel was doing. He'd just been working on a dead guy for more than an hour.

*That will be me next time. What am I signing up for?*

I'd been deeply ashamed of my panicky reaction on that plane and had never mentioned how I felt to anyone.

I tuned back in to the ceremony, noting that my name would be called soon. *Do I want to do this work for the right reasons? Is it OK that I chose medicine because it seems that I'll enjoy it and be good at it? What about helping others and doing good in the world? Am I altruistic enough? What about my classmates who speak of their lifelong wish to help others? Do they deserve this white coat more than me? Or the classmates who say they're just following in a parent's footsteps? Do I deserve that coat more than them because they don't even seem to want this job?*

The ceremony again required my attention—it was my turn to go forward and assume the mantle of my chosen profession.

As I walked up and received my coat and stethoscope, all of the chatter in my head was quiet. I saw the faces of other people's families looking at me with respect. I felt the slight weight of the coat on my shoulders and the heavier weight of the stethoscope in my hand. I was different with the coat on. Every person in that audience viewed me as a physician in that moment. Every person who saw me wear that white coat from then on would view me as a physician. I began to feel the power of the coat. And I began to feel the responsibility. It didn't feel like college any more.

*I can do this. I deserve to be here. Tonight, I take on the Identity of Physician.*

I straightened my shoulders and, for the first time, I pretended to feel confident in my white coat.

**Gross Anatomy and Grandma Anna**

Gross Anatomy is a rite of passage so universal in medical training it has become a cliché. There is good reason for the course's fame—it is a profoundly altering experience to take apart a human body. Our gross anatomy lab was located on the first floor of one of the biology buildings on the main campus—not in the medical center. It was in one of the old stone buildings, and the huge windows were all painted black so no one could see inside from the nice courtyard lawn on the other side of the wall. We worked in teams of four first-year medical students, and I had a good team. Two women, two men. Two leaders (me and one of the guys) and two followers. No budding surgeon who insisted on doing all of the "work." (I didn't yet know I would become a surgeon.) Two quick-studies and two more sedate in their pace. We all got along very well, which was not true of some of our neighboring teams in the lab.

Each team was assigned a cadaver (a dead body) for the six-month course. The lab was large with very high ceilings, a linoleum floor, and about two dozen waist-high stainless steel tables just large enough to fit one person lying down. On the day we first "met" our cadavers, we all walked into the lab and found our team's assigned table, upon which lay a human body inside a plastic body bag—just like the morgue on TV. With the bodies in the room, we were introduced to the odor of the chemical preservative that was necessary to prevent decomposition. It was the sort of odor that got into your nose, soaked into your hair and clothes, and imprinted itself on your brain forever. We all kept a set of scrubs in lockers at the lab building. The scrubs were necessary not so much because what we were doing was so messy, but because we didn't want that smell on our clothes and in our homes.

On the first day of anatomy lab, our main task was to unzip the bag and look. We were also given the information cards that come along with each cadaver. On the card is recorded the age, gender, and cause of death. That's it. No name. No story. Our cadaver was a man in his 70s who died from sepsis. I had never heard of sepsis, but I learned very soon that sepsis means overwhelming infection in the blood—usually from bacteria.

When we unzipped our bag, we saw that our cadaver's head was wrapped in large pieces of cloth, as were his hands. The rest of him was naked—no hospital gowns needed in anatomy lab. Near the end of the first lab period, we were instructed to unwrap our cadaver's head. He had a full beard, a bald head, and a sharp, prominent nose that was flanked by bushy eyebrows and deep-set blue eyes. His expression was peaceful. And his brain was missing—standard procedure for cadaver preparation, apparently.

Before that day, I'd wondered if I might be upset seeing a dead person for the first time. Surprisingly, I felt pretty good—curious and calm with just a touch of queasy nerves. In retrospect, I realize that I was soothed through that first exposure to human death in part by the church-like reverence of the old lab space. I unknowingly sensed my place in the solemn dignity of that room's past, present, and future. As I left the lab, I wondered if I might be upset cutting our cadaver for the first time. I soon learned that the first incision is easy.

The day we began our first dissection, we were instructed to turn over our cadavers so their backs were facing the ceiling. Each team was then given a copy of the dissection manual that would lead us through every step we were to take for each class. The manuals were dog-eared, spiral-bound books that had seen many years of use, and they were indelibly infused with the anatomy lab smell. No way those books would ever be brought home for studying.

The very first dissection was of the muscles of the upper back and shoulders. Someone on each team needed to be the first one to pick up a scalpel and make an incision as illustrated in our manuals. To be honest, I can't remember who on our team made the first incision—I don't think it was me, though. I do know that I took part in that first dissection and that I was so fascinated by the truly extraordinary structure of the human body—even back muscles and nerves—that I lost awareness of the fact that this had very recently been a living, breathing human being. At the end of that first lab session, the four of us on the lab team had bonded together in an act of extraordinary intimacy and privilege, and we knew it. I felt energized by the intense experience and glad for the support of my team. I was aware that I had crossed a boundary into the taboo territory of death and mutilation; I was transformed rather than disturbed.

A few weeks into the course, my great-grandmother died. Her name was Anna and she was the first relative to die in my family since I was six. Grandma Anna was my mother's mother's mother, and she was the last of the immigrant generation of my family. She had been born in Lithuania and had come to America in 1900. She was 105 when she died, and she had remained lucid throughout her long life. She lived in the Chicago area along with my great aunt, so the funeral was held locally. I was able to attend the funeral without traveling, and therefore only missed one day of school: the day of the funeral itself. This was the first funeral I had ever attended, and it was an open-casket service. I had known Grandma Anna throughout my life and had visited her at least every other year. She had always been very old in my memory—she was in her 80s when I was born—and I had had few meaningful conversations with her, maybe none. But my mother had grown up with her as a member of the household, and I had come to know her through the stories my mother told.

As the service began, I sat with my family in the front row. This was the first time I had seen the casket, any casket, and I couldn't look away. From where I sat, I couldn't quite see into the casket far enough to see Anna. I could just see part of her pink suit—I recognized the suit from one of her recent birthday parties. Once she hit 100, the family made a point of having a birthday party with everyone there each year. Sitting at the service, I remembered saying goodbye to her each year as if that would be the last time. I remembered her thick Yiddish accent and how she was embarrassed of her snarled teeth, so she would try not to smile with her mouth even as she smiled with her eyes. I remembered her hands. She had been a seamstress and hatmaker. She'd made all of my mother's childhood clothes. I had a pile of dolls' clothes that Anna had made from the scraps of material used for the family's clothes. I wondered what her hands looked like in the casket, but I couldn't quite see.

As the service ended, our front row of family filed past the casket first. I looked at Grandma Anna's closed eyes and uncharacteristically peaceful expression.

*Her face is the wrong color.*

Fleetingly disoriented, I scanned the rest of her form. Her hands were folded across her stomach quietly. That was wrong, too. Her hands were always busy—plucking at lint, rearranging a knickknack, offering a candy. I knew that her hands couldn't move any more, but their stillness disturbed me.

*I wonder what our cadaver looked like alive. How he moved.*

I watched my mother and grandmother cry, and I felt so sad for them. But no tears came for me.

When I returned to anatomy lab the next afternoon, I was glad to be back with my friends and ready to catch up on what I'd missed the day before. We were working on the front side of our cadaver that day, and his face was uncovered. As I got to work on the next dissection, I found my thoughts drifting relentlessly back to Grandma Anna's face in the casket the day before. I felt my heart rate speed up and my breathing get shallower. My hands started shaking just a little. I couldn't keep from seeing Anna's face on our cadaver as I worked.

*Just hold on and keep going—this is only a reaction to the funeral. Keep it together. You can't miss any more lab time. Keep going.*

I then realized I was no longer moving, I was just standing there and staring at the cadaver—frozen. My team stood there looking at me questioningly.

*I have to make this stop. I have to get out of here.*

I put down my instruments and told them I needed some air. I walked out of the lab building to the courtyard outside, my head filled with images of Anna and the cadaver, all blended together. I was crying and shaking and pacing around near the door of the building in my stinky anatomy scrubs. I wanted to run away. I wanted to go back in. I was furious with myself for having this meltdown now.

*Why couldn't I cry at the funeral like a normal person? This is humiliating and interfering with my education. Get a grip, Jennifer. You're wasting time out here.*

As I berated myself in the chilly stone courtyard, my anatomy team showed up, all three of them, in their stinky scrubs. They simply came to me and put their arms around me. Someone said, "Your grandma?" And I nodded. We huddled there silently together; my team's support and understanding warmed me as much as their bodies did. After a minute or so, I realized that I was keeping us all from our work in the lab. I took a deep breath, broke free of the group, and said, "Let's go back inside. I'm better now." Following my smelly teammates back inside, I squeezed the choking sadness from my throat down into my chest, willing it to stay out of my way. I didn't have any more time for crying—I had anatomy lab. That invisible act of will was Disconnection 101, the first of many lessons in how to detach from my emotions in order to function as a physician.

**First Patient Interview**

Another of our first-year courses was called Introduction to Clinical Medicine. In contrast to the ancient tradition of gross anatomy in medical training, this class was quite progressive for its time. Rather than waiting until the third year, our medical school integrated clinical training from the start of the first year. We were taught how to take a medical history and conduct a patient interview in a professional, medical manner. One of our early assignments was to go into the hospital and interview an inpatient (who had agreed ahead of time to participate). I was in my third week of medical school on the day of my first patient interview.

Since the majority of our classes were not held in the medical center, I had not yet been to the inpatient wards of the hospital. I set out from the medical student lounge, which was located in the basement of the building adjacent to the hospital. (Our lounge was right next to the morgue—to give a sense of our relative position in the medical universe.) On that day, I had worn a skirt and blouse rather than my customary jeans and sweatshirt. Before I headed toward the hospital, I pulled my white coat out of my locker, where it had hung since the White Coat Ceremony a few weeks earlier. I nervously put it on and looked at the young doctor in the mirror.

*Wow, I look a lot more confident than I feel.*

As I walked down the long corridor toward the hospital, I passed the dozens of framed medical school class portraits that lined the walls. I looked at hundreds of faces of past graduates—now all physicians. They all looked so competent and smart and… solid. It was hard to imagine any of them feeling as unsure and lost and scared as I did at that moment.

*My picture will be on this wall in four years. How?*

I kept walking at a brisk pace with my head up and my face composed. I carried—or rather, clutched with a death-grip—the leather folder I'd just been given as a college graduation present.

*Who gave this folder to me?*

Inside the folder, which my sweaty hand was probably staining, were the notes with my patient history questions.

As I neared the hospital building, I began to pass more medical people and fewer administrative people. I saw an increasing number of physicians walking past in their white coats. I kept glancing down at myself, wondering if my hospital ID was properly displayed and whether my white coat looked right.

*Buttoned or unbuttoned?*

I reached up to button my open coat.

*No! Don't fuss with the coat now—you'll look even more clueless.*

My hand dropped back to my side. I kept walking, staring straight ahead, heart pounding.

*Oh God, they're all looking at me and they all know I have no idea where I'm going or what I'm doing.*

The paranoia took hold. I expected one of the hospital staff to stop me and question my presence there. It was only moments before someone would figure out I was an imposter—disguised in a white coat.

As I approached the nurse's station near my patient's room, I saw a handful of nurses and doctors sitting and standing around the counter. I needed to check the "white board" at the nurses' station to confirm the room number. A couple of people glanced at me as I arrived at the counter to look at the board. One of the nurses who sat behind the counter seemed annoyed to see me, but she seemed annoyed by everyone else, too.

*OK, I'll keep away from that one.*

Mostly, they all ignored me and went about their work of making notes in patient charts and talking on the phones. The group exuded a general air of weariness, but a few of the faces were cheerful and I could make out at least one friendly conversation. I tried to figure out which person was going to blow the whistle on me as the unqualified interloper. I nodded and smiled at a few residents in scrubs and white coats, got a look at the white board, and headed off toward my patient's room.

*Nice job, Dr. Hasenyager.... You kept cool, blended in. That was pretty slick.*

My tiny self-satisfied smile evaporated when I realized I had set out in the wrong direction and would need to double back in order to get to my patient's room.

*Shit.*

I started losing my composure, tearing up slightly as I did a U-turn in the hallway and walked as fast as I could past the nurses' station—my eyes fixed straight ahead and my leather folder held defensively across my chest. Those last few seconds before arriving at my patient's room expanded as fear warped my sense of time.

*I don't think I can pull this off—of course I can pull this off. What if the patient is mean? What if she won't talk to me? How do I introduce myself? Dr. Hasenyager? Jennifer? Dr. Jennifer? Student Doctor Hasenyager? What if someone asks me a question... a MEDICAL question? Oh my God, I have no idea what I'm doing.*

I watched my hand knock on the cheap hospital room door.

*Just play the part and hope for the best.*

I walked in, smiled, took a deep breath, and started acting. I don't remember a lot about our interview. I know that I asked the questions I was supposed to ask and that I managed to take notes while simultaneously maintaining the impression I was a confident professional. I remember my patient was a very sweet and chatty woman in her 70s and that her husband was also in the room. They both seemed to believe I was a doctor and knew what I was doing. My patient was scared about losing her independence at home and didn't know if her husband could manage to take care of her. She didn't come out and say those things to me, but I could tell from the way she answered my questions. Her husband had no idea she was worried. I was completely unaware that my knack for picking up unspoken information was both a gift and a vulnerability. Ignoring my instincts, I focused on the data—the black-and-white answers to the questions on my list. I spent about thirty minutes talking to them, firmly shook their hands goodbye, and escaped back into the hallway.

As I walked back toward the student lounge, I reflected on my performance. No one seemed to notice how clueless and scared I was. As long as I played the part and concealed myself, I was passing as a doctor.

*I can fool them all with this white coat on—amazing.*

In that long hallway, I noticed the doctors swung their clipboards and folders loosely by their sides rather than holding them tightly to their chests as a schoolgirl would hold her books. I looked down at my tightly-held folder and let it swing by my side.

**Hands in Anatomy Lab**

As the first year went by, we all settled into the routine of our classes and our new roles as physicians in training. The sharp creases in our new white coats relaxed, and so did we. There were many classes—biochemistry, immunology, histology, physiology—but anatomy remained the symbolic and literal engine of our transformation from college kids to physicians. At about the midpoint of our six-month long gross anatomy course, the time came to dissect our cadaver's hands. Until that time, his hands had remained wrapped in cloth and plastic baggies. Our instructors had explained to us early on that the tissues of the fingers (and toes) were very thin and delicate and would easily deteriorate if they were exposed to air. We were, therefore, asked to leave the hands and feet wrapped in the preservative-soaked cloths until the time came to do the dissection.

On the day of the hand dissection, my lab team gathered around our cadaver and paused. I felt nervous, almost reluctant, to unwrap his hands. I think my three teammates did, too. We didn't talk about being nervous and the pause was brief. Then two of us began to unwrap—one on each side. I clearly remember being one of the unwrappers, though I'm not sure which hand I worked on. As I removed layers of damp cloth, I became increasingly tense.

*I don't like this. How did I end up doing this job?*

I felt a vague dread as the last layers came off and I held his bare hand in mine.

His nails were neatly trimmed. His fingers were long and thin. There were the usual age spots one would expect on a 70-year-old person's hands, but they were otherwise very nice looking hands. I turned his hand back and forth.

*What did he do?*

I saw images of him working at a cheap metal office desk with a gooseneck lamp.

*Accountant at a small company?*

I saw him holding a book in a comfortable chair, reading for pleasure. I saw him holding his wife's hand as he spent his last few days in a hospital. I saw him petting his dog.

*He was kind.*

Even though I had laid my hands on every one of his internal organs, traced his blood vessels and nerves through his body, and discovered that he'd had a hip replacement, until that moment, I hadn't felt connected to him as a living human being. Now, I was connected. My breath caught. I wanted to show my gratitude by acknowledging his…personhood.

*Oh, you dear man. Thank you. Thank you for your gift to me.*

Here was a person whose name and life I would never know, yet I knew all about him. I knew things about him that none of his loved ones could ever know, like the way his heart looked on the inside. I knew him. And at that moment I could not bring myself to destroy his hand. I wondered if he was grumpy when he woke up in the morning until he had his coffee, or if he was an early riser who relished the quiet of the dawn. I wondered if he'd had a good life, filled with love and satisfaction—I hoped so. I wondered why he'd chosen to donate his body for our education. Despite knowing that it was his wish to give his body in this way, I still held his hand, unwilling to deconstruct it.

All of those thoughts and feelings must have flashed by quickly because none of my team members seemed aware I was hesitating to begin the dissection. They were busy reviewing the lab manual and arranging instruments. His other hand had also been unwrapped.

*How can I do this to him?*

I felt deep regret as I set down his hand and tried to focus on the lesson plan. My teammate read from the manual about where the first incision was to be made.

*There is no way I'm making that incision.*

The internal mutiny was gaining momentum, and I tried to reason with myself.

*What's wrong with you? You've been doing anatomy for months now. Hands are just another body part. Get a grip.*

Time was running out—the team was going to notice my squeamishness very soon.

*They won't understand this. Freezing up over a dead grandmother is one thing, but a sudden personal relationship with your cadaver is over the line.*

I was looking down at the lab manual, pretending to study it as I silently scrambled to get control of my powerful aversion. Staring at the hand diagrams on the white page, the images began to blur out, leaving just the whiteness. There was something soothing in that cool, white space. In my desperation to conceal my distress from my teammates, I concentrated intently on the white, and it began to seem that I was entering that white space, becoming surrounded by it. The calming whiteness contained a beautiful silence, as if it insulated me from the paralyzing clamor of my emotional reaction.

*That's better. Stay here.*

I took on the calm of the white room that had formed around me. I kept my eyes on the lab book rather than on his hands until I was sure that the first few incisions had been made by someone else. When I finally looked up from the book, the white room faded from my vision, but its calming effect lingered. My pain at dissecting his hands wasn't gone, but it seemed much farther away. I picked up the instruments and did my share of the work. My stomach hurt a little, but my head was clear and my hands were steady. Most importantly, no one knew that I'd struggled at all that day. ▪

# My Teaching Career

...late in that hot, aimless summer of love....

BY BILL STACK *(Issue 27)*

MY LOTTERY NUMBER WAS 169. It was not low enough to be certain of being drafted but low enough to make it probable. The year was 1969. The number had prevented me from making a serious effort at interviewing for the investment career I planned; no company was going to hire me, train me and then see me off at the station for a two-year leave of absence. All I could do was graduate from Georgetown, go home, and wait it out.

There were lots of rumors, lots of advice, but no one knew anything. Each draft board was different. My family doctor, as he signed a letter describing my lifelong problem with asthma, said that he had seen guys who could play linebacker for the New York Giants be rejected. Others who he would personally give his seat to on a bus were doing search-and-destroy missions in the Mekong Delta. To him the process seemed completely arbitrary.

Sometime late in that hot, aimless summer of love, after the moon shot and the Charles Manson murders, maybe just before Woodstock, a now unidentifiable, disembodied voice told me that teachers were not being drafted directly from classrooms. It probably took place in some sleazy bar or over a smoke-clouded pool table. It checked out to be true. I now had a course of action; I would become a teacher. Hopefully in the next two weeks, as the school year was about to start.

I had already applied for a Reserve Unit, but the waiting list was very long. If I had a good nine months of deferral as a teacher, I had a shot. That was the new backup plan if the letter from my doctor didn't work.

Today, after all the political mud that has been thrown over Dan Quayle's Reserve Unit service, the letter that was written to Bill Clinton's draft board and George W. Bush's performance in the Texas Air National Guard, any attempt made at the time to seek a Reserve Unit status or legally avoid the draft is portrayed as sniveling cowardice. That sentiment would have produced blank stares in that smoke-filled pool hall in the summer of '69, if not outright snarling laughter. There had already been a quarter of a million people on the Washington mall and protests, even riots, on most major U.S. campuses. Vietnam was by then a very unpopular war. A lot of guys got drafted and a lot of guys went, but nobody I knew wanted to go. Nobody.

Back then there was, believe it or not, a teacher shortage. I simply opened the paper to the want ads and answered a few. I could not teach in a public school without certification, so I focused on private and parochial schools. I got some responses, interviewed, and took the first offer. The St. John's Prep/Georgetown University part of my resume produced the expected response from Catholic schools. Let's face it, it was August and they were pretty desperate too. The next thing I knew I was a sixth-grade teacher at St Mary's School in Windsor Locks, which was about ten miles from my home in Manchester, Connecticut.

My salary was a paltry $6,100 a year. I met with the principal who had hired me, a very nice but no-nonsense nun with crystal clear, steel-blue eyes, Sister Cecilia. She gave me the textbooks I was to use and a few lesson plans. There were two sixth-grade classes. I was to teach Math, Social Studies and Science, and an older nun would handle Religion (thank God) and English. I tried to prepare a little, but I pretty much figured I could wing it. I was focused on other things.

A week or so after I accepted the job at St. Mary's I got a call from the principal of a major regional Catholic high school. He was looking for a history teacher and was intrigued by the fact I had taken courses in Asian history. Would I like to teach a number of American history classes and then perhaps one in Asian history for top students? It sounded great and I told him so, but I also said I had signed a contract with St. Mary's and didn't feel I could pull out just a few days before school started. He told me if I wanted to break the contract, I should. He could also offer me more money. This guy was a priest, but I had learned not to be shocked by such things. I had to turn him down, as much as I hated to. I could run tollbooths to save a quarter, but I really couldn't break faith with a very nice person who had put her trust in me.

It's interesting to think that the other job might have been so much fun, I might have considered staying with teaching for a career. My life would have been very different. You just never know.

My first day at St. Mary's I showed up a little early and said hello to the principal and the nun who was the other sixth-grade teacher. She was about fifty and seemed very capable. I then went to my homeroom and waited for my class to show up. I think it was only then it began to dawn on me how completely unprepared I was.

*Sixth grade, hmmm... How old are you in sixth grade?* I was counting it out on my fingers. *Eleven! Eleven? How big is an eleven-year-old?* I looked out the window to the children gathering on the playground. They were all so little. I remembered my own sixth grade as though it had been the previous weekend. *Was I that small when I was in sixth grade?*

I had absolutely no idea what I was doing. I knew nothing. I was seized with panic. *God! I'm responsible for these kids!* I thought of Mrs. Boyle, my sixth grade teacher. She was so good! She had made an enormous difference in my life! My eyes focused on my reflection in the windowpane. I was no Mrs. Boyle.

I believe I became an adult that very moment. I was, for the first time in my life, responsible for someone else. I could be as reckless and irresponsible as I wanted with my own life, but I couldn't be that with these kids. I suddenly realized this was going to be a serious challenge I would have to meet head-on. After suffering through years of boring, incompetent teachers who could not hold my attention, I was not about to do the same damage to these kids. Not if I could help it.

A bell rang. The children began to come in and take seats one at a time. They still looked small. I noticed they seemed to all know exactly which seats to take. The little ones were in the front rows; the tall ones were in the back. Their feet were firmly on the floor, their backs straight; their hands were folded on their desks. These kids were very well trained. They didn't make a peep, but all stared at me with obvious fear and reverence. I wasn't accustomed to being looked at like that. I eyed them coolly.

Another bell rang and I stood to speak to them. This was as close to an out-of-body experience as I have ever had in my life. I was watching this thin fellow of twenty-two years with his new, tailored sports coat and tie, his neatly creased bell-bottom slacks and leather boots, his wavy hair, sideburns and dark-rimmed glasses. He was addressing his class. He was confident, measured, responsible and articulate. He was saying just the right things for the beginning of the school year. He was doing an excellent job. Who the hell was he? Where was he getting all this stuff? He certainly didn't sound like me.

Then another bell rang and the class stood up and filed to the door, one row at a time. They stood there, girls on one side, boys on the other. The two at the front looked around at me, waiting for my permission. For what? To go where? I had no idea what they were doing. I was still standing there, finger raised to punctuate an extremely important point to a class of empty desks, my head now turned to the two rows of eyes at the door awaiting my command. I assumed there was an assembly somewhere—I actually hadn't even looked around the place to discover where—so I lowered my hands to my side and gave a knowing, authoritative nod. They all turned forward and moved out in silent precision.

As we padded down the hallway I did notice, with some alarm, that there were no other classes joining our procession. Then my little platoon took a sharp left and went out of the building onto the street. There was nobody following! We motored down the street. Not one kid gave so much as a sideward glance while I was frantically looking around to find some clue as to what the hell we were doing! I figured the moment had passed when I could have reasonably asked what was going on. Now I had to simply go along for the ride. But I began to visualize Sister Cecilia, hands folded in front of her, calmly asking me, "They went where? They did what? You just followed them?" Was I going to be thinking of this moment while lying in the muck of a rice paddy, Cong bullets splashing around me?

The dog team came up to the next cross street and took a right. Just as I was swinging around the corner, feeling like the guy holding on to the ladder in the back of a fire truck as it careened into an intersection, I caught sight of some neatly uniformed children marching out of the front door of the school. I exhaled for the first time in five minutes. When I had finally righted my vision long enough to look forward again, I saw it. At the end of this new street, facing us, was a church! It had a tall steeple and its two front doors were opened wide, waiting for us. We were going to church! Of course! We were going to church! How perfectly obvious. How could I have, even for a minute, felt like the Pied Piper, only in reverse, the children leading me to my doom? I quickly composed myself. I was back in control.

We proceeded to the end of the street, mounted the steps and swished down the aisle to the foot of the altar with the smartness of the graduating class on the parade ground at West Point. The troops then pealed off into the pews with the exactitude of a sorting machine, leaving, of course, the spot at the end of the first pew open for me. I, with just the right amount of nonchalant care, inspected that all things were in proper order, and then assumed my place in front with quiet dignity. After a while the church filled up with the rest of the school. I snuck a peek at the congregation. They were all, every one of them, staring at me. I turned and looked forward with regal aplomb.

The priest and two altar boys swept in front of us from the wings of the sacristy so we all stood. The mass had begun. While I was standing there it suddenly occurred to me that, despite years of attending mass, I had never paid the slightest attention to when, in the course of the proceedings, one was to stand, sit or kneel. I had always relied on everyone else and simply followed along. Actually I had never been in the front row of a church before. This could be a little awkward. I took another extremely disinterested look behind. They were all still staring at me. I figured my little mechanical sixth-grade soldiers would march me through this one as well.

Well, they didn't. They were looking for my leadership on this one. I heard rustling behind me and sat down. Fine, but the next time I wasn't sure the sound was of standing or kneeling. Whatever it was, I guessed wrong, as the titters all around proclaimed. The rest of this interminably long ceremony was a laugh fest of my sixth grade standing when everyone else was sitting, kneeling when they were standing, some kneeling or standing or sitting all at the same time. Finally I threw off all pretenses and simply turned around to the now extremely bemused gathering to get my directions. When it was over, on the way out, I was, of course the last one to leave. Sister Cecilia was waiting for me at the door outside.

"Mr. Stack," She bowed her head slightly.

"Sister Cecilia," I bowed back.

"It appears we haven't been to Mass lately, Mr. Stack."

"Well, we haven't sat in the front row for quite some time, Sister."

"Perhaps we shouldn't sit in the front row in the future, Mr. Stack."

"You know, Sister, it is quite extraordinary, but the very same thought occurred to me."

"Good day, Mr. Stack."

"May yours be very pleasant as well, Sister."

By the time I got in my car at the end of the day I was wringing wet. I pulled out of the parking area offering the occasional red-faced wave to my flock on the sidewalk. They were smiling. "See you tomorrow, Mr. Stack!"

Half way home I literally had to pull the car off to the side of the road, I was laughing so hard.

As a parent and now a grandparent, this story is frightening. How could anyone have entrusted children to such a untrained boy? But I was a good teacher, for a rookie. Sister Cecelia, after observing me many times, said I was a natural. I'm certain I learned more than my students that single year of teaching, but I put a lot into the effort and they liked me very much. I think after that first day, they were on my side. I owe them a lot.

As it turned out, my doctor's letter worked. I received a medical deferment for asthma and began my investment career the following summer. I was prepared for it because of what happened that day in September 1969.

That was the day I grew up. ▪

# Pink Flamingoes

Faster than a seagull diving for a potato chip....

BY J.C. ELKIN *(Issue 28)*

A POSTCARD TAUGHT ME EVERYTHING there was to know about Florida. It looked like Gilligan's Island, but with mermaids, and I thought my grandparents were the luckiest people in the world to vacation there. Then they came home with my souvenir, and I knew Florida was ten times better than New Hampshire because our stores had nothing half as beautiful as my new pearly pink, plastic change purse. Iridescent as a gasoline rainbow on the water and decorated with a flock of shocking pink flamingoes, it was my most prized possession. I loved the way it shone in the sunlight, the way it caressed my cheek, the way it smelled so good that I couldn't inhale deep enough, like the new car I'd sat in once.

Its benzene scent was still heady six months later when I opened my closet and donned a pair of shorts and a T-shirt, instead of my school uniform. It was a strange Friday all around. We were going on a field trip, my first, and I needed to retrieve the wallet from its secret hiding place behind my shoes. It contained 26 cents, all the money I owned, which I wouldn't ever have thought to bring, except Sister Theresita insisted. Three times she told us, "Be sure to bring some money, in case there's anything at the beach you want to buy."

Of course we all knew there weren't any stores at the beach, but no one would contradict her. She was the teacher, after all. And speaking for myself, at least, I would have died rather than disappoint her. Maybe she planned to take us to some other beach far away that we didn't know about. Maybe a place that looked like Gilligan's Island with mermaids.

Mama warned me it was a dumb idea. "There's just an overpriced snack bar," she scoffed. "And besides, you're bringing your lunch."

"But Sister said three times, 'Be sure to bring some money,'" I said. "I don't want to get in trouble."

"Bah. She's not even from around here. She's in for a surprise," Mama said, turning back to her pan of scrambled eggs.

I rode in a purple convertible that all the chaperones coveted, but I didn't like it much. The wind whipped my hair in my eyes, and my sweater wasn't warm enough for the overcast morning. There were four of us crammed in the back seat, all misfits. I was the youngest in the class, branded early as the baby. Then there was Wayne the wild kid, Celia of the scratchy voice and kinky hair, and Keith, the cute but poor boy who made my heart beat faster. When we passed a Coppertone billboard, the famous one showing a little girl walking topless on the beach with a dog pulling down the bottoms of her swimsuit to expose her white behind, I looked the other way. Blood rush to my cheeks as the boys pointed to it and snickered.

"Oh, isn't she cute?" our chaperone said, patting the lavender headscarf that tamed her bouffant.

I pretended not to hear. One person's cute is another's immoral, even at age six.

When we got to the beach it turned out to be the same old one I visited year round with my family. The most impressive thing about it was the boulders, which Sister wouldn't even let us climb. The snack bar was closed, and there weren't any other stores in sight.

We searched the tide pools for starfish, and walked along the water's edge like clutches of sandpipers, racing the waves as they advanced and receded. We dug with our toes for the elusive clams that blew taunting bubbles, and tested our balance against the tide that swept the sand from beneath our heels. It was an impossible contest to win. Sooner or later we had to step back with grace or fall back with an undignified splash.

At noon, one of the chaperones unpacked a Styrofoam cooler stuffed with twenty-seven brown paper bags, identical except for our names printed on the outside. I welcomed the chance to hunker down in the warm sand with my tuna fish sandwich and tonic. Then I ate my Ring Ding and took a quick stroke and sniff of my change purse before tucking it back in my lunch bag for safekeeping. I was still peeling my orange when Sister Theresita announced clean-up time.

Faster than a seagull diving for a potato chip Wayne swooped in, arms outstretched like an airplane, and grabbed my lunch bag. He stuffed it under his arm and grabbed a dozen more from all the other girls on nearby blankets, kicking sand in our faces as he sped away. He was gone before I could speak a word. My wallet, my favorite possession, was still in that bag.

I jumped up and tugged a chaperone's sleeve. "Wayne took my lunch bag with my wallet in it!"

"…nine, ten, eleven…" She was counting heads.

My lips were moving, but I might as well have been dumb. The breeze carried my voice with it down the beach in the opposite direction.

I ran to our teacher. "Sister, my lunch bag got thrown away, and I…"

"It's just a paper bag. Now go back to your group," she said. "It's time to go."

"But it has my…"

"Go on," she said, with her business face.

Wayne was everywhere all at once, uncountable. It was so unfair! He was a nuisance: a loud, intrusive, obnoxious thief. Why didn't someone stop him?

I ran to the garbage can, taller than I was, and peered through its wire mesh to see if I could spot my bag among all the others. I knew only that it was out of reach somewhere at the bottom, under twenty-six identical, crumpled, brown paper bags.

Our driver herded me back to her cold purple car, babbling about what a lovely day it had been.

"But, my wallet…" I started.

"Yes, indeed, a gorgeous summer day," she continued. "You kids sure are lucky. We didn't take field trips to the beach when I was your age."

I wished I'd gone to school with her.

I slid into the back seat, silent as a sand dollar, and turned my head away from the others as if to watch the receding waves. The more I tried to forget, the more my eyes blurred. But crying wasn't an option. I hadn't been called a baby since turning six back in November.

Wayne dove in right behind, like Superman, landing against me with a mighty whump that punched all the air from the upholstery and my lungs. I sighed with the naugahyde. It was a long drive back to school. ■

# Part Three

# FICTION

# Easter Lilies

To peel green bananas

BY JACQUELINE BISHOP *(Issue 21)*

WHEN I CAME FROM CLASSES I found the letter under my door. Matron must have collected it for me. I dumped my books on the bed, opened the window of my dorm room to let some fresh air in, before throwing myself down on the bed, to read the letter. As I suspected the letter was from my mother. She wanted me to come home for the Easter holidays when the fields would be full of the fragrant white Easter Lilies, those large funnel-shaped flowers that I hadn't seen much of since living in Kingston. Papa was doing better but still not very well since his stroke; now he was totally confined to bed and could barely speak. He keeps asking about you though, she wrote, always wanting to know when he is going to see his Cassie; you always were your father's favorite. Then, she added, as-if-it-were-nothing-special, Raymond was home. He'd come all the way from America for the Easter holidays and this time he had come all alone and he let it be known he would be staying for a while. What's more, he had come by the house to see her, to ask how I was doing and did my mother think I might be coming home from the university any time soon? It seems he'd broken up with the American girl he'd brought home last time he was on the island.

I put the letter down quickly. Raymond! After all these years! I couldn't even remember the last time I'd seen or heard from him. I hadn't even been allowed to say goodbye to him when he was leaving the island for school in America what must have been fifteen years ago. Raymond! After all these years!

* * * *

Back then, it was as if my life was a saucer broken completely in two: what it was before my body started to change and what it became after my body started to change. Because from the moment my breasts started forming, nothing I did was ever right. Mama would quickly lose patience with me and before I knew what was happening she would be shaking me hard to pay attention to one thing or another that she was now forever showing me to do. I was becoming a "woman" now, Mama kept saying, and it was time I learned how to do things around the house, especially in the kitchen.

To peel green bananas, she was standing as tall as a breadfruit tree over me, I was to make a deep cut into the thick green skin of the banana, deep enough to remove the banana's thick peel, but not too deep into the firm pearly-white flesh of the banana. I should slip two or three fingers under the peel and pull the skin from the bananas without managing to break the banana into a million tiny pieces.

To cook the bananas, she continued, looking at me struggling with the peel, I should wait until the water was boiling-up in the pot before placing the bananas in. If I didn't wait until the water was boiling-up then the bananas were going to be hard because bananas needed hot water to boil soft in. If I was going to become one of those lazy women who cooked green banana in its skin, then I was to cut off the tips of both ends of the banana, slit the banana down the length of its back, then drop it into a pot of boiling water with the skin on. I should always remember to put a touch of cooking oil into the water so the peel would not darken the water and blacken the pot.

On and on Mama would go, giving me one instruction after another, while, from the kitchen window, I could hear our neighbor Elizabeth shout to our friend Nadine from up the road: “Statue! Nobody melt you but I!” I so wanted to go outside to play with them, like I’d done every evening before the “thing” started happening to me, before my body started changing, but now I am not allowed to play outside anymore.

And suppose Mama should see me walking home from school with Raymond, like we have been doing forever, Raymond’s bag over my shoulder and my bag over Raymond’s shoulder, both of us laughing and talking and shoving each other, Mama will come tearing down the street like a mad woman and ask me what I think I’m doing, walking home brass-face as I please with a boy like that! Giving Nonsuch people more than a mouthful to talk about!

“But Ma, its only Raymond!” I said to her the first time this happened, Raymond standing there beside me.

She said nothing but began pulling me along by my ears.

All of this would not be happening, I say looking down on myself, if my breasts hadn’t decided to start growing before everyone else’s; if my body hadn’t suddenly decided to start behaving as if it had a mind of its own.

* * * *

Mama showing me now how to do embroidery and how to do piecework. Mama showing me which herb is good for a bellyache and which herb is good for an upset stomach. Which bush boiled with which bark can cause a man to love you. One day she stopped talking and looked around quickly to make sure no one could hear what she was saying to me. It was a warm Sunday afternoon and we were alone in the back yard. My white school blouses had been washed long ago and were blowing on the line, along with my navy blue tunic and blue school socks. The back yard was swept clean and everything was neat and in order, just the way Mama liked it. Mama reached into the front of her apron and pulled out a beige mushroom-looking plant, “And this—this will make you flow regular.”

Absolute confusion must have spread over my face because she added, “flow regular, you get me, chile?”

“No Mama, I don’t understand.”

“Flow re-gu-lar, Cassie, as in every month.” She said this last bit in a hurried fearful whisper and I knew she was telling me something to be both feared and worshipped. Something both good and bad. Something that would take me full force into the world of whispers and herbs and monthly “pains.” I sighed. We were back there again. The monthly “thing” that would soon happen to me. This “thing” Mama never fully explained to me, except to say I should be on the look out for it any day now. The "thing" I'd only vaguely heard of before, and did not fully understand. This "thing" I couldn't wait to happen so "it" would be over and done with.

"Yes Mama," I answered her finally, "I understand."

* * * *

I think life is totally unfair! Totally unfair! For here it is I have two older brothers, Paul and Cranston, who get away with everything and don't have to learn one God thing! I never see them in the kitchen learning that a spoonful of brown sugar will darken the meat faster and give the stew a nice rich taste. I never see Mama bending over them making sure they scale the parrotfish correctly, or teaching them how to choose Bay leaves. I still can't understand why I am the only one expected to learn how to cook and clean and wash. And—as if that wasn't enough—pick up after my two older brothers too!

And the worst part about the entire situation is that after I have done all of the work—going to the Bay and choosing the snapper or parrotfish for Sunday dinner, arguing with the men over the price like Mama say I should always do (No matter what price they tell you, you can always get it cheaper!); then taking the fish back home and scaling and gutting them and squeezing lime over them to clear away the raw-scent and stop the flies coming down in droves (The yard will smell something-terrible if you don't squeeze lime over those fish!); then cutting the fish on both sides and sprinkling salt and black pepper into the cuts and into the cleaned-out gut like Mama says I must always do (You have to learn how to season food properly); then laying the fish into the hot sweet oil by the tail, jumping back so the oil does not splash up and burn my hands or my face or my chest (There is an art to doing the thing!); then going outside and picking the red plummy tomatoes (Make sure you search them for worms!); then picking two or three scotch bonnet peppers (Again, make sure you search them for worms!); then picking okra from the okra tree (Remember okra trees harbor giant red ants, and that sticky white feathery thing that comes off all over your hands, you have to be careful because nothing scratch like that!); after choosing the best okras (the firm green ones that snap off easily at the end); then carrying all of this back to the kitchen and chopping everything together, my eyes watering from the onion and escellion that I use to escoveith the fish; after I lift up the cover of the pot where the fish are frying, stepping back from the heat on my face, then getting close again, adding all the seasonings plus some water, then covering the pot and letting everything steam; Mama coming into the kitchen from the room where she is ironing Papa's shirts, wiping the sweat from her face into her sleeve, a satisfied look on her face; after I have done all of this, grumbling but believing for all my troubles, I will, at least, get first pick of the fish—this, of course, is not what happens.

The biggest fish goes to Papa, which I don't really have a problem with because he does work very hard in his field all day long. But the next ones go to Cranston and Paul, the two laziest persons on the face of the earth! Then Mama and finally me!

One Sunday Mama must have seen the look on my face and knew what was boiling up inside of my heart, because she asked, "Cassie, why you got that terrible look on your face this nice Sunday evening? Look the wonderful Sunday dinner the Good Lord provide for us, the rice and peas so nice. Why your face must look like that?"

"Not fair!" I mumbled under my breath, throwing Paul and Cranston a terrible look, "Not fair at all!"

"What's that Cassie?" Mama asked, her voice rising in anger.

"For God's sake leave the chile alone!" Papa said. "Give her a moment to herself! Let her be! She do more than those two louses in the corner do, just sitting around and waiting to put food in their bellies!"

"You always taking up for her!" Mama said, really angry now.

"Hush woman," Papa shushed her again, "let me eat this wonderful meal my one and only daughter done prepared for me this Sunday afternoon in peace and quiet. Like I say, she do more than those two worthless creatures who only care about them bellies! Leave the child alone! Let her be!"

* * * *

In the evenings after dinner Mama force me to sit outside with her on the verandah to-enjoy-the-cool-evening-breeze. I want to tell Mama that last evening when I was coming home from school and had to stop at Ms. Pearl's shop to shelter from the rain, there was a new lady that I was listening to on the radio call-in show. This lady was saying things like, "In today's society men must learn to look after themselves in the home like they do in the larger society. Boys need to understand that girls are not there to wash, cook and clean for them!" I want to tell Mama about the tingling sensation that went straight through my body when the lady said that; as if something finally made sense to me. A gap finally closing.

"In addition," the lady on the radio continued, "mothers need to train their daughters from early on to fend for themselves, to be more aggressive in the larger world like boys are!"

I kept saying the word "aggressive" over and over again. For even though it was the first time I'd heard the word, there was something about it that I liked. The way the word rolled around inside the soft of my mouth; as if it were a new blue marble, hard against the soft pink palate of my mouth.

Mama got up and went inside the house, coming back out with her sewing basket. O Gawd, I groaned under my breath, she is not going to start with that again! Telling me how baff-handed I was because I am always sticking myself with the needle and find the thimble too cumbersome to sew with! That I have been working on the same shirt for months now and-isn't-it-a-crying-shame I can't finish one little shirt for my brother! What kind of woman was I going to become? Who did I think would seriously marry a woman who couldn't sew one-little-shirt?

"Mama," I jumped up quickly, "can I go play with Elizabeth and Nadine just this once? Just for today? I promise I won't bother you ever again about this, Mama please!"

She looked me straight in my eyes, shook her head very slowly and said, "No Cassie, playing days are over."

In that moment I felt as if a heavy gray curtain had fallen over my childhood and I was in a different stage of my life. I was clearly no longer a child and was at a place where I was still waiting to become a woman.

* * * *

First there was a strain across my blouse as if something was pushing up from deep within the walls of my chest. Then there was a gathering of flesh, the tips of which darkened like a wilting dark-red hibiscus flower. At first the tips were very tender and whenever I tried to touch them or if I accidentally brushed against something, my young developing breasts would hurt; they were that sore and tender. I stared and stared at myself in front of the mirror. I was twelve years old; soon I would be thirteen. Earlier in the year a nurse had come at school to talk to all of us girls about what she called our "flowering."

"You know the field near the river you pass on your way here to school," the nurse was looking at all of us girls who had gathered in the hall just staring up at her on the lectern. "The field that for most of the year lie bare and fallow, except, like now, when, after a hard shower of rain, the place is suddenly and entirely covered with white Easter Lilies?"

We all nodded our heads "yes," because we all knew what she was talking about: the plants that, when in full bloom, produced large funny-shaped blossoms, white in color, with waxy dark green leaves. In soils deficient in some kind of mineral, they became a nice golden yellow color, the Easter Lilies. Yes, we all knew the flowers she was talking about because they were so spectacular when in bloom.

"Well, your bodies now are just like that field two weeks after a hard shower of rain; your bodies are changing and you are all becoming just like those flowers."

For the rest of the day all I could think about was those flowers, how much like them I was. And that night, my hands began wandering all over my body, between my legs, the sepals and petals of what I instinctively knew was the most beautiful part of my flower. In biology class our teacher had taught us how to gently use our finger tips and nails to open up a hibiscus flower, ever so slightly slitting open the plant; tall thin pistils; thick seeds in the rounded yellow/green ovaries. How surprised I was to see all the things that had been carefully hidden inside of the flower! I was like that flower now, I thought, a soft drowsy feeling coming over me.

After that, I convinced Nadine and Elizabeth to meet up on full moon nights by the river, where we would show off the buds on our chests. In hushed voices we would pull our blouses over our heads and look and look at each other. Without saying a word we would reach over and touch each other, all the time something thick and sickeningly sweet around us. Something that had the moisture and taste of a large brown naseberry.

Somehow Raymond found out about this, and one night when I went to the river who should I see there but Raymond, a bouquet of white Easter Lilies by his feet. None of the other girls had shown up that night.

For the longest time we sat there together, in silence, neither of us saying anything to the other.

"These are for you," he said finally, handing me the flowers.

I smiled and took the Lilies, knowing full well that I would never be able to take them home. That would start my mother asking too many questions.

Suddenly Raymond looked over at me and got serious. Much too serious. He pulled me close to him. "You've become so moody, lately." He was playing with me, although there was nothing playful about the look in his eyes.

"Moody, nothing!" I replied, laying down in his arms.

It was a clear night with a full pale moon in the blue-black sky. A cool breeze came in off the water and immediately my skin was flushed with goose bumps. Raymond and I looked at each other. He reached down and we started kissing. Soon we were on the ground, Raymond fumbling with the buttons on my shirt. Before long he was staring down at my breasts, the most amazed look in his eyes. He reached down and ran his tongue over the tips of each of my breasts, and I felt something like an electric charge run straight through my body.

"Look at the impression your body made in the grass!" Raymond pointed to where I had been lying down. The female shape my body had made in the damp green grass. Raymond then reached for the bouquet of white lilies and started using the flowers to outline then fill in the curves of the female body-impression in the grass.

"What are you doing?" I asked him a couple minutes later, when he was still hard at work.

He did not answer me but kept filling in the body-impression with more and more white petals. When he was done, I gasped. I'd never seen anything like this before; it was quite stunning. It was as if he filled the inside of a female body, my body, with flowers. It looked as if the white Easter lilies were growing out of the soft green bed of a female body.

"You should go to art school!" I told him softly.

"You know I cannot do that! You know I-am-going-to-go-to-America-to-become-a-medical-doctor!"

We were quiet for a while longer before he threw the leftover flowers in the river. We watched as the flowers struggled a bit in the water, before moving swiftly down the river, carried away by the current.

"Come, let's go" he held out a hand to help me up, but I did not want to go. I just wanted the two of us to stay there all alone by the river, looking and talking about this flower child of a woman that he had created.

I had the dream that night. Something dark and heavy was coming towards me. It had a vague undefined shape, and it kept coming closer and closer, as if it was trying to cover me up. In the past, whereas this dream used to frighten me, it no longer did. It moved very slowly, this purple-blue thing that was now wrapping itself around me, dancing with me, filling me up. It was so slow this thing, almost as if it was molasses that someone was pouring ever so slowly over my body. I was running as hard as I could, and was often out of breath from how fast I was running, still this slow-moving dark and sticky thing was catching up to me. Finally I could run no more and lay down, breathless, and watched as it came over and covered me.

* * * *

Then Mama came home from the Bay one afternoon with some ugly black panties. The type that looks more like girdles than panties. When she took them out of the bag I felt certain they must have been for her, or one of her church sisters, since these were the only ones in my mind who would wear such panties. I would never get caught in one of those things. So you can imagine my shock when my mother said, “And these are panties for you, Cassie.”

Was this some kind of joke my mother was playing on me? Surely these could not be the panties she’d pinched me and told me she was going to buy for me? No, these big ugly things could not be for me.

“Oh, don’t look at me like that, they will become useful one day soon, these black panties!”

“Mama” I mentally braced myself for a slap in my face, ” I won’t be wearing those panties anytime soon. I will never be wearing those panties—ever.”

Mama looked at me a long time, then she laughed. “Believe me, one day you will, you will wear these panties.”

* * * *

The day “it” finally happened I was a tired and restless spirit. There was this horrible tightness in my stomach and I walked around the yard grumbling and mumbling about the simplest of things. I was feeling totally miserable. I’d woken up with a feeling I’d never felt before. It was as if something was gathering, then pulling and tearing inside me; what an awful cramping feeling! From where she was in the back yard Mama kept watching me as I paced back and forth as if I was being ridden by something ancient, strong and terrible. Mama was boiling white clothes in a tin-pan over a roaring wood fire, using a stick to stir the clothes in the pan. And all the time she kept watching me.

“Mama” I said to her finally, “My belly is hurting me in a way it hasn’t hurt me before.”

” You eat anything to give you bellyache?”

“No Mama.”

“Your belly ever hurt you just so before?” Her eyes were averted, looking at everything but at me.

“No Mama, not quite like this before. ”

The day was too hot, I was thinking, and I was sweating much too much. Yet, at times, despite the heat, I felt cold. My body did not feel like the one I’d lived in for the past thirteen years—the slender dark body Mama always teased me about saying she didn’t know where I came from because both her and my father were big-boned people, look at the two giants I have for brothers, and how small and skinny I was. No, this did not feel at all like my body.

"Come Miss Cass," Mama was finally looking at me, several different emotions in her eyes and playing across her face. She was looking on me as if I was a brand new person standing there before her. So many different emotions on her face! There was a kind of fierce pride in the way her eyes traveled over my body. Then, swiftly following this, was a look of fear. I was afraid too, sensing the "thing" we'd not-been-talking about for the last couple of months, the "it" was fully upon me. Now I would become one of "them," one of my mother's women friends who were sick every month with the "curse," and who would emerge from their strange sickness talking about the trials and tribulations of being a woman. I wanted to stop what was coming upon me; the wetness now between my legs.

"Its OK, just go in the bathroom and tell me what you see … Cassie?"

"Yes Mama?"

"Anything happen to you yet?"

"Yes Mama" I answered, horrified at the magenta stain in my panty.

* * * *

Dear Diary, I plan to run away if Mama do not stop her foolishness.

What kind of "foolishness" are you talking about?

You know, all the rules and regulations, all the things I shouldn't do now that I'm a "woman."

And how do you know that you are a "woman" now?

Because "the thing" we've both been waiting for has finally happened to me.

And does that make you a woman?

Not fully, but in a way it does. It certainly changes your position around here, causes much confusion in the family, and that is why I'm running away.

But where will you run to?

Oh, I don't know, up to the hills … live in one of the caves up there. In one of the books I have to read for school, *Escape to Last Man's Peak*, some children did just that.

That's a fool-fool plan…

Not so, that's a good plan.

And just how will you live?

I'll figure something out like the children did in that book.

Have you tried talking to your father at least?

It's no use, he's changed too.

How so?

Remember how happy he used to be to see me when he came home from work in the evenings? How the first thing he used to do when he came through the gate, even before he dropped his machete was call-out: "Cassie-oh! …But where, oh where, is my Cassie-oh?" Then I would come tearing out of the house and straight into his arms? Remember how Papa would throw me up in the air and catch me? Then I would search his pockets and find a sweetie, a ripe guava, or a piece of sugar cane he'd brought home especially for me? That's all ended. Now Papa doesn't even hug me anymore. He keeps his distance and is forever bothering Mama saying, "I hope you keeping a sharp eye on that girl!"

Well, your brothers, at least …

Are now idiots too.

How so?

Telling me everyday to stay inside the house. Warning me against so much as talking to any of their friends.

Really?

Girls come and visit them too you know! And they lock up with the girls in their rooms!

Your mother, she knows about this?

Yes she knows, and I see her smiling when she think I'm not looking, although sometimes she quarrels with them about this and says she doesn't want any nastiness going on inside of her house.

What does she mean by that?

Oh, you know…. Mama keeps saying she hope that they have money put-down to take care of children.

Well … Raymond at least?

Has gotten a scholarship to some specialized high school in America.

Well that must have made you very sad….

And the worst of it is that Mama isn't even letting me say goodbye to him!

Yes, that is bad. Very bad. But you'll soon get a scholarship and go away to America too. And when Raymond sees just how much more beautiful you are becoming….

**II**

I decide to go home for the Easter holidays after all and when the bus pulls into the square Mama is there already, sitting under the piazza and waiting for me. As soon as I come off the bus, she sees me and begins waving wildly. I stand for a moment and just look at her: tall stout woman, very dark, wearing a tangerine-colored dress, her silver-gray hair pulled tight in a bun. I couldn't lie: I loved the woman. One of my many nieces, Roselle, is with her.

For a while we just stand under the bus shed and hug and touch and kiss each other, my niece with her finger in her mouth. When I finally pull away from my mother, there are tears in both of our eyes. She is right, my dear mother, we really should see more of each other. As soon as I finished my studies at the university, I promise myself, I will take a break and spend some time with both her and papa.

"You still so slender!" she says, pushing me away from her and looking me up and down, taking me in, we see each other so infrequently.

"And Papa, how is he doing?"

"As good as can be expected, I suppose." She turns away from me, her eyes clouding over. "I told him this morning you were coming and he smiled, which is really a good sign because I can never tell these days whether or not he fully understands what I am saying to him anymore." Her voice is trembling badly. For the first time I am forced to contemplate how truly difficult this must be for her. She and Papa alone in the house. No one for her to talk to, even after they have been married for so many years.

"We should find a car to take us up to the district," she is hurrying to get away so I won't see her crying.

On the bumpy ride up to the district I lean against her, our arms in each other's, both of us looking out the window at the greenery all around us. Roselle, who is sitting up front with the driver, is having a ball. She doesn't get to drive in a car very often and certainly not in the front. She will have so much to tell all her other brothers and sisters and cousins, like so many leaves on a tree, that she has about the district.

"Oh my goodness!" Mama says suddenly, clapping her hand in joy. "How could I forget such a thing?" For a moment she is a young woman again, a young and excited woman.

"Forget what?" I am glad to see her happy for a moment.

"You'll never believe who is home, Cassie! Never! Raymond! Raymond is home for the Easter holidays!"

"Mama," I look at her unbelievably, "you already told me that in a letter!"

"I did?" She looks sheepish, incredulous and only partly innocent.

"Yes, you did!" I laugh and push her.

"But did I tell you he was home alone?"

"Yes, you did!" I shake my head at her.

"But did I tell you he was divorced? Did I tell you he left the American? Did I tell you that he came by the house asking about you?" Her eyes and skin are flushed, she is so excited. Was this really the woman who would've killed me when I was younger if I so much as stood close to a boy? I keep looking at her and shaking my head unbelievably.

"And did I tell you how handsome he is that Raymond, and how he talks with a nice American accent? I invited him over for dinner this Sunday, you know! Oh, yes, and he accepted the invitation fast-fast Raymond did, and he is coming for Sunday dinner, this Sunday."

Oh, these women! These Jamaican women! How hard they were on their young daughters! I remember as an adolescent how hard she was on me! All the rules and regulations to make me into a nice-and-decent-woman! How I had to stay far, far away from boys. They could blight my future! But now it seemed that everything was reversed. Now it seemed that every other day she was asking me about some or the other fellow. I needed to take my head out of whatever book I was reading. Look up. Show my pretty dark face. This from a woman who had told me when I was thirteen years old to never stop reading; to never stop studying. Education was the key. But now it was, did I plan on becoming an old maid? Did I never plan on getting married? On giving her some grandchildren? I looked at her and shook my head once more. Was this really the same woman I had grown up with?

But just now there was the business of that fellow from America. How many years had it been since I last saw or heard from Raymond? How many times had I thought about him, and that time at the river; him, I, and the Easter Lilies? The truth is, I wanted to see Raymond. I desperately wanted to see him in fact. Was he really the same like Mama said? No, he must have changed. What kind of man had he grown into? Would I be able to talk to him about any and everything like I once used to? But that was years and years ago. His life in the United States, a wife; did he have any American children? So many things I wanted to ask him about. But first I would go by the river and make a bouquet of white Easter Lilies. I would put the bouquet in the center of the table, and watch him, when he came to dinner this Sunday, to see if he would remember. ■

# Obsession

I want to wallow in my organs.

BY DUFF BRENNA *(Issue 22)*

WHEN I GET HOME THAT NIGHT, Ray's kisses still on my lips, I take my clothes off and go to bed, not bothering to shower, not bothering to remove my makeup, or brush my teeth. I want to wallow in my organs. I want to review the kisses over and over, the vodka-mouth, the sucking lips, tongue touching. Musk of Ray Poe.

I keep the lamp on and stare at his portrait. I read the titles on the spines of his books. I wonder for the umpteenth time what it would be like to be married to a man so gifted and handsome, so intelligent and obviously wise, obviously kind. Everything dull and drab would vanish, would be transformed into something new and vibrant with Ray in my life. It doesn't matter that he is eighteen years older. Norman was twenty-five years older and that hadn't mattered. Also thinking age: only a number.

But before anything more can happen, Ray will have to get rid of that wife, that Bobbi. And I will have to get rid of Buddy Carr, my current boyfriend and employee. I wonder if I will miss his beautiful body. Possibly, but not his narcissistic prancing in front of the mirror, his lying back on the bed and wanting me to suck him. At first it had been wild and exciting, like making love to a movie star. But now it's boring and I can hardly work myself into a passion when he wants me. Ho-hum, I'd rather sleep. Everything about him: too familiar. His conversation running the gauntlet from me to me. Look at my trophies.

Look at my six-pack belly, how narrow my waist is, I'm a perfect V from waist to shoulders, have you ever had a man last as long as I do? I have to admit I haven't. But more often than not as he pounds away at me, I will be thinking of my first love, sweet sybaritic Hamlin. Oh, to be that young again, everything fresh, everything new and full of fire. Also thinking: Jesus, get it over with, Buddy! Also thinking with Ray Poe it will be different. It's his mind not just his body I want. But I do look forward to that insatiable honeymoon period I've had with all my other lovers. I wonder how long on average couples sustain those initial desires?

Danny was fun and inventive. He had satisfied me for the first ten years of our marriage. Until he started accusing me of sleeping with nextdoor Jerry. And all the while Dan is sleeping with April! What a time that had been! The experience cracking something in me, that innocence about men lost forever. Losing it? Like losing your virginity, no more *beata virgo*. Men are not to be totally trusted. Always keep something in reserve in case the relationship sours. Learn to shut down quickly, stifle emotion, cast a cold eye on what had once been fiery—thrillingly so. Also thinking thrillingly nasty.

The marriage became a grinding agony. Near the end I couldn't even stand to look at Dan's face. A face I had once thought handsome. How could I have ever sucked those sarcastic lips, his arrogant prick? The sound of his voice abused my eardrums. His eyes mocked me, belittled me. So why did I stay as long as I did? Who remembers? Who knows the why of anything? For the kids. For the sake of the kids. How many women spend their lives living a lie for the sake of their children? How many men? What a muddle we make of it.

And yet, here I am preparing to make even more of a muddle. A married man is not to be trifled with. Breaking up a family is dishonorable, in some cases criminal. Maybe evil. But whatever it is, I am determined to have Ray Poe. Also thinking wife Bobbi be damned.

My thoughts stay on Bobbi and the time we met after Norman Ten Boom's poetry reading. I had felt incredulous that such a tub could be Ray's longtime wife. She was pretty enough, but what a lugubrious body! A body not good enough to please him was my opinion. Not good enough to hold his attention for five seconds. Bobbi didn't deserve him! A woman who won't take care of herself any better than that is just asking for it. I don't buy the excuses. Arthritis. Acute anxiety. Slow metabolism. Etcetera. Bobbi might be sick, but she shouldn't have let herself go so utterly. Also thinking frankly she's repulsive.

"I love eating, but I refuse to get fat," I tell Ray's portrait, his smile the smile of a kind man, a mellow man. A man with a good heart. I can see it in the radiance of his eyes, in the brilliance of his entire countenance. The soul of an artist. Which is what I have also. Leaving my husband's control taught me that there is more to Annette Annaba Walker than just a pretty face and a nubile body. (Is thirty-eight still young enough be nubile?) My love of reading has filled up a spiritual well that is overflowing into brilliant verses. I write at least one poem a week. I don't show them to anyone. I will show them to Ray when he becomes my lover. Also thinking he will edit them and tell me where to get published.

Norman the Dutchman had told me there was no doubt about my talent. All I needed was "time in the saddle." His time in the saddle with me had been unexpectedly fulfilling. For a man of sixty he had been surprisingly vigorous. I remember him pumping away for all he was worth, trying to make me climax, which I did occasionally, though I also faked it when I was ready to stop. I might have been able to love him if he hadn't talked so much. He would never stop talking! Drove me crazy! I had wanted to tell him to let some silence into the room once in a while! The barrage of words had driven every nascent thought straight out of my head. I hadn't been able to write a single poem when I was having my affair with him. Everything he read of mine had been a product of the early years with Danny: Dan you are the man holding my hand/The only love of my life/As we walk along the sand/And absorb the roar of the ocean/And the waves pounding the land like a potion.

He never liked anything I wrote. I know now that Norman had faked his admiration, telling me what I wanted to hear. Also thinking how those years with Dan had given me a tin ear.

Part of my lack of invention during the affair with Norman had been the by-product of guilt, the sneaking around, the painful lying. The stress on my nerves had given me heart palpitations and high blood pressure. My doctor couldn't understand what was happening. "You've always been so healthy," he had told me. "This isn't natural. What's going on in your life, Annette?" "I wish I knew," was what I had answered.

After I broke off with Norman and stayed with Irene for a while, the poetic impulse came back little by little. The palpitations, the blood pressure problems faded. But they returned when I went back to my husband and children. The writing stopped. I started drinking and taking Xanax in order to sleep at night.

My leaving home had been a wakeup call for Dan. He had never believed I would actually leave him. I returned to a subdued husband. I felt as if I had broken his spirit, and, truth be told, I didn't give a damn, didn't care that he was inordinately kind, didn't yell anymore or try to make me feel inadequate, hopelessly defective. He no longer accused me of having affairs. He bought little gifts, gave me candy and flowers. Even wrote me some clumsy poems. He tried very hard to become a new man, a man who could win my love back. But by then none of it mattered. Repulsive kisses. When he made love to me the feel of him inside, the smell rising between us was nauseating. The marriage was irrevocably shattered, but I hung on for another year before leaving and filing for divorce.

Living with Irene again, I explored a side of myself I had vaguely known existed whenever I watched women making love in the porns. Irene was a good listener and undemanding. Many nights we went to sleep in each other's arms. When we made love, I was the aggressor. Irene lying back passively receiving. Poems poured out of me, all of them subtextually Lesbo:

My tongue swims
Out to taste
The wick of your soul
Your scent lingering
On my lips
Becomes the bouquet
Of dawn
Every blessed morning
Lying here hand in hand
The aroma of light
Growing in my heart
An intimate reverence
Savored forever.

I was writing stories as well, even planning a memoir based on my life with Dan Walker—how naïve I had been, how immature, how easily fooled. A simpleton for nearly sixteen years, fawning on a husband unfaithful to me, while also nurturing and spoiling two little vipers who ultimately broke my heart. Children, who needs them? Not Annette Annaba Walker.

Dan had phoned my mother and played the aggrieved husband. She took his side, as did everyone, agreeing that I had lost my wits, was mentally unbalanced, needed professional help. "Go home to your family," Mommy kept telling me. "You're going to lose those children, Annette!" And all I could think at the time was so what? The little monsters had been against me for years. They were tools of their father who had used them to make my life miserable. I was sure they were happier without me. And if not? Tough-titty.

"You won't have Annette Walker to kick around anymore," I hear myself murmuring, thinking of a quote I had read in a Richard M. Nixon biography, Nixon saying he was getting out of politics. And then he went on years later to become President, one of the most reviled in memory, second only to that son of a Bush the country is dealing with, the war monger warrior wannabe.

The divorce settlement had given me every other weekend with Keats and Emily. It would have been more the judge told me if I hadn't so obviously abandoned them. He called me selfish and unnatural. Two adjectives that stuck to my continuing story. Whenever I talk to my mother on the phone or go over to her house for dinner or meet her at a restaurant, the judge's words will find their way into the conversation. Selfish and unnatural. Only a selfish, unnatural mother wouldn't be torn to pieces inside over the loss of her children. "You've always been willful, Annette. You've always made sure you got your way, no matter who pays for it."

Mommy still thinks Dan is a prince. "What a devoted father. What a loss to any woman, but especially to my daughter. If he was as mean-spirited and unkind as you say, Annette, I know you, and my guess is you drove him to it. I've never seen him be anything other than a perfect gentleman."

"And you wonder why I hardly ever call or come over," I told her, she who is always there in my mind, a dominating force whose raison d'être seems always to find fault with her only daughter. I believe my father's death at 59 was at least partially self-willed. Death being the only way of getting away from his wife forever.

What is right? What is good? Who is wrong? No one is wrong. Feelings cannot recognize wrong when it comes to loving or hating. The feelings tell you that you're alive and need to make the most of every opportunity that might enhance your life. You might die in your sleep tonight. Yes, maybe a sudden sleep-death is already programmed into you. The Damocles Sword of genetics hanging over you every second. Maybe you are doomed to die early. Also thinking no time to waste!

I climb out of bed. Put my clothes on. Grab a pen and a yellow sticky and write a short note to Ray: His kiss, his kiss—impossible! I get in my car and drive to his house. I stick the note to his windshield.

Staring at the house a long while, I wonder in what room he is sleeping. Is he still awake, maybe lying in the dark thinking of me, thinking of the kiss in the bar tonight? I tiptoe up to one of the bedroom windows. I remember the dinner to celebrate the launch of Norman's book, the conversation that he dominated, the growing coldness towards him I had felt that night. The egomaniac! The growing interest I had felt for Ray Poe, the distaste for bloated Bobbi. I recall that both Ray and Bobbi have offices in their home. Do they sleep together? I can't imagine them sleeping together. Having sex? Not impossible, but definitely improbable. How can a man rise to the occasion lying next to such a whale? Touching the cool glass, I tap it with my fingernail. I am breathing hard (actually panting), my heart hammering. Mouth so cottony I can't swallow. What if he comes to the window? What if he opens it and I crawl in, crawl into his bed into his arms? What if?

What are you doing, Annette? What are you doing, girl? This is beyond crazy. This is cockeyed, this is sick. This is what some lovestruck teenager would do. Get away before someone spots you and calls the police!

I scurry to the idling car. Put it in gear, drive away. A plan forming in my mind, a way to attract his attention, a way to get what I want. I know I can do it. I know he wants me. His kiss told me he wants me. Also thinking this is my rendezvous with destiny and anyone in my way doesn't have a chance. Whatever I have to wreck I'll wreck. Come what may that man is mine! Also thinking fait accompli! ▪

# Stuck Kiss

A very long kiss....

BY RACHEL WINEBERG *(Issue 24)*

THE BARTENDER SLAMS DOWN THE DRINKS, but they don't stop. He knows they won't. He just hopes they will stop kissing long enough to give him a tip. He hopes they will finish before his shift is done.

The man's breath smells of cigarettes. Hers of the mint she surreptitiously put into her mouth just before they entered the bar. His mouth engulfs hers. His lips are hard as she presses back. His tongue searches, she opens, his tongue digs, and her body is feverish. They are falling. There is no going back from this moment.

The bartender mumbles something about a bedroom. They don't hear him. A dwarf sits down on the stool next to them. They don't see him. All she knows is her thirst for the man and all he knows is hunger.

In the end, the bartender gives up on that tip. He gets a different job; one that comes with a wife, two children and a house. Sometimes he goes back to the bar, to see if the couple is still kissing and how the neighborhood has changed. A GAP opens and is torn down; Wall Street Brokers discover the neighborhood and move in. The economy changes and they move out.

Still they sit with his mouth engulfing hers. His tongue explores her endless possibilities; she answers his questions with her own. He is imposing, she is small but determined. Her closed eyes flutter, the smell of his stale cigarettes vanished a long time ago.

The bar changes hands. It closes for a while and then reopens for brunch with bright lights and flowered napkins. The new owners circle the kissing couple and scratch their heads. Finally, the new owners decide to keep the bar, the stools and the couple—for it is clear they cannot be moved. They name the restaurant Stuck Kiss.

Tourists come from China to have their picture taken in front of the couple. Brides cut off a lock of the woman's hair for good luck. His mother dies and the woman's sister has a child. But they are oblivious to these changes. All they know is the temperature of each other's mouths.

Even now they continue to fall into each other. The heat of his body inflames hers. They are in a dark cavern; they are each other's only light. They are kissing each other. They are kissing still. ▪

# Pinkman at Home

You always hear old men talking about their girlfriends who aren't really their girlfriends.

BY JP BORUM *(Issue 27)*

HERE'S THE THING. The days I spent with Joel Pinkman were not date dates. Not really. And yet. I think he thought of them as dates. You always hear old men talking about their girlfriends who aren't really their girlfriends. It didn't matter to him that I look more like a boy than a girl. A little blonde shagetz, he would joke. Never shiksa. I think he liked to look at me, liked my company, and so these were dates to him. I didn't care. He was paying me fifty dollars cash to push him around the Upper West Side in a giant wheelchair for three hours. Two twenties and a ten.

Before we started having our Sunday dates, I never went into The Home on the weekend. The coffee shop was closed so I had no business there. It was always so crowded with families visiting bubbe or zayde. Too many strangers and their bored offspring. I always felt jealous of these hordes. Was I not family to the old people? I made their coffee every day. I fed them, listened to their stories, made them laugh, and watched them die.

Pinkman would always be reading in bed when I got there at eleven o'clock. This was an act, a carefully constructed scene. I called this act Pinkman at Home, or, Retired Board of Ed Social Studies Teacher Joel Pinkman Takes in the Classics on a Sunday Morning. He would feign surprise when I knocked, and casually drop his book onto his lap so I could see the title when I reached him. Always something literary, but sexy too. *In Search of Lost Time. Madame Bovary.* He loved French whores.

"Jesse, did you know French whores read books back then?"

"Yes Joel, those French whores were clever ladies," I would answer, pushing the red button to get the nurse to help me roll him out of bed.

Pinkman didn't care that it was December and cold out. He never let me cover him properly for our walks. I was afraid he'd get sick and die like everybody else in The Home. He didn't like to cover up his legs. I should say leg because there was only one, now paired with a bandaged stump that was still healing. I don't think they changed the bandages on the stump often enough. And the foot on the remaining leg was not fit for the public. Old men don't take care of their feet, which after a lifetime of walking have usually been reshaped to look troll-like. Pinkman's foot belonged to this brotherhood of old troll feet, and the sight of his yellowing, jagged toenails made me sick and nervous. It was the remaining five toenails that made me want to cover him most. I was sure they had some kind of disease. After the nurse and I rolled him onto his wheelchair, which was technically a wheel-bed, I would try to cover up the whole mess with a blanket from the linen closet.

"It's December, Joel."

"No damnit. I want air! There's no air in this fucking place! I want to feel air!" he would yell with his head back and his eyes closed.

It was an ongoing battle which I think he enjoyed because it drew me closer to his body, and I think his body was lonely, and welcomed any kind of attention it could get.

"I can't let you freeze." I would say, covering up the good leg and the stump.

"Fuck you." He would apologize later.

We would compromise and keep the blanket over his crotch, but rolled up pretty high so that the rest was visible, dirty bandages, the toes, everything. It was obscene but it was his calling card.

Getting an elevator was the worst. We had to wait until we could get an empty one, and this took forever. Once in the lobby, he would begin to groan and moan. This was a constant and would get louder out on the street, when we started to hit the bumps. Not so bad on 106th Street, except for one big bump when you got to the Access-A-Ride pickup place. Pinkman would wait for this bump and scream, so loud that the other wheelchair people lined up there would look over at him in unison with blank faces. Behold, the martyrdom of Joel Pinkman.

106th Street crested in the middle so it was pretty easy to get down to Amsterdam. Crossing Amsterdam was a bitch, though. You had to really move. I would wait for the light to change and start running, which would make the wheel-bed bounce a lot, but it was the only way to escape the deadly lava flow of yellow cabs rolling at you, unable to stop itself. I knew that if I didn't run with Pinkman, we might both get hit. If he got hit and I didn't, I would get sued by the family, and maybe even The Home. This is what I thought about as I ran, listening to him scream after every bump. I thought that if I didn't make the light, I could dive behind the wheel-bed to save myself. Maybe the metal frame would slow the car down, and he would be OK too. Or not. Either way, I had to run, even though running meant inflicting pain on him from the bumps. But he could see the cars coming just as well as I could, despite the Mets cap pulled over his face. I think he appreciated the running.

After Amsterdam it was all uphill to the bookstore. First, a stretch I called No Man's Land, the pre-Columbia University neighborhood with no stores, no shops, not much to suggest civilization. Pinkman endured quietly. He was waiting to get up to the school, all the young people. Until the college students appeared, he would fall into a coma-like state, his head rolling forward to his chest, but flipping back again when I had to take a curb at the cross streets. When he screamed, people would look at me, the abuser. This was his intention.

When the first college students appeared, up by about 110th Street, Pinkman perked up. Before lunch, we always went to Labyrinth Books on 112th, just past the Post Office. It was always the same thing, squeeze the wheel-bed in through the front door with him yelling orders and up to the register where the hipsters would be waiting, trying not to look at his toes.

"I'm here. Are you thrilled?" he would say to register kid. "Pinkman account. P-I-N-K-M-A-N. I want my order. Pinkman. Is it there?"

He would make me wheel him into the store to look around, which caused traffic jams by the book displays. This ritual was purposeless, never leading to any purchases, all of which were done by phone ahead of time. But he liked to talk to anyone he could. This lasted about ten minutes, until he demanded to be wheeled around to the front again to pick up his books. More Zola, perhaps some poetry by Baudelaire, no doubt written for a

French whore. The register kids would have the books in a bag for him by the time the wheel-bed was facing front. By now the whole downstairs of the store was filled with angry disgusted people, trying to get around us.

"Get my wallet, Jesse."

Pinkman kept his wallet where it would normally have gone, were he not an amputee. In order for me to dig it out, I had to get my hand down there in the sheets of the wheel-bed by his ass. He would lean forward, but never far enough.

"Can you find it? Got it? We're holding up the line." His eyes would follow my hand, watch my progress as I dug around down there. The wallet was old and brown and fat.

I knew they hated us in Labyrinth. I knew they couldn't wait for us to get out. I tried to let them know with my expressions that I understood, but Pinkman monitored my face so that it was impossible to get in even an eye roll. He wanted me on his side all the way. Rolling him out took forever. But it meant that lunch was coming. Free lunch.

Le Monde is one of those corporate tourist trap French restaurants. There is a chain, and they're all the same, all meant to look like the Folies Bergère. Full of models from Connecticut and snotty European men with greasy ponytail hair. I hated this place. And yet it always felt like a haven, because I was always hungry. The only good thing about this place was one waitress. Older than the others, voluptuous. Long skirts, a peroxide buzz cut, tattoos. Pinkman always caught me looking at her.

"There's your girlfriend. Say hello. Maybe she likes boychicks like you."

Getting Pinkman settled by a table was a trick. I think he was a rolling health violation and if the city inspectors would have been there, he would have been asked to leave. The blonde waitress never came to help us, even though I'm sure they put us in her section a couple of times. I told myself that it was because of Pinkman's lower body, not indifference to me. She smiled my way from time to time, and Pinkman never missed an opportunity to embarrass me when she did.

"Your girlfriend's saying hello! Aren't you going to wave back?"

The way the tables were set up, we always got a table for two, and they would help me angle the wheel-bed so that he could eat, which left his foot sticking into the aisle, and pointing at the center of the table right next to us. Customers always asked to be moved so they just stopped seating people there. But the foot was visible from other tables, and I could see the disgust on people's faces. And, ever the teacher, Pinkman talked too loud.

"Proust used to throw dinner parties from his bed. He entertained everybody from his bed. Just like me!" He would look around to see who was listening.

"I bet Proust invited whores to dinner in bed, Joel," I would tease.

"So what if he did, is there anything wrong with that? Do you have a thing against whores?"

"No, Joel. The whores were different back then. They hung out with princes."

"You're damn right they did. They served a social function." He was indignant.

I tried to let the decorations at Le Monde trick me into thinking I was in Paris, but it never worked. All the fake signs in French. Who were they kidding? The café au lait wasn't bad though. It came in a white au lait bowl with lions' faces for little handles. This was the best I ate all week. French onion soup with melted cheese floating on top that stuck to the sides of the two-toned brown crock. Goat cheese salad drenched in herb vinaigrette. A basket of frites with a fat little ketchup bottle and tons of salt. Tourist food. Pinkman would go for the Sunday special, duck breast with potatoes. The French know how to cook potatoes. Even the pretend-French.

For dessert, we both ordered from the Les Tartes section. We got a bunch of them to share, lemon, chocolate, apricot. And another round of au laits. He wasn't supposed to eat sugar but I looked the other way. He was dying of diabetes.

"Too late," he would say with a shrug, pointing to the stump. "I may as well."

Pinkman's life was a life of the mind. His body just got in the way. On our dates, I agreed to ignore his body, to suspend any differences that might separate us. He wanted to know things about me, and even though I could have told him to back off, I kept talking, let him pry a little deeper every time. The truth is that I wanted somebody to ask these questions, and he was the only one asking.

"So how will you live?"

"What do you mean, Joel?"

"Without a husband? Who's going to take care of you?"

"I will, Joel. I'll take care of myself." I'm not sure I believed this.

"What about your mother? Your father?"

"What about them?"

"Aren't you going to break their hearts? No grandchildren?"

He didn't care one way or the other about the gay thing. I was in the habit of saying queer. I never liked the other choices. My obvious queerness was never a problem for him. It hardly ever was for inmates at The Home, most of whom were Jewish and therefore not crippled by the whole gays-will-burn-for-all-eternity thing. I loved them for this. Yet the questions kept coming.

"But why queer? Did you know that used to mean something very bad indeed?"

"Yes, I know. But we use it. I use it. I like it."

"Is it like when the blacks use the N word? All the kids today?"

"Sort of, yeah. Like that." Even though, not really.

"So you're insulting yourself? Do you hate yourself?"

"No, Joel. I like myself. And I don't want a husband. I can take care of myself. Just like the French whores, Joel. They didn't need husbands either."

At this he would laugh—really laugh—and when he did I could tell he lived for this kind of sparring. During these moments, I could almost picture a young Pinkman, out on a real date, keeping some poor girl on her toes.

Even though it meant that I would be free soon, I didn't ever want to leave Le Monde. It was warm in there, and leaving meant more hard labor. It meant apologizing to people on the street for running them off the sidewalk with the wheel-bed and to Pinkman for every hurt I caused him.

Going back was worse than coming up, even though it was mostly downhill on Broadway, past Tom's Diner, past No Man's Land. I could get up a good head of steam and really fly down the sidewalk with the wheel-bed. The problem was that if there was no flat part to slide down at the cross street, that left us flying over the curb, slamming down hard. Once I almost dumped Pinkman onto 108th Street like a bricklayer dumps a pile of bricks. The wheel-bed flew into the air, tilted down sharply, and then jammed into the street. It stopped and Pinkman kept sliding. But he didn't go all the way down. Some benevolent supernatural force kept him up there, except for his leg, which dangled over the edge like a broken tree branch, his toes submerged in the puddle. I had to ask strangers to help me level out the wheel-bed and get it going again. He yelled at me the whole way back. That night I kept waking up from the sound of my own teeth grinding.

When we got back to The Home, he always had me wheel him over to the aviary down the hall from the lobby. This was a floor-to-ceiling extravaganza, filled with fake branches and flowers and way too many finches. The birds had adapted to this prison by lining up on the topmost branch and dive-bombing, one by one, to the bottom, only to hop back up and get in line again. On Sundays, this Sisyphean bird show was the main attraction at The Home, and it was impossible to wheel him close to the glass thanks to all the other wheelchairs already parked there. Sitting there, in the back, he would begin to talk at the top of his voice just to piss people off.

"Excuse me!"

And so would begin his slow push to the front. He didn't really need me for this, because he could wheel himself forward on the smooth hospital floor. If the person in front of him was asleep, he would ram the wheel-bed into the back of the chair until its occupant woke up, confused and afraid.

"Wake up! God damn old people! You're already dead! Coming through!!"

It was a lot for him to go from the real world of sun and air and the street back into this world of stagnation and fluorescent light. I could still hear him yelling as I walked out through the lobby to the front door when it was time for me to go. When they told me that he'd died after a second amputation, I was happy to think that he'd finally broken out for good. ▪

# Belva's Meat Market

He is blunt as a dull knife....

BY DENA RASH GUZMAN *(Issue 29)*

IT SMELLS LIKE MEAT. Raw. Outside, the sheep talk to each other in the rain. They bleat and mew, strong and steady. I wonder if they say, "Why are we in this pen? Why are we in this pen? We want to go back to our pasture."

Inside, they are dead, and for sale. Chops. Sausage. Also for sale, water buffalo. Ground, steak, roast. Water buffalo? In a rural Oregon butcher shop, this is not what I expect. This shop is the nearest business to my house. Five miles from my farm, up a windy hillside and down a narrow lane and up a country highway. Trees, trees, trees, so green is the drive to Belva's Meat Market. Moss on everything but the pavement and the animals. Moss on a broke down truck abandoned on an overgrown, foreclosed upon nursery across the street from Belva's. Constant green, growth, growing.

The woman behind the counter here, the most amazingly beautiful woman I have seen in my life, has just ripped me off. She wrapped my order and took my credit card for payment. Upon overcharging me, she declared that she did not know how to refund my money, and I would have to pick more meat. I had been warned she would do this and to bring cash, but I forgot the cash, because I was excited to gaze at Ivan. Harmless gazing: I am married, but how could I not be excited to gaze at Ivan? Upon my entering the shop, the woman behind the counter caught me gazing at Ivan, giggling a bit as I said hello to him, and he then introduced her as his wife. I wonder if the overcharge was her power play. Her accent is deep as Russian snow and I cannot detect the truth inside it. She hands me my extra meat and stares, so beautiful, but dead on, surely as the devil must stare before he rapes you of your soul for a handful of coins.

This is my first time at Belva's Meat Market. I am new to town. As I leave with my four extra pounds of sausage and water buffalo, I see the Russians also sell wine. I take note. It is expensive, but wine is wine when wine is such a distant commodity. Fifteen minutes by car to the nearest town from my house; Belva's is only seven minutes away. I consider the convenience, but somehow, though excited and a borderline alcoholic, I know I will never come back to Belva's.

I met the owner of Belva's last week. Ivan came to speak to my husband about lettuce, and to invite us to be patrons of his meat market. We grow lettuce. Ivan is a butcher. He let us know he would slaughter and butcher our livestock for us. We told him we had none yet, with no immediate plans to procure any.

He looked blank and still. "But you have barns and pasture and sixty acres. I do not understand this lack of animals."

We explained it as a financial investment we are unready to make.

He scratched his head. "This is stupid. You need some meat."

Ivan is six feet five inches tall and from Bogorodsk, in the Moscow Oblast. He came to Oregon six years ago, at age twenty. I wanted to listen to what he was saying. His delivery was compelling.

He is handsome as hell. Blond, stormy. Muscles and grit. Narrow, bright eyes. Ivan. Sigh. He looks mean, but honest. Earnest. Curious.

He is blunt as a dull knife, too. He looked around our farm, a recent purchase. In need of repair; gone to seed. We have fifteen buildings, sixty acres, two rivers and a flock of transplanted urban chickens. We have never farmed before, garden hobbyists who came into a windfall and decided to invest it in a dilapidated former flower plantation. We have one greenhouse up and running, a bounty of greens and deformed carrots, all organic, all kind of ugly, some moldy. The greenhouse is 1930s vintage, part leaded glass, part missing glass and part plastic sheeting, rigged to let the sun in and keep the cold and wind out.

"You need to fix this glass, Steven. That sheeting looks like shit," Ivan said to my husband. Ivan is sedate and intense at the same time, like when a parent whispers their anger instead of yelling it. Then, the child really listens. Steven looked at the greenhouse, half laughing and half, I imagined, wanting to do as Ivan said.

Ivan turned to me. Some might say he turned on me. "What are you?"

"What am I?" I had an existential crisis. What am I, I thought? What am I? Why was this handsome man asking me to self-actualize?

"Yes. What are you? You are dark." His accent is so thick that for a moment, I did not understand the word dark. I stood, dumb and starry-eyed. Ivan. "Where are your people from, Elizabeth? We are not used to dark people in Boring."

He rolled the letter z in Elizabeth into something like a letter r. I stood silent, thinking zephyr, or Zorro. Steven spoke for me.

"Elizabeth is Dominican and Greek, Ivan."

Ivan laughed. "I do not want to be here when she gets pissed at you. There will be more broken glass." Steven laughed, too, but I giggled. Steven looked at me sideways. I snapped out of it.

"Really, though, Steven. I have to ask you. Why did you buy this shit hole? You like this? You like these falling down buildings and this mud? This place is shit. I left Russia to get away from this kind of shit. You need to fix this shit up. Does your wife like this shit? Maybe it is better than Greece or Dominica, but she should have stayed home where it is at least warm and sunny, if this is true."

We fell silent. Ivan left shortly after, and we drank two bedtime bottles of wine in our falling down shit hole, looking out at the stars, knowing there was very little between us and their light but decades of wear and some windowpanes. ▪

# An Honest Conversation

Grandma painted on slabs of butter.

BY KEERTHANA JAGADEESH *(Issue 29)*

WE WERE WALKING on the two finger trail around Ulsoor Lake; she was telling me why squirrels had lines on their back. "Squirrels are the only animals born from the tips of trees. Baby squirrels sprout at the tip of branches and slide down the tree bark on their backs. The bark scratches lines onto their backs. And that's why squirrels never leave their trees, their mothers."

I only half understood my grandmother's explanations. I half believed them, I half loved her.

We lived in an old Brahmin house that had more garden than house. Our house was just four ground-floor rooms placed next to each other like the squares of a Rubik's cube. Eraser-sized windows, pencil-sized window grills, no glass pane. The door was a slab of wooden butter that looked like it was melting because rats had been eating away its edges for the past thirty years. And it all used to be white, underneath all the rain damage and the yellowness of age.

Grandma and I were the neighborhood light bulbs that emitted an odd light that attracted flies and strange questions. One frequently asked question was: how did my grandfather die? She'd say he died on the inside, like a flower that shriveled and died because it swallowed its own honey. They'd ask another question, vainly trying to understand us: "But what happened to your grandson's parents though?"

"I'm sure they're behind the curtains. We've never bothered to check though." She answered like this each time. Some people would stop talking to us after this conversation while others grew fascinated, surrounding Grandma like the protective petals of a flower.

I reasoned Grandma's behavior, telling myself that she probably talked like this because she was a painter, a job none of my friend's parents ever seemed to have. But I've always wanted to know my grandmother beyond her words. For most people, their words were a bridge to their mind. My grandmother's words were a bridge to her paintings, the ones in which I couldn't make out circles and rectangles.

Apart from canvas and paper paintings, Grandma painted on slabs of butter and called them butter paintings. She'd mix food-coloring powders into see-through liquid, not water. Different pools of color in separate small steel bowls. I would watch her trace color, the paintbrush touching the butter like it was in love. She would usually paint tree canopies or the sky over a sea or just swirls of circles. Once she was finished painting a slab, she'd run to the kitchen and grab a blowtorch. She'd laugh excitedly and say, "This is the best part! You enjoy watching this don't you?" I didn't enjoy watching it but I never admitted that to her. I could never look away from her face as she used the blowtorch to melt the butter painting. It was done methodically. First the four corners were warmed, then a hole was melted into the center and by then you could see Grandma's face become happy in the sad way. We'd watch the colors curve and bloom and fade into the butter. "This is like as if I was inside my brain, watching my thoughts," she'd say as she dipped her little finger in the melted pool. "Hmm, curious," she'd say as she licked the butter off her little finger.

I had a rare glimpse into Grandma's mind when her old friend from Davengere came to stay with us for one night. He was unlike other old people in that he didn't stoop or smell of Ponds cream. We sat around our old dining table in the kitchen, eating some wobbly milk pie he'd brought for us. Grandma and he ate it right out of the baking pan while they'd given me a mushy slice in a steel bowl; this was Grandma's way of excluding me from their conversation. They both had their elbows on the table top, occasionally pointing their spoon at the other's face to emphasize a point. If I stayed quiet, I would be allowed to stay up till 9 p.m. and listen to their talk.

Grandma held her chin in her palm as she spoke. "So, you're applying to teach at Srishti? I gave up years ago. The more I talked about paintbrush angles, the less the kids learnt. But you've always been a good teacher."

He replied with a knowing smile, "Some people are painters and some people are painting teachers. Anyway, this visit isn't about my teaching position at Srishti. It's about your gallery showcase in three days. Everyone's getting excited. How do you feel?"

Grandma put down her spoon and held her elbows in her hands as she said, "Hmm, I don't know. We'll see. I'm a little nervous."

"You say that all the time but I'm sure it'll be a success. More people are coming to see you, the odd little butterfly you are. Your paintings are a nice supplement to meeting you."

"That's an odd compliment. I'm not the person you remember me from ten years ago. Time has changed me and my paintbrush strokes," said Grandma.

"That's true but some people don't lose their inherent colors. I'm sure deep down you're still the girl who ran after squirrel secrets. Remember how you used to steal bird nests and keep your earrings and pens in them, convinced they'd give birth to eggs? Do you still have that bird nest?"

"No, my mother burned it. She said I had one home, I didn't need another home."

I'd never heard stories of Grandma as a girl. I interjected, "Grandma, what are squirrel secrets?"

I knew I shouldn't have interrupted them as Grandma seemed to remember that I was there. She turned to me, "You've finished your pie, let's get you to bed. It's late."

"But I want to know!"

But my bowl was already taken away and she was driving me to my room, her hands cupping my shoulders like it was a steering wheel.

The next day, after our guest had left, she knew I was mad at her for excluding me. I was sitting in the garden, on our bed of weeds, digging holes by punching my fist into the soft earth. I'd spit into each fist-sized hole and cover the white froth with more earth. I was getting my fists and my white shirt dirty. Grandma let me get dirty like this and pull out weeds when I was mad at her. She'd sit on our white swing set and draw sketches on the large sketchpad on her lap. Once I'd run out of spit to fill the holes, I'd stop and sit next to Grandma, watching her draw my face in different stages of a lie.

"I'm sorry about last night. I wanted to talk to my friend alone. You don't like it when I hover around when your friends are over to play." In a way, neither of us has accepted each other. But I, at least, tried to understand her; I said, "But you know all my friends, you talk to them. You don't want me around your friends or your paintings."

"That's because you'd be bored. And you say you don't understand my paintings. And you touch the paint on the canvas. Your fingerprints dirty the painting."

I stayed quiet because it was true. She continued, "But I'll tell you what a squirrel secret is. Let's go to Ulsoor again."

* * * *

"Can we get a pet squirrel for our garden?" I asked.

"Only if we can catch one here!" she said as her stooped back did a trotting run on the green mossy grass surrounding the Lake. Against the strips of teal water and tree canopies, Grandma looked like a painting that I could understand. And to someone looking at us from afar, I was a part of her painting too. We'd make a nice watercolor.

"Well, we have to run if we're ever going to catch up with any squirrel."

We ran after one that had a star shaped splotch on the back of its head. It was carrying something round. It stopped at the foot of a Banyan tree and dug a hole in the cone formed by two slithering roots. It stuck its head up a lot, nervously, as it buried its treasure. It looked up at the surrounding water one more anxious time before it ran away.

"So, what's a squirrel secret?" I turned to my grandmother.

"Well, to find out you have to dig up what that squirrel buried."

I ran over to the spot between the huge roots and dug out a handful of earth.

"Grandma! The squirrel had buried a peanut, look!" I ran over and opened my palm to her.

She smiled and said, "Well, you're not going to know the secret until you eat it." I stared at her.

"But I don't want to eat the squirrel's food. It's going to come looking for it at dinnertime. It'll be sad when it finds this gone."

She laughed and said, "But don't you want to know what a secret tastes like? I can't explain things. You have to eat it, to understand."

We were suddenly two different paintings. She was a portrait that hung in shadowy light and I was an abstract piece with clearly defined circles and rectangles.

I said, "No, I don't want to know. I'll just put this back. I want to go back home."

* * * *

Maybe Grandma became a little scared of me after that squirrel day at Ulsoor because she let me eat packets of chips and she listened to me recite multiplication tables without interrupting me with her explanations of how numbers 1 and 2 were a married couple and how numbers 3 and 4 were best friends. I knew she was really trying when she let me attend her gallery showcase on Friday night. We even wore coordinated outfits to let other people know that we were related— she wore a white sari with thin gold leaves trimming the edges and I wore a white kurta with gold water waves trimming the bottom. When we entered the Srishti gallery, she put her arm around my shoulder as people streamed around her. People were wandering around almost like they were lost, lost in the understanding of Grandma's paintings. A small group crowded around Grandma, asking her questions. They started at the first painting hanging at the entrance; it was of an old man's wrinkles and his beard.

They'd ask her, "The lightness of this piece… how do you do it?" Grandma would say, "I wanted to bring out the heaviness of age; I don't understand how it became this light. I didn't expect it, really."

As the evening went on, people asked more questions.

"How did you understand the shadows in the lake?"

"Where did you find the darkness for this tree?"

"How did you draw the veins for his skin?"

"What color is this lightness?"

Grandma would usually say, "I don't know, I just felt like water. It really flowed." Or if she really wanted to answer a question, she'd say, "I wanted to know why people got lost so I painted lots of light. I'm not sure I found out why though."

So many questions about things Grandma couldn't understand. So many things I didn't understand about Grandma's answers but we just stood there together in our matching white outfits with gold trimming. ▪

# We Will Get To Know You

A segment from the novel *The Shaman Factory*

BY MP SNELL *(Issue 29)*

THERE WAS A MAN. I knew him for over twenty years. I also knew his wife. She turned yellow and died. The first thing I said when he led me into his bed was "I am sorry she died. I am sorry she is no longer with you."

"Perhaps there was a reason she died," he said as our bodies closed in on each other he was dreaming seducing imagining as men do before and women do after.

This man, Paul, fought to find a reason. Even as she was dying touching a near stranger's lips any escape any reason until six months later realizing he was simply insane with grief.

(On a ferry it was dark. They were traveling, he and the woman who turned yellow in the hospital. He needed a break, the smell. She was asleep. She was sleeping more and more. The fresh air. The dark night. Waves going deeper into the sea. Someone to hold. Someone to press his lips against. She was dying, it was hard just looking at her. How could he kiss her. Find someone else. In the dark water against the boat the waves striking its side.)

Paul and this woman, Jo, met on a plane. On their first date she was so nervous she went to her dentist's office for drugs. She was living with a painter above a diner he was with his second wife—a doctor. Within a month he was divorced. Jo moved in, first to a small apartment where he opened cans of Chef Boyardee for his children then to a brownstone no one would buy because of its location.

When there were areas in the city no one wanted.

When Jo was alive I was with another man. In theory. This other man, Dean, flew in from Nebraska and showed up at Paul's front door. Paul had casually told him in a hotel dinning room "you must come to New York." Dean took these words as an invitation. Jo answered the door. She was charmed by the sketches he showed her, drawings he'd made to illustrate his compositions. She invited him in took his tape to Paul who listened to the curious sounds that were so different than his. Paul is as famous as a classical composer can be. Paul and Jo did not have children together. Dean slipped in and became their child.

I met Dean after Paul had connected him with a theater troupe that performed his work. Their main actress wasn't available; the director asked me to be in the show. "Listen to this tape, this guy is a genius, I want you to consider being in this show." I didn't need to hear the tape. I had nothing else to do.

The director had seen me scream into a microphone once. He had, to be exact, shown a flashlight onto my body from the ground while I screamed. It was a thin gallery full of paintings what I imagined I was expressing I can't remember.

In the first show of Dean's I wore a sequined aqua dress and fishnet stockings. I remember being lifted into the air. In another show I wore a flesh-colored skin tight suit and was the head. As Dean's pieces developed, I actually spoke. I was the Night Nurse. I was a Manson Family Girl… which in fact I looked exactly like if I parted my hair in the middle and had spent the night with Dean arguing.

We thought well together, we argued well. Bums on the street were scared of us. He never hit me, I always hit him. Umbrellas. Those worked well.

Dean had recently left a cult, which was the most exciting thing to do in Nebraska. He had learned tricks from "Storm Alligator" on how to control people. Storm had a band tattooed around his eyes. He was an ex-marine who, along with his ex-prostitute "Flame," enticed young boys into their house. They would sit around all day studying their dreams then walk military style in a single straight line to the A&P for groceries. Dean said that Storm knew where he was at all times.

A photograph of Storm and Flame was one of the few things he brought to the city.

Dean watched me. Dean watched me dance in that first rehearsal and asked Paul if he should ask me out on a date. Paul told him I was very talented but he should not date me. Dean asked me out and bought me a hamburger, which was the first and last time he bought me anything. I remember his thin body and sucking each other. I remember ripping the skin off his penis. Our sexual chemistry was nonexistent but we were inches away from each other for five years.

We were both obsessed with work. I told him what direction to take his music; he put me in his pieces. Every time I tried to leave him he threatened suicide or would fire me.

I finally flew across the country, around the time Jo was dying, to get away from Dean. He made one visit out. He gave me lice and we went to Disneyland.

I see now that Dean and Paul were inseparable in my mind. I never knew who I was there for.

My father came down from New Hampshire for every performance—to the bars, the gas stations, the avant-garde theaters, we even made it to Lincoln Center. My mother doesn't travel. She is nearly agoraphobic, which works well now that they are in an assisted living center.

I left for New York City the minute I could, because of my father, who had brought me to the city every year from the age of eight. My father, the mathematician who wanted to be an Opera Singer. Once a year he went to the "real opera singers'" throat doctors. Some of the singers kindly invited him backstage. We would visit them in their dressing rooms, their large bodies, their tired faces, and their amusement for my dear Dad.

Jo never told Paul how much time she spent with Dean; Dean was troubled. Together the three of us were like wayward children living in someone else's house. Paul was away often. He was happy Jo was taken care of. We distracted her from the inevitable isolation of being with Paul.

As a younger man Dean was seductive, elfish. As an older man he became heavy not in body but in spirit. Bitter. Paranoid.

When Paul returned from his tours Jo suddenly realized the house was hers, she was an adult. She would put on a sexy gray miniskirt she had found on sale at French Connection. Dean and I ran back to our walkup on Ridge Street. We stepped over the junkies in the hall then as quickly as possible opened and closed the multi-locked door. We warmed the apartment with pans of water and waited for the phone to ring. Paul. Asking us to come over for dinner. We pretended we hadn't just been there.

We all loved secrets.

"We will get to know you." Jo said, staring at me the first time I was over after declining several invitations. They thought I didn't like them. I knew if I entered their house I would never leave.

The house has four stories. It is brick. It has black railings in front. A man broke in through the small window to the left of the door. Many changes have been made to the house since I knew it so intimately. The back wall in the basement has been knocked out, glass opens into a patio. But it has never had the light it had when Jo was alive.

The house was a movie, a fantasy of what it would be like to live in the city.

When Paul was traveling Jo took the subway up to her graphics studio at Carnegie Hall. She drew whimsical book jacket covers, smoking cigarette after cigarette pausing to change the radio station, staring off into space her eyes framed by her thick black glasses.

She preferred everything framed.

Dean had keys to the house.

We would arrive late morning and leave just as the sky was going dark. Jo smoked, so Dean's cigarettes did not give us away. Dean smoked so much he clogged the wheels of the computer. We'd blast the music make cappuccinos; create soundtracks and listen to music.

Dean would say I was a worthless talentless pathetic piece of shit. Or was it talentless pathetic worthless? Then tell me little white birds were flying around my head. Why I thought he was charming I do not know, but I loved him.

We charged into the world of success as if it were a game of tag.

I don't think he was with men at that point. I remember him being homophobic.

After I left him, Dean replaced me with a woman who looked like me but was shorter, then a woman who looked like us but had shorter hair, then a woman who was tall with long hair, then a woman who looked like him, then an Asian woman who looked like a boy and finally a boy from Thailand who dressed up like a girl.

Dean was adopted. He said his mother was either a whore or a stupid Kansas farm girl. After her parents' divorce, Jo's father put a gun in his mouth and shot himself in her mother's driveway. They had dramatic stories to share. I grew up in a square white house built in 1777 with window seats in a small New England town so I didn't say much.

Jo spent hours with a therapist so she wouldn't bother Paul with her sadness. Dean smoked a lot of dope. When Jo was dying, her therapist said he couldn't see her anymore. He was not a "therapist for the dying."

Jo drew pictures of his box of tissues over and over again.

I have never seen a woman love a man more than Jo loved Paul.

The last time I saw Jo I was upstairs in the library next to their bedroom. She was on the couch watching one of her bad television shows, a dating game, a show that made her cackle. Paul ran downstairs to get ice cream as if this would turn the gathering into a party.

As Jo died Dean moved into the house to help take care of her. It was Dean who took her on unending walks. All she wanted to do was go outside. Dean was desperate for sleep, hiding in the basement behind the sofa; Jo kept calling for him. She was hungry for air, flashing signs, traffic, and oblivious to everyone staring at her. Her eyes were too huge for her body, wild grinning features on a collapsing body.

The teeth themselves can sing. That's when you know it's near the end.

Jo had two parrots, each with its own black cage. Jack and Jill. She asked Dean to take care of the birds when she died. If there was a guest she didn't like she'd let the birds out. They would attack like dogs.

When Jo wanted Paul to herself, which was hard to achieve as he always surrounded himself with people even as he was also always alone, she would start up the stairs to their library. She would make the sound of a bird and he would follow without knowing why.

Paul and Jo got married 15 days before her death on my birthday. She knew it was my birthday. He did not.

Those last months she drew with charcoal—empty stages dark large urns.

After she died, Paul would regret not helping her more with her work.

Dean took care of the parrots, as promised, but it became too hard. They were finally sent to her mother whom Jo hated but who took excellent care of the birds. ▪

# Part Four

# HUMOR

# Witticisms Lost to Time

BY DAN MCCOY *(Issue 12)*

**Oscar Wilde:**
"There is only one thing worse than being talked about, and that is being arrested for sodomy."

"Either this wallpaper has to go, or I redecorate the place myself. And I have no throw pillows to speak of."

**Dorothy Parker:**
*When asked to use the word "horticulture" in a sentence:* "Horticulturally speaking, that garden is terrific. No wait. I've been drinking. Let me get back to you in a week when I sober up and can think of a pun."

"If they laid all the girls at the Yale prom end to end, I'd wonder why they didn't give me a ring. I could be there in less than an hour."

**Samuel Johnson:**
"A woman delivering a sermon is like a dog standing on its hind legs. You can see its bait and tackle, and let me tell you, that's nothing to sneeze at."

*When asked if he believed in infant baptism:* "Believe in it? Madam, the only way to soften up the little buggers is to marinate them until juicy."

*When asked to refute a popular idea of the time, regarding the intangibility of the material world:* "I refute it thus!" (Striking a rock with his toe.) "OW! Ooh. Ooooh. Holy *shit* that hurts."

**Mark Twain:**
"When angry, count ten. When very angry, break a bottle on the bar and rearrange someone's face with it. I recommend a vodka bottle."

"Man is the only animal that blushes, or needs too.... That is, excepting the frog. But it only blushes when it's done something very, very dirty."

"Anyone attempting to find a moral in this narrative will be shot. That also goes for trespassers. Yeah. Trespassers too."

**Abraham Lincoln:**
"A man's legs should be long enough to wrap around a woman's torso." ■

# Praise for *Codename: Vengeance*

BY PAUL MACTAVISH *(Issue 13)*

"Sharp-eyed and suspenseful, Trevor Banks' tale of ultimate payback raises the bar for the genre. Just as he did with *Sins of the Geisha*, Banks has given the world a meaty piece of red-hot fiction."
— Carl Sutton, author of *Sudden Justice*

"Ballsy and big-hearted, Detective Slade Sheehan is a character for the ages. Only Trevor Banks could create a protagonist with so many layers. A champion of justice, but with a soft spot for small-time hoods, you'll be rooting for Sheehan to conquer his fetishes and win back his one true love, all the way to the blood-soaked but tender climax."
— Thom Halpern, author of *Sharkville*

"With Dex Hauser, Trevor Banks has created the type of bible-quoting, gun-toting, unrelenting killing machine too long missing from contemporary literature. Hauser's near-daily axe fights with the troubled but brilliant Sheehan result in a riveting, terrifying page-turner. The verdict is in: Banks' long-awaited follow-up to *Blood Splatter* is guilty of greatness."
— Patricia Quinn, author of *She's Been Captured By Mountain Men*

"Crackling tension. I couldn't put it down. Except during the opera scene. I didn't get that. Why was Sheehan wearing that reversible red

Illustration: Dan McCoy

cape, and how did snapping the cellist's neck contribute to the plot? But I was absorbed."

— Will S. Donovan, author of *Murder at the Waffle House*

"The cellist was *obviously* working for Dex Hauser and would have been a great source of information, but Sheehan was so drunk that he didn't consider that. Plus, he always wore the reversible cape when drinking. It was symbolic: black for routine investigative work, red for off-duty thrill kills and sex with whores. It's so obvious. Read it again. Banks scores."

— Frank Collins, author of *Kill, Sweet Raven*

"Anyone who has woken up next to a dead swimsuit model and succumbed to that old necrophilic urge will relate to Dex Hauser's struggle for redemption. It's impossible to not see yourself on every page and sort through all the harebrained schemes and drug-clouded orgies you've been a part of. The whole thing just tore my heart out. I love you, son. And thanks for the smokes."

— Henry "Cougar" Banks, author of *Cellblock Zero: My Life in the Hole*

"Astonishing. That my own son could write something so violent and perverse. Everybody's killing everybody, and all the characters have multiple sex partners. I didn't raise him this way."

— Florence Banks, author of *Timesaving Tips for Tuckered Moms*

"Trevor Banks? Decent jump shot. Tough under the basket. Flipped out and broke another player's nose once. But I remember him as a nice kid overall. Real quiet. His book? Haven't read it. I like romance and sports biographies."

— Roy Sybil, author of *The High School Basketball Handbook*

"A work for the ages. All hail Trevor Banks!"

— Harold Bloom, author of *The Western Canon* and *Shakespeare: The Invention of the Human* ■

# College Envy

## From the poison ivy league

BY DAN MCCOY (*Issue 14*)

IF YOU CAN MAKE IT IN NEW YORK, you can make it anywhere, but you'll have to fight your way past a bunch of former Harvard, Yale, Columbia, or NYU students to get there. Sure, said graduates may be easy to take in a street fight, but their superior understanding of the law will mean a stiff civil suit, so yours will be an amoral victory at best. My days are spent in a miasma of Ivy Leaguers and graduates from non-ivy prestige schools—the sort of people who could probably explain how I just misused "miasma." They all have better jobs than me; but, to be fair, I'm a professional unemployed person.

Last year, a former *Washington Post* reporter named Jay Matthews wrote a book called *Harvard Schmarvard: Getting Beyond the Ivy League to the College That Is Best for You.* My college placed second on his "Most Overlooked" list. Although I enjoy any book that puts the word "Schmarvard" right there in the title, being the second most overlooked school in America is the world's second most backhanded compliment (the first being, "Sex with you met my expectations"). Overlooked is the sort of adjective reserved for sentences like "You know what Harrison Ford movie has been kinda overlooked? *The Devil's Own.*" What's worse, my alma mater didn't even make the top

Illustration: Dan McCoy

of the list. We're number two. Apparently, we're the *Hollywood Homicide* of colleges.

My college actually has a bit of a philosophical reason for being overlooked. Due to its Quaker affiliation, it places strong emphasis on doing good work without seeking recognition. However, I've discovered, as a chronic job-hunter, that when you're sitting in an interview and you begin to explain the philosophical and religious reasons why your interviewer has never heard of your school, you've lost the battle. I usually stick to letting them know that I can type 60 words per minute. (Another tip: the "skills" section of your resume should not be sexually explicit.)

Certainly, graduates from name colleges deserve success. They worked hard (or at the very least, paid a large sum of money) and showed a presciently realistic understanding of the world by choosing a university whose name everyone recognizes. Were I a high school guidance counselor, I'd cancel my subscription to "Selecting the School That's Right for You," and begin handing out the "It's Only Student Loan Debt If They Haven't Heard of You" pamphlets. Also, I'd quit my job.

Since my feeling of entitlement rivals that of any Yale alum, I decided to pretend to be a Yalie for a day, to see how an Ivy League degree might have changed my life. This is my journal:

**6:00 a.m.**

I have decided that the sort of person who went to Yale is the sort of person who gets up at six in the morning. Also, probably they jog. Since I spent the previous evening at Chevys, drinking margaritas to celebrate my decision to keep this journal, I push my fiancée out of bed with the instructions to go jogging and to describe the experience to me upon her return. I sleep the sleep of the well-educated.

**10:30 a.m.**

Am trying to decide what a Yalie eats for breakfast. Granola suddenly seems too politically charged, and a bagel too ethnic. Being from Yale is hard. I decide to take a nap.

**11:00 a.m.**

Refreshed, I begin my day. Pushing aside my purple flip-flops and unlaundered jeans, I reach to the back of the closet for my pinstriped suit, and I dress to the nines. Showing the foresight that only a top-class education can buy, I look out the window, note that it's raining outside, and grab an umbrella.

**11:05 a.m.**

I encounter my downstairs neighbor on the front stoop. Have a brief conversation:

Me: Hello, did you know I went to Yale?

DN: I doubt that.

Me: Oh yes. I remember my days on the punting team fondly….

DN: You didn't go to Yale. Your umbrella says "Earlham College."

Me: Ah. Can you excuse me? One moment.

**11:06 a.m.**

I return upstairs to exchange my umbrella for one I have spray-painted with the word "Yale."

**11:10 a.m.**

Me: As I was saying, I'm a Yale man, myself…

DN: Can I go? I'm really late for work.

**12:00 Noon**

Lunchtime already! I've decided that a man who chooses only the finest in colleges would settle for nothing less than the finest in fine dining. So I've booked a lunchtime reservation at Aureole. Starting with the osteria caviar, I move rapidly to the lobster ceviche salad, and finish with a triple chocolate mousse. Everything is extraordinary—so much so that I retire to the restroom to disgorge, then order everything over again. (Note: The food was slightly less revelatory the second time. Perhaps the chef was tired?)

**1:30 p.m.**

I leave the waitress a generous tip, then skip out on the bill. Although today I may be a Yale grad, I'm no richer than yesterday.

**1:35 p.m.**

A gentleman in a waiter's uniform attempts to accost me as I round the corner. He is not dissuaded by my cries of "I have no money, ruffian!" nor, "I have important friends in Skull and Bones!" I beat him to death with my umbrella.

**1:25 p.m.**

I am a bit shaken by the day's homicidal turn, but I remember the words of John Merriman: "Yale is more than going to classes. Yale is staggering on in the best fashion possible." In that spirit, I stagger into the gutter and pass out.

**4:00 p.m.**
I awake several hours later, to find that I am late for my job interview (which I had scheduled with one of the city's top law firms, upon receiving my imaginary diploma). As I stumble into their restroom I realize that I've left the murder weapon lying in the street. "Stupid! Stupid!" I mutter to myself, as I splash cold water in my face in an attempt to quell the memory of the man's desperate death cries. "Pull yourself together! You can do this. You can do this, McCoy." I stare at my reflection in the mirror, but I cannot recognize the wild-eyed specter that looks back at me. I smash my face into the glass. Blood drips down my face and onto the floor, pooling next to my diamond-studded spats.

**4:15 p.m.**
"Hi, nice to meet you!" I say to Julie, the pleasant woman who will be interviewing me. "As you can see by my resume, I went to Yale!"

**4:30 p.m.**
Interview did not go well. Apparently many legal phrases are in Latin. My two years of high school French helped not one bit. As a last ditch effort, I attempted to give her the Phi Beta Kappa handshake as we said our goodbyes. She misinterpreted the gesture as a come-on and asked whether the "special skills" listed on my resume were accurate. After some heated innuendo, we come to a physical agreement. Afterwards, I feel dirty.

**6:00 p.m.**
I choke down some saltines.

**7:00 p.m.**
I am awakened from a restless sleep by a knock on the door. I open it to find two serious-looking men, who identify themselves as homicide detectives. They wish to question me in conjunction with a waiter's death. Pulling the murder weapon from an evidence bag, they ask, "Is this your umbrella?" "No, it couldn't be mine," I say. "I didn't go to Yale. See?" I present them with my real diploma. Their brows unfurrow. "Oh. Okay,

sir. Sorry to have bothered you." I can see their eyes fill with pity, as they realize they've never heard of my school. I hope they don't notice my sweat-soaked shirt. "Quite all right, officer," I say, with forced good cheer.

**7:05 p.m.**
I weep for all mankind.

So, is the Ivy League right for you? Ask yourself these questions:

- Can you afford it?
- Do you enjoy a challenge?
- Do you want a good job?
- Does human life mean little to you?
- Do you crack easily under interrogation?
- Which sentence best describes you: "I am well liked by my friends" or "I am well liked by my cronies"?
- Is death just the gateway to a better life?

And what of me? To be honest, when I ask myself, "Was it worth it—the day I spent lying about having gone to Yale?" I have mixed feelings. On the one hand, my hands will always be stained by the blood of the innocent, I have whored myself for personal gain, and I have descended into a miasma (?) of pain and deceit from which I may never claw my way out.

On the other hand, it got me out of the apartment, which is something. ▪

# Devon for Pope in '06

BY DEVON T. COLEMAN *(Issue 15)*

GOOD EVENING. Unless it's afternoon where you are, then good morning. As you know, the Pope is dead. The Catholic Church is running around, trying to find a new Pope—British Royal Family Picture Day style. So I'm throwing my pointy hat into the ring. I'm qualified. I have my own staff and everything. And I'm comfortable with people kissing my ring. Even dudes. Even old dudes. But not dudes in wheelchairs. I am so serious about that, I can't even tell you.

There are a myriad of reasons why I should be Pope, including that I just used the word "myriad." I know you're thinking, "But Devon, there's already a new Pope." And you're right, but he isn't exactly a Hitler *youth* anymore. It's simply forward thinking (another reason!) on my part. So if you're through thinking things I already know, I'll continue. I would make a great Pope because I'm all about the people (and the papal). Everyone was very much "up in arms" about that brain-dead woman in Florida. If I were Pope, this problem would've been solved with two 1-900 numbers. One to let her "live," and one to let her finish dying. It was good enough for Jason Todd, it's good enough for her. It is my firm belief that the People should make these decisions. Though there will be room for the People's decisions to be overturned. The People don't always make the right choice. I mean, really, Constantine? Before Anthony Federov? Have you *heard* Federov?

Dan McCoy

Popes have to name themselves and as everyone knows, names are important. Pope Benedict Borington The Third or whatever doesn't seem to get that. I would be a great Pope because I'd have a great name. Here are a few I'm considering:

Pope Space Glider

Pope Hannibal (to show my love of plans coming together)
A Pope Named Scooby Doo
Ninja Pope!
Pope John Paul IV: Citizens On Patrol

If you were a guy who hated Catholicism, would you mess with a Pope with any of those names? I can already tell you the answer is no.

There are lots of other reasons I'd be the greatest Pope since that Pope who built the Pyramids, but you know, religion is all about faith. So you should just believe me.

Look for me on XBox Live. My screen name is "Gr8X_Communicator28." I'll completely let you win at Halo 2, but it'll seem like you beat me really bad. Because that's what Popes do. They give. ■

# An Email that Received No Response

Wild about baskets

BY RITCH DUNCAN *(Issue 15)*

*We're really wild about baskets! We want you to be wild about them too!! Email us at: (withheld)@aol.com — from wildaboutbaskets.com*

From: Ritch Duncan
To: (withheld)@aol.com
Subject: Basket questions
Hello—I am an unemployed writer living in Brooklyn, and I just came upon your website after a Google search looking for the history of the term "Hell in a hand basket." My dad says it all the time, usually in reference to how I'm living my life, and it cracks me right up. What's the story with that?! I figured you would be the person to ask, as you say on your website: "We're really wild about baskets! We want you to be wild about them too!!"

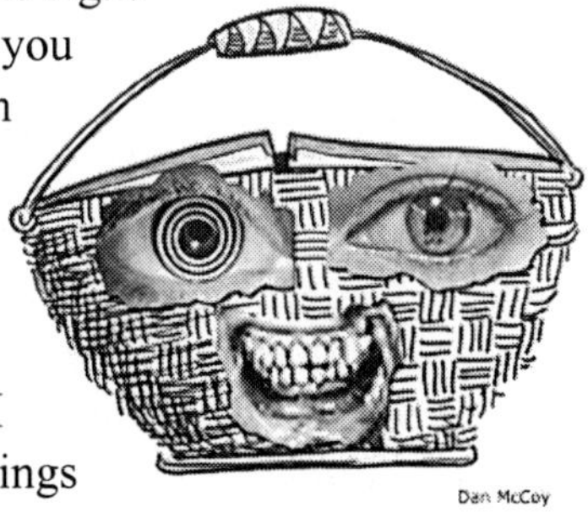

Currently, it would be a stretch to say that I am "wild" about baskets, but I certainly have nothing against them. All things considered, I am staunchly pro-basket.

In fact, I own a basket and I enjoy it quite a bit. Right now, it is sitting in my bedroom, and I put magazines and books in it so I can peruse them before bed. Still, my enjoyment of my basket is fairly conservative. Don't get me wrong, it's a nice basket. It was a gift from my mother and I enjoy having somewhere to put my magazines. Still—I think "wild" would not be the right adjective to describe my basket-related emotions.

Is there anything you could suggest that would increase my overall wildness about the one basket I do own, or does building a wildness vis-à-vis baskets require multiple baskets to get all fired up over?

I'd guess that you would suggest more baskets, or your website might not be called "Wild About Baskets"; it might be called "Get Wild About The Basket You Own!" or "I'm Wild About My One Solitary Basket!" or "Hey You! Get Your Goddamn Hands Off My Basket! It's My Favorite Basket, And I Am So Wild About It That Any Attempt To Wrest It From My Grasp Could Lead To Violence! Go Ahead And Test Me, Padre."

Come to think of it, seeing as I have never met anyone who is wild about baskets, I have several other basket-related questions if you have the time:

What is a tisket?

You probably saw this one coming, but while you are at it, what is a tasket?

Of these major sports terms employing the term "basket," which is your favorite and why?

Putting the biscuit in the basket — Hockey
Making a running basket catch — Baseball
"Basket!"— Basketball

Do you like basketball, or has the replacement of the original basket with a hoop and net caused you to abandon the sport entirely?

If they were to go back to using an actual basket in basketball, what kind of basket would you recommend? Keep in mind, it ought to be strong enough to withstand an NBA dunk.

What is the best basket movie of all time?

(NOTE: My vote goes to *Basket Case*, about a pair of conjoined twins who are separated when they are young, and the one twin lugs around his mutilated brother named Belial in a huge basket. Belial is pretty much just a head with an arm, and he goes nuts and kills people who get too close to his brother, because he has abandonment issues. I'm not sure how you are on horror films, but the basket gets a lot of screen time, so I thought you might be into that. There are a bunch of sequels, but stick to the original. Just a tip.)

(It also could be *The Wizard of Oz*. Lots of basket in that one, too. Thoughts?)

Would you agree with art critic Robert Hughes's assertion that the early images of 1980s artist Jean-Michel Basquait look quite vivid and sharp at first sight, but despite the fact that Basquait could bring off an intriguing passage of spiky marks or a brisk clash of blaring color from time to time, the work quickly settles into the visual monotony of arid overstyling?

If you were to ever punch a guy, would you aim for the bread basket, or would your ardor for baskets lead you to punch elsewhere, like the throat or spine?

OK—I think that's all the basket questions I have for now. I bet I could think of some more, but I'm late for a picnic, and need to pack a bag.

Best,<br>
Ritch Duncan ■

# Maternal Leggings, Paternal Sweatpants

## Was I allergic to fatherhood?

BY JAKE KALISH *(Issue 27)*

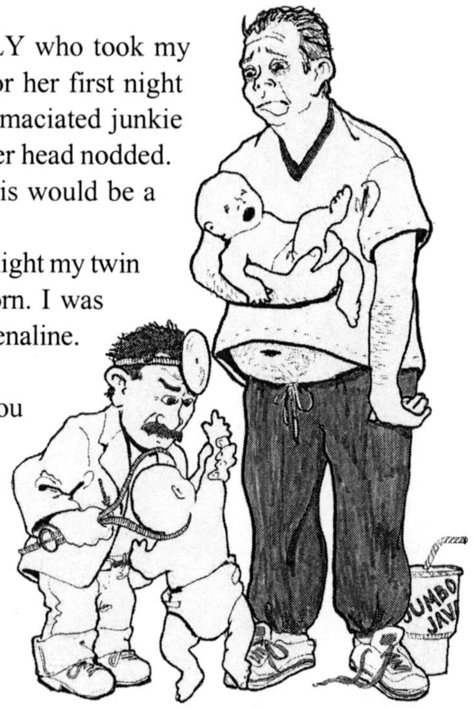

THE HOSPITAL ORDERLY who took my wife, Nola, to her room for her first night as a new mother was an emaciated junkie with eyelids that fluttered while her head nodded. I should have known then that this would be a hell of a year.

But I didn't know anything the night my twin daughters Una and Esme were born. I was bubbling over with joy and adrenaline. My mind was a complete blank.

No matter what sort of books you read, classes you take, training you think you're doing, nothing prepares you for being a parent. There's no transition. You fully aren't a parent, then: BAM! You are. It's like becoming a different creature. You feel like Gregor Samsa.

A better insect analogy: you're a fly, whizzing free and aimless through the air. Then, suddenly, you're an ant—ready and willing to trudge slowly, carrying a hundred times your own weight on your back.

Pregnancy is no preparation. Pregnancy is its own thing—an existence that's like neither the one you had before, nor the one to come. It's purgatory on Earth. And it lasts forever. Pregnancy is not like any 9-month period I've ever experienced. Those lasted 9 months. This took 15 years.

My wife's C-section, however, was literally 8 minutes—slightly less than the album version of "Purple Rain." The strings would have still been going by the time Nola and I became parents of 2 screaming, kicking, glistening, 5-pound aubergine people. Purple rain, indeed.

The doctors showed us Una and Esme—take a good look, parents, get that terrified expression off your faces—then whisked delirious Nola to a "recovery" room, where they allowed her to "recover" for a few minutes. Or until they could locate a junkie orderly.

A side note: The difference between day-shift and night-shift workers at the maternity ward is like the difference between, well, day and night. The day-shifters keep your newborn alive with pizzazz and aplomb while perfectly explaining to you how they are doing so. They are loving, understanding, calm, and efficient in dealing with the hysteria of brand-new life and brand-new parents.

Night-shifters…not so much. It wasn't just the junkie. It was also the angry, muttering nurse who felt it necessary to barge into Nola's room multiple times nightly to turn on the lights and move stuff around. (The one thing she didn't do was turn off the 20-minute, English-language instructional newborn care video that was on an all-night loop for the Hispanic woman in the next bed who spoke no English.)

* * * *

When we took our babies home from the hospital, all hell broke loose. What are the first few months with twins like? Imagine two people screaming in your ear all day and night. Now imagine being required to keep those people as close to you as possible. I loved Una and Esme immediately and completely. But I still spent many days wondering when the next bus left for Atlantic City.

Nola and I also had our unique dramas. For example, my exploding lip incident. One night, when the babies were 20 days old, and they were finally asleep, we watched *Gran Torino*. It was such a pleasure to watch a film that I barely noticed my mouth getting numb. I paid more attention a half-hour later in the bathroom, when I saw my upper lip was literally four times its normal size. But for being white, I was a living 19th century racist cartoon. Drawn by the biggest racist ever.

I got whisked through ER triage—that's how bad it looked—and told I had acute angioedema. If this allergic reaction had spread to my throat I could have stopped breathing, which often leads to death. It took two weeks for my lip to return to normal size.

A month later I had another, milder, angioedemic reaction. I went to a number of allergy specialists, who noted I didn't seem allergic to anything.

I offered that the Internet told me these reactions could be triggered by stress.

"That's possible, but unlikely," they all said. "Had there been a major change in your life prior to this episode?"

I wondered, Am I allergic to fatherhood?

* * * *

Two months later something far worse happened. I dropped Una. It was Father's day weekend (I know, the irony) and we were at my family's country house—a rustic log cabin in a charming state of disrepair. I tripped over a crack in the stone walkway and pitched forward with my 12-week old girl in my arms. I had her all the way until my left knee hit the walkway, and, rather than breaking my fall with an infant, I released her.

Una fell face-first. Then she just lay there. She looked up, bleeding from her cheekbone, and silently stared at me. I was relieved when she started crying, since I already was.

Nola rushed Una to the nearest hospital, Putnam County, which is, I believe, the hospital other countries cite when denigrating the American health care system. Putnam's star doctor was literally a dwarf with eyes set so close together they almost overlapped. He ordered a number of X-rays, the last set of which revealed what appeared to be bleeding on Una's brain. They'd have to keep her overnight. A nurse told Nola she'd pray for her child. My wife called me sobbing.

Later that day, Doc Closeeyes said that, while he was pretty sure that it was a brain bleed, perhaps they'd better take the ambulance 30 miles to Westchester Children's Hospital, where "they have much better facilities." (And, he neglected to mention, much better doctors. Wise is the man who knows he knows nothing.) Tiny Una was strapped to a gurney, plugged with IVs, and carried to the ambulance by huge paramedics who did their best to console Nola.

I met my wife and baby at Westchester Hospital. Una was strangely calm and casual, smiling even. (Baby, your brain is bleeding!) The doctor, who was not a dwarf and whose eyes were appropriately distanced, ate an ice cream sandwich. He smiled and said everything was fine. He strongly doubted there was any brain bleeding, but they'd do an X-ray just to be sure.

"Nope," he said, when he returned 20 gut-wrenching minutes later. "No bleeding on her brain."

No? So what is it?

"Well, li'l Una does have a pretty nasty scrape on her cheek."

He told us that what Putnam's doctor thought was a brain bleed was likely "a smudge." Or possibly "some blurring."

Blurring?

"I'm not sure what he thinks he saw," said the doctor. "You know, Putnam doesn't have great facilities."

* * * *

We managed to avoid any more ambulances for the rest of the year. The babies, healthy and thriving, have settled into being cute little identical twins who drive strangers apeshit.

If you don't like talking to strangers, don't have identical twins. The endless comments are not all positive. That old standby, "Double trouble!" (always delivered with a chuckle, like it's so clever because it rhymes) is actually a crappy thing to say. Who would point at a single baby and yell "Trouble!" at her parents?

"Double trouble" is a comment that often comes from the African-American community, who, besides that and the occasional "You got your hands full!" are overwhelmingly positive when it comes to identical twins. This is a good thing, because, right before we found out Nola was pregnant, we moved into a not-quite-legal sublet in Harlem. If you want to be illegally subletting white gentrifiers in Harlem, don't have identical twins. They're not known for their inconspicuousness.

Still, it was nice to receive a warm reaction in the neighborhood. The girls even got some fans. One woman, who always smiled and said hello when she saw Una and Esme, one day shouted across the street (while jumping and clapping) "Are those my babies? Those are my babies!"

Hispanic people are the undisputed best when it comes to identical twins. Everyone smiles. A high percentage offer: "Awwww" or "So cute!" And several times a day, we get a "God bless you." That's the clincher. Even if you don't believe in God, who doesn't want to be blessed by Him?

White people, on the other hand, suck. Twins frighten white people. Here are some of the comments we've received:

"It must be so hard."

"Sooo hard." (Literally, many white people have just uttered those two syllables.)

"I bet you're exhausted."

"How do you do it?"

"I can't imagine."

"I don't envy you."

It seems many Caucasians see twins as punishment. One woman, as she walked past us, turned to her friend and remarked: "My God, I would never want twins!" Apparently thinking part of our twin punishment was losing our hearing.

And everyone, of all races, wants to know two things:

1. "Can you tell them apart?"

Yes. Always. They look very different to us, even if they don't to you.

2. "Are they different?"

Well, yeah. They're two different people.

But even I was surprised at just how different Una and Esme, from the beginning, have been. Una is affectionate with her parents but reticent with strangers. Esme flirts with everybody and squirms when we pick her up. Una can sit quietly for long periods of time. Esme charges all over the place, often emitting high-pitched squeals. Una sometimes refuses to go back to sleep in the middle of the night just so she can spend an hour cuddling with her mother. Esme likes to try to catapult off things.

One of our friends described their differences as internality (Una) vs. externality (Esme). That sounds about right, at least for now. My fears for the future are that Una will have her heart broken and Esme will run into the street without looking.

What our girls have in common is that they couldn't care less about most baby toys. For this simple reason: baby toys are bullshit. Brightly colored, plastic, fake bullshit, when babies just want what's real. Here are my daughters' favorite things to play with:

1. An empty tube of Neosporin
2. Any remote control
3. Empty diaper boxes
4. Eyeglasses
5. Necklaces
6. Their parents' and grandparents' faces
7. Anything they're not supposed to have

Their desire for the forbidden is all-encompassing and doesn't bode well. This is the beginning of mischief, a concept they've grasped early. How do they know throwing things they're not supposed to throw is funny? What keen senses of humor!

* * * *

Of course, with all of this throwing, grabbing, and high-speed crawling in opposite directions, Nola and I, who vowed not to be nervous parents, find ourselves constantly chasing, bending, and reaching for our children to prevent them from doing the horrible things we envision them doing to themselves. It makes the muscles ache.

Then there's all the baby gear we have to carry or push. Which leads to the most important lesson of new parenting: If you have small children, don't expect to be comfortable unless they're in daycare or with a nanny. Comfort is the stuff of dreams. My biggest fantasy has nothing to do with a woman. It's a pitch-black, silent room, a cool breeze, and a California King bed with a firm mattress. Reality is lugging around a gigantic stroller, my raw thighs chafing, a river running through my ass cleavage.

The quixotic quest for comfort leads new parents to dress the way we do: maternal leggings, paternal sweatpants. This is precisely what we swore we wouldn't wear in public when we were in our 20s and didn't recognize the garments as parental uniforms.

With this much stuff to do, inevitably, Nola and I learned some things. Over time, we developed systems for caring for our daughters. I'd share some of these systems, but parents' choices are not that interesting unless they're horrible. Besides, I don't want to share our secrets because Nola and I are competing with other parents who have their own secrets. This is terrible but true—as much as we try to not think of this as a race, we do.

Our kids are bigger, but their kid walks already.

But our kids say more words.

"Is 'ba ba ba' a word?"

"Yes! Count it!"

* * * *

Our winning systems got us through Una and Esme's first year. Then, a week after our children celebrated their first birthday by slathering chocolate cake all over their adorable little faces, I got the whole family kicked out of our home. How? By yelling back at the angry, unreasonable old lady downstairs, who promptly reported us to the landlord, just as she had threatened to do.

Some might say, "Don't scream at the ancient, frail downstairs neighbor when you're subletting illegally," and those people might technically be right, but I live by the sword and I die by the sword. Whatever. She was mean and she yelled first.

And our new place is bigger and better than our old place, so there. We Kalishes keep on rolling.

We've rolled through more than one year together now, Nola, Una, Esme, and I. Throughout the year Nola and I have said things we never thought we'd say. Ridiculous things, like "Daddy's going toilet now," and "Want some milky-poo? Or some na-na?"

There have been countless conversations about who defecated when—even more than before I had children.

We've spent our days lugging and schlepping until we thought we could lug or schlep no more. We've passed out, jumped up, changed diapers half-asleep, passed out, then jumped up again when the babies did their business in the brand-new diapers.

In exchange, we've gotten to spend the last 13 months with two magical little girls.

Many of the commentators on the street, especially the ones who have twins themselves, say, "It gets easier." It has to, right? We made it through the wilderness. (Somehow we made it through-ooh-ooooh.) Now my wife and I just have to raise two functional, intelligent, self-sufficient, well-adjusted, caring human beings. Hell, we did the first year. All that's left is a lifetime. That's nothing. ▪

PART FIVE

# POETRY

# What?

BY NIC DARLING *(Issue 14)*

she is trying to tell me
that the world can end
one thousand times before lunch.
she is meaning to say
that nothing
is as we left it. ▪

# ask for a god

BY NIC DARLING *(Issue 15)*

1. i ask for a god,
and they give me five hundred sixty five channels
which they say have him surrounded.
so, i will try to find the shape of a deity
as an absence in the midst of discovery; cinemax,
cartoon network and one hundred different mtvs.

2. *we can do anything we want*, she says,
*we are adults*, but this is america two thousand five
and there are official versions of god
chiseled deeply into the bases of all our sacred monuments.

3. oh my god.

4. someone says, god is the chaos we arise from,
the primordial soup progenitor
of our present entropy.
millennia ago tiny gasping fish
crawled from his seething belly
and began to live a different death
toward dusts return. though,
when they say it, there is often
something about a garden as well.

5. god is in the details, and this is why
we must always look at everything more closely.
somewhere powerful microscopes are searching
for the next burning bush,
flaming sword or jesus shaped mildew.

6. my father carries a god around with him
but its alright. he will only show it to you
if you ask.

7. like anything, we only know god
by what he is not. god is the binary opposite
of everything and god is
the binary opposite of nothing.

8. god damn

9. she hides tiny gods
between her words
and as she talks my pantheon
is always expanding. the statuary
i need to represent each of her ideas
is staggering as it spirals out from the central pillar
of agnostos theos, the unknown god.

10. nietzsche says that god died comfortably
in his sleep. there was no pain.

11. for the love of god.

12. i will search for a god in drug temples,
alcohol mosques and the church of the perfect orgasm.
i will sit with my legs crossed in places of power
and sleep fitfully on the pillows of the divine dreamer.
i will climb incense ropes, suck snake venom
and collapse in the epileptic epiphany. my hands
will form all the proper shapes, my mouth will wrap
itself around the sacred om and i will wear holes in the knees
of all my holy garb.

13. maybe i will just get drunk and make phone calls
to all the women i used to know. god in the dial tone
and the church of two a.m.

14. i am not a god. i just play one on tv.

15. he speaks of god like god's name is dave
or robert and they talk each morning over coffee
at the diner. he orders eggs, hash browns and bacon
but dave, or robert, is really into french toast lately.
god is a close friend whose thoughts he relates
with the expertise of a shared diner tab.

16. her body is a temple
and i will enter into the presence of her god
prostrate and humble.

17. everyday people are trading gods
like baseball cards, like stock certificates,
like tapes from really good concerts
and i am discouraged because i have a god
shaped like a rusty old car
and no one will give me anything for it.

18. please god

19. when i was ten or eleven years old
i thought i felt god
brush the divine fingers
down the ridge of my spine
and disappear without a word.
i spent years trying to call him back,
trying to feel that again
but the closest i got was my first orgasm and i have been distracted ever since

20. in the end there is death
and god, deus ex machina,
it is all so easy this way. ▪

# Caruncle

BY COREY MESLER *(Issue 15)*

*"It all goes slo-mo...."*
*— Kate Bush*

The grass growing as you sleep.
The damp spot on the porch.
The tree branches, sky-hung,
after the storm years ago.
The sinkhole, the broken squirrels.
The path the dog took.
The way it all gets to you on a
morning in May.
The way your wife keeps talking
about her life, the
reasons you no longer listen. The
way it builds in you like corruption. ▪

# Imagining the Death of My Father on the Pascagoula River

BY BENJAMIN MORRIS *(Issue 15)*

Sometimes I think his truck will backfire,
so that you will be able to hear him
and answer the door. Other times I think
he will come silently, so not to disturb
the catfish in the weedbed, and he will sit
with you a while on the skiff and maybe drop a line
into the water too. He will not catch anything,
because not even death could coax those old cats up.
I see him living on a houseboat like the others,
evading his taxes and slicing open his hands
on the bright scales of his dinner. I see him
looking up from checkers to wave at you
on the bayou. He will walk in the woods with you,
hear the wild hog grunting; you will show him
how to break Catawba worms in half like celery,
then thread them inside out so the bream
will smell them sooner. When he returns home
he will tell your mother you still remember how.
He will trim your azaleas in the evening,
then sit in your chair as you practice the trumpet;
he will daub your bloody lips upon his sleeve.
Yes, this is how death must arrive on the river:
like the eyes of the alligator, slipping smooth as shadow
into the summer air, watching, watching the dog. ■

# Scenes from an Ideal Marriage

BY SHARON DOLIN *(Issue 21)*

*after Cy Twombly, 1986*

**I.**

Ideal because it's hard to tell
what's there. On wherever lane
we read a reader in with a
sofa or reclining chair—back
to the ringing chaos that's
the smudgy forest of home life.
Gender is obsolete. And the child
rules the living room.
It's always possible to make French
toast. Maple syrup drips like paint
over our days. and white nights?
We've had so many they color
our view—rouged with naps,
stippled with flowers. Watch your
back: The child-prince is about
to wield a bat.

**II. Anything Goes**

out the window (except the child)
the order of newspaper sections the
mail arriving by 3, your after-dinner
drink or lozenge of chocolate. The
jump rope of plastic cups the fetching
of endless snacks (remember when we were
two not three?) Now walking hand-
in-hand is reserved for one large,
one grimy paw. And you're still
looking for her to fix the . . .
for him to do the . . .
Purple no longer majestic but
the mixture of primaries still
a serenade by the window that suggests

**III.**

He. He hee-hees. He almost sees
it. He. He rufous-red. He shrugs
off the dead. He sits. Faces the wolf.
He backlashed by she. He passes
the past off. No repast.
He helluva weekend. He
relieved to bring the key.
He in his study. Office. Zendo.
He carries everyone's story. He
lunches and does not see.
He walled by his inner wall.
Not at all. Says he. Re-
vered by patients, readers, meditators.
He leaves his crown when he
goes home. He
pours a drink.
By son dethroned.
He. Sleep alone.
He. Sometime wonder
where is she.

**IV.**

Not tied by blood.
Not tied by time.
Half a day painted over
with fidgets, chores, blame.
The pièent of-white-thickens
Oh if only she had a little poodle,
a little noodle, a little . . .
Airplanes are for thinking
of other getaways. Where's
the coupling in coupling.
The bedsheets are creased
paper with very little writing
on them. Except for the restless
boy who nightwalks to find her.
And the smudged kiss—
does she even miss? ▪

# Dear Rubens

BY DAVID KIRBY *(Issue 21)*

*Medici Gallery, The Louvre*

You like women the way I do: busty! With big fat asses.
You aren't so good with kids, though, making the infant
Marie de' Medici just a pint-sized version of her adult
self, right down to the cleavage,
but maybe you just don't like to think about children or have to—I can't

imagine Peter Paul Rubens going fifty-fifty on diaper duty!
You're excellent with dogs: there's a good dog
in nearly every painting, by which I mean a well-drawn
dog, for all dogs are by nature bad. Good
with weapons, jewelry, horses; not so good with lions, but who ever saw

a lion in those days? Good with imaginary creatures
such as cherubs, who look like babies with hummingbird
wings. Wait a minute: if you never saw one, a lion
would be an imaginary creature to you,
so why didn't you do a better job? I know: the lion is not an imaginary

creature to us, whereas a cherub is to you but us, too.
A lot of people mix you up with Rembrandt,
but they don't know the difference between Bach
and Beethoven, either. Quick,
which one wrote "Ode to Joy"? You don't know because you died

before Whatzizname was born. Big fat asses:
big ones! An artist friend tells me you used a brick red
to fill in the butt cracks, and when I peer closely
at the behind of a water nymph
in "The Disembarkation of the Queen at Marseille," I see that it's true,

that the ruddy color makes her whoopie cakes look all muscular
and yummy. Neptune has long grey hair
parted in the middle and looks like a biker.
That's another thing you do really well, mix
the godlike with the mortal. I'd like to think the Virtues and Graces

are traipsing with me through these galleries,
the trains of their beautiful see-through gowns trailing
behind them. And should Ignorance
or Calumny or Envy come writhing
around my ankles like snakes, I'd want to put my foot between

their horns and squash them like ticks.
You're so super-excellent with fabrics of all kinds
that you remind me of what Aldous Huxley wrote
in The Doors of Perception after
he takes mescaline and looks at a reproduction of Botticelli's "Judith"

but gazes "not at the pale neurotic heroine
or her attendant, not at the victim's hairy head
or the vernal landscape in the background,
but at the purplish silk of Judith's pleated
bodice and long wind-blown skirts" and asks "is it because

the forms of folded drapery are so strange
and dramatic that they catch the eye
and in this way force the miraculous fact
of sheer existence upon the attention?"
Well, I think that question answers itself, Aldous! Especially

in the case of Rubens, who had sheer existence
out the whoopie cakes.
Only where's Henri IV in all this? Marie married him and had
Louis XIII but then Henri was stabbed
by François Ravaillac when his carriage got stuck in a traffic jam.

Le Ravaillac is actually the name of my favorite
Polish restaurant, a great place
to sit down to veal chops and potatoes
in creamy onion sauce that you wash down with shots
of buffalo-grass vodka instead of le vin rouge, only what kind of person

would name a restaurant after a king-killer? Being
a regicide in France is not that big a deal, though;
it's a job, like being a pharmacist
or architect. Whereas Louis XIV was a fun king, nobody
remembers the XIII or the XV, though by the time

Louis XVI came along, oh, dear. Kings were bad
in those days, or maybe the people were. Why can't
we all just get along? Goodbye, big pretty women.
Goodbye, courtiers and peacocks and greyhounds
and sea dragons. Goodbye, Anne of Austria,

whoever you are! And to you present-day Austrians
and Spaniards and Japanese and Greeks and all
the people speaking languages I can't understand,
goodbye, goodbye. Oh, wait,
something just rushed by overhead: I know, a cherub. ■

# Naiads

BY SCOTT HIGHTOWER *(Issue 21)*

**(For Jean Kiernan Gabbay)**
*A lot of us were upset when it*
*was ploughed over and leveled.*
*The black mold foxing up the walls*
*of the new school's foundation*
*neither takes a figurative shape*
*nor scripts a vandal's invective;*
*but, there's no doubt about it,*
*it's pure naiad scorn.*
*
There's an old story about
a king marrying one. In one
of Virgil's stories, didn't a mother
guide her frustrated son to the key
of how things change; some trouble
with lethal, unintended consequences
springing up like agitated
snakes or a colony of bees?
*
An Austin friend of mine
goes on about the monarchs
and about how gods
and goddesses are eternal,
even when people
completely fall silent,
stop worshipping them.

She has a lot to say
about a native spring
that use to be a charming spot.

Once, in Luarca, a small village
in northern Spain, I visited a legendary
urban spring, *La Fuente del Bruxo.*
Someone had marked the source
with a four-leaf clover carved in stone,
had installed a spigot. The locals
(whose ancient language is Bable)
say that water use to always
run there, that it was a Celtic site.

My last visit, I was piqued
to see that someone had built
on top of the ancient location.
Another disconcerted pilgrim
had scrawled VERGOÑA
in fierce black spray paint
across one of the new walls.
*
*Back then, we didn't have*
*a place to hang out. No mall.*
*There was one remote spot. . .*
*a little spring. An ancient wall spigot*
*was mounted near a limestone cliff*
*green with maidenhair fern and frogs.*

*It was a beautiful place!*
*We'd trounce there to skinny dip,*
*picnic, eat the wild figs*
*that grew there;*

*sometimes, we'd hike on*
*down to Bull Creek..* ▪

# The Fall, *Revised*

BY SHIRA DENTZ *(Issue 22)*

The date today
A sky like parchment, goat skin,
an aged *sedur* cover;
pale gray-blue.
Uncomfortably translucent.

Looking up a different face from where it happened.

Trees thick as cream,
crickets pulse

the seventh month
before January and February were inserted
beginning the same day of the week as December every year
flower: morning glory
birthstone: sapphire
*September your opportunity to reinforce proper food safety training*
*inform everyone food safety is not an option, but an obligation.*
*Molecules of the month* Two thousand and four:
Ubiquitin (H) A ubiquitous protein
Two thousand and one:
Methyl Jasmonate (H, C, J, V) The smell of jasmine flowers
*Image of the month* Two thousand and five: *The Parting Cheer*
*Decorating idea of the month*: *Say Curtains to Kitchen Clutter*
*Movie of the month:* LIFE IS WAITING.

Seven, *sheva,* mourning,

the seven deadly sins

Seven wonders ▪

# Fathers

BY DENISE DUHAMEL *(Issue 22)*

My father walks through the scrub, a shortcut, to get to Walmart
where he meets up with his friends for coffee on Friday afternoons.
He says teenagers are always hanging around back there, barbequing
something. I'm assuming my father has never smelled pot
and that's what he's smelling now, so I say, *Dad, stick to the streets,*
because I am afraid for him, even though these kids
are probably mellow from weed. My father, 80, says
there are too many zooming cars on the road, and besides,
he likes the pond, the wildflowers that will probably be gone
when the plaza expands to a Super Walmart next year.
I want to make sure the teenagers don't rob my father for his two dollars,
the way they robbed my father-in-law right in the Albertsons bathroom,
pushing him into the white tiled wall while he was at the urinal,
then fleeing with his wallet. It took my father-in-law a long time to get up
and regain his balance. It took him a long time to replace
his credit cards and ID. He was 90 by then. My husband said,
*Can't you catch these kids on the surveillance camera?*
The manager was lazy and said the supermarket wasn't responsible.
My husband said, *No one is saying the supermarket is responsible—*
*we just want an arrest so these kids can't mug anyone else.*
My father-in-law filled out a police report,
his provisions idle in the silver cart.
When the supermarket wanted my father to retire,
they sent him to get the carts in the rain. Though there was a union
to protect wages, employees had no fixed assignments.
Having meat men suddenly clean bathrooms or produce men
suddenly wash floors was one way management
could humiliate older workers enough to make them leave.
A grown man doing the work a teenager could.
A grown man working 40 hours a week, eating up
the supermarket's profits with his benefits. A teenager was warm inside,
part-time, bagging, flirting with the cashier, maybe laughing
at my father because my father wasn't the teenager's father.
That would have been a different story all together. ▪

# Bar Napkin Sonnet #20

BY MOIRA EGAN *(Issue 22)*

I gave up buying COSMOPOLITAN,
the air-brushed cleavage, SEX TIPS FOR WILD GIRLS,
the articles on HOW TO ROCK HIS WORLD:
a budding feminist at twenty-one.
Last weekend, *en route* to our assignation,
I found one on my seat, its pages curled
with use, its sacred mysteries unfurled.
I read: DON'T DRINK IN HOTEL BARS ALONE.
So I'm to meet him in the hotel bar.
I grab a barstool, ask about the wine,
a sadly disappointing list. Meanwhile
the loosened-tie brigade of hungry sharks
encircles me, but O, Power Divine,
his hand along my spine: "She's mine." I smile. ■

# Rehearsal Night

BY ROMY RUUKEL *(Issue 22)*

My mother is all smells and sounds of waiting,
the click click click of distinctly confident
heels in the dark hallway,
the anticipated familiar mix of perfume and cigarette smoke
when I reach for her hand at the crosswalk,
the poised T-shape of them on the small stage
as her partner lifts her up,
and I am in the corner with pencils and a coloring book
forgetting what I've been told,
pressing down too hard on the paper. ▪

# The Amazing Perseverance of the Sandhill Crane

BY MARILYN L. TAYLOR *(Issue 23)*

Endangered species? Not this chick—she's got
a built-in arsenal: claw, bill, and feather,
and soon she'll pull her leggy act together,
gear up for the hunt. She'll troubleshoot
the dales and dunes where eligible males
from her subgenus are inclined to loiter,
then browse around, observe, and reconnoiter
until she's got her target by the tail.

Not for her, macaws that squall for freedom,
Not for her, the frowning peregrine;
She wouldn't know an albatross from Adam
and doesn't need some snail-catching machine
puttering in the garden, spitting seeds.
One crane. One skinny crane. That's all she needs. ▪

# Before the Funeral

BY KATHRINE VARNES *(Issue 24)*

The embryonic poem: two rhymes,
one metaphor, one memory:
lethargy,
door chimes.

I cannot open the door
for death or lovers.
Who needs an invitation?
They walk in anyway.

Look at the scandalous cleavage of the volta!
Look at her hips! How she ruffles her pretty skirts!
*Delete the dead man's email, quick*, she says,
*and buy a new watch and eat a mango*
*over the kitchen sink. Don't iron.*
At words like *infarction* she hiccups once, and winks. ▪

# Elegy Theory

BY BRENDAN CONSTANTINE *(Issue 25)*

Einstein was born in 1879, which is already pretty
brilliant.
Most people couldn't drive or tell you where
the lights were but when his mom brought home a baby
sister, he knew to ask
*Where are her wheels?*
My big
red dictionary defines time as *a period,* then later
as *an interval.*
Granted, it's the 1920 edition—love
is defined as *a losing score in tennis*, the Giant Panda
as the *opposite of Lesser Panda*—but in 1921 Einstein
won the Nobel.
All America did was smile at Europe
& then invent the Vibraphone.
It's still embarrassing,
though it helps to pretend Time & Space are just ideas,
like islands or maps.
When Einstein asked a conductor,
*What time does Oxford stop at this train,* he meant
every moment of it.
He meant, *Look out the window*
*& tell me the wheels aren't turning the earth. Tell me*
*God plays dice. Tell me the force of a kiss will put*
*any body at rest.*
In 1955 all the blood left his heart,
& ran to his feet, though no one knows when it arrived;
news out of Jersey has always been sketchy.
However
I can tell you, for poetry makes nothingness happen,
that's-when-time-slowed-down-to-the-present
crawl.
Before the year was out, Emmett Till was put
to death under the law of inertia.
So was James Dean.
Everyone was singing *Ain't That a Shame.* ■

# The Mannequin at Grand Central Station

BY SARAH STERN *(Issue 25)*

This morning at the Pink Slip
she's dressed in a teal bra and panties—

her breasts—a statement of defiance
to gravity, aging, modesty.

In this economy, screw the whole world.
Yesterday she wore a purple thong—see-through.

I imagine she's what men want,
the men in liquor ads, drinks barely

visible—nautical themes, subliminal sex
ricocheting about like song birds.

That's what's been imprinted on the brain
since my birth in 1964, the last of seven,

my poor mother, I think as I nod
to my mannequin friend.

Across from her is Zaro's,
another display tempting us.

What would you choose—
a bustier or a baguette with butter?

Maybe an evening with both, one under each arm
as you commute with the human race.

The *Times*'s been running articles
on female arousal—guess what?

It's *non-specific* and *narcissistic.*
Let's pause for a moment.

Oh yes, much centers, too,
on *wanting to be wanted.*

Men don't look at me anymore.
In poetry they say

keep the line that turns you red and
x-out those you can't part with,

which brings us back to the Pink Slip.
She's poised just so

as if you could name her.
That's the thing about getting older.

Nobody names you—
a freedom worth earning on this side

of constellations we pass under
with tourists, the homeless, the National Guard,

all framed by bouquets in buckets
next to shoe shiners, loaves stacked

high, and her babydolls and teddies
already wrapped in tissue, waiting for someone else. ▪

# Bright Windows

BY GERRY LAFEMINA *(Issue 29)*

Jackhammers rattled the walls with stammered curses & I
awoke from a dream of soft-spoken longing—what I want,
ungiven. The window, a rectangle of brilliance I couldn't enter; thus now, to
retain some sense of holiness I go
to Tompkins Square, but even the monkey bar set escapes the playground,
sneaks in
the fenced areas to dance where it says not to tread. The

daffodils so alluring, I can't blame them. One mother yells, *I'm gonna tan
your back-*
*side*. She pauses before they both laugh—he hasn't taken the proverbial yard,
just wants to loaf in the grass, little Whitman. Now
& then I can still hear work crews—steel grates crashing into place, &
a vagrant offers to trade a hug for a dollar. Maybe
today I'll tell the woman I love that I love her & she will take down

her voice to whisper something about romance, about passion. The
city of my heart is always under construction, it seems. Alley
cats yowl in heat, its children grow into leather jackets. Where
are the priests who'd forgive us these trespasses? The park holds little
solace, the
grey squirrel on his haunches begs for scraps—this city of charity,
Tompkins Square awash in morning light. On the swings those children
shout louder than hardhats, their voices bright windows of play. ▪

Part Six

# ART GALLERY

**Karla Siegel**
***Three Part Portrait***
Oil on canvas, 30"x40"
*(Featured Artist, Issue 30)*

**Rob Matthews**
***The Artist's Wife (Tracy), 2008***
Graphite on paper,
7" diameter on 9"x9" paper
*(Featured Artist, Issue 22)*

**David Poolman**
***Malice (For Vera Manshande), 2012***
Graphite on paper, 30"x22"
*(Featured Artist, Issue 28)*

**Mary Smull**
***Lute Player, Summer 2011***
Found, unfinished needlepoint completed by the artist using only white yarn, 20"x21"
*(Featured Artist, Issue 27)*

**David Poolman**
***Protest Cancelled Due to Rain, 2012-13***
1,500 miniature balsa wood and acrylic paint protest signs, variable dimensions
*(Featured Artist, Issue 28)*

**Aaron Morgan Brown**
***Arcadia Revisited, 2009***
Oil, 50"x60"
*(Featured Artist, Issue 24)*

**Aaron Morgan Brown**
***Suffragettes, 2012***
*(Featured Artist, Issue 24)*

# Contributors

**Derek Alger** is a graduate of Columbia University's MFA writing program. He serves as Editor-at-Large of *pif Magazine*, Nonfiction Editor of Ducts.org and Contributing Editor at *Serving House Journal.* His fiction has appeared in *Confrontation*, *The Literary Review*, *The Del Sol Review* and *Night Train*, to name a few. He has worked as an editor and reporter in the Bronx for more than 20 years.

**Jennifer Berman**'s work has appeared in *The New York Times*, Ducts and NBC's Petside, and she has appeared on stage at The Far Space and The Cornelia Street Café as part of the Never Alone series. She lives in New York City with her husband, Bob, and their two rescue cats, Frankie and Alex.

**Jacqueline Bishop** is an award-winning poet, novelist, essayist, painter and photographer. She was born in Kingston, Jamaica, and now lives in New York City. She has held several Fulbright Fellowships and has exhibited her work widely in North America, Europe and North Africa. She is also Master Teacher in Liberal Studies at New York University. Contact Ms. Bishop at *jacqueline-bishop.com.*

**JP Borum,** MFA, is a writer who teaches writing in New York University's Liberal Studies program. He lives in New York City.

**Duff Brenna** is the author of nine books, including *The Book of Mamie*, which won the AWP Award for Best Novel; *The Holy Book of the Beard*, called "an underground classic" by *The New York Times*; *Too Cool,* a *New York Times* Noteworthy Book; and *The Altar of the Body*, which received the Editors Prize Favorite Book of the Year award from the *South Florida Sun-Sentinel* and a San Diego Writers Association award for Best Novel 2002. He is the recipient of a National Endowment for the Arts award, Milwaukee Magazine's Best Short Story of the Year award, and a Pushcart Prize Honorable Mention. His book *Minnesota Memoirs* was named Best Short Story Collection at the 2013 Next Generation Indie Awards in New York City, and his memoir *Murdering the Mom* was selected as a Finalist for Best Nonfiction at the same event. Duff's work has been translated into six languages.

**Aaron Morgan Brown** currently lives and works in South Central PA, where he is constantly inspired by the sound of trucks, Amish wagons and distant gunfire. He received an MFA from Syracuse University, graduating with honors. Other kudos include a 2005 grant from The Pollock-Krasner Foundation, Inc. and a 2009 grant from the Franz and Virginia Bader Fund. He was a Finalist in the National Portrait Gallery's Outwin Boochever Portrait Competition Exhibition 2013.

**Devon T. Coleman** has been making things for years. Things like bios. He is a (comedy) writer whose work has appeared on stage, (computer) screen, and in print. He grew up in Southwest Detroit and currently lives in the suburbs, proving that if you have enough street cred, you can eventually cash it in for living near a grocery store. He is for Batman and against speaking in the third person. Oh, and I/He/We love(s) you.

**Brendan Constantine** is a poet based in Hollywood. His work has appeared in *FIELD, Ploughshares, Rattle, ZYZZYVA*, the *Los Angeles Review* and other journals. His most recent books are *Birthday Girl With Possum* (2011, Write Bloody Publishing) and *Calamity Joe* (2012, Red Hen Press). He teaches poetry at the Windward School and is an adjunct professor at Antioch University Los Angeles. He also conducts workshops for hospitals and foster homes and with the Alzheimer's Poetry Project.

**Nic Darling** currently lives in London. He does not know what he wants to be when he grows up.

**Shira Dentz** is the author of two books, *black seeds on a white dish* (Shearsman, 2011), and *door of thins*, a blend of prose, poetry, and visual elements (CavanKerry Press, 2013). She is also the author of two chapbooks, *Leaf Weather* (Tilt Press/Shearsman), and *Sisyphusina* (forthcoming from Red Glass Books). Her writing has appeared widely in journals, including *The American Poetry Review, The Iowa Review,* and *New American Writing,* and has been featured online at Poets.org (Academy of American Poets), NPR, Poetry Daily, and Verse Daily. Her awards include an Academy of American Poets' Prize, the Poetry Society of America's Lyric Poem and Cecil Hemley Memorial Awards, *Electronic Poetry Review*'s Discovery Award, and *Painted Bride Quarterly*'s Poetry Prize. A graduate of the Iowa Writers' Workshop, she has a PhD in Creative Writing and Literature from the University of Utah and is currently Reviews Editor for *Drunken Boat* and Lecturer in Creative Writing at Rensselaer Polytechnic Institute. Find her online at *shiradentz.com*.

**Sharon Dolin**'s most recent poetry books are *Whirlwind* (University of Pittsburgh Press, 2012); and *Burn and Dodge* (University of Pittsburgh Press, 2008), winner of the 2007 AWP Donald Hall Prize in Poetry. She received the 2013 Witter Bynner Fellowship from the Library of Congress. She teaches at the Unterberg Poetry Center of the 92nd Street Y and directs The Center for Book Arts Annual Letterpress Poetry Chapbook Competition. She lives and works in New York City.

**Denise Duhamel** is the author, most recently, of *Blowout* (University of Pittsburgh Press, 2013) *Ka-Ching!* (Pittsburgh, 2009), *Two and Two* (Pittsburgh, 2005), *Mille et un Sentiments* (Firewheel, 2005) and *Queen for a Day: Selected and New Poems* (Pittsburgh, 2001). The guest editor for *The Best American Poetry 2013,* she is a professor at Florida International University in Miami.

**Ritch Duncan** is a comedian and writer who lives in Upper Manhattan with his wife and four-year-old daughter. His work has appeared in *The New York Times* and on Salon.com, Puck Daddy (Yahoo Sports), *Saturday Night Live*'s Weekend Update, the Onion News Network and more. Manageable samples of his vast body of work can be found at *twitter.com/ritchied.*

**Moira Egan**'s poetry collections are *Hot Flash Sonnets* (Passager Books, 2013); *Spin* (Entasis Press, 2010); *Bar Napkin Sonnets* (The Ledge Chapbook Competition, 2009); *La Seta della Cravatta/The Silk of the Tie* (Edizioni l'Obliquo, 2009); and *Cleave* (WWPH, 2004). Her poems and essays have appeared in numerous journals and anthologies in the U.S. and abroad, including *Best American Poetry 2008* and Lewis Turco's most recent edition of *The Book of Forms*, and she is co-editor of *Hot Sonnets* (Entasis Press, 2011). With Damiano Abeni, she has published more than a dozen books in translation in Italian, by authors such as John Barth, Aimee Bender, Lawrence Ferlinghetti, Anthony Hecht, Mark Strand, Josephine Tey, and John Ashbery, whose collection, *Un mondo che non può essere migliore: Poesie scelte 1956-2007,* won a Special Prize of the Premio Napoli (2009). She has been a Mid Atlantic Arts Fellow at the Virginia Center for the Creative Arts; Writer in Residence at St. James Cavalier Centre for Creativity, Malta; a Writing Fellow at the Civitella Ranieri Center; and a Fellow at the Rockefeller Foundation Bellagio Center. She lives in Rome.

**J.C. Elkin**'s award-winning prose and poetry has appeared in dozens of literary journals, including *Kestrel*, *Kansas City Voices*, and Empirical Magazine. Founder of The Broadneck Writers' Workshop, she now makes her home on the Chesapeake Bay. Her chapbook *World Class: Poems Inspired by the E.S.L. Classroom* is forthcoming from Apprentice House Books.

**Benjamin Feldman** has lived and worked in New York City for the past forty-four years. His essays and book reviews about New York City and American history and about Yiddish culture have appeared online and in print in CUNY's Gotham History Blotter, *The New Partisan Review, Columbia County History & Heritage, Ducts* literary magazine, The SoHo Memory Project, The Green-Wood Cemetery Historic Fund Blog and in his blog, The New York Wanderer. Ben's first book was *Butchery on Bond Street— Sexual Politics and the Burdell-Cunningham Case in Ante-bellum New York* (2007). Ben impersonates Broadway impresario William Niblo several times a year at Green-Wood Cemetery during Open House New York as well as at an annual picnic at the Niblo Mausoleum, where a performance from Niblo's Garden is recreated from its mid-19th century heyday.

**Kipp Friedman** (born 1960) is a native New Yorker who holds BAs in History and Journalism from the University of Wisconsin-Madison. During his career, he has worked as a newspaper reporter and in public relations and marketing. He is also a professional photographer. "Breaking Up is Hard to Do" is the first of two personal memoirs Kipp has contributed to Ducts. Both stories appear in Kipp's new memoir, *Barracuda in the Attic*, about growing up among a family of creative artists in the New York arts scene of the 1960s and '70s (Fantagraphics Books, Fall 2013). Kipp currently resides in Milwaukee with his wife, Anne, a research coordinator at the Milwaukee VA Medical Center. They have a grown son, Max, who is studying to be an architect. *Barracuda in the Attic* is Kipp's first book.

**Mindy Greenstein, PhD**, is a clinical psychologist and writer whose essays have appeared in *The New York Times, The Washington Post, Los Angeles Times*, *Self* Magazine, the anthology *DIRT: The Quirks, Habits, and Passions of Keeping House* (Seal 2009), and elsewhere. Her book *The House on Crash Corner and Other Unavoidable Calamities* (Greenpoint Press, 2011) was chosen as one of *O: The Oprah Magazine*'s "Books to

Pick Up." Her upcoming book, *Lighter as We Go: Character Strengths and Aging*, will be published by Oxford University Press in 2014. Mindy lives in New York City with her husband and two sons.

**Dena Rash Guzman** lives on an organic-produce farm in a temperate rainforest outside Portland, Oregon. Her debut poetry collection, *Life Cycle*, was released by Dog On A Chain Press in June, 2013. She works as an editor.

**Jessica Hall** is a social worker living in NYC who sometimes swims for justice and sometimes just for fun.

**DeWitt Henry** is a Professor at Emerson College and the founding editor of *Ploughshares*. He has published a novel and two memoirs, and has edited five anthologies. For details, visit *dewitthenry.com*.

**Scott Hightower** is an award-winning poet, translator, and the author of four books. He teaches as adjunct faculty at NYU. A native of central Texas, he lives in Manhattan and sojourns in Spain. His bilingual book, *Hontanares/Fountains*, is forthcoming this fall from Devenir (Madrid).

**Keerthana Jagadeesh** comes from Bangalore, India, where the skies are expanding with the new metro rail. Her favorite writers are Cólm Toibín and Nell Dunn. This is her first publication. She is currently a junior at NYU.

**Jake Kalish** has written for *Details, Maxim, Playboy*, and *Men's Fitness*, among other publications. He is the author of *Santa vs. Satan: The Official Compendium Of Imaginary Fights* (Three Rivers, 2008) and the proud father of Una and Esme.

**David Kirby** was known as "Dynamite" in high school and, for about a week in college, "Popcorn." He teaches at Florida State University, and his book *The House on Boulevard St.: New and Selected Poems* was a finalist for the 2007 National Book Award.

**Jonathan Kravetz** is the founder and Editor-in-Chief of DUCTS.org and a New York City-based writer and playwright. Jonathan's plays have been produced in New York City, Dallas and Brighton, England and have won numerous awards. He has published several short stories and has written a dozen science nonfiction books for children. Jonathan has edited and ghostwritten several essays and memoirs. Jonathan is also the founder of the monthly reading series, Trumpet Fiction, which is held the second Saturday of every month at KGB Bar in the East Village. He holds an MA in Cinema Studies from NYU and recently received his MFA at Queens College, where he was a writer-in-residence at the Louis Armstrong House and Museum. He teaches fiction and dramatic writing in New York City and drama at FIT, State University of New York. He is also on the Board of New York Writers Resources.

**Gerry LaFemina** is the author of one book of stories, two books of prose poems and six books of poems—most recently, *Vanishing Horizon* (2011, Anhinga). He directs the Frostburg Center for Creative Writing at Frostburg State University, where he is an Associate Professor of English. He divides his time between Maryland and New York.

**Melissa Larson** teaches high school English to the fine youth of New Jersey, where she resides with her husband and her dog. She enjoys writing memoir and humor, and her work can be found in *Ducts* and on Happy Woman Magazine and Funny Not Slutty, to name a few sites. She is finishing up her first full-length memoir and can be reached at *mlarson103@gmail.com*.

**Robert Lascaro** is the design director of Greenpoint Press, where some of his book designs include: *The House on Crash Corner*, *We're Not Leaving* (featured on *60 Minutes*) and *Starfish.* He has worked as an art director at Scholastic, Ziff Davis, Thompson Reuters and the *Wall Street Journal.* Before his career in publishing he worked as a financial analyst on Wall Street, a newspaper reporter and the manager of The Center for Public Cinema, which operated the repertory Bleecker Street and Carnegie Hall Cinemas. He has also worked as a lifeguard on the Jersey Shore, a Fuller Brush salesman and a street magician on 42nd Street. He is an Eagle Scout.

**Roger Lipman** grew up in London during the Second World War, went to Imperial College, London and Cambridge University, immigrated to the USA and became an industrial chemist. Now he lives in Manhattan and still does a bit of chemistry.You can reach him at *r.lipman@ymail.com*.

**Paul MacTavish** is the pen name of **Jerry Farrell**, who has been a frequent Ducts contributor since 2004. He is currently working on the comedic novel *I Want That Fucking Beachball,* inspired by his media career at Condé Nast. He resides in Farmingdale, New York with his wife, two young sons, and toddler daughter.

**Fredricka R. Maister** is a New York City-based freelance writer. Her essays and articles have appeared in a variety of publications and websites, including *The Baltimore Sun*, *Miami Herald*, *Chicago Tribune*, *The Philadelphia Inquirer*, *Baltimore Jewish Times*, *The Jewish Journal of Greater Los Angeles*, New York/Long Island Woman, *Big Apple Parent*, *Coping with Cancer* magazine, Travel Thru History, and The Huffington Post.

**Mia Mather** hasn't done a thing. Stories still come, sometimes in pieces, sometimes in swoops and sometimes (sigh) not at all.

**Rob Matthews** is represented by Gallery Joe in Philadelphia and by Daniel Cooney Fine Art in New York City. See more of his work at *matthewstheyounger.com*. He lives in Nashville, TN.

**Dan McCoy** is a writer for *The Daily Show with Jon Stewart*. He is the creator of the bad movie podcast *The Flop House*, which has received press in *The New York Times*, *The Guardian*, *Entertainment Weekly* and elsewhere. He is also the creator, animator and co-star of the webseries *9AM Meeting,* which won MTV's Best Animation award at the 2010 New York TV Festival. Visit: *www.flophousepodcast.com* and *9ammeeting.com.*

**Corey Mesler** has published in numerous journals and anthologies. He has published 7 novels, 3 full-length poetry collections, and 3 books of short stories. He has also published a dozen chapbooks of both poetry and prose. He has been nominated for the Pushcart Prize numerous times, and two of his poems were chosen for Garrison Keillor's The Writer's Almanac. His fiction has received praise from John Grisham, Robert Olen Butler, Lee Smith, Frederick Barthelme, and Greil Marcus, among others. With his wife, he runs Burke's Book Store in Memphis TN. He can be found at *coreymesler.wordpress.com*.

**Cindy Stockton Moore** is a Philadelphia-based artist whose recent shows include "Toward Futility," a solo project at Artspace Liberti (Philadelphia) and the two-person exhibitions "An Island Now Peopled" at Chashama Chelsea Project Space (New York City) and "Water/Line" at The Center for Contemporary Art (Bedminster, NJ). Her writing on art has appeared in *ARTnews*, *NY Arts Magazine* and *The New York Sun*, in addition to university and web publications. She is a part of the artist-curatorial team behind Grizzly Grizzly Gallery in Philadelphia. See more about her work at cindystocktonmoore.com.

**Benjamin Morris**, a native of Mississippi, is a writer, researcher, and the author of numerous works of poetry, fiction, and nonfiction, with recent work appearing in such publications as *Oxford American*, *The Southern Quarterly*, and *Tulane Review*. A member of the Mississippi Artist Roster, he is the recipient of a poetry fellowship from the Mississippi Arts Commission and a residency from A Studio in the Woods in New Orleans. His next book, a history of Hattiesburg, MS, is forthcoming from The History Press in 2014. Visit *benjaminalanmorris.com.*

**Alicia Finn Noack** lives in Austin, Texas and is pursuing her MFA in Creative Writing at Queens University of Charlotte. She is working toward her black belt in taekwondo, so don't mess with her.

**Nita Noveno** is a NYC-based writer and educator originally from Southeast Alaska. She is a graduate of The New School MFA Creative Writing Program and founder, curator, and co-host of Sunday Salon, a monthly prose reading series in its eleventh year. in NYC. She is the co-editor of the anthology-in-progress *Bitter Melon: A Literary Feast by Filipino Writers* and is completing a novel based on the true story of her father's journey from the Philippines to pursue life in the strange, beautiful landscape of post-Depression America. Nita has been published in Kweli, The MacGuffin, and Ducts.org.

**Jericho Parms** received her MFA from Vermont College of Fine Arts. Her work has appeared in *Hotel Amerika, American Literary Review, Bellingham Review, South Loop Review*, and other journals.

**David Poolman** was born in Wallaceburg, Ontario. He is an MFA graduate of the University of Windsor and a graduate of Vancouver's Emily Carr University of Art and Design. Working in drawing, video, print media and installation, Poolman has exhibited in art galleries and screened in festivals both nationally and internationally. He currently lives in Toronto and is a Professor of Drawing at Sheridan College. His video work is distributed through VTape and Ouat Media in Toronto.

**Anne Posten** translates contemporary German poetry and prose, and writes fiction. She has been published by *FIELD*, *Words without Borders*, -ality, Stonecutter Journal, and *Hanging Loose Press*, and has work forthcoming with *Free State Review* and Black Lawrence Press. She lives in Queens, NY, where she teaches in the CUNY system.

**Romy Ruukel** is an Estonian-born writer currently residing in the San Francisco Bay area. She is a member of the radical performance collective 30/70 and the anarchist collective bookstore Bound Together. Her work has appeared in *Apalachee Review* and *Bayou Magazine*. She bakes a lot of cupcakes, which is one of her biggest vices or virtues, depending on whom you ask.

**Charles Salzberg** is a freelance writer whose work has appeared in such periodicals as *Esquire*, *New York* magazine, *GQ*, *Redbook*, *The New York Times Book Review*, *Good Housekeeping*, *Elle* and *The New York Times Sunday Arts & Leisure*. He is the author of more than 20 nonfiction books, including *Soupy Sez!: My Zany Life and Times*; *From Set Shot To Slam Dunk,* an oral history of the NBA; and *On A Clear Day They Could See Seventh Place, Baseball's Worst Teams* (with George Robinson.) His novels includes *Swann's Last Song*, which was nominated for a Shamus Award for Best First PI Novel; the sequel, *Swann Dives In; Devil in the Hole*; and, forthcoming in the Fall of 2014, *Swann's Lake of Despair*. He has taught writing at the S.I. Newhouse School of Public Communications at Syracuse University, where he was a Visiting Professor of Magazine Journalism; Sarah Lawrence; Hunter College; The Writer's Voice and the New York Writers Workshop, where he is a Founding Member. He is also the Editor-in-Chief of Greenpoint Press. Visit *Charlessalzberg.com*.

**Carl Schinasi** is a retired college professor. His work has appeared in Ducts, *Slow Trains*, *Mr. Beller's Neighborhood*, and *Baseball/Literature/ Culture*, among other publications. He is contemplating entering clown college.

**Karla Siegel** is a Philadelphia painter who trained at Temple University's Tyler School of Art, obtaining her BFA in 2004. Her work has been widely exhibited in the Philadelphia region as well as in New York. Karla has also worked with a number of Philadelphia art institutions, including the Mural Arts Program, the Philadelphia Museum of Art and the Main Line Art Center. She currently lives in Philadelphia's Fairmount neighborhood, where she maintains a working studio practice at The Church Studios artist's co-op.

**Jennifer Hasenyager Smith** is a sometimes-psychic, Ivy-League surgeon and award-winning change agent recognized by the American Academy of Ophthalmology for her visionary leadership. Despite her success, she betrayed herself for years, living in an Identity that didn't fit her. She finally stepped off the treadmill of her "perfect" life when she quit practicing medicine and got divorced just before she turned 40. After recovering from her years of disconnection as a physician, she had a reluctant intuitive awakening, discovered her purpose, and wrote a book about her unusual path through medicine and beyond the White Coat. She now uses her uncommon gifts combined with her neuroscience knowledge to inspire and empower other professionals to activate their potential through creating Identities that fit them.

**Mary Smull** is an artist, writer, and curator living in Philadelphia, PA. She merges object and action in a practice centered around textile processes to expose the diversity of attitudes toward labor and the complex relationships surrounding art and craft, amateur and professional, producers and consumers. Recently, Smull's work has been exhibited at the University of Pennsylvania, Philadelphia International Airport, the Philadelphia Museum of Art, Temple Contemporary at Temple University's Tyler School of Art and Philadelphia's Bridgette Mayer Gallery. It has also recently been exhibited at the Houston Center for Contemporary Craft, the Public Fiction Gallery in Los Angeles, the Racine Art Museum in Racine, WI, and Cranbrook Museum of Art in Bloomfield Hills, MI. Smull holds a BFA from The University of the Arts in Philadelphia and an MFA from Cranbrook Academy of Art in Bloomfield Hills, MI. She currently teaches in the Fiber Department at the Maryland Institute College of Art in Baltimore.

**MP Snell** has had short stories published in various literary magazines. She has recently completed her novel, *Planet of Blue and Green*. She can be heard on John Moran's opera *The Manson Family: An Opera* with Iggy Pop. She has also performed with Ridge Theater, and in locations such as Lincoln Center and the Guggenheim Museum.

**Coree Spencer** has lived in New York City for almost twenty-five years and has taken time off from her great acting career to write: at least you don't need current headshots or movement class to write short stories. "Sunshine Factory" was written in Charles Salzberg's class at the Westside YMCA.

**Bill Stack** is retired from a career as Chief Investment Officer and CEO for an investment-management firm. He lives in Mendham, NJ and New York City with his wife of forty-three years. He reads, travels, plays with his nine grandchildren and, from time to time, writes.

**Sarah Stern**'s chapbook *Sarah Stern's chapbook Another Word for Love was published by Finishing Line Press in 2011. Her poems have appeared in magazines, anthologies, and online, most recently in The American Dream anthology, The Best of Ducts, Epiphany and Verse Daily. Sarah is a four-time winner of the Bronx Council on the Arts' BRIO Award for Poetry. She was a finalist for the Alexander and Dora Raynes Poetry Prize and received Honorable Mentions from the Anna Davidson Rosenberg Awards and Lilith Magazine's Poetry Prize. She graduated from Barnard College and Columbia University's Graduate School of Journalism. Sarah is the public policy and communications officer at the EastWest Institute.*

**Marilyn L. Taylor**, former Poet Laureate of Wisconsin (2009 and 2010) and of Milwaukee (2004 and 2005), is the author of six collections of poetry. Her award-winning poems and essays have appeared in many anthologies and journals, including *Poetry, The American Scholar, Measure,* and Ted Kooser's American Life in Poetry. Marilyn taught poetry and poetics for fifteen years at the University of Wisconsin-Milwaukee, and currently serves as a board member for several writers' organizations.

**Lee Upton** is the author of thirteen books, including the collection of essays *Swallowing the Sea: On Writing & Ambition, Boredom, Purity & Secrecy*; the novella *The Guide to the Flying Island*; five books of poetry, including *Undid in the Land of Undone*; and four books of literary criticism. She won the second annual BOA Short Fiction Prize for her forthcoming short story collection *The Tao of Humiliation (*BOA Editions, Spring 2014). Her awards include the Lyric Poetry Award and The Writer/Emily Dickinson Award from the Poetry Society of America; the Pushcart Prize; the National Poetry Series Award; and the Miami University Novella Award. Her collection of essays, *Swallowing the Sea*, which includes the essay from this volume, received *ForeWord Review*'s Book of the Year Award in the category of books about writing. She is the Writer-in-Residence and a professor of English at Lafayette College, SUNY-Binghamton.

**Kathrine Varnes** is the author of the book of poems *The Paragon* and co-editor of the poetics handbook *An Exaltation of Forms*. Other works include a screenplay, two stage plays, a pile of literary essays and the first thirty pages of a novel-in-progress with the working title of *Joint and Several*. An instigator of collaborative poetry, Varnes lives with her family in Larchmont, New York.

**Jack Willis** is President of the Willis Group, a television and documentary film production company. He has been a producer and executive in commercial, cable and public television. He created and executive produced the Emmy award-winning, innovative news show *The 51st State* for WNET/13. He was Co-Executive Producer of PBS's groundbreaking, Emmy award-winning *The Great American Dream Machine*; and his series *City within a City*, which also won an Emmy, was widely credited with helping to achieve passage of Milwaukee's Open Housing law in 1967. Willis has produced and directed numerous award-winning documentaries and has also produced films for CBS News, as well as *The Human Animal* series with Phil Donahue for NBC (1986). With his wife, Mary, he has written several highly rated network movies of the week and co-authored the book *But There Are Always Miracles*. He has a BA and LLB from UCLA and an Honorary Doctor of Law from St. Johns University in Minnesota.

**Rachel Wineberg**'s short story "When the Thaw Comes" was nominated for a 2011 Pushcart Prize. She teaches writing at Westchester Community College.

**Helen Zelon** is a freelance writer. She has won prizes for investigative reporting, urban-education coverage and meritorious journalism from the Newswomen's Club of New York, the New York Independent Press Association, the Education Writers Association, the National Council on Crime & Delinquency, and the University of Maryland's Journalism Center on Children & Families. She has written for *New York* magazine, City Limits, InsideSchools.org, a swath of women's magazines, and other local and national publications. Her nonfiction has been included in many anthologies, including *The Portable MFA* and *How Not to Greet Famous People: The Best Stories from Ducts.org*. She taught writing at two New York City public schools and, for two years, at Sing Sing Correctional Facility in Ossining, New York.

**The Man Who Ate His Book**
***The Best of Ducts.org Volume II***

**STAFF**

**Book Editors:** Jonathan Kravetz and Charles Salzberg
**Art Editor, Art Gallery Curator:** Cindy Stockton Moore
**Book Designer:** Robert L. Lascaro
**Editorial Assistant:** Ann Posten
**Copy Editor:** Gini Kopecky Wallace

CPSIA information can be obtained
at www.ICGtesting.com
Printed in the USA
FFOW01n2226050516
23833FF

9 780988 696846